INTOLERANT

INTOLERANT

H. PETERSEN SMITH

XULON ELITE

Xulon Press Elite
2301 Lucien Way #415
Maitland, FL 32751
407.339.4217
www.xulonpress.com

Paperback ISBN-13: 978-1-6628-6224-3
Ebook ISBN-13: 978-1-6628-6225-0

DEDICATION

This book is dedicated to Ginger Kolbaba, my initial editor and the person who mentored me to the present day. I will never forget your patience with me and your gentle hand on my much-needed corrections.

PROLOGUE

12:35 p.m.
Wednesday, July 15, 2026
Arlington, Texas

ROSIE CHAVEZ HURRIED down the steps of Carlisle Hall at the University of Texas—Arlington to find better cell reception. Her parents were scheduled to call in a few minutes, and she didn't want to miss it. Today was day three of their dream trip to New York City, and Rosie loved keeping up with their adventures. Through video calls, Rosie got to experience the various landmarks in the background as she watched her parents walk on Fifth Avenue, climb the steps at the Statue of Liberty, look out over the city from the Empire State Building, and even ride a horse-drawn carriage through Central Park.

These brief moments away from her studies brought Rosie sanity, especially now that she was in the final exams for her Master of Science in nursing. The pressure to finish well added stress to her already busy, high-paced life.

She spotted a nearby bench under a tree and plopped down in exhaustion just as her phone rang. "Hey, you guys!" she said as soon as her parents' faces showed up on her screen. "Where are you today?"

"Let's see what we have here behind us," her father said in a deep, reporter voice. Dressed in a polo shirt and shorts, with a camera strap hung diagonally across his chest, he looked the picture of a tourist. He grazed his fingers through his thinning gray hair, then cleared his voice theatrically. "We see the street signs for Wall Street and Broadway. That must mean we are in the Financial District, ladies and gentlemen."

Rosie's mom moved the phone camera off Rosie's face-mugging father and pointed it toward the Wall Street sign, then back.

Rosie's dad turned the camera on her mom. "For my first man-on-the-street interview, let's talk to . . . well, who do we have here? Ah, the lovely and beautiful Belinda Young. Sometimes, in very important circles, referred to as Grandma! She is dressed in a new turquoise skirt and blouse because right after this report, we will be filming in front of the one and only Tiffany & Co. to look at rings."

Belinda leaned her head into the camera. "Don't forget my 'NYC Rocks' visor. Plus, he promised to buy me a four-carat diamond!"

"He did not," said her father, returning to his normal voice.

Rosie laughed and rolled her eyes. She could always count on her parents to bring joy to every situation.

Her mom held up a Statue of Liberty snow globe. "Look what we got for Cooper," she said as she turned the globe upside down and shook it. "I got the one that had the most snow." She turned it right-side up and held the glittering globe up to the camera. The globe snow fell over the miniature version of the Statue of Liberty.

"I tried to tell your mother that all the globes have the same amount of glitter in them, but she insisted on shaking every single one," Rosie's dad said.

"Cooper will love it," Rosie said, knowing once it made its way into the hands of her four-year-old son, it would be broken within fifteen minutes.

"We have something for you and Ramon too," her mother said. "But you'll have to wait till we get back to Fort Worth to see it."

"Sounds good, Mom. I'm so excited to have you two back home."

Rosie heard them giggling as if they were teenagers again.

"Stop it, Clifford!" her mom said, though her voice was clearly teasing. They were having the time of their lives. Rosie was glad to know her parents were still in love. "Guess where your romantic father promised to take me tonight, after Tiffany's?"

"Where?"

"He's taking me—" The screen went bright white and the "Call Failed" button appeared on Rosie's screen.

Rosie pressed the "Try Again" button, thinking the call must have dropped. The call began to ring, then went dead. No answer, no voicemail. Just as she started to disconnect, a rapid beep, beep, beep of a busy signal began.

That's odd, she thought and hung up. *They'll call back when they realize what's happened.* She sat and waited for the return call, looking out over the campus, enjoying the quiet of the afternoon.

Three people rushed through College Hall's doors, followed by other groups of two and three, and soon a steady stream of students. "What's going on?" Rosie asked, knowing that it was not time for the current class to end. "Bombs just exploded in New York City and LA!" a student explained. "We are going to the commons to watch the news."

Rosie felt the blood drain from her face and began to tremble. She quickly followed, pushing her way through the crowd heading into the chemistry and physics building where the commons was located. She had to get in front of one of the many television screens. It didn't matter which screen she chose; every screen had the same images. The evidence of a nuclear blast was obvious.

Her legs wobbled dangerously as she reached for the nearest chair. "Oh no," she whispered, covering her mouth with a shaking hand. She was trying to process what she was seeing, but her body began to react as a knot formed in her stomach. From distant helicopter cameras, the split screens slowly panned the devastation. In New York City's Lower East Side, what had been tall, magnificent buildings were now plumes of dust and smoke, reduced to barely recognizable heaps of rubble, reminiscent of the 9-11 tragedy. Through the dense dust and smoke, the remnants of brick and steel beams stood up like tinker toys thrown during a child's temper tantrum. A local news anchor soberly explained that one bomb had leveled multiple structures in Lower Manhattan.

"The Financial District has been hardest hit," the reporter declared.

Rosie gasped. *The exact spot where Mom and Dad are!*

Rosie reached into her pocket and pulled out her cell phone. She desperately pressed the last call button, and her dad's picture appeared with the call process icon showing. Then the obnoxious triple beat indicated network difficulties. She hung up and tried again and again. After the fourth attempt, she burst into tears. She knew it was over. She knew they were gone.

The brutal reality sunk in. There was no way they could have survived that kind of incineration. She tasted the hot, salty tears pouring from her eyes as she vaguely heard reports that another bomb had obliterated every structure in its path near Marina Del Rey, Venice Beach, Santa Monica, Culver City, Inglewood, and LAX, the busiest airport on the west coast. Bile rose in her throat as she clenched her stomach.

She didn't want to hear any more, but she couldn't turn her gaze from the images. She sat with the others as they continued to stare in utter disbelief.

The news reporter was interrupted mid-sentence, announcing that another nuclear device detonated at Gateway Arch in St Louis, right at the water's edge on the Mississippi River.

How could this happen? Rosie wondered. *Why?*

As if reading her thoughts, the news anchor announced that a radical Islamic extremist group was claiming responsibility. According to the group's social-media feed, they claimed they were prepared to detonate five more bombs in five major cities. Only one thing would stop them—the President of the United States and Congress had fifteen minutes to accept surrender terms. If they did so, the United States would be no more. It would become part of the Islamic Caliphate. If they did not agree to surrender, more lives would be lost.

Rosie's body felt heavy as she crumpled from the chair to the floor, and as darkness descended over her, she thought, *This is WAR; the president will never surrender.*

CHAPTER 1

9:00 p.m.
Sunday, February 28, 2027
Fort Worth, Texas

ROSIE GRABBED HER keys and rushed to her Toyota
Corolla. She was late for work. She'd been a pediatric nurse at the
Children's Medical Center for five years. When her good friend
and supervisor, Betsy Thompson, called and told her she needed
to cover for another nurse's shift, she knew she didn't have the
luxury to say no, even though she now possessed her master's
degree. Rosie was the go-to girl in times of trouble. After the call,
Rosie quickly reorganized Ramon's death certificate, his life insurance policy, and a pile of monthly bills into the two folders. She
had planned to work on them, but now she needed to jump in the
shower and change into her uniform.

She was two blocks away when she realized that in her haste,
she'd forgotten to put on her hijab, the head covering now required
for all women in public. Worse, she didn't have the required male
escort she needed. She considered turning back but decided against
it with one glance at the clock on the car dashboard. She was
already fifteen minutes late. To everyone's dismay, the President
and Congress had surrendered to the demands of the radical
Islamic terrorists, and they now lived under an Islamic regime.

1

She pulled to a stop at the next intersection's red light and noticed the required "infidel" tag displayed on the windshield had expired.

Great, she thought. *Strike three.*

The hospital wasn't much farther. She hoped she'd be able to dodge any informants and make it to work without incident. Seven months had passed since everything she'd known and loved about her life was gone. Now Sharia Law reigned.

With one look in the rearview mirror, she noticed a car tailing her with its high beams on. It followed closely for several minutes.

"Oh, this can't be good," she muttered aloud.

The light turned green, and she tried not to floor the accelerator. She tried to reassure herself. "Calm down, Rosie. It's probably nothing. You're just being paranoid." But with each turn, the car stayed behind her. Her heart began to race, and a lump appeared in her throat. *Could this be the patrol?*

The patrol was created during the nearly six months of martial law between the surrender and January 1 of this year. She'd heard they were mostly made up of disenfranchised gang members. All infidel cell phones had been confiscated at the first of the year, so it had been nearly two months since she had a cell phone. Still, she instinctively reached into her purse and felt for it to call 911.

Beads of sweat formed on her forehead. She couldn't afford to let her mind wander. "Ramon, why did you have to leave us?" she cried out, her bright blue eyes brimming with tears. "STOP!" she said, audibly scolding herself. She had to get a handle on her emotions. "Oh, God, help me get control of my mind." She forced herself to breathe in deeply. "The LORD is my shepherd; I shall not want. He makes me to lie down in green pastures, he leads me besides still waters, he restores my soul." Her heart continued to race. Reciting Psalm 23 had always helped her calm down and focus whenever she was in a stressful situation, but it wasn't helping her now.

Why is this happening to me? Haven't I been through enough? Through her mind, the faces of her parents drifted by. Then her beloved husband's face came into view. The love of her life, Ramon, was gone. As if the devasting bombs and Islamic takeover were not enough, a car accident had stolen him from her just four weeks before. Cooper had been in the car too. He'd survived, but barely and was now in the PICU of Children's Medical Center, Fort Worth's best neurological and pediatric hospital and Rosie's place of employment.

Shaking her head to clear her thoughts and stay focused, she glanced again in her rearview mirror. The car was still there.

If that car was the patrol, she was in a lot of trouble. The patrol's main job was to enforce Sharia Law. These men had the full support of the caliph. They were authorized to drive around and look for obvious violators of the new status quo and correct the problem while teaching the violators a lesson. She had no escort and no evidence of paying her "infidel" tag, plus she wasn't wearing the required hijab. She was too far from home to turn back, but she wasn't close enough to work to make it safely.

She sped up to make the next light as it turned yellow, but the car in front of her stopped. She was stuck. And beyond scared. She'd heard stories of women getting caught at stoplights and the patrol getting violent with unescorted female drivers. Those awful incidents usually included sexual assault, beatings, and even death.

"Oh, God, help me get out of this."

An idea popped into her head. Her friend Lori lived nearby. Lori was a Muslim, so she would know what to do to get out of this mess.

Rosie took a swift left turn from the righthand lane to make the Southwest Blvd on ramp and speed onto the expressway, going in a perpendicular direction from where she'd just been. Checking her rearview mirror once more, she saw the same headlights trailing her. No confusion now. This was the patrol. She exited the expressway at Ridglea Country Club Drive. After crossing several streets and turning right onto Tumbling Trail, she pulled into the circle drive in front of a ranch-style house. She prayed Lori would be home. Screeching the brakes, she turned off the car, jumped out, and ran to the front door.

"Lori!" she yelled as she beat on the door and rang the doorbell over and over. "Please! Hurry, Lori. I need help. I need help!"

The front door opened, and Rosie burst inside.

"Rosie, what on earth are you doing out at this hour?" her friend said. Lori Larson was a friend she'd met at Children's Medical Center the previous summer when Lori and her husband, Tom, lost their son in a playground accident.

Rosie slammed the door and peered out the side windows.

"Where is your escort? What's going on?"

The men in the car pulled up to the curb in front of the Larson home and turned off the engine. They weren't going anywhere.

"They . . . they are after me," she said, barely able to speak. "F-following me." Even though Rosie had escaped the men, she couldn't get control of her unsettled breathing and panic. "Every time I turned, they turned right after me. They've been on my tail since I got out of my neighborhood."

Tom entered the hallway and gave a surprised look at his visitor. "Rosie. What's going on? Why are you here?"

"The patrol, you know, the compliance network." She stepped away from the window. "The people who are supposed to ensure that we keep up with the new rules . . ." Rosie stopped her explanation as she remembered, "Oh no!" Panic rose again within her. "I left my purse in the car."

"That's okay. Tom will get it." Lori said and looked at her husband.

"Of course," Tom said and headed toward the door.

Rosie looked from Tom to Lori and then down at her shaking hands. "I was so rushed to leave the house to get to the hospital to cover for a nurse, I didn't think about the rules. I didn't have time to call for my escort. I didn't have time to find my scarf. I didn't have time to pay my tax. *I didn't have time!* It wasn't until after I left the house that I realized I was violating the compliance rules, but by then, it was too late." Her breath came in gasps, as she felt herself starting to hyperventilate. "I was on my way to—." *Gasp . . . gasp.*

Lori motioned for Rosie to follow her into the living room and sit down. "Breathe, Rosie. Calm down a bit and start from the beginning so I can understand."

Once she was seated on their couch, Rosie drew in a couple of long breaths and let the air out slowly. It took a few moments before she could regain some composure. "The hospital called me. Betsy, the nurse manager, told me the scheduled night nurse had called in sick. They needed me to fill in. I'd just finished a double shift yesterday, but because Cooper's there, I said okay since it allows me to be near him again this evening. But I was tired and going through some of the paperwork from Ramon's death. As soon as I hung up the phone, I rushed to take a shower and get ready. By then I was running late and wasn't thinking about the rules. I just put on my smock uniform, put the documents away, grabbed my purse and ID key card, and left."

Tom rushed back inside, holding Rosie's purse. "When I stepped outside, one of the men in the car jumped out and yelled at me about you being in our house and that we can't hide you forever. What is that about?"

"I'm sorry to drag you into this. The nursing call list has gotten short with all the confusion over the takeover and imposition of Sharia Law. No one wants to be out at night. Because of Cooper, I get the calls, and I'm grateful for the opportunity. The hospital lets me check on Cooper while I'm there. I am so scared and confused right now. I need some help, and I don't know what to do." Rosie walked to the window and peered out. The patrol was still there.

Lori shook her head. "It's okay. We just cleaned up the meal after our Ramadan fast. Whitney is in bed, and we are settled down for the night." She stepped toward the front window and parted the curtains ever so slightly. "How can we help you?"

"I . . . I don't know. I haven't thought that far. I know I can't stay here, but I—"

"Tom?" Lori cut in. "Is there something you can do?"

He looked unsure and uncomfortable, which made Rosie feel worse. She shouldn't have brought this trouble on them, she knew, but she had run out of options.

"Let me call Jamal, the city imam. Perhaps he can get somebody to call these guys off." Tom started to leave the room.

Rosie knew about each major city having its own imam who oversaw Sharia Law and the operations in those cities. "Don't do that!" Rosie blurted out. "If you could just call a cab so I can get a ride to the hospital. And if I can borrow a hijab . . . I can pick up my car later."

Tom shook his head. "Too risky. The patrol tends to be lawless toward what used to be called the Civil Rights of the Unbelieving Infidels—especially women. The hour is getting late. The taxi is a bad idea." Tom looked at Lori. "Excuse me while I call Jamal."

Lori offered Rosie a seat at the kitchen table. "Tom and Jamal have been best friends for years. They grew up together; they were in each other's wedding. He doesn't mind calling Jamal. The patrol is dangerous," Lori told her. "You were right to come here. You're safe now."

"But I don't want you or Tom to get into trouble."

Lori smiled. "You don't need to worry about that. What are friends for?"

Rosie smiled and tried to relax. She would call the hospital as soon as Tom came back in. If Ramon were still here, she wouldn't be in this predicament. But he wasn't. She was alone. Being alone was tough enough. Being a single woman under Sharia Law was almost unfathomable.

She could hear Tom's lowered voice in the next room as he spoke to Jamal on the phone. She had met Jamal at Tom's son's funeral prayers last summer. He'd been kind to her then. But that was a different set of circumstances. Now she hoped he'd be agreeable to help a singled-out infidel. If not, her life was about to get worse.

CHAPTER 2

9:30 p.m.
Sunday, February 28

"JAMAL, IT'S TOM." Tom could hear a siren and some road noise in the background on Jamal's end. "Sounds as if you're out driving."

"I'm on my way to the office," Jamal told him. "I have another late-night video conference call from the caliph. I'll be on camera again, so I need to make sure the office is tidied up and that I'm completely ready. Why are you calling so late?"

Tom began to pace in a tight circle as he knew the conference call must be something highly important and classified for Jamal to drive to his office rather than take it at his home. Now he felt uneasy about asking Jamal for this favor. "I'm calling about Rosie Chavez. Remember, she was the nurse who helped us so much after Alex's accident?"

"Yes, I remember," Jamal said. "Your wife took a particular liking to her, and they became friends?"

"That's right. Rosie worked tirelessly with Alex, then comforted us so much after he died. I'm not sure if you recall, but she is also the woman who lost her husband and has a critically injured child from that drunk driver case that got all that attention back in January."

"Ah yes. That case got a lot of media splash at the time. The fact that we were able to make such an example of the drunk driver has certainly cut back on alcohol consumption and alcohol-related accidents here in Fort Worth and in the entire DFW area, for that matter. As I recall, Rosie came to the funeral prayers for Alex. I remember meeting her briefly there."

"Yes, that is correct. Anyway, Rosie showed up at our house in a panic about fifteen minutes ago. Seems she left her home without an escort, and the patrol saw her and followed her."

"Did she tell you why?" Jamal asked.

"She got a call to cover for one of the nurses who couldn't make it to the hospital, so she was in a rush. Says she was so focused on getting to work that she forgot her escort."

"Hmmm, I don't see a problem with taking care of that for her."

"Well," Tom paused as he picked up the speed of his nervous circle. He swallowed hard. He knew having more than one issue was a problem and hated asking his friend for the favor. "Rosie also left her house without the hijab, and her jizya tax hasn't been paid for the month of February. She claims the payment omission is because of her husband's death."

"I see," Jamal said. In the background, Tom heard another siren whir by.

"As she left her house this evening, she was easy pickings for the patrol. She came to our house because she was scared, nearly hysterical. The patrol is still out front, waiting for something to happen. Could you do us a favor and call them off just this once? She needs our help. I wouldn't normally ask, but she has been so helpful to us, and she and Lori are friends."

Jamal didn't speak. Tom stopped his pacing and waited, quietly tapping his foot. He squeezed his eyes shut tightly in an attempt to get some relief from an oncoming headache. He was asking a lot, and suddenly, he wished he hadn't called Jamal.

"Yes, text me the decal number of the patrol car," Jamal finally said with a terseness that belied his normally friendly voice. "I'll call the director of the Compliance Network and have him pull them back."

Tom breathed a giant but silent, uneasy sigh of relief. *This is becoming a bigger deal than a simple call to Jamal.*

"Look," Jamal continued, his controlled voice sounding friendly again. "I've got a few minutes before I have to be at the office, and I'm pretty close to your house. I'm curious to see how this Network and patrol thing works. I'd like to watch their reaction."

Tom resumed his pacing in the tight circle. "You are more than welcome," he chuckled tensely. *Just like Jamal to want to see the action.* "Thanks, Jamal. I know Rosie will really appreciate—"

"But, Tom, we have to impound the vehicle because of the tax issues. The tax is becoming a grave sticking point. These infidels need to realize this is a serious impediment to their freedoms. We need to keep this tax constantly in front of them. The Koran must be followed; the tax has been taught and collected for centuries. The choice for Ms. Chavez is simple: convert to Islam or live with the consequences. The tax is just one of the many consequences she has chosen to face by not converting."

"Of course. And I'll make sure to tell her that again, so she understands the seriousness of it."

"Because of the car being impounded, I insist that you drive her to work. She must get there without any more problems. I'll see you in a few minutes."

Tom hung up, feeling irritated that this situation aligned him with a female infidel who had broken Sharia. He'd had to defend Rosie's actions, guilty as she was, to his best friend, who was charged with strict adherence to these rules. Although the Sharia was clear about dos and don'ts, following those directives was up to the infidels, difficult or not. The fact that Rosie was his wife's friend had nothing to do with it.

CHAPTER 3

9:40 p.m.
Sunday, February 28

ROSIE GAVE HER full attention to Tom, who appeared exhausted and frustrated. He threw an irritated glance her way when he came back into the kitchen.

"Here's the story," Tom said. "Jamal told me the guys in the patrol car are from the Compliance Network. Those two men are going to leave, but first, they have to get the wrecker service here to impound your car."

"Impound my car?" Rosie jumped from her chair, then thought better of any other show of temper. She breathed in deeply to control her anger. *The Larsons have been nice to help me out. I need to keep my mouth shut.*

"Yes," he said. "The jizya has not been paid for the month of February. March 1 is tomorrow, and you are already behind on that tax. In order to get the car out of hock, you will need to pay the back tax and the tax for March, then pay the expense of getting the car from the impound."

Rosie wished she'd said no to covering at the hospital for tonight. The news just kept getting worse. She had no escort because her husband had died, but that didn't matter. *And hey,* she thought wryly, *who needs an escort when you have no car?*

"You know, of course, that the tax goes away if you convert to Islam?" Tom had been kind to call the imam on her behalf, but she had no interest in converting, not even to fake a conversion to get out of paying some stupid tax.

She nodded and then shook her head with a grimace.

Tom sighed. "But we have discussed this before, and we know how you feel about it. That is just how things are right now under Sharia."

Rosie's head dropped. "I know, I know. I'm so preoccupied with settling Ramon's affairs, and I was waiting for the payment from his life insurance policy. I completely forgot the jizya. It's tough to lose so much so quickly, and now all this new stuff is expected of me. Since July, there has been a lot of learning for us infidels." She tried not to choke on that last word. She breathed in deeply and continued. "First, we had five months of martial law and then the last two months of Sharia. All of this is hard from a standing start, without much warning, I might add."

She blinked hard to keep the tears from flowing. "I miss Ramon so much. I didn't realize I was so dependent on him. We were always a team, like you and Lori, and we worked together so well. He had taken care of the January tax, and here I am . . ." Like a dam bursting, she could no longer hold back the flood of emotion, and the sobs came hard and fast.

"Oh, Rosie," Lori said, reaching over to hug her.

Lori's embrace felt warm and comforting. It was the kind of hug her mother used to give her. *Oh, my mother . . .*

No, she determined. She wouldn't let herself go there now. She took another deep breath in and let it out slowly. She stood deliberately, smoothing out her wrinkled smock uniform.

Tom went to the window and stared outside. He pulled out his phone and typed in something, then turned his attention back to her, his voice more forceful and unsympathetic. "Well, you can't forget! You have to get control of the situation and yourself. The escort, the tax, the hijab—*all* the rules of the Sharia are televised constantly on channels 1 and 2. You have to learn the rules and live according to them." His voice softened as he looked at his wife, then back at Rosie. "These are different times, Rosie. All the rules have changed, and there will be no future exceptions for you. Jamal wasn't happy when I called to ask this favor. You nonbelievers are going to need to pay more attention to this new way of Islamic life. Islam and Sharia are not going away."

Rosie felt a knot in her stomach and nodded again. She worked to accept the fact that her car would be hauled off, and she would have no way home. It seemed harsh, but it was far better than being dragged from her vehicle by hysterical men who certainly wouldn't be looking out for her best interests. "If they impound my car, how will I get to work tonight?"

"You are very fortunate," Tom said. "Jamal has agreed for me to drive you there. This cannot happen again. Do you understand? As much as we care for you, if events like this come up again, consequences could easily get worse for you. And we won't be able to step in."

"I understand." Rosie squared her shoulders, trying to be brave but not feeling it inside. "Thank you, Tom. I know this puts you in a difficult situation. I never meant to bring you or Lori into this."

Without acknowledging her, Tom turned to his wife. "Lori, take Rosie to the garage and get her one of your hijabs. I'll get my keys and wallet."

Lori wrapped Rosie's head in one of her own hijabs, then led Rosie to the car in their garage. Rosie sank her body into Tom's car and looked gratefully at Lori. *How has my life come to this?* She pulled a tissue out of her purse and dabbed her eyes and nose.

As Tom backed out of the garage, Rosie saw in the side mirror that the patrol car had pulled up to block the driveway. Two surly, bearded men got out and began walking toward them.

"They're coming!" Rosie gasped.

"I know," Tom said tensely. He grabbed his cell phone and handed it to Rosie. "Call 911 and put the call on speaker!" He shifted the car into drive and inched back toward the garage door, which had just closed.

After one ring, an operator's voice came on the speaker. "Nine-one-one, what is your emergency?"

"We're being attacked by two men, and they will not let us leave the house!" Rosie blurted out. "Can you send the police immediately?"

"I see your address on Tumbling Trail. A police cruiser is within two minutes of your location. Just stay on the line."

Both men had on what looked like bomber jackets and had hungry looks in their eyes that terrified Rosie. They looked like men whose only intent was to haul Rosie off to some far-off location for a nefarious purpose. They began banging on the car. "You don't have the right to leave this property until we get that woman," one of the men yelled, looking directly at her.

Bile rose in Rosie's throat. Not even Tom could save her from these men if they got ahold of her.

"Get away from the car!" Tom yelled back.

"Can't you just open the garage door so we can go back in?" Rosie said, feeling helpless.

He shook his head. "I'm concerned that if I raise the garage door, these guys will see that as an invitation to go into the house."

Rosie yelped in fear, sensing she was on the verge of hysteria.

"Ma'am, is everything all right?" the 9-1-1 operator asked.

Are you kidding me? "No! Can you hear all of this?" Rosie pressed the phone against the window to make sure the operator heard the pounding. "How close are the police?"

"They're just a few blocks away," the operator stated, a little too calmly.

"Please help! I don't know what these men will do next, and I am very scared. Please, get the police here soon!"

"They're almost there, ma'am. Just stay on the line."

"You will be getting a call from your supervisor," Tom yelled through the glass. "You must leave now. Your supervisor will tell you to leave the premises immediately and to not harass anyone on this property. Leave us alone!"

Unfazed, the men continued to yell and bang on the car. "Open the door and let us have her! She is ours!"

Rosie shrank farther into her seat and away from the door. "Can you hear all this commotion?" she asked the operator.

In the distance, the sound of sirens, signaling rescue and safety, came nearer. Within a second, she saw the red-and-blue strobe lights reflecting off the trees and houses. "The cops are here!" she yelled as much for her benefit as for theirs.

"Ma'am, stay on the line until confirmed," the operator repeated.

"Get back in your car and wait for the call from your boss," Tom said, still gripping the steering wheel.

Rosie watched as the police cruiser pulled in front of the patrol car. Both doors flew open, and two armed officers raced out of the cruiser with pistols drawn, running toward Tom's car.

"Back away and get into your car. You are no longer needed here!" the lead officer yelled, his gun trained on the two crazed men.

The lead man from the patrol bowed his back. "Look, copper, we followed her, and she is ours. You don't understand Sharia Law?"

The officer pointed his pistol at the man's chest. "You should get back into your car and let things settle down, or I will arrest you."

The two patrol men paused as though they weren't going to obey, then reluctantly walked back to their car and leaned against it.

The lead officer returned to his car and mercifully turned off the siren but allowed the lights to continue flashing.

Rosie kept her eyes on the two patrol thugs. The bigger guy dug into his pants pocket, pulled out a cell phone, and spoke into it. He said a few words, snarled, then said something to his partner. Both men jumped into their car, backed away from the police car, and drove off without a glance at Tom and Rosie.

Rosie breathed a sigh of relief, dropping her head back against the seat. Suddenly, a man in an Islamic white robe and skull cap appeared at Tom's window. His concerned face flashed red and blue as the strobe lights reflected on him.

This must be Jamal. Rosie vaguely remembered their meeting at the mosque after the funeral prayers for Alex, but it was difficult to recognize him with her emotions running so high.

Tom rolled down his window and wiped his hand against his forehead, giving a nervous chuckle. "You just missed all the excitement."

"The police are now in control of the situation. You can hang up now," the 9-1-1 dispatcher squawked over Tom's phone speaker.

Rosie looked down at her hands. They were shaking.

The police stepped to Tom's car. "Everything all right now?"

"Yes, thank you, officers," Tom said, putting the car into park and getting out.

Rosie knew the police would need to debrief Tom for a few minutes to fill out their reports. She looked at her watch and realized that it had been well over an hour since she last communicated with her supervisor. She could only imagine what Betsy was going to say. *There is no way I'm going to impose upon Tom and ask to use his cell phone.* She sighed. *Well, at least this additional delay will make my story of being late even more unbelievable.*

The debriefing took about fifteen minutes. Rosie sat alone in Tom's car, helplessly watching. And to make matters worse, she watched as her car was towed away. She was sick to her stomach at the thought of not having a vehicle for a while and how that would affect her life, not to mention the financial impact. How would anything ever feel right again? She turned her attention toward the house and noticed Lori peering out of the window with a worried expression.

Tom opened the car door and turned to Jamal. "Thanks for your help and sticking around to explain what was going on here. I'll pull the car into the garage and meet you inside. Lori can let you in the front door." He lowered himself into the car, raised the garage door, and pulled forward into the garage.

"Why did Lori stay inside?" Rosie asked. "Especially after the patrol left?"

"She has a genuine aversion to the police. Something from her childhood set it in motion. Then the way the police handled the investigation of the accident with Alex didn't improve her fears. That day was supposed to be a fun afternoon at the park. They were at the playground." Tom took on a strange look as he recalled what Rosie already knew. "Alex was climbing on the monkey bars on the highest rung. He lost his grip, fell straight to the ground, and smashed his head. Lori was sitting right there. Whitney saw the whole thing too. Lori was telling Alex to be careful, as she always did. When a police officer came to the hospital to talk to Lori, he seemed to imply that she was careless with our son, which couldn't be further from the truth. Needless to say, she tends to shy away from the police." As he began to get out of the car, he looked at her. "You are welcome to come in, or you can sit in the car for a few minutes. Jamal and I will be inside the house to tell Lori what has happened."

Rosie smiled slightly but shook her head. "If you don't mind, I think I'd rather sit out here. My legs are still shaking."

Tom maneuvered himself out of the car. "That's fine," he said over his shoulder.

As soon as Tom closed the door to the house behind him, Rosie tried to calm herself for the second time that night. She began repeating, "The LORD is my shepherd, I shall not want. He makes me lie down in green pastures . . ." As she quoted Psalm 23, she absentmindedly pulled her wedding ring off and on, adjusted her hijab close to her face, then pushed it away from her eyes. Back and forth she went with her hands, anxiously contradicting her attempts to relax her nerves and lower her heart rate.

My haste caused a lot of chaos. I don't know how I will ever make it up to Lori and Tom. Getting the city imam involved seems almost unforgivable.

After about ten minutes, Tom returned to the car, buckled his seat belt, and reached up to raise the garage door. Through the side mirror, Rosie watched Jamal disappear into his car and leave. Tom backed out of the driveway into the street, which was again quiet and dark.

The ride to the hospital was only fifteen minutes, though it seemed like an hour. Neither person spoke, and Rosie wondered again how she was going to get out of this mess.

Tom stopped the car under the covered portico at the hospital entrance, but Rosie didn't move. She knew she needed to thank him, but she didn't know how to do it without sounding trite. She almost felt as though she were in high school again, caught in some stupid act.

19

Finally, Tom broke the silence. "Rosie, you realize you were in serious danger tonight, right? I'm sorry I had to be so firm with you. As you know, this is Ramadan, plus I am in the middle of a busy tax season. Your timing was off. On a different night in a different month, perhaps I would have been under less stress and kinder about this situation."

"I understand," Rosie said, remembering Tom was a CPA and that when her uncle had a tax accounting business, March was always a busy time of the year for him. "I was stressed out myself. Before I got to your house tonight, I had repeated thoughts about a coworker's experience. In January, she'd gone walking alone on her lunch break, as she'd done for years, when two men in matching jackets attacked her. She was beaten and then dragged into some bushes, where they raped her. Her partially clothed and crumpled form was later discovered when another walker happened by and heard her cries for help. All this occurred in broad daylight. She was alive but terribly roughed up. She wanted to bring charges against the men, but the Fort Worth police informed her that under the new Sharia, she would need two witnesses to confirm the crime." She exhaled harshly. "Then there are the stories we hear where unescorted drivers get boxed in at stop lights and horrible things happen to them. Women are treated like they have no rights. Is this the new normal for us?"

Tom nodded. "To your point on women's rights, the Koran and Sharia Law are clear on the necessary number of witnesses. It takes two women to equal the testimony of one man. Now, I could say, off the record, that this is a crime against women. And you may call it the new normal, but the Koran and Sharia Law have been in existence for more than a thousand years. For Muslims, this is the way we please Allah."

Rosie thought about what Tom said. She knew speaking against the Koran and Sharia could get her in even more trouble, but she felt that she couldn't stay silent. "I could not disagree with you more. Jesus's teachings preceded the Koran by six hundred years, and he was full of love and had a completely different attitude toward women and their rights in society. That's one of the many dividing lines between Islam and Christianity."

Rosie paused as she realized Tom's hands were clenching the steering wheel, and his shoulders had tensed. She quickly changed the subject, recognizing this was not the time to debate religious beliefs. "Tonight, you have helped me, and I thank you for your assistance. I apologize for inconveniencing you and Lori. You didn't have to make the call to the imam, but you did. Your kindness saved me a lot of anxiety and pain, perhaps even my life, and now you have graciously brought me to work. Despite our differences in what we believe, your sympathy is appreciated, and I am very grateful."

Tom turned in his seat to face Rosie. "You touched our lives during a very dark time. You held Lori and helped her understand that your team had done everything to keep Alex alive and make him well." Tom's chin began to quiver with grief as he teared up, and a sob broke from his lips. "I vividly remember all you did to help Lori when it was time to take Alex off the ventilator. You were with us as we watched Alex breathe his last. It is not fair for parents to have to bury their child."

Rosie thought of her own son, Cooper, lying in a bed several stories above her. She leaned over and put her hand on Tom's shoulder, forgetting that under Sharia she was not allowed to touch a man outside of her family. "I feel your pain, and I am sorry that you and your family had to go through that."

Her tears now mirrored his as he nodded.

Rosie reached in her purse for a tissue and took several deep breaths as she mentally recited, *The Lord is my Shepherd* . . . When her breathing returned to normal, she turned in her seat to get out of the car.

Tom stopped her. "Lori and I wish there were something we could do for you. We know it isn't easy to lose your husband and care for your injured child. We lost Alex, but we still have each other. I know this has to be difficult, and it may soon get worse for you. You mean a great deal to our family."

Rosie smiled gratefully at Tom, dabbed her tears one last time, and got out of the car to walk toward the hospital as the building's automatic doors slid open.

CHAPTER 4

10:45 p.m.
Sunday, February 28

ROSIE WALKED UNSTEADILY onto the pediatric intensive care (PICU) floor and headed straight to the breakroom, opened her locker, and looked in the mirror on the back of its door. Her mascara was drooling down from her puffy eyes, her nose was red, and her face was splotchy with the leftover remnant of fear.

I look awful, she thought. She wiped the mascara off, then she collected her stethoscope, hospital cell phone, and other personal items and stepped to the open area of the PICU, where she heard the normal rhythms of the monitors' beeps and dings.

As she passed room 3, her heart beat heavily. Inside that darkened room was her son, Cooper. Her pacing slowed as she yearned to peek in and see him, touch him, and tell him she was there, but because she was so late, she went to the central desk where the other PICU nurses gathered. Along the desk sat monitors showing each of the beds on the unit. She plopped down next to Betsy. Betsy was the charge nurse and her manager, but mostly she was her good friend, despite being twenty-plus years older than Rosie. "I'm sorry I'm late. I'll explain after I review the charts."

First, though, she snuck a peek at Cooper's room monitor. Everything was peaceful. She breathed a quiet sigh of relief and turned her attention to the process she had done thousands of times before: reaching for the first chart to review and get up to speed on the vitals and protocols for every tiny patient in her area.

She went through each file, and when she was about two-thirds through the process, she noticed a new patient. "Is there anything I should know about? I see we admitted a new patient around 9:00 p.m., brought up from the ER. Infection with fever, pelvic pain, and lethargy? It reminders me of a couple of other girls we had a month ago."

Betsy held up her hand, an angry frown covering her face. "I am just now beginning to cool down about the harm done to that little girl. Seeing a child needlessly suffer is way beyond my temper threshold." Betsy's curly red hair bounced as she shook her head in disgust, and a hot pink color began to crawl up her neck as it often did when her temper flared.

"The Medical Center had two Muslim girls arrive this afternoon," Betsy continued. "Both came about the same time, one ended up here in PICU, and the other went to surgery. Both were brought in with complications resulting from the required genital circumcision, which their fathers performed at home. Our patient has what appears to be a severe infection. We immediately administered a bolus of fluids. As you no doubt read, we are waiting on labs to see if she is septic. We started an IV antibiotic about an hour ago to be on the safe side." She paused and looked around, taking deep breaths as though trying to regain some composure.

Rosie's anger rose to meet Betsy's. Genital circumcision, or what they referred to as female genital mutilation or FGM, was something they had witnessed before, and it was maddening. "How is the other girl doing? Have you heard anything?" Rosie asked.

"The other child had some reconstructive work done. Evidently, the father, or should I say 'butcher,' didn't get the sutures tight enough to close the wound, and apparently, no one has heard of cauterizing the injury to staunch the bleeding. It is highly probable the damage done to that young girl will keep her from ever bearing children. Both girls were lucky to see the inside of the hospital, where they could get some genuine treatment for their wounds and infections."

Rosie felt her own rage growing. "I am so disgusted that these young girls, children really, have to suffer at the hands of their fathers in some sort of seventh-century barbaric religious ritual." Rosie pounded her fist on the table. "How many girls get butchered that we don't see? Talk about a war on women!"

"I cannot understand how anyone, much less *a parent*, would think female genital mutilation is a good idea." Betsy lowered her voice and furtively looked around again. "At last count, this is the eighth child brought in since the takeover. I have a feeling that things are only going to get worse for young girls and for us as we try to treat them."

"That entire process of 'preparing' girls for womanhood is sickening," Rosie said, trying to gain control of her volume. "There is not a single thing we, as medical practitioners, can do about the carnage going on in the real world among the radical Islamic population now that they are in control."

Betsy nodded. "It is so sad to see girls come in here with such unnecessary damage and pain from FGM. God help us all in knowing how to deal with this."

Rosie sighed. "This is a rough way to start my shift, but it pretty much fits the day I've had."

"I want to hear all about it," Betsy said sympathetically. "But first we need a change of subject, and I have just the subject—Cooper. You have got to see your boy."

Rosie eagerly followed Betsy into the bed in unit three and stood next to her beloved son. Cooper was lying still, looking like an angel. The jet-black curls, escaping over the bandages, fell on the bed in stark contrast to the white pillow. His arms were to his side, and his leg, which was cast from the accident, was out from under the sheet.

"Hi, Cooper. How's my little man today? You sure are looking good." Rosie reached down and stroked his tousled hair with one hand as she patted him on the chest with her other. Her eye caught the monitor's movement. Cooper's heart rate quickened, and his respirations increased.

She gasped. "What is going on? Is he responding to me, or am I causing something like a neuro storm?" Because she worked in the PICU for a while, Rosie knew that comatose patients could be stuck in fight or flight mode due to brain trauma, and at times, outside stimuli can cause a response that seems intentional but is just a reaction. She prayed that this was not a neuro storm but an intentional reaction to hearing her voice.

Dr. Wilson strolled into Cooper's room, as though on cue. "No, you are not causing a neuro storm, or as my colleagues at Craig call it, 'storming.' Cooper is simply trying to wake up. And hi, *young* lady," he said, smiling. It was their inside joke, a play on Rosie's maiden name of Young. "I thought you were off today. Why are you here?"

Dr. Boyd Wilson was the head of Pediatric Orthopedics and Neurology at the medical center. Although his surgery suite was on the first floor and his post-surgery rounds were on the floor above, his critical patients often ended up on the PICU.

Rosie and Betsy looked at each other and then to Dr. Wilson. "It's a long story with a lot of twists and turns," admitted Rosie. "First, tell me about Cooper. I realize patients normally respond to touch and voice stimuli, but Cooper's coma is so deep. When I was here yesterday, he didn't respond. What's happened? Are you really saying he is actually trying to wake up?"

Just as Dr. Wilson opened his mouth to respond, the alarm from the newly admitted Muslim girl blared. Rosie ran to the center desk as Dr. Wilson and Betsy hurried to the girl. Rosie grabbed the chart and followed them.

She was shocked to see how small and defenseless the girl looked. Initially, Rosie estimated her to be about twice the size of Cooper, maybe eight or nine years old. Despite the alarm's obnoxious noise, the girl lay in the bed without the slightest movement or concern. Looking at the monitor, it became obvious that the patient was in a great deal of distress. Her heart rate and blood pressure were dropping quickly, along with her oxygen saturation, and her respiration and temperature were going up.

This poor child seems strangely unconcerned.

"When was she admitted to the floor?" Dr. Wilson asked.

"Nine this evening," Betsy said.

"How has her wound been monitored since admittance?"

"Initially dressed in the ER," Betsy answered again. "I checked her once she got here to make certain there was no obvious bleeding. She is due for a change of dressing, but I have a few pressing things to check on at the central desk. Rosie, even though her catheter bag looks fine, why don't you have a look and check the Foley to see if we are getting good flow without any blockage?"

Rosie went to work to remove the pelvic dressing from the wound. An overpowering odor that smelled like rotting meat seeped out. As she exposed the skin, she noted the gray and purple mottled tissue. She put the back of her gloved hand down beside the wound and felt the feverish infection. "I think I found the problem. Come look at this. I think it's Fournier's gangrene." Rosie was horrified to discover this acute, rapidly progressing, potentially fatal infection.

Dr. Wilson looked at what Rosie had discovered and tensed up. "You are correct. That looks severe."

Out of the corner of Rosie's eye, she saw a strange movement from the curtains in the unit, then she heard the booming voice of Betsy. "Hey, you cannot be in here! You need to be out in the waiting room. This is a sterile environment. Come with me, sir. This area is not for you. Come with me right now."

Rosie and Dr. Wilson glanced at each other curiously, then went back to work on the girl.

When Betsy returned to the unit, she made a terrible face. Rosie knew Betsy was obviously gagging over the rotten smell. "Wow, that caught me off guard."

"Tell me about her BP," said Dr. Wilson.

Betsy moved back into nurse mode and replied hurriedly, "BP is falling. She is at eighty over fifty and falling."

"Rosie, we need to start a BP pressor and vancomycin antibiotic immediately," Dr. Wilson said. "Start another bolus of fluid in her IV as well. I'll need you both to assist to scrub in for a surgical debridement now. We need to scrape off the infected tissue immediately to give her body a chance to fight off the infection and heal. We don't have time to get her to the OR. Let's get moving, STAT!"

Their next steps were like a well-rehearsed fire drill. Rosie, Betsy, and Dr. Wilson fell into line, prepping themselves and the girl as if they were in the operating room. Betsy walked directly to the door marked "EMERGENCY" and unlocked it, which had all the preparations and equipment for this eventuality. Rosie and Betsy grabbed the needed drugs and equipment. They added the vancomycin, the pressor, and the fluid to the IV, administered local anesthesia, and poured betadine on the infected area. Dr. Wilson began surgically removing the gangrenous tissue from the wound. When that was completed, Rosie reinserted the Foley catheter as Dr. Wilson used the blade to push the girl's tongue to the side so he could intubate her lungs.

"Is the IV going at full strength?" he asked.

"She is receiving the antibiotics as well as can be expected," said Rosie.

"Sounds as if the ventilator is going well."

Betsy checked the ventilator. "Yes, we are getting full returns."

"Good," Dr. Wilson said. "How many units of saline has she had since admission?"

"Three," said Betsy. "One in the ER, one when she arrived to ICU, and then her third bolus just now."

"She seems to be tolerating the infusion of saline. Prior to the alarm, was the BP stable?" he asked.

"Stable and normal," said Betsy.

"Order up two more units and add another pressor," Dr. Wilson said. "Has her BP begun to stabilize yet?"

Rosie read from the monitor. "BP is rising to 90/60 and temperature is 101."

Dr. Wilson exhaled. "Okay, let's see where all this takes us and hope for the best. That's all we can do right now. Keep watching her closely. Work your magic and give her the special treatment but realize she is in a very critical place."

"Ah, Doc, all we got here is the special treatment," said Rosie, discarding her surgical gloves and mask and heading back to the central desk.

Before she could get there, Betsy steered Rosie toward the breakroom and stopped in front of its door. She spoke in a low tone. "When you and the doc were working on the girl, I saw a man in a blue shirt come out of the waiting room and peer into the unit through the privacy curtain where we were working. That is when I yelled at him and got him out of there. I shooed him back into the waiting room, but he had already observed the commotion. I think he must be a relative of the girl."

"I'll take care of it since Dr. Wilson is headed upstairs," said Rosie as she walked into the waiting room and spotted an anxious-looking man in a blue shirt sitting alone. He rose immediately, wringing his hands. For a moment, her heart broke for him until she realized he might be the reason the girl was in the hospital in the first place.

"My name is Rosie," she said, trying not to show any disgust or emotion. "I am a nurse on the PICU floor. I understand you were in the PICU, possibly checking on one of the patients?"

The nervous man nodded. "She is my daughter. She is very sick, and I am suspicious of the doctor. I think he is an infidel. If he is doing procedures on my little girl, that would bring shame on her and my family."

Rosie was confused. "I'm not sure I understand what you're saying."

"He saw my daughter's private parts. As her father, I will bring this to the attention of the supervisor on this floor. A Muslim cannot have an infidel man looking at the body of his daughter. It is forbidden. It is against the will of Allah. This man should not be allowed to do this ever again."

Are you kidding me? she thought as his words registered in her brain. *What kind of monster is this guy?* Rosie stopped herself, thinking about her earlier run-in with trouble and knowing she might say something that could put her in more danger. "Excuse me, but please understand that the man you refer to is one of the finest doctors in the United States. People bring their children from all over the world to have *that doctor* treat their child."

The father appeared unimpressed. "Please remember that we are now in the United States of Islam."

Angered by the correction, Rosie inhaled deeply before she replied. "Well, never mind that. The doctor didn't have much time to think of the new requirements while he was trying to save your child's life. He was trying to correct something barbaric that was done to her. You are correct; she is very sick, and I only intended to assure you that we are doing everything we can to save her life, which is still in question. I need to get back to her and tend to her needs. Is there something else I can do for you?"

The father replied coolly, "Where is the supervisor's office?"

Rosie knew that all the PICU staff reported directly through a chain of command to the human resources administrator. After careful consideration, she determined that he would eventually figure out who he needed to complain to, so she would rather be cooperative than adversarial. She told him that the supervisor was on the first floor near the cafeteria. She turned on her heels and quickly went back through the door, which held a huge sign that read, "RESTRICTED AREA. AUTHORIZED PERSONNEL ONLY."

Rosie returned to the central desk where Betsy and Dr. Wilson were doing paperwork. With her back to the door, Rosie pointed over her shoulder and whispered angrily, "That man is the little girl's father. He has only Sharia on his mind. He never once asked how his child was!" She looked at Dr. Wilson. "His biggest concern was that you are an infidel and that you did certain 'intimate' procedures on her, which would bring shame on her and her family. I tried to explain we were under a time crunch and trying to save his child's life. He is going to report you to the floor supervisor." She paused. "This could mean your job."

Betsy looked from Rosie to Dr. Wilson and then back at Rosie. The back of her neck was growing beet red. Betsy held up her hand, mouthing a countdown from ten. "I am getting too angry to function in this environment," she said in a strained staccato voice. "Let's go to Cooper's unit."

As they walked toward Cooper's unit, Betsy's volume picked up again. "We all worked valiantly trying to save that girl, and all the father could think about was that the doctor saw her under her gown?"

"We are dealing with a different culture now, aren't we?" Rosie pushed her own anger aside as soon as she saw her son. "Hello, Cooper. Did you miss Mama while I was working?" Rosie stroked Cooper's hair again. She found herself feeling disappointed when Cooper gave no measurable response. "He must be asleep," she said softly to Betsy.

They took a few moments of respite while Rosie explained to Betsy everything that had happened as she tried to get to work that night—the patrol chase, the frantic stop at the Larson's house, the call to the imam, the Fort Worth police rescuing them, and Tom driving her to work.

Betsy grimaced as she listened. "I remember the Larson family. Their son's name was Alex, wasn't it? Poor boy. It's been about eight or nine months since his playground accident, right? How are they doing now?"

"The pain and hurt are still obvious. You can see it in his mom's eyes. I believe my invasion into their home this evening caused some tension between Lori and Tom."

"How so?"

"Tom was angry. He was busy with tax season. It's Ramadan, and I realize now that my unexpected presence could give anyone a reason to feel irritable. Tom was short with me and not very sympathetic about the danger I was in. But when he dropped me off here, he got choked up. I think coming to the hospital where Alex died was too familiar and reopened his wound."

"I'm sorry they're still hurting," said Betsy. "Wait, though. If he dropped you off, and you have no car, how are you going to get back home?"

Rosie shrugged. "I guess I have to call for an escort." She didn't relish that thought at all.

"This is so ridiculous. The fact that you and I, as single women, can no longer leave the house without a male escort has become a huge intrusion into my personal space and finances. I have been perfectly capable of handling myself and my own safety for my entire adult life. Now to depend on some goon whom I hardly know, from some rent-an-escort pool of men, is just insulting."

"I know," said Rosie. "Ramon used to tell me to be careful and not roll down the window if someone approached the car. He used to say, 'Be aware of your surroundings at all times.' That is how I picked up so quickly that the patrol was on my tail. I was aware of their presence almost like a sixth sense. Ramon drilled this into me constantly. It doesn't matter now. The Compliance Network is impounding my car, and it will be expensive to get it back. That is not what I need right now." She lowered her voice. "Honestly, I wonder what God is trying to tell me. I feel like I'm at a point where I can't take any more. I have that same feeling of abandonment I had on the day I lost my mom and dad."

"You have gone through a lot of trauma for your age." Betsy smiled kindly. "Your response to the murder of your parents, along with millions of other people, is admirable. I can only imagine what you are experiencing, then suffering through the months the press took every occasion to replay the videos and news coverage of that day, along with the coverage of the million-and-a-half people suffering radiation sickness." She shook her head. "This must bring back the fresh feelings of horror and grief again and again. And on top of that, losing Ramon and waiting on Cooper's recovery and the uncertainty in that. All you've been through weighs heavy on you. I get it. I see why you feel abandoned and why you might wonder where God is in all of this. I've often heard people say that God never gives us more than we can bear, but it seems you've had more than your share, dear friend. Come to the window with me for a moment."

Rosie joined her, wiping the tears Betsy's acknowledgment of her pain caused, and they both faced the outside lights and early morning traffic of 8th Street as the vehicles moved north and south along their lanes.

"That world may not seem like your friend at this time, but you have a choice to trust God and lean into Him or look at these circumstances and say that you want no part of what else God may have for you. I'm here for you, and I do know, beyond a shadow of a doubt, that God loves you. I can promise you I will do everything I can to help you get through this life-altering tragedy. I'm here, and I love you like a daughter. You can take that to the bank."

Rosie hugged Betsy in a long embrace. Her tears trickled at first and then came faster as the events of the entire evening caught up with her. "Thank you. There are so many times of doubt when I need Ramon with me. He would have sat me down and put his arms around me. He would have told me he was going to take care of the situation. He was such a rock for me when my parents were killed. Nothing was right. Everything had changed, but having Ramon there certainly helped put the tragedy in perspective. Now I don't have him either." Rosie took a few moments to get her tears under control. "But as terrible as everything is, I have to admit that there have also been times when I've experienced unexplainable peace in my soul."

Betsy grabbed a tissue from Cooper's bedside table and handed it to Rosie.

"When Ramon would hug me like you did, he always said to me, 'This is how we recharge our batteries.' I loved that man." She wiped her eyes. "You hearing me out and comforting me shows me that you *are* here for me and Cooper. That's such a consolation to me. As strange as it may sound, even though I miss Ramon, and nothing can replace him, I feel like a piece of him is here with me through your words."

She shook her head as she thought again about the earlier events of the night. "Everything that happened tonight was my fault, though. I should have known better. I feel stupid about the danger I put myself in, the extra scrutiny that I brought on the Larson family, and the concern I caused you."

"Don't be so hard on yourself," Betsy said. "There's a lot going on in that precious heart of yours. I'm glad to hear about that peace. It had to come from somewhere outside of yourself. And *I* didn't give your circumstances a second thought when I called you to come fill in tonight. I wasn't thinking about the Compliance Network. I was only thinking of giving you another opportunity to be here with Cooper."

An alarm monitor went off in the next room. "Back to work," Rosie said with a forced smile.

As they left Cooper's room, out of the corner of Rosie's eye, she saw a stern-looking man with bags under his eyes march past them, looking around as though trying to find somebody.

"May I help you?" Rosie said.

"I'm Roger Barnett, one of the assistant administrators. I'm on call for the weekend, so I'm here to answer the concerns of a patient's father. Can you direct me to Dr. Wilson?"

Pulling out a sheet of paper from his pocket to reference, he said, "A Mr. Siddiqui called the hospital to talk about a doctor on the PICU floor who worked on his daughter."

Rosie grimaced. "Oh yes. I do know about that case. My colleague," she nodded toward Betsy, "and I were both involved in that procedure."

"Let's go to our breakroom," Roger said.

"I'll page Dr. Wilson and bring him in when he's available," Betsy said.

Rosie escorted Roger to the room and turned off the television as Roger sat in a chair nearest the entryway. "While Betsy calls for Dr. Wilson, I'd like you to hear everything that happened. He can clarify when he gets here."

Rosie did her best to explain the situation without allowing her emotions to get the best of her. She'd just finished her story when Betsy and Dr. Wilson entered.

Roger stood to greet them.

"You seem to have met my patient's father," Dr. Wilson said. "Although I didn't catch his name, I believe I can tell you about his concerns."

Roger sighed. "Mr. Siddiqui is his name. He identified all three of you as having worked on his sick little girl." He nodded toward Dr. Wilson. "Mr. Siddiqui is extremely upset."

We're listening to this complaint because a father doesn't want his daughter, when she becomes an adult, to have any physical pleasure when she marries and has sex. We're getting reamed out, but nothing is happening to the father who botched a home surgery! We tried to save his child after untold hours of suffering at home without medical attention. Unbelievable!

Roger droned on. "I handle patient and family concerns, and he was definitely not satisfied. He said he mentioned to Rosie his concern of infidels working on his daughter. I realize all three of you are in a tough spot—"

Dr. Wilson slammed his fists down on a nearby table. "You are absolutely right we are in a tough spot! But do you know who is in a tougher spot? That poor little girl." Dr. Wilson pointed in the direction of the girl's unit. "She didn't get Fournier's gangrene over the last few hours. The horrible and painful gangrene takes at least three to four days to develop. And during that time, she was manifesting all the signs of the infection. This eight-year-old was lying in her bed, presumably at her house, suffering miserably. Meanwhile her vitals were all screaming that something was wrong. She has the lethargy of someone who has given up. We have done all we can, and yet she is likely to die because we didn't see her three or even two days ago. I would have loved to see her yesterday, which would have given her better odds." Dr. Wilson took a deep breath to calm himself. "So . . . *you* were saying?"

Roger cleared his throat. "I know you are trying to save the child's life. But it would have been better had you gotten a Muslim doctor to work on her."

"What would you have had us do?" Betsy said. "The two male nurses who are on the surgery ward downstairs are Muslim, but they are not trained for the emergencies of ICU. They couldn't have helped in this situation, and we didn't have time to think of them anyway. Are you suggesting that we should have not acted, consulted around the hospital to find a Muslim doctor or nurse, and then waited until somebody—not qualified—would have shown up?"

"Not the right procedure, I understand," Roger said. "Before coming up here, I looked at the roster of our PICU medical staff. There is only one Muslim nurse who is even employed on this floor. She is not scheduled to work until tomorrow night. The next available Muslim physicians are on a different floor, and they don't work until tomorrow morning at 6:30 rounds. What are we going to do to alleviate his concerns?"

"Alleviate his concerns? Did you not hear what I said?" Dr. Wilson told him through pursed lips. "Is it more important that his daughter is worked on by a Muslim and dies? Or is it better that she gets the necessary treatment at the hands of infidels and lives?" Dr. Wilson put his head down for a moment, then looked back at Roger. "Seriously, what does the father want from us? And did he tell you how this entire ordeal got started?"

"Mr. Siddiqui wants all three of you fired immediately. That is a position I am not prepared to take at this time. You three are well-established and trusted members of our staff. Relieving you of your duties is not in the best interests of this hospital. As to the second point, I believe I have a fairly good understanding of how the child's fever and infection became an issue, but that's not our problem at this moment."

Roger walked slowly to the two doors and dramatically secured each door by pulling hard on the knob. He came back to the table, put both hands on it, leaned in, and lowered his voice. "I will tell you three something that must not be repeated. We are a hospital that treats sick and injured children who come in our doors. A year ago, this hospital would have called Child Protective Services, and Mr. Siddiqui would have been arrested and charged with child abuse. What a difference a year makes! Our country, and therefore our hospital, is under the control of Islam. At this point, you three have nothing to fear regarding firing. We at this hospital have a national reputation to uphold. In six months or even a year, I pray to God that we can still be pleased with our reputation."

"Roger, please understand this girl is still in critical condition," Dr. Wilson said. "She needs a miracle to have a fighting chance.

Go by her unit and see her vitals for yourself. We did everything by the book." He sighed. "Should we bring up the Muslim male nurse from surgery and have him available, just in case?"

"Yes. We can be proactive to make a point, so that's a good idea—even though, technically, no male should touch a female to whom he is not related. Hopefully, the presence of a Muslim employee will be helpful to the father."

"I know the nurse," Rosie said, "I'll get him." She looked at Betsy and rolled her eyes. *How in the world is this going to help? The nurse doesn't even know ICU procedures!*

"Be careful," Roger warned, then left the room.

"I'm glad I don't have that job," Betsy admitted, smiling, "because nobody is happy right now." She turned her attention to Rosie. "I guess you get the fun job now."

Rosie sighed. "I'll be back in a few minutes—with our one Muslim nurse who will be of little use to us."

"I'll walk down with you," Dr. Wilson told her.

They walked to the bank of elevators, and Dr. Wilson pushed the down button. "Betsy tells me that you got chased down by the patrol tonight."

She sighed. Usually, she hated when someone leaked a private matter, but in this case, she didn't mind. She knew they were both trustworthy. "Yes, and what a fiasco that turned out to be. Now I get the privilege of acquiring an escort, then pulling my car out of impound. Not exactly what I had in mind for my day off. I imagine it gives me another opportunity to trust God for more things in my life. It is hard to imagine what else could go wrong."

Dr. Wilson nodded. "Something tells me we should anticipate that plenty of those types of opportunities are coming our way."

They parted at the surgery floor as Rosie headed to find the male nurse, Asim, and bring him up. She was surprised that he came willingly at her request and wondered if he'd already been pulled to different areas of the hospital. He alerted his supervisor and then headed with Rosie back up to PICU.

As they entered the PICU, an alarm sounded from unit eight. "That's Jimmy's room," Rosie said. "Come on, you can help with this one."

Jimmy Fisher had a congenital heart defect and, with a cruel twist of fate, epileptic seizures as well. The alarm required every available nurse and orderly to restrain Jimmy. As Rosie rushed into the room, she saw several other nurses already working on him. Jimmy was tensing every muscle with super-human strength.

Asim immediately stepped in and held one of Jimmy's legs to stretch out the muscles and relieve and release the cramp that had gripped the boy's body only moments earlier.

Rosie moved in closer to the boy and spoke gently. "Jimmy, can you hear me? Do you know what just happened? We are trying to help you rest. Now take a deep breath for me." The attending staff seemed to hold its collective breath as they waited for Jimmy to breathe.

The little boy gasped for breath at first, then began slowing his breathing as Rosie gently stroked his arm and chest. "That's good, buddy. Now take another quiet breath."

As Jimmy responded to Rosie's nurturing, calming voice, Rosie looked up to find Betsy next to her. "Would you and our new nurse check on the little girl in unit five, please?"

Rosie got Asim's attention and beckoned him out of the room.

CHAPTER 5

11:15 p.m.
Sunday, February 28

LYING ON THE bed face up, arms folded across his chest, Tom pondered Rosie's intrusion into their home and her unsettling exit that night. He thought about the way he'd emotionally come apart in the car when he had dropped her off at the hospital.

Am I becoming an emotional basket case? he thought, as he felt fresh tears fill his eyes.

He forced himself to center his emotions. *Breath in as you lift your hands; breath out as you lower your hands.* But memories of Alex kept taking over his mind. He couldn't remove the image of his son lying in the hospital bed and having to make that horrible decision about ending life support.

We had no choice. The hospital did all they could. And Rosie was right there holding our hands, talking us through every possible explanation and outcome. He sighed heavily. *There were no miracles. Oh, Allah, it was horrible and excruciating.* Tears ran freely down his face, spilling over into his ears. He balled his fists, wanting to hit something to release his pent-up anger and grief.

Lori breathed in deeply and shifted her body slightly toward him.

Not wanting to wake Lori, he slipped out of bed and made his way to the spare bedroom, his mind still reeling. He lay on top of the bedspread, knowing sleep was unlikely. What other explanation could there be for why he so easily wept in front of Rosie? He hadn't wept in months. And now he'd shown weakness to an infidel—and a woman at that. He cringed with embarrassment.

Alex's death last summer came a week before the three bombings and the takeover. He realized he had never taken the time to grieve his son's passing. Certainly, he and Lori felt the loss of Alex's presence within their family. There were the obvious cruel reminders of Alex's absences—the unoccupied room, the empty chair at mealtimes, the unused car booster seat.

It seemed that as soon as his son was buried, Tom was caught in the financial planning and launch of martial law in the DFW area. Jamal, as the city imam, leaned heavily upon Tom, who did all the planning to nationalize the financial infrastructures the radical Islamic warriors had hijacked. This created the needed funds to pay the Islamic soldiers who enforced martial law. Martial law kept the infidels in line and corralled them long enough to implement Sharia Law, which they'd launched on January 1. Though complicated, Tom took pride in his work and secretly enjoyed when people told him that he made everything look easy.

Thinking about all he had accomplished while the lives within his family were neglected, Tom began to tear up again.

Perhaps I should allow myself the time to see what is behind that mystery curtain called grief.

Tom drew his arms behind his head. Though he was emotionally spent, he wasn't sleepy. He closed his eyes, thinking again about Alex.

Alex . . . He had such trusting brown eyes as he would say, "Come on, Daddy. Let's read another book," handing him the longest book on his shelf. He made story time so fun with his infectious giggle, which emptied the other rooms in the house as his

INTOLERANT

sister and mother had to come see what was going on. Eventually, the entire family could end up lying on his bed as Tom did the different voices of bedtime books. Those were wonderful memories . . . He breathed in and out. As he inhaled for the dozenth time, his body responded to something that had changed in the room. Even with his eyes closed, he knew a bright light had filled the room, a light so brilliant that it seemed blinding. He jolted upright and squinted, holding his hand up to filter the light.

In front of him stood the outline of a man, surrounded in the whitest brilliance he'd ever experienced. He gasped. *Can this be Prophet Muhammad, who has finally come to give direction?* He remembered that it was Ramadan, and his people often received visions during the night watch. *Maybe he has come to kill me for some misdeed or omission.* He swallowed hard at the thought. *Have I spent too much time thinking about Alex and not enough time praying?*

Tom flung himself off the bed and got down on his hands and knees, with his head to the floor, assuming the prayer of contrition posture. He didn't know what to do next, so he remained transfixed on the floor, trembling, waiting for something dreadful to happen. Waiting for death.

"Tom, do not be afraid," the man's voice said in the kindest tone Tom had ever heard. It was filled with comfort that calmed Tom with each word. "I am the Man in the White Robe. I am Jesus, the source of the peace you seek, and I love you. I know of your grief and sorrow for Alex. I know you and Lori miss him, and I want to let you know that Alex is in heaven with me."

Tom had heard of this phenomenon in backroom Muslim discussions. The Man in the White Robe was secretly discussed as a visitation of Jesus. In the Muslim parlance, dreams and visions were highly valued because that was how the prophet Muhammad received his revelation. He had heard frightened whispers that for

43

those who had a visitation from the Man in the White Robe, it was life-changing.

Now Tom was face to face with him. And this man was talking about his son.

This Man in the White Robe, Jesus, touched his shoulder. An electric shock flowed through him, which made him jump and sit upright on his knees. Jesus extended his hand to help Tom stand. Wary of any further shocks, he reluctantly accepted the support. He stood, then fell weak-kneed onto the bed.

Either the brightness of the light had toned down, or Tom's eyes had adjusted to it. He didn't know what to say, so he blurted out, "Hallelujah," thankful that he remembered one word from his Christian upbringing before he had converted to Islam. "What can I do for you? Should I call you Master or Lord?"

Jesus smiled. "One of the reasons I am here is to explain who I am. We have much to talk about, and you have much to learn in the weeks to come. Concerning Alex, he is doing wonderfully and is with Granny, Granddad, and me."

Tom remembered that after his parents divorced when he was eight years old, he spent many summers with his grandparents on their farm in the small town of Shamrock, in the panhandle of Texas. He loved those times. Those summers had been lifesavers. They'd brought stability in a life marked with constant transitions, shifting from his mother's house to his father's and back again. He thought about how much his grandparents showed him love.

"They cared for you when you lived with them, and your grandmother sent you letters and presents when you could no longer stay with them," Jesus said, as though he'd been there.

Sobs slipped from Tom's mouth. *There is a God who knows all about me*, he thought. *This really is Jesus.*

"Yes, I really am," Jesus answered Tom's thought. "That small boy with his grandparents on the farm had my love then, and he has my love now. And that love encompasses your family. I died for you all that I might be a gift of grace for both you and your family. You cried out to me as that young boy in the country church your second summer in Shamrock, and I was there. You and your grandfather would meet with me out by the dry creek bed near the old cottonwood tree. You kept that notebook—a prayer journal—and you saw answers to prayer."

Memories of that creek bed overwhelmed Tom, feeling the sun on his back and smelling the mixture of his grandfather's sweat and Old Spice cologne. "I begged you to keep my parents together and to spare the life of my grandfather." Tom's sorrow grabbed at his throat. "I needed Granddad!" he blurted out with an anguished cry. "When my parents split up, he was all I had!" His bitter words trailed off into grief-stricken sobs.

Jesus put his hand on Tom's shoulder and let him weep.

After a few moments as he regained his composure, Tom stood and faced the Man in the White Robe. "But you didn't answer the biggest prayer request in that notebook. You didn't make my parents reconcile. They continued arguing and treating each other worse and worse. Then my grandfather died, and my summers in Shamrock ended. I lived through the vitriol of every hateful conversation, helplessly watching the parents I loved as they tore each other down in front of me. Where were you in all of that? Why did you let them get a divorce? Why did you let Granddad die? They were all I had. And then Alex. He was such a sweet child with a bright future. Why take him?"

Jesus looked at Tom with compassion. "My love for you has no limits. You can't see the entire picture of what I am doing in your life—or what I was doing in and through theirs. I was right there with you when your grandfather died. I was there when you and Lori had to make the decision to remove Alex from life support. Alex had already passed into eternity; he was already with your grandparents and me in heaven. I have plans for you and Lori and your daughter, Whitney. They are plans to give you a future and a hope. Trust me to lead you."

Tears came to Tom again as he remembered the pain of that moment when he and Lori held hands and agreed that disconnecting life support was the only thing left for Alex. Tom slumped on the bedside with his head in his hands.

"That tragedy with Alex took part of your heart," Jesus said. "Yet you still have a place in your heart for him. You miss him and would like to talk with him in the same way you love your grandparents and would like to visit with them. That is one of the joys of being reunited with your loved ones in heaven."

"How do I make sure I get there to see them and experience what you are talking about?"

"Believe in me and receive the gift of forgiveness I am offering you. I died to allow you to live free of the bondage of the wrongs you have done. This is a free gift to you, something you could never earn or deserve. But you have to choose to accept it. Then we need to talk about your time in Shamrock."

"What about Shamrock?" Tom stood and walked to the other side of the room to get another look at Jesus. He looked suspiciously at Jesus, unsure that he could trust this vision he was having.

"I was right there with you when you kept the journal," Jesus said. "When you were writing down that particular prayer request about your parents. You and your grandfather talked it over. Remember, he told you to be careful what you ask for. Do you recall what he said?"

Tom looked down nervously and felt his heart rate speed up. He thought of his grandfather's admonition. "He told me that I was dealing with my two parents and their separate wills and that they were impossible to control because they were allowed to make their own choices." He scoffed. "That sure turned out to be correct." He realized he had asked for the very thing his grandfather had warned him might not be possible. He didn't want to face that truth. "Then you took Granddad from me, right when I needed him the most."

Jesus took Tom gently by the shoulders and looked him in the eyes with a burning intensity. "You had five good summers with him, Tom. You saw and felt what it was like to be part of a loving family so you could be a good role model to your family now."

He couldn't take the intensity of the eye contact with Jesus, and he dropped his gaze. He felt ashamed as he realized he had been focused on what was taken from him rather than the five wonderful summers he'd experienced. He certainly felt Jesus's compassion now, and the reminder of the loving environment he had shared with his grandparents felt overwhelming. Tears began to fall freely down his cheeks again. His grandparents had meant so much to him, yet their removal had been abrupt. That didn't seem fair. He could feel his heart growing distant and hard again as he focused on his loss, just as it had when he was a youth. He took a step back.

But Jesus wouldn't let him get away. Jesus lifted Tom's chin slightly to regain his attention and smiled warmly. "That deep resentment and bitterness you are feeling has done you great harm. In the big picture, you couldn't see that your grandfather had a serious heart defect. Without my intervention, you wouldn't have had those five summers with him. He was a respectable man, a good husband, a loving father to your mother, and an excellent role model in your life. You needed another encourager back in Fort Worth, but you chose Jamal instead of another boy who was on the journey I created for him that was meant to cross your path. I still had my eye on you. and it was your choice again to respond."

Jesus's mention of Jamal surprised him. "Jamal was there for me. He was good to me. He met a need in my life and made me feel like I was part of something like I was important."

Jesus shook his head kindly. "Jamal was not the wisest choice for you because he shook your faith in me in your time of loss. But you must know that I also have plans for Jamal and his family. They need to come to me as well. I know life is hard, and it will soon get more difficult for Jamal. I want to use you in his life. This path will be difficult and full of great conflict, but you will be in the safest place, in the middle of my plan for you. Follow me."

"But what about the free will of my family—and Jamal and his family? Isn't that what you just told me about my parents?"

"There will be times, exactly like the situation in Shamrock, when your prayers may or may not be answered as you want due to the autonomy of others or my Father's immediate will. Walking with me and trusting in me will be the best choice you can make."

"Even when the world I am living in is turned upside down?" Tom said testily, feeling bolder.

Jesus squeezed Tom's arm compassionately. "That is when you need to trust and depend upon me the most. It may not look like it, but I can assure you that my Father is in control. Following me and establishing your eternal salvation will put you in the middle of the greatest earthly adventure you can ever imagine. In the coming weeks and months, you and I will be in close contact if you allow it. Your dependence upon me will be critical. If you choose to follow me, you will affect the course of millions of lives."

Tom unknowingly stepped back. "Millions?! How is that possible?"

"You have to trust me one step at a time, and you will see," Jesus said with a smile.

"Well . . . I do see that bitterness is getting me nowhere," Tom confessed. "I'm sorry that I didn't understand all that was going on then, and I certainly don't understand it now. I want what you are offering, but I don't know what to do next. Please forgive me for putting myself and my desires first. Help me, Jesus."

Jesus put his arms around Tom. "Remember how easily you trusted and believed in me when you were a child? That's how you must come to me now. Come to me with the faith and trust of a little child, Tom, believing I am the one true God. Trust in me as Alex did."

"Alex? I don't understand."

"Alex responded to the words of the gospel while he was at WhizKidz Day Camp early last summer. His best friend from school told him about me, and Alex opened his heart to me. During his last days in the hospital, while he was in the coma, Rosie Chavez kept whispering to him the reassuring words of my love for him. She carries my presence with her because she is my child."

"I don't know how . . ."

"Remember how you cried out to me while you were living with your grandparents on the farm? Cry out again, and this time, give your life fully to me."

Tom breathed in deeply. He finally comprehended that Jesus was offering him a true life, a life of peace and purpose. "Jesus, I give myself to you and choose to trust you fully. I give this bitterness to you and ask you to forgive me of all I've done wrong. Help me learn to love you and follow you."

More tears came, but this time they were tears of relief. Tom knew the struggle and anguish were finally over. He didn't want to fight with God anymore. He surrendered his complete will to Jesus.

Jesus's compassionate voice surrounded him. "What started in Shamrock is now settled. You have let go of the pain and bitterness."

An amazing peace came over Tom. He felt clean. His bitterness was gone. He looked at the Man in the White Robe. "Lord, what do I do now?"

"Let Lori and Whitney know about this encounter. Tell them about the comfort and relationship available to them." Jesus gently tapped Tom's chest. "Tell them about the peace in your own heart and that I am the one, true God. They also need to know that it is okay to grieve Alex and to know that he is safe with me."

Tom nodded. "I will. I promise."

"Now we need to talk about your friend Jamal," Jesus said. "He needs your help because he is in serious trouble."

CHAPTER 6

1:20 a.m.
Monday, March 1

JAMAL KADIB ARRIVED at his office with plenty of time to make certain the seven different camera angles would not show what a messy housekeeper he was. He moved the stacks of papers and books out of the camera's view and resituated his chair so he would be sitting directly in front of a seventy-inch flat-screen monitor. This monitor would be the means for Jamal and the other ninety-nine city imams to watch the Zoom call. This set-up was all the work of a genius coordinator whom everyone simply referred to as the Observer. On previous conference calls, if someone had a question or comment, the Observer enlarged the inquiring person on the screen so everyone could see who was speaking. The Observer made the entire call appear seamless as if the call was staged.

Jamal walked around the room, looking at his chair from every possible angle, trying to imagine what the camera would see while he was on the meeting with the caliph and the other imams. Though he hoped he had done all he could to prepare, he nervously straightened his notes on this night's meeting agenda, readied his pad and pen, and sat down rigidly, anxiously anticipating the call.

At exactly 1:30 a.m., the cell phone rang in Jamal's pocket. "Hold the line for his eminence, the caliph," came a stiff announcement in a female Arabic voice.

Jamal responded in Arabic, "Praise be to Allah." This drill wasn't new to him, though he didn't relish today's meeting.

The agenda focused on each imam's need to oversee the relocation of infidels from the metropolitan regions of the largest one hundred cities or city zones—those places with populations of at least 220,000 people. The infidels were to be placed into camps. If the city and its surrounding area generated a census of less than 220,000, no camp would be established, though the area would be placed on a watch list to make certain no rebellions against the Islamic leadership would occur. Jamal was responsible for overseeing the Dallas-Fort Worth area relocation. The purpose of the camps was to control the vast majority of the infidels. This control was to be achieved by making certain there was no counter uprising, by population control through disease and starvation and gathering up the spoils of war by securing assets.

Jamal sat straight in his chair as he looked at the screen. It was still on audio only. "Praise be to Allah and to Muhammad, his prophet. Peace be upon him," said the caliph, speaking in Arabic, the language of the Koran.

Jamal, along with the other participants, responded dutifully, "Praise be to Allah. Peace be upon him."

Jamal's screen sprang to life with the video feed. There, in vivid color, was the caliph's face in the upper right of the screen. The rest of the screen continually switched to view the other imams, including a small identifier of their city of origin. Jamal recognized a few of the images as the video feed panned all ninety-nine imams, highlighting fifteen of them at a time. He relaxed a little as his friends from the Houston and Austin areas appeared until he realized they looked exhausted and gaunt. Gone were the smiles and carefree days of being college students together. This work, after the takeover, had clearly affected them as well.

He wondered if he looked as haggard as they did. *What happened to being the religion of peace and having our own mosque of followers as we led them and their families into an agreeable way of life?*

Jamal pinched his leg to try to regain some concentration. He knew the onscreen faces changed periodically, so he needed to keep alert. *Sit up straight and look interested,* he chided himself.

The caliph continued, "As you have all heard by now, the announcement of the relocation will be delivered in a few hours, at 6:00 a.m. on the East Coast. This announcement will broadcast on our state-sponsored television on Channel 1 and Channel 2 in each of your cities. We also have simultaneous internet announcements. We have moved the relocation announcement forward to today to be preemptive in our second strategic strike at the Great Satan, the former United States. We have hastened the release of the announcement to keep any potential uprisings short for the next thirty days. Have your jihadists at the ready to quell any resistance to the announcement and implementation of the edict."

The caliph went on to explain that the final size of each camp would depend upon the percentage of that area's population, as well as conversion rates to Islam. Those who converted would, for the present time, be allowed to stay in their own homes, allowed to keep their current jobs, and have the privilege of adhering to Sharia Law. He continued, "Many of the camps are ready, and relocations can begin at the discretion of the imam prior to the April 1 deadline. Nonetheless, all relocation must be completed by April 1."

Jamal's mouth went dry. *This can only be done if I drop everything and make this my only priority. What about my message preparation for the mosque, the daily prayer commitments? And what about my family? This is Ramadan, which is a time commitment in itself.*

"I understand delays, and some sectors of the business and medical communities may require more time," the caliph said. "We will consider those delays per individual imam request." The caliph paused and scanned the faces, though Jamal was unsure what exactly the caliph was looking for. Perhaps the Observer had told him to wait?

The caliph inhaled and looked sternly into the camera. "We are expecting full cooperation. Each of you know where the relocation sites are, and each of you have the resources to complete the relocation by this deadline. We expect—"

"But your eminence," a voice interrupted, quickly followed by the camera going to the speaker identified as the Seattle imam. The other imams shown on the video feed disappeared, leaving a split screen of only the caliph and this imam. "Pardon my interruption, but we will need extra time. The roads and bridges are not capable of holding the mass evacuation we're talking about."

Is this guy completely crazy? Jamal thought. *To interrupt the caliph is tantamount to a death wish. Surely, he doesn't understand what he has just done!*

The interrupting imam paused, as though contemplating his speech, but then said, "I have previously questioned your decision to move up the timing of this relocation but have had no input or response from you. Perhaps we should slow down a bit to make sure we are better able to—"

Two gunshots sounded. The screen showing the Seattle imam was now splattered with blood. The imam slumped in his chair.

Jamal jumped in shock. Logically, the shooting made sense, but he was caught off guard by the immediacy of it. Instinctively, Jamal wheeled his chair around to see if a gunman lurked behind him as well. The hair on the back of his neck stood straight up and sweat poured out of every pore on his body.

The caliph's face now occupied the entire screen. "Aswan Akeem, the Seattle imam has exercised a liberal tone far too long."

His voice sounded eerily calm. "The problem is now eliminated for all of you to hear and see. In case you have not gathered from these proceedings, insubordination will not be tolerated." The caliph's voice turned terse. "Islam is submission, and your submission is to Koran, to Allah, to the stated purposes of Muhammad, and now to me. Any form of conduct, which does not include this perfect submission, will be a grave mistake."

Without taking his eyes off the screen, Jamal reached for a bottle of water and drank long and hard. *How can he seem so calm after murdering one of his imams? He is a bully! How can I be cut out for this type of work?* He thought of his wife and children. This is not who he wanted to be.

"One more item of extreme importance to me," continued the caliph. "More than a month ago, I instructed the regional imams to give an important task to the patrols. In each of the one hundred cities, the patrols have now found and captured at least ten homosexual men.

So now we are working over the homosexual population? Jamal thought. *Why the sudden emphasis on this particular sin against the Sharia? What else does this caliph have planned?*

"These men will be executed publicly tomorrow in the downtown areas of each of their cities," the caliph said. "Some of your cities will have two sets of executions because of the configuration of your regions. St. Paul and Minneapolis; Kansas City, Kansas, and Kansas City, Missouri; Seattle and Tacoma; San Francisco and Oakland; and Dallas and Fort Worth. These areas will have double executions of ten men in each location. Imams will host the executions, which will occur at noon across every time zone in the new United States of Islam. Channel 1 will announce the event early to get the maximum exposure out of the public executions. You will be emailed your scripts, and I expect 100 percent participation. This must be done to bring the purity of Allah to the new nation of Islam in America. In the cities where we will have double executions, the assistant imams will handle the executions in the extra cities. Any questions?"

Jamal couldn't imagine anyone daring to ask a question after what they'd just witnessed with the Seattle imam. He anxiously studied the faces panning by on the screen. All of them seemed gripped with apprehension. Nonetheless, Jamal forced himself to appear as calm and cool as he could, as he suspected the other imams were doing. *Now he was expected to personally host an execution event, which was going to demand more of his time and emotion, not to mention the thought of those who would be killed. He couldn't bring himself to think about that now.*

After an hour, the caliph finally closed his session. Everyone concluded with the normal unison statement, "Praise be to Allah and to Muhammad his prophet. Peace be upon him."

As he made his way from the office, a chill shivered through him. *I am carrying a lot of responsibilities, and I better get this correct the first time. I never would have thought my life would be on the line.* He instinctively looked over his shoulder for a possible gun aimed at him. *Are they watching me? Can I possibly go on as the DFW imam? Now I will have to live under the tyranny of the caliph's pressure and be the source of tension to those under my authority.* He knew that for this entire process to work, he must be as demanding as the caliph, or he could be the next one shot.

Jamal's mind wandered to his youth when he felt similarly overpowering anxiety but failed to handle it correctly. During Jamal's teen years, when he was teased for his weight, he had gotten drunk on more than one occasion to drown out the taunts. His father had spent time and effort to cover up the alcohol use to protect the family name and honor. Jamal's father could have allowed a legal honor killing, but instead, he protected his son. Jamal couldn't forget his previous behavior, even though he believed this bullying as a youth gave him compassion for those who were overweight, who were slow to be chosen to the athletic field, or who were the underdogs in other areas. He had seen in Islam a space to love and bring all types of people into the fold of his flock. He loved his congregation, and they loved him. They knew he was looking out for them, and they admired and trusted him.

Now he had to obey, even if he inwardly disagreed. How would he keep the trust and admiration of his congregation? If he wanted to live, he had no room to think about anything other than exact submission to the strictest rules of Islam. Jamal had been the cleric in Fort Worth until he was promoted to the position of DFW city imam—something he wanted—but now he feared he was in over his head.

Unable to rid himself of the feeling that he was being watched, perhaps at gunpoint, he quickened his pace to his car and drove straight home. He arrived at his house at 3:00 a.m. and hoped to slip in without being detected. To his dismay, he found his wife, Safi, awake and sitting in the living room.

"How long have you been waiting for me?" he demanded.

"Why are you so defensive?" Safi said as she rose from the couch and walked toward him. "You leave the house without so much as a word to me. This is Ramadan when we are supposed to spend extra time with the family and play games with the kids to get their minds off the fast. Then after we break the fast with the meal, you are gone. I can see the pressure in your eyes and in your response to me and the children. Where is the compassionate man I know and that people look up to?"

Jamal tried to walk past her, but she blocked his way. She was trembling.

"You told us this new job would be good for the family," she said. "I want to tell you that I am having serious concerns about the time it is taking, the stress you are under, and the direction this radical path is leading you. I love you, but I feel abandoned. I am alone almost all the time, and the girls miss their daddy. In the last several weeks, I've wondered if the cost might be too great for all of us."

Her words struck at what he also felt, but he knew he could not afford to give in to them in order to protect his family. He had to be firm, even harsh. He scowled at her. "What you just said sounds as if you want to spit in the eye of Allah and the caliph, peace be upon him. There will be sacrifices to make for Islam, but it will be better for you and our children in the long run. You should think long and hard before you say anything else, Safi, because you are close to blasphemy." He looked hard at her. "I don't think you want to go there."

Safi's eyes widened momentarily. "Is that a threat?" she said snarling, surprising Jamal with her blatant defiance. "You think this Islam submission thing is going to make me cower so you will arrange my death as an accident? Remember, I covered for you early in our marriage and kept your parents from having to see the guilt and shame of another drunken incident that could have brought down your family. If you remember, they never found out about it, and neither did the cleric leaders."

Enraged at her insubordination, coupled with the reminder of his past failures, Jamal slapped her hard across her face. The physical contact seemed to feed his fury, and he struck her with repeated blows to the face, head, chest, and stomach. She tried to block his fists from hitting her, but she could not—he was much bigger and stronger than she was. He had never beaten her before, but as hard and fast as his fists connected to her body, his wrath demanded more violence, more submission.

"Daddy?" a small, terrified voice broke into his anger.

Jamal watched in shock as their three small daughters stumbled into the room. Jamal's mind slowly awakened to his children's cries, and he ordered his fists to stop. He quietly straightened himself, still towering over his cowering wife's body, and shamefully looked at his horrified children. "I'm sorry," he said calmly and collapsed into a chair.

Slowly, Safi roused herself and tried to calm their young children. He knew she would want to get them peacefully back in bed so the scene they just experienced could get out of their minds. He watched dispassionately as they clung to her.

"Daddy is under a lot of pressure, but he didn't mean to be so cruel," Safi said to them as they continued to cry. "Mommy and Daddy had a grown-up disagreement, but things will be all right. Everything is okay. Now you girls need to get some sleep because tomorrow is a school day."

As his emotions slowly quieted themselves, Jamal began waking up to the horror of what he had done. As Safi put the girls to bed, he walked to the bathroom and prepared a cold washcloth for Safi's head and face. He opened the medicine cabinet and pulled out the hydrogen peroxide to put on her abrasions.

Safi stepped into the bathroom and jumped in fright when she saw him there. Her face, though swollen, gave away her anger and fear. This physical violence was new to them both. He had displayed his angry temper to her in the past, but he had never struck her. He reached toward her with the cold compress, but she instinctively drew back.

Jamal hung his head. "The caliph's call was rough," he said in a whisper, not looking at her. "He gave each of us a very difficult assignment. When one imam disagreed with the plan, he was killed immediately, in front of all of us. Even if I shared your misgivings about my new position, my life would be in danger if I tried to get out of it." He paused and swallowed hard, unsure of what to admit. Finally, he exhaled roughly and allowed a sob to escape his lips. "I feel like a trapped animal."

Before Safi could respond, he turned on his heel, walked to the garage, got into his car, and drove away. He had to control his rage. He was still seething and knew he needed to get away quickly because he wasn't sure how far his violent mood could take him.

CHAPTER 7

3:45 a.m.
Monday, March 1

THE OBSERVER PUT down his earphones connected to the listening device planted in Jamal Kadib's home and rubbed at the long scar on his right cheek. He turned off the recorder and sent the chronicled file to the caliph's administrator with a flag on the email and a note to the caliph's immediate attention.

"For your ears only: DFW imam may be showing signs of emotional instability. Further evaluation required. Jamal Kadib is on my watch list." He signed it simply, "The Observer."

He sat back in his chair. He'd been in this role long enough to know when an imam was dangerously close to quitting, or worse, losing his ability to rule with an iron hand. Though Jamal appeared calm and collected during that night's meeting, the Observer noticed something in his eyes, something that didn't look right. The Observer had lived by and depended upon his instincts for years. He was correct most of the time, and he knew the caliph depended on his sixth sense. Rarely did the caliph question the expenses of planting bugs and various listening devices in workers' homes and cars because those expenses paid off by exposing the mole, traitor, or weak link to the caliph and his organization.

Taking the DFW imam's folder in front of him, he made a careful list of things to do:

(1) Contact Jamal's administrative assistant.

(2) Have her create a pattern of Jamal's comings and goings from the office.

(3) Wiretap all telephone conversations.

(4) Set up a bug in Jamal's car.

He paused to consider planting a bug in another part of Jamal's house because he couldn't hear part of their conversation after the beating. Something was said that might have made a difference or given him more clues into the disposition of Jamal's temperament. Perhaps his bedroom would be the perfect place. At least he could hear what was going on in that end of the house.

"Planting the bug in his bedroom will be number five on the list," he said aloud and smiled, feeling pleased with himself as he added that to the list.

If he was wrong, and Jamal was simply a compliant but stressed imam, then no harm would be done. But he sensed he was *not* mistaken.

Feeling satisfied with his intended course of action regarding the DFW imam, the Observer turned his attention to three other imams. He rolled his chair to the main control board to type in the addresses of the men in Salt Lake City, Louisville, and Miami. As he listed each man, the computer quickly collated separate files for viewing. He dialed up the Miami file to start isolating that specific imam from seven different camera angles, watching the imam's face and body language frame by frame. As he made notes, his cell phone rang. It was the caliph.

"I received your file and listened to Imam Kadib's conversation with his wife. I don't like what I'm hearing. She does not seem supportive. He beat her, which is good. It appears, though, that after the beating they had another conversation in another room. I want to know what they talked about and why he then left the house. That is bad. Where did he go? We need more facts, so get more facts."

Before the Observer could respond, the caliph hung up. He smiled to himself. *A man of few words. No wonder we get along so well.*

The Observer went back to his freeze-frame study of the Miami imam, looking for another possible chink in the caliph's support system. *I have your back, sir. I'm watching out for you.*

PART 2

THE RELOCATION

CHAPTER 8

5:10 a.m.
Monday, March 1

ROSIE WAS LEANING on her elbows against the counter of the PICU's central desk when she noticed Betsy speaking with a young man in blue nurse scrubs.

The nurse nodded and watched Betsy walk down the hall. He, in turn, sauntered up to the desk. "Good morning. I am Asim. I'm replacing the other nurse from surgery."

Dr. Wilson was going through some charts and didn't look up.

Rosie noted his look of irritation. *Probably because of this nurse's nonchalance.*

Asim was only there at Mr. Siddiqui's insistence, but he was acting as if he was doing PICU a giant favor with his presence.

"I'm Rosie." She slid the girl's chart across the desk to him. "Her name is Ilhan Siddiqui. Everything you need to know is in the chart. I saw that Betsy already checked you in."

Dr. Wilson finally looked up and gave his attention. "Gangrene has spread through her body. We are trying to push heavy-duty antibiotics as a last-ditch effort to make a difference. Whether it works or not is up to the way her body responds."

"Because of her father's wishes, your responsibility is to sit with her and monitor her vital signs," Rosie told him. "You are to tell us if you see the vitals beginning to fall or change in any way. Mr.

66

Siddiqui may try to come into the unit. However, he is not permitted, so if you see a short man in his mid-to-late forties wearing a blue shirt, kindly ask him to go to the waiting room, then make reference to his intrusion on the chart. Are you with us on this?"

Asim nodded, "I can do that."

"Good. We're counting on you," Rosie said and led Asim to the girl's unit. "We're sorry to take you from your normal duties."

"That's fine. I get moved a lot."

I'll bet you do, she thought, feeling disgusted yet again by the new rules.

As Rosie returned to the main desk, a pale Betsy stumbled out of the breakroom, clearly shaken with a shocked expression, as sweat dripped down from her forehead.

"What is it?" Rosie asked, her voice filled with concern. She watched Betsy brace herself against the wall.

Betsy put her hands on her hips, taking several deep breaths to build some steam. Rosie saw the telltale red blush creeping up Betsy's neck, showing she was about to blow. "That creep on the El-Shafei news outlet just announced that we infidels"—gesturing wildly to include all those in the main central area and increasing her volume—"all of us are going to be forced to move to some camp within the next thirty days."

"What?" Rosie said, not sure she was hearing Betsy correctly.

Betsy steadied herself as she shares more of the life altering-news, "Muslims from the rural areas will be moved to the cities and into *our* homes."

"What on earth are you talking about?" Dr. Wilson asked. He let a file he was holding slip onto the nurses' desk.

Betsy nodded. "We're being relocated!" she said, lifting her fingers and making air quotes.

"You mean like to concentration camps?" Rosie felt sick to her stomach.

Betsy slowly nodded her head as Rosie's words sunk in. "Yes," she said, lifting her fists and then grabbing her forehead. "Ooh! How can they do this?"

"This can't be true," Rosie said. "This is too farfetched. You must be wrong."

Betsy stared straight into Rosie's eyes, and Rosie knew that Betsy had heard correctly. She motioned to Rosie, "Well then, come and hear it for yourselves."

Rosie followed Dr. Wilson and Betsy into the breakroom, where other staff had already gathered. They all stood, eyes glued to the wall-mounted television, watching the summary and other details on the information crawler across the bottom of the screen. The news anchor was midway through interviewing different extremist leaders who explained logistics. The infidels would effectively be marched to a location in a predetermined camp, which would be their new home. The infidels could forestall this expensive move by converting to Islam, and "perhaps" they would then be able to retain their home and job, but they definitely would avoid the camp relocation.

Rosie couldn't believe what she was hearing. *We have until April 1 to move out of our homes?*

One leader continued, "To ensure complete compliance, we have elevated the patrol to the position of enforcers for the move."

Thugs is more like it, thought Rosie.

"This is not right." Betsy shook her head and seethed as she stood next to Rosie. "I have lived in my house for the last twenty-five years, and I have to leave it and go to some controlled area just because of what I believe? This makes me so angry! They can't do this!" She balled her fists again, this time shaking them at the television screen.

Rosie placed her hand on Betsy's arm to help her calm down. She knew spies were everywhere, and the last thing they needed was to get into trouble again—especially after she'd just gotten her car towed. But Betsy pushed her hand away.

"First, they take away my right to travel by myself because I'm a woman," Betsy said, her voice shaking. "Then they make me hire an escort, which is the biggest inconvenience I have ever experienced. I can't get anywhere on time, coordinating my schedule with some man I've never met who has yet to show up at my house on time! They don't care about us nonbelievers! They simply don't care. Now they are taking my house from me?" Betsy began pounding her fists on top of the breakroom table. She was trembling, her crimson face matching the color of her fiery red hair.

Rosie had distractedly been focused on Betsy's outburst, but soon the reality of the announcement sank in, and tears welled up in her eyes. "My house is where Ramon and I brought Cooper home from the hospital. It is the only house my son has ever known."

She looked at Dr. Wilson, whose expression had turned ashen. "What are we going to do?"

Dr. Wilson looked around before cautiously whispering, "This is Pakistan and India in 1947 all over again. Only back then, the militia had the place of the patrol and the military. The choice has been made clearer than ever before. We can stay and convert to Islam and presumably keep our jobs and our houses, or remain Christians, or as they call us, 'infidels,' and go to these rural camps, wherever those might be." He closed his eyes and exhaled harshly. "May God have mercy on us."

"Can they really do this to us?" Rosie asked.

"Well, we surrendered," Dr. Wilson replied with a shrug.

Before she could say anything else, she heard the alarm sound at the central desk. "I guess the time for our pity party is over—for now."

She hurried out of the breakroom toward the central desk. From the array of screens there, she saw that the alarm was coming from Ilhan's unit. The girl's vitals were failing fast.

"Ilhan Siddiqui is about to drop again," she yelled to Betsy as she ran toward the room.

As Rosie rounded the corner, she looked through the window, expecting to see the male nurse hard at work to stabilize the girl. But the room was empty except for the girl. "Where's Asim?" yelled Rosie.

"He told me he was going down for morning prayers," Betsy said, catching up to Rosie. "I figured we'd be the ones working with her anyway. I guess he had to get ready and wash his feet and hands before the prayers began."

Betsy stepped to the head of Ilhan's bed and rapidly took her flashlight from her pocket. She gently pried open the girl's eyes. "Come on, honey, we need you to stay with us. A lovely girl like you has so much to live for." Without looking at Rosie, she told her, "I got nothing on the eyes—no movement and no dilation."

Dr. Wilson hurried into the room putting on his gloves.

Rosie hurriedly readied the emergency medical gear. "So, Asim's MIA," she said, adding under her breath, "Typical. It's 'just' a girl. We call this guy up to our floor. We have him sit in her room, waiting for something to happen, and then when we need him, he takes off!"

The monitor alarm changed. Rosie looked up to see the green track flatlining. "Patient failing on every score," she called out urgently.

Dr. Wilson rushed to the head of Ilhan's bed and flipped the RED switch on the wall that issues a "code blue." Almost immediately they heard "Code Blue. PICU South Wing. Unit Three" echoing in the hall over the intercom. Within moments, the emergency team banged the crash cart through the PICU entrance doors and rumbled toward them. Rosie and Betsy pushed the chair Asim should have been in against the wall just in time for the Code Blue team to fill the room.

Rosie asked one of the nurses who came running to see if she could locate the Muslim doctor who worked on the cancer ward. Perhaps he could come for an assist. *No point in offending Mr. Siddiqui again while his little girl is in the process of dying.*

The nurse agreed and left the room.

Rosie watched as the Code Blue team worked to intubate Ilhan's lungs. Dr. Wilson asked for a heart stimulant and another bolus of fluid, as well as another pressor for the blood pressure.

Betsy lifted a syringe of atropine, used to quicken the heart rate, from the crash cart and pointed to the IV port close to Ilhan's arm.

Dr. Wilson nodded. "Yes, now!"

As Betsy injected the medicine and Rosie plugged in the IV bags in the same port, the alarm made the same obnoxious prolonged beep. Rosie groaned with exasperation; the girl was not responding to anything they were trying.

"Give me a dose of epinephrine!" Dr. Wilson barked out.

Betsy promptly grabbed it from the cart and injected it.

All eyes in the room stared up at the monitor. Still no change.

Rosie double-timed it over to the defibrillator on the crash cart, handing the paddles to Dr. Wilson as she stretched the connecting lines tight, away from the cart. Then she began to feverishly cut the gown off of Ilhan, who now appeared gray.

Dr. Wilson set the paddles onto the girl's chest, as the staff stepped back. "Clear!" he said and released the charge.

Ilhan jerked involuntarily.

Immediately, Rosie looked at the monitor, which was still running a flat line. The whine of the defibrillator accelerated to the ready position.

"Clear!" Again, Dr. Wilson shocked her body, and though the girl flinched violently, she remained unresponsive.

Dr. Wilson handed the paddles to Betsy, as Rosie climbed onto the child's bed, straddling the girl with her knees. She positioned her interlocking hands on the girl's chest and began a tempo of chest compressions.

"Come on. Come on!" she insisted in between counts. "Not on my watch. I'm not going to lose you on my watch. Please, God, let her live."

Rosie turned her face toward the monitor, holding her breath and praying desperately for any sign of change. It came. Lines began to move and register the sinus rhythm of her heart along with the hiss of the ventilator, clicking away as the respirations were recorded. The girl was struggling for her life, but the infection that was waging a war inside her body was winning the battle. Despite the brief flicker of a heartbeat, Rosie could see the child was dying right in front of them.

Dr. Wilson ordered another pressor, which Rosie knew would max the girl out on fluids. They had no other choice. Sweat ran down Rosie's face and arms as she continued the laborious compressions. Tears streamed down her cheeks as she realized that her compressions were the only sign of the heartbeat this little girl had. The sad reality was becoming clear: as Rosie slowed the tempo from her fatigue, the heartbeat dropped accordingly. She looked at Dr. Wilson and then at Betsy.

"Let's see what she can do on her own," Dr. Wilson said.

Rosie reluctantly placed her hands on either side of Ilhan's small chest to rest on all fours and catch her breath. The heart monitor began to flatline again.

Dr. Wilson gazed sorrowfully around the room. "I don't have anything else. Does anyone have a suggestion?"

Rosie watched him glance around the unit, silently polling the room as the nurses dropped their heads in an exhausted expression of defeat.

Dr. Wilson sighed heavily. "We've done all we can. Thank you for your excellent work." He glanced at the clock on the wall. "Let's call the time of death at 7:23 a.m."

As the staff slowly filed from the room, Nurse Asim entered the unit. He was coming in from his 7:00 a.m. call to prayer and wore a questioning look, as though he thought just because he left his post, nothing should have happened to his patient. Betsy helped Rosie off the bed as they both began to cry.

"These are the days that are hard to get out of your head," Dr. Wilson said, his voice sounding tired. "I better get upstairs. I'm late for my rounds." He looked at Rosie and Betsy. "Thank you for your time and effort to save this child." Then he turned to the male nurse. Rosie saw a flicker of disgust pass over Dr. Wilson's face, then he quickly gathered his composure. "We tried to accommodate the wishes of the father." He removed his gloves and dropped them into the disposal can next to the door. He patted Betsy and Rosie on the shoulders and walked out.

Rosie walked to the head of the bed to switch off the monitor and disengage the ventilator. Just as suddenly as the alarm bells and noise had started, everything went silent. Dead silent.

Rosie pulled the sheet over the deceased girl. "I will page Dr. Wilson and ask him to meet me and explain to Mr. Siddiqui exactly what happened. He will receive it more easily from a man."

Rosie looked at Betsy, who was putting the room back in order. "It's hard to work so long on someone I've known for less than twelve hours, then see her slip through our fingers like that." She shook her head in exhaustion. "This is the part of the job I like the least when we lose someone, especially a child we want to help, and we can't send her home to live another day. She will miss out on the freedoms we enjoy—" Rosie caught herself. "Or used to enjoy."

Betsy pushed the last piece of furniture back in place and nodded slightly, her eyes filled with understanding. She held out the chart to Rosie. "Can you finish the paperwork?"

"Sure," Rosie sighed. "I need to do something productive before I get any more depressed. That phantom Muslim nurse can catch up with me later."

Rosie followed Betsy out of the unit and dimmed the lights low as Ilhan's body lay waiting for the family to come and make arrangements for her burial.

CHAPTER 9

7:10 a.m.
Monday, March 1

JAMAL DROVE AIMLESSLY east of Fort Worth on Randol Mill Road in the flood plain area of the Trinity River. He sighed as he realized with the dawning of light on this morning of Ramadan, he had missed his one chance to eat for the day. His head was throbbing. His squinting-tired eyes were growing weary, so to avoid the blinding sun, he turned right onto Winters Street, which helped momentarily. When the road made a quick left again, he was staring back into the glare. He looked up to adjust a stubbornly sticky visor to block the streaky sunrays on his windshield. Reaching up, he jerked on the visor. It only moved a little, stirring his frustration, so he yanked down on the flap, which eventually broke loose from the clip and pivoted freely all the way over to the driver's window.

"That is no help at all!" yelled Jamal as he slammed it back in front. The glare was so strong that he had trouble seeing.

Just as he tried adjusting the visor again, his car drifted toward the shoulder of the narrow road. He felt an impact, then ran over what felt like a large bump, followed by a loud scream.

Swerving abruptly to the left, he stopped and looked in the rearview mirror.

A small body lay sprawled on the ground, mere feet from where he had just driven. Putting his vehicle in park, he shot out of the car, gathering up the skirt of his cleric robe so he could move faster. *Please don't be dead*, he thought frantically.

Collapsed on part gravel and part pavement was the crumpled body of what looked like an elementary-aged child, crying and writhing as he held his leg, blood running from his forehead.

"You're hurt," Jamal said as he bent down. "How can I help you?"

The child, clad in blue jeans that were now badly torn and a blue-and-silver Dallas Cowboys jacket with blood on the collar, stopped wailing when Jamal's face came into view. "I can see that you need help." He stood and looked up and down the road where he saw no obvious witnesses. Jamal took a quick assessment of the situation. He could see the boy was still breathing. His backpack on the ground next to him revealed dirty tire marks across the straps. The boy, he realized, to his horror—*this boy is probably the age of my oldest daughter.* He cringed. Jamal presumed the child was on his way to school or to the bus stop.

He considered calling 911, but he had way too much on his plate to get involved in an incident that probably had to do with an infidel. He made a snap decision to escape before someone came along who could identify him. "I'll go get you some help. An ambulance will be coming very soon to assist you." He decided to drive to the nearest convenience store and call 911 to report the accident anonymously.

Jamal ran back to his car and sped away. He made a right turn onto Sandy Lane, rounding the corner from the accident and stopping long enough to take his cleric robe and skull cap off. He threw them onto the backseat's floorboard. As Jamal shoved his tunic into the backseat, his hand brushed against his sunglasses. Jamal put them on and shook his head. If he had these on in the first place, he wouldn't have needed to mess with the visor, and this whole debacle wouldn't even exist.

He then took a quick look in the rearview mirror so he could straighten his hair and appear as normal as possible. What he saw was a tired, frightened, and hungry man who had now hit a little boy on the side of the road.

What have I become in such a few short hours? I've beaten my wife, terrified my children, plowed into a child, and left the scene of the accident. He sighed. His whining would do nothing to help him. He turned his attention back toward the road. *I just need to report the accident and get that kid some help.*

He unsteadily sped another mile and came to an intersection at a more populated area. Spotting a corner convenience store, he pulled his car to the side of the store to avoid any surveillance cameras. Leaving the engine running, he walked briskly into the store and up to the counter.

The store clerk, with his back to the cash register, was busy taking cigarette packs out of the cartons and shoving them into the long slots above the counter. Though the clerk looked at Jamal when he entered and stood at the counter, he kept stocking product.

"Excuse me," Jamal said loudly, feeling frustrated. "This is an emergency. I'm in a hurry here!"

The worker turned around. "Yeah? What's going on? How can I help you?"

"You know where Sandy Lane goes back north toward the river, then left on the street called Winters?" Without waiting for the cashier to respond, he continued. "There was an accident there about two minutes ago. Would you call 911 because it looks like a little boy was hurt? Have an ambulance come quickly. I'm heading back there to check on the boy. Please, just make the call."

"Calm down, mister," the clerk said, picking up the store phone and dialing.

"Thank you!" Jamal bounded back to his vehicle and drove one block north to make it look like he was going back toward the accident. Once his car was out of sight of the convenience store, he made a quick U-turn to head west, back toward Fort Worth.

So, I'm not only a hit-and-run driver, now I'm a liar. What am I doing? He sighed heavily and reached up to pull down the rearview mirror to look at himself. He brushed his hair with his fingers. *Now I've got to get cleaned up and look presentable.* He readjusted the mirror as he continued to drive toward his home. "You're disgusting," he said to himself. *I don't want to host an execution of homosexuals in downtown Fort Worth. That's the last thing I want to do right now. I can't even think straight. I need to talk to someone who can help settle my nerves.*

Jamal reached for his cell phone and dialed Tom's number. As the phone rang, he realized his only way out of this terrible situation was to tell Tom the truth. This was something he didn't relish. As soon as Tom answered, he shot out, "Tom, I am in big trouble."

"Yeah, you were missed at the mosque for morning prayers. Someone else had to lead the Al-Fajr prayer and wing it through part four of your khutbah series on the importance of the morning prayer. Kinda ironic, don't you think?" Tom chuckled.

"It's not funny. I only wish that was all that was wrong. I had a very disturbing call with the caliph last night. I went home after that and beat Safi badly. I've been out in the Trinity River area since then to clear my head." Jamal lowered his voice as if to hide the darkest part of the truth. "I ended up hitting a little kid as I was driving into the glaring sunrise. I checked on him, and he was still alive, but I left him on the road and drove to a convenience store to report it. I'm heading home now."

"Why did you hit Safi, and then you left the scene of an accident?" Tom's voice sounded harsh. "Do you realize that is a felony? What in the world is going on with you? Why did you choose the Trinity River this morning?"

"I don't know! I-I ran because I was scared. My life is a huge mess, and you've got to help me! My nerves are cracking, and I have to go to an event downtown at noon—"

"What's going on downtown?"

"Tom, listen to me!" Jamal's patience had reached its limits. "These questions are not helping me right now. I need someone to help me, not interrogate me."

"Okay," Tom said, his tone calming down. "What do you need?"

"I've got to get home, take a shower, and get to the office. I'll explain most of it later, and we can work on the answers when we get together. I just need someone to hear me out, and you're my best friend."

"I'm here for you, Jamal." Tom's voice sounded weary but concerned.

Jamal breathed in deeply. "You may have heard that the caliph has rounded up groups of homosexuals in each of the large cities who will be executed today. Hang on, this traffic is beginning to snarl up."

Switching lanes, Jamal pulled his car into the right lane of a familiar thoroughfare. He switched the cell phone to a hands-free connection. "As the city imam, I must host and present greetings from the caliph, along with admonitions about the Koranic lifestyle and the disapproval of anything that does not conform to Sharia Law. I sent a text to Omar, the assistant city imam, early this morning to ask him to cover the Dallas execution. Now I have to go by the office to check in and pick up my script and make sure everything is all right. Can I swing by your office to pick you up this afternoon after the executions?"

"I'll be looking for you," Tom said. "Call when you're on the way. I still have lots of questions, but I want to help you. Hang in there."

Jamal drove straight to his house. This time, as he entered, he announced his presence with a quiet hello but didn't receive a response. He took a few steps into the kitchen. "Hello?" He said again, still with no response. He walked down the hall toward the bedrooms and noticed the children were not there.

A bad feeling settled into his stomach. *I bet Safi has packed up the girls and left me because of the beating.*

Jamal ran from bedroom to bedroom, looking in each closet to see if he could tell if any appreciable amount of clothes were missing, if their backpacks were gone, or if Safi's suitcase was absent. He slowed down when everything seemed to be in its place. He walked back to the kitchen and looked to see if she had left any messages. Everything seemed to be in order, and he had no messages. *Where have they gone? Has she told anyone about the beating?*

He showered and put on a fresh robe and skull cap. As he was leaving the house, he walked by his home computer and paused long enough to touch his fingers to the keyboard, wanting to check for news stories about the little boy he hit, but he had no time. Although Sharia Law was in force, civil law remained with traffic cops and the normal maintenance of responsibility in respecting others' lives, infidels or not. Hurting a child and leaving the scene bothered his conscience greatly.

He'd wanted to stop his life long enough to own up to the hit and run, but his duties weighed upon him. He had to keep moving and stuff down any emotions that didn't relate to the relocation, execution, or other wishes of the caliph, like getting the camp ready for occupancy. He shook his head and backed away from the computer. It was time to leave. Back in the car, the images of the boy returned, and he slumped wearily. *Maybe Safi is right? This job is driving a wedge between me and my family. Is the caliph too radical for my beliefs? I can't deal with this now. I need to focus on what is next.* He finally arrived at his office at 10:25 and hurried inside, glancing furtively at his personal assistant, Uma. He decided to take charge rather than let his fear show. He walked straight toward his office, asking Uma as he passed her, "Did you print out the pdf for the downtown event? Did Omar come by and pick up his copy for hosting the Dallas executions?"

"Your copy is on your desk. Omar got his copy about an hour ago and is on his way to Dallas already. Where have you been? This is important!"

Jamal stopped mid-stride and gave her a deadly stare. He didn't take kindly to being questioned by his secretary, a woman. He opened his mouth to say as much, but something snapped in his brain. *What if Uma is the spy for the caliphate here in the DFW office? What if she gives a bad report about me to the caliph?*

He breathed in deeply to get a hold of himself. "Uma, I know you are my assistant, but I do believe I am capable of keeping track of my own life. Please allow me some space in that regard." Jamal's voice rose in volume at the end of the sentence, belying the sense of calm he was trying to project.

"You can't be late." Uma stared back at him, seemingly ignoring his words. "The executions are quite a spectacle to tighten up gender orientations that have gone wild over the last decades. I, for one, am glad to see this come to an end." She stopped to smooth out her hijab and glanced at him. "Will you take your personal car or the city imam vehicle?"

He glared at her. *She has the courage of a pit bull! I better be careful what I say to her.* "Since it is the business of the caliph, I'll take the official car."

Quickly stepping into his office, he snatched up the instructions, shoved them in the folder under his arm, and headed back out to the waiting car without another word to her.

He drove a few blocks and turned into a parking lot to read the instructions. The last thing he'd wanted was to give Uma the satisfaction of explaining the details of the noon execution to him. He pulled the sheet from the file and began to read.

The patrol director will put up the barricades on the ground level underneath one of the tallest buildings in the downtown area. The patrol will lead the ten men, captured for execution, to the roof above the thirty-eighth floor of the tallest building in Fort Worth. Their hands will be zip-tied behind them. Then, one by one, each man will be pushed off the building in such a fashion that the body will land inside the barricaded area below.

A sick feeling came to his stomach, and he paused, thinking again of the boy's body lying in the road. He blinked hard and shook his head to focus. He noted that he would be provided with a bullhorn to use as he presented the official host's message to the onlookers.

The patrol would make certain that a crowd of people attended and that the proper mob atmosphere was in place. Agitators were paid to yell slogans, hold up signs, and otherwise discourage others from any violation of Sharia. Jamal lowered the paper and stared out the window. The instructions were very clear, but he dreaded every aspect of this event.

He wheeled the official car back on the road and called Omar to ensure that he understood the instructions and his part of the event. "Where are you?" he asked.

"Right here in the thick of the Dallas executions," Omar exclaimed.

"So, you've found your spot? Tell me about it. What's it like there?"

"Hang up, and I'll do a video call. You have to see this for yourself."

Omar's video call came through immediately. Jamal pulled the car to the side of the road so he could watch with undivided attention. Omar's smiling face showed his excitement. "I'll hold the phone up and do a slow 360-degree scan of the crowd," he said. "Look and listen."

Jamal could see people in every direction. "It certainly looks like the advance team got the crowd there."

Omar returned the phone to his face. "Yes, I'm here along with at least two thousand people, and I can see more coming. They are yelling something about getting this started, but we're still an hour out. The barricades are established, and news people are here setting up too. Maybe this will stop all forms of perversion and queer activities, at least from the public view."

"That is the hope of the caliph." A horn blast came behind Jamal. He checked the rearview to see the problem. "I've got to go."

Omar spoke quickly. "One more thing. A friend from Seattle called me about Aswam Akeem, the imam who was shot last night. His house was torched in the early hours this morning. The fire killed his wife and four kids. It appears that his parents and in-laws were hunted down and killed as well. Jamal, be careful."

Jamal's mouth went dry, and the honking car behind him grew louder. The thought of driving home to get his wife and kids and escaping became paramount in his mind. But he had to do this one more appearance. "Thanks," he said quietly. "I'm about ten minutes away from where I need to be. See you at the office later."

He disconnected the call and drove to the corner of Houston Street, where he could see lots of young people walking in the direction of the event. A police officer spotted Jamal's official car and waved him into the parking space designated for him. As Jamal stretched to get out of the car, he reached into the passenger's seat to get the folder with the prepared remarks when someone tapped him on the hip.

A patrol escort was holding a bullhorn. "Here is your horn, sir, and I will make sure you get safely to the podium."

As he followed the patrol, Jamal was shocked by the size of the mob and their vocal fervor. They were repeatedly chanting, "Come on. Come on. Let's get this going!"

Homemade signs bobbed up and down throughout the crowd. The mildest read, "Queers, your time is up!" and "Fags in body bags!" The other signs were much more visually and verbally graphic.

Thirty minutes from the appointed time, the crescendo is building, and I haven't even said my opening remarks. How much worse will this get?

"We're anticipating this crowd to double in size," the patrol said, as though reading Jamal's thoughts. "Sir, please be aware that the news people will have two separate drones aloft to get the different angles for the best results. The Observer thought that would please the caliph. So, when you are looking up, don't be distracted by the movement."

Jamal nodded, keeping his face solemn to avoid his disgust. "Thank you for that warning." *What a circus. I can't wait to finish this and get out of here. Then I can talk to Tom.* He looked back over the crowd and then down at his instructions. *I better practice my part so I don't disappoint the crowd—and the caliph.* He found his comments in the notes and read silently through the text of his remarks again. He had to be prepared mentally and emotionally to make it appear he was completely onboard with this event. Everything was at stake.

CHAPTER 10

10:45 a.m.
Monday, March 1

ROSIE WOKE UP in the hospital sleep room, an area set aside for staff who required rest during a double shift. Since Rosie had no car to take her home, and she had to work later that day anyway, she decided to stay put.

She stretched and yawned as she wandered out into the break-room to get some toiletries from her locker to freshen up. She had dreamed about Ramon, and she wanted time alone to think about him. She sat at the breakroom table, her mind bouncing between the pain of losing the Muslim girl, her trouble getting to work last night, the relocation mess, and the dream about her husband. She let the dream capture her imagination. It was similar to when she first met him. Her first job was near the Texas Christian University campus at a Fuzzy's Taco Shop. She'd been cleaning tables when a guy from two tables over interrupted her.

"Excuse me, miss, can you check on my order, and by the way, you have beautiful blue eyes." That was the first time she'd laid eyes on Ramon Chavez, and it had changed her life.

"Thank you, sir. Do you remember when you placed your order? If they asked for your name, they will call your name when it's ready." She finished wiping down the table and picked up her tub of dishes.

"I do remember, and I did give my name," he said. "But it's been a while, and I see people who were behind me in line picking up their food."

Taking her wet rag, she made a cleaning motion over the table to pick up the crumbs from the last customer, then she threw the rag into her tub and balanced it on her hip as she smiled at him. "I can see how that would be frustrating," she had to admit. "What did you order, and what name did you give? I'll check."

"I ordered a Big Salad with chicken fajitas and avocado-ranch dressing."

"And the name?"

"Hugo."

"Hugo?" she asked in surprise, assuming he wasn't telling the truth. "As in Victor Hugo?"

"No, as in Hugo Chavez." He grinned a wide smile.

"Why Hugo?" she asked.

"Well, my last name is Chavez."

Rosie shifted the tub of dishes, took two steps toward the food counter, then turned and snickered in Ramon's direction as she caught the joke that the deceased Venezuelan president shared this guy's last name. She thought he was cute and clever.

As Rosie arrived at the food counter, the name "Hugo" came over the loudspeaker. Ramon sprinted to the counter. "That was fast! You must have a lot of pull here." He smiled again and winked. Then he asked for her phone number.

She had never given her phone number to a guy, but he had sparked her interest. "On one condition." When he raised his eyebrows, she smiled. "What's your real name?"

He laughed out loud. "Ramon."

A week passed before she heard from him. They made plans to go out, and he'd come to the door of her parents' home, graciously met and interacted with them, and escorted her to the car. He even opened her door on their first date. She was impressed and then swept away.

"Hey, Sleeping Beauty, are you awake?" Betsy slid up to Rosie, interrupting her pleasant daydream. Betsy looked exhausted, but by the look on Betsy's face, Rosie had a feeling rest was not coming soon. "It's a good thing I haven't left for home yet because we have problems with Siddiqui again. This time, he called in some Islamic reinforcements." Betsy rolled her eyes and shook her head as she continued. "Evidently, our hospital acquired a new administrator, Saeed Ali-Com, and Siddiqui got in front of him. He wants to see all of us together. Walk with me to the unit where the girl died. Dr. Wilson is on his way down now."

Saeed Ali-Com was sitting in the only chair in the unit when Dr. Wilson, Betsy, and Rosie arrived together at the room. He neither stood nor offered his hand but coolly regarded them as he tapped his glasses on what appeared to be hospital personnel files that rested on his lap.

"You asked to see us," Dr. Wilson said. "This is the charge nurse for PICU, Betsy Thompson, and her nurse, Rosie Chavez."

"I know who you are," Saeed said in a curt tone. "Even after being warned to cease treating the Siddiqui child without an Islamic presence, the three of you still worked on her. What is your explanation?"

Rosie was shocked at his question. Did he not understand what had taken place?

"Respectfully, sir," Dr. Wilson said, "the chart will show that Ilhan Siddiqui went into cardiac arrest a few minutes before 7:00 a.m. The Muslim nurse, who was stationed in that very chair, left prior to that emergency to participate in the morning call to prayers. Similarly, the Islamic doctor, whom we tried to reach, was otherwise predisposed. We had no other Islamic medical staff. Unfortunately, this was the time of her passing. Even though we fought for her life, she succumbed to her infection. What would you expect us to do?"

"What were your instructions from last night?"

"We were to secure Muslim medical staff, which is exactly what we did, but her cardiac arrest occurred at a most inopportune time, which was out of our control. We couldn't let her die without giving assistance, could we?"

"I'm asking the questions here. All three of you are on probation."

Rosie's eyes popped open wide.

"Notwithstanding your work record here at the hospital," he continued, "the fact remains that all three of you are infidels, and you have less than thirty days to convert to Islam, or you will take a long and not very enjoyable march to the camp down south." He stared at them for a moment, then stood and left.

As soon as he cleared the unit door, Rosie's mouth gaped open in shock and covered her mouth. "I can't believe this. If this is any indication of how much fun it will be working for Mr. Sunshine Ali-Com, then I guess I'll take my chances with the camp. Cardiac arrest, and he doesn't want us to respond to a dying child? How dare she code during their morning prayers. What about our oath as healthcare professionals and our pledge to do no harm? He definitely has no consideration for the health or feelings of others, nor does he care in the least."

Betsy's neck reddened. "Not so much as a 'kiss my foot,' or 'Gee, it was nice meeting and talking to you three,' or 'I'm sure going to miss you and your wonderful expertise here at PICU when they ship you down to the camp,'" she spat out. "We'll see how this hospital does without our experience. Hope one of his kids doesn't need help."

"It doesn't appear that he would care—at least if it's a daughter," Dr. Wilson said and looked at his watch. "I need to get back upstairs to prepare for two surgeries this afternoon."

"It will be difficult to imagine what this place will look like in two months when they clear out the infidels and bring in the replacements."

"How about we take a break?" Betsy said.

Just as they slipped into the breakroom, the wall-mounted television began to blare with another jolting news alert.

"We have breaking news," said the somber-looking El-Shafei news anchor. "In thirty minutes, public executions will take place in all major cities. Ten men from each city will be executed. In the DFW metroplex, we will cover these events live—one in Dallas and one in Fort Worth. Before they begin, his eminence, the holy and gracious caliph, peace be upon him, will deliver a message. The crime is homosexuality, the shameful and disgusting act of sodomy. The method of execution for these men will be quick and merciful, due to the kindness of our caliph. Each man will have his hands tied behind his back and will be thrown off the highest building in each of the downtown areas."

"Oh No, this is awful!" Betsy said.

Rosie gasped and let out an audible groan as the breakroom began to buzz with conversations.

"How can this be right?" asked Betsy. "This is exactly the way the radical Islamists behaved in parts of Iraq during the US occupation. Those are some sick minds that think this type of execution is okay. I can remember when the United States embraced Muslim immigration, and all the network news channels praised Islam as a religion of peace. I even believe some of those American network news anchors were gay, but I don't remember a single anchor saying a negative statement regarding the Islamic belief that homosexuality is a capital offense. I wonder where those guys are today?"

Rosie's ears perked up as the news anchor continued. "It is the decision of the caliph, peace be upon him, to bring this plague of sin to the attention of the public in each of the one hundred major cities around the United States of Islam. With this public form of execution, the caliph believes that the plague of homosexuality will stop, and the nation will be purified from this sin against Allah. We will begin our coverage in approximately fifteen minutes."

Rosie watched the news cameras pan the crowds at both locations, zooming in on the signs the jubilant spectators carried and amplifying the noise of their chants.

Oh, Dear God, what have we become? Please be with those men and their families. You are a compassionate and loving God who sees the hearts of men. Have mercy on us all.

CHAPTER 11

11:35 a.m.
Monday, March 1

THE OBSERVER WATCHED the DFW imam's office on the same cameras he had used to view Jamal the night before during the conference call. His multiple cameras also included the reception area where Uma now sat. He leaned forward with renewed interest. Uma's belligerence toward Jamal was curious to him.

She is so spiteful with Jamal, snipping at him over his hours in the office and scolding him. I wonder why he puts up with her? Is she the only person available to work within the DFW office? I don't particularly trust her, but I have no one else to ask. He watched as Uma filed her nails at her desk. *She has no other work to complete?* He exhaled loudly, feeling disgusted by her. He picked up his phone and called her.

As the phone on her desk rang, he listened as she sighed and dropped her nail file before answering.

"Good morning, Uma," he said. "This is the Observer from the home office. You have probably heard of me since I coordinate all activities between all the major city imams. I noticed that your imam, Jamal, took the caliph's car."

"Yes, sir," she said, slowly drawing out her response; a quizzical look covering her face as she glanced around the office.

He ignored her questioning look. "A week ago, all the city imams' assistants were sent a package. You received one, which you were to store away until this call. It is time for you to get that package and follow the instructions to the letter. Please get that box out right now."

Without a word, she held the phone in one hand as she strained to pull the box out of the bottom file drawer with her other hand.

"Be advised that I have access to several cameras and microphones within the office suite you occupy," he continued. "For example, your interaction with the imam this morning was too harsh. If you are going to follow my instructions, the imam must have some level of trust with you. You need to tame your responses to him. No more catty comments. Do I make myself clear?

Uma immediately sat up straighter and squinted around the room looking for possible cameras. "I have the box here." She displayed the box, waving it in random directions, trying to locate the Observer's camera.

"Good. Now put it down," The Observer rolled his eyes at her apparent inadequacies. "Since you are alone in the office, it would be much more comfortable for you to put me on speaker phone. That way, you will have both hands available."

"Oh yes, sir, the office is empty except for me." Uma's voice shook slightly, and her eyes darted furtively around. She put the handset in the cradle and punched the button to activate the speaker on the telephone console. "Are you still there?" she asked awkwardly.

"Yes, I'm here." He loathed having to use a woman and smiled at her nervous reaction. "As you know, the caliph has set up a city imam in each of the one hundred major cities in our new United States of Islam." While he was speaking, he watched Uma reach in her drawer and pull scissors out to attack the box's wrapper. "Wait!"

he nearly shouted in frustration. "Before we get involved with the box, there is something else we must discuss."

She dropped the scissors as if they had burned her hands. Then in an act to recover herself, she spoke enthusiastically. "I certainly know all about that, and the DFW is one of those cities."

"Let me finish," he spat out, fearing he wouldn't be able to get through the rest of their conversation without losing his temper. "In each office of these large cities, I, as the Observer, have a helper within the imam's office—someone who can give me information when I need it. It is imperative that this person be discreet in getting the information to me without the imam knowing that he or she is helping me. Do you realize what I'm asking you to do for me?"

"Oh, I like the way this conversation is going." Her face brightened as she again scanned the room. "If you're asking me to be your helper, I am more than willing. What can I do?"

"I was hoping you would say that. I'm expecting you to get the information I am requesting and in a timely manner." His jaw was so tight from gritting his teeth that it was beginning to ache. He hoped he wasn't making a mistake by recruiting her. "Remember, this is just between you and me. All this is for the good of the caliph, peace be upon him." The Observer bowed his head in submission to the caliph.

"I certainly would like to try," she said.

"Fine. Get some paper to make some notes. This is very important. You and I will need to work closely as a team in the next several days. Here are my expectations."

Uma scrambled around in her desk drawers until she located a pad of paper and pen. She put the paper on the desk, arranging the box on the left side of the table with the pen in the middle of the writing space. She folded her hands to indicate she was giving him her full attention. "I'm ready to start now." She glanced toward the door. "I just hope we don't get any visitors during this discussion."

"If we do get a visitor, I'll stop talking. You are to address them and act natural. It is all very easy, Uma, don't worry. When they leave, we will resume our conversation. No one will ever know we are on the phone. Simply follow my instructions and take good notes. You will do just fine." *You better do fine—or I will dispose of you when I am finished with you!*

"This sounds exciting, very secretive," Uma blurted out with a big grin.

"Okay, let's begin." The Observer cleared his throat. *Will this woman ever shut up and just listen, or will there always be constant running commentary?* "Your responsibility is to keep track of all your imam's hours both in and out of the office. I want to know where he goes, what he does, and who he sees. You must keep an up-to-the-minute log of where he is at all times."

Uma took notes on what the Observer was saying and nodded as he continued to talk.

"I will keep track, with our recording devices, of all his telephone conversations. However, I am concerned that your imam is compromised and has put up some safeguards. Let's just say he is more cautious than usual."

Uma put down her pen. "I think you might be right. He seems to—"

"Uma," the Observer interrupted, "We are not interested in anything but facts, not what 'seems' to be true or what you think. All the caliph wants are the facts. Remember, we are a team, and you are the only one on the ground in Fort Worth who can give us the facts about your imam. Consider yourself a private investigator working directly for the caliph and for the glory of Allah, peace be upon him."

Uma sat up even taller at the suggestion of being the PI for the caliph. She set her jaw as if determined to make this work.

"This factual information that you will gather is vital for DFW's survival. We are counting on you. Now that you know the nature of the request, are you the right person for the job, or should we look for someone else?"

"I can do it, and I will do it!"

"Very good. Keep the log hidden and send it to me every night at 8:00 p.m. Right now, the GPS tracking sensor that is hidden on the official car tells me that Jamal has parked the car in the downtown area of Fort Worth. But did you know that the car was parked for eleven minutes at the corner of Penn and Seventh Street earlier today? Why did he stop? Did he pick up anyone at that address? Did he arrive at the downtown location alone? These are questions that you can research for us. Remember, we need only the facts. I will make arrangements for the GPS report to be downloaded directly to your computer, then you must send me the day's activities at the prescribed time."

Uma smiled conspiratorially. "It would be an honor to do those reports for you."

"Now let's get started on the contents of the box." The Observer waited while she picked up the box and held it in front of her. "Look over the instructions, and I will answer any questions you have. The contents of the box are complicated."

Uma mopped her brow with the back of her sleeve, as her body began to react to the exhilaration of being chosen by the Observer. Her hands shook so much that she struggled to open the box. When she finally did, she quickly pulled out the contents and read the instructions.

"Are you feeling okay?" asked the Observer. "I can see that your hands are trembling. Is this too much for you?" *I am beginning to wonder if this woman has the mental capacity to handle these tasks.*

"No! I'm just excited to be part of your team with the caliph here in Fort Worth. This is the most important job I've ever had. I want to be a good private investigator for you and his eminence."

Stifling a sigh, he reverted to his saccharin sweet voice. "You are doing just fine. Please take your time. We want you to understand what you will be doing."

The Observer waited until Uma put down the instructions and looked up expectantly. "As bright as you seem to be, I am sure it is probably self-explanatory, but I want to warn you that when you connect the devices to your imam's vehicle, you should be wearing gloves to avoid leaving fingerprints. Put the gloves on after you get inside his car, so you do not look suspicious.. These devices are fairly easy to install, but when you are in the parking lot, or wherever his car is parked, you need to avoid looking or acting suspicious. Walk up to the vehicle as if it is yours. Do you have the key to his car?"

Uma coughed slightly, as though embarrassed. "No, he has never trusted me with the key."

"That is okay. Simply use the automatic door opener that is in the package." He paused as she dug back into the box and brought out a small device. "It is easy to use. It will unlock any car door. Push the 'unlock' button and hold it for five seconds, then push the button again, and you will hear the click of the doors unlocking. Once you are inside the car, use the gloves in the package and go to work installing the bugs. Exit the vehicle, lock it, remove the gloves, and dispose of them, and you have completed this task. As soon as your imam comes back and uses his car, I will be able to hear every word he says inside it, and we can determine his true intentions toward the caliph. Do you have any questions?"

Uma smirked. "I'm perfectly capable of carrying out these instructions, sir, and am glad to do it. I never trusted Jamal anyway."

He smiled at her eagerness to work for him. "When you have completed the task, call this number and let it ring once, then disconnect the call." With that, the Observer hung up and watched on the monitor as Uma reread the instructions, put on the gloves, and picked up the box containing the door opener before heading out of the office. Just before she closed the door behind her, she looked around the room once again and gave a little wave goodbye.

The Observer dropped his head into his hands. *I think I'm going to regret using this imbecile. This incompetent woman should have put the gloves on once she was in the car, as I instructed her to do multiple times.* Even so, he had to admit that he was mostly pleased that this portion of the plan was coming together.

He turned his attention to the public television monitor on his array of screens and checked his watch. "It's almost showtime," he breathed, as he settled back into his armchair. He tuned to the Fort Worth feed to see how Jamal was going to handle his presentation of the caliph's remarks. *This should be very interesting.*

CHAPTER 12

11:50 a.m.
Monday, March 1

THE OTHERWISE DOCILE business atmosphere of the high-rise buildings had been converted to a makeshift amphitheater with a fifty-foot square street-level barrier next to the second-tallest building in Fort Worth. Jamal estimated that more than five thousand people were crammed together. They stood shoulder to shoulder as they aggressively jockeyed for a better view. People pressed up against the metal of the police obstacles with their hands on the top of the rails, hot from the sun beating down, trying to keep their balance as others shoved from behind. Everyone wanted to be ringside. The crowd was so wired up that chaos was one firecracker away from a disastrous stampede.

He stifled the urge to run and raised the bullhorn, engaging the speaker button on the wired microphone. "On behalf of his eminence, the gracious and merciful caliph, peace be upon him, I welcome you to the execution of these sodomites who have forsaken the laws of Allah."

With that statement, the audience's deafening roar drowned out anything else Jamal tried to say. They began to surge and pulsate almost in unison to a spontaneous beat, yelling, "Go! Go! Go!" and raising their fists in the air. Others brandished their derogatory signs, which celebrated the execution in tempo with the chants.

After several attempts to regain control, Jamal finally pointed skyward and spoke once more into the mic to say needlessly, "Look up! Here comes our first perpetrator."

On the roof of the assigned execution building stood two patrol officers secured with a harness to ensure their safety, each wildly waving the new green-and-black flag of the United States of Islam. Between them stood two more patrol officers similarly secured to the building.

The first victim was shoved into view, struggling frantically. With hands zip-tied behind him, he headbutted the officers, and wildly wriggled, yelling, screaming, pleading for his life, and trying to get loose from their grasp as they methodically shoved him to the edge. Each of the ten bodies was supposed to land within the fifty-foot concrete square, now surrounded by the throbbing multitude who were eager to watch. The mostly male Muslim throng certainly knew what was about to happen. As soon as the crowd saw the man, they instantaneously changed their chant to, "Jump! Jump! Jump!"

The sourness in Jamal's empty, troubled stomach percolated into his throat, reminding him of all the other tortuous events that had caused him to miss his meals. Against his better judgment, Jamal joined the masses and looked up, watching the struggling man lose his fruitless attempts at resistance.

The sodomite screamed all the way down the thirty-eight stories as his legs bicycled and flailed, trying to find some balance as he tumbled. His restrained arms fought wildly against the zip ties. Within seconds, he slammed inside the concrete square with a horrific thud, forever ending his screams. The sober death was met with a victorious cheer, as though the home team had scored the last-minute touchdown. Jamal felt nauseated and began to dry heave, but that only produced a worsening taste in his mouth.

After the crowd's triumphant howl, the chant came again, "Jump! Jump! Jump!" as the next victim was thrust to the edge of the precipice for all to see.

I don't know that I can do this nine more times. Once was horrific enough. He'd been a Muslim all his life, always believing homosexuality was wrong, but there was no way he could have prepared his mind for this shocking scene. Certainly, he could avert his eyes, but he could not keep from hearing the thud, cheers, and chants.

As he tried again to continue with his prepared statement, the crowd's shouts overpowered him. He put down the bullhorn and his paper. His job of hosting was basically complete, and all he wanted was to leave. But this spectacle was televised, and if he left now, the world—especially the caliph—would know. On the other hand, the crowd didn't seem the least bit interested in his presence or in anything he had to say.

As the next man was propelled off the building, Jamal closed his eyes and put his hand on his forehead acting as though he was squinting from the bright sun's rays. Though this blocked his sight, it did nothing to drown out the sickening thud, announcing the man's end. Again, his gut was wretched as he heard the thunderous approval that turned to chanting. *How can this possibly be part of the plan of Allah? I thought we followed a religion of peace and kindness, of helping humanity find its place in Allah's world.*

Jamal's hands gripped the podium tightly as he steadied himself, feeling faint and trying to keep his knees from buckling underneath him. *I am about to lose it right here on stage. Right now. If I don't get some help, I may be the next casualty.* He turned to his patrol guard and asked for some water, trying to get control of the cold sweats he felt even though the spring afternoon was warm.

The patrol officer brought back a bottle of water and handed it to Jamal. "You don't look so good. You're as pale as your white tunic."

"Thanks for the water." Jamal ignored the man's comments and took a long drink. He also poured some on his skull cap.

Thud. Cheer. "Jump! Jump! Jump!"

"Is that number four or five?" Jamal asked the patrol.

"Number three."

"Could you get a chair for me?" Jamal asked.

"I'll see what I can find." The patrol officer left the platform again.

Thud. Cheer. "Jump! Jump! Jump!" went the thunderous beat of the mob.

The water helped a little, but Jamal could not get accustomed to the violence of the execution. His hands were shaking, his heart rate was elevated, he still felt lightheaded, and if he had anything at all in his stomach, it would be long gone.

If I could just lie down and put my feet on the seat of a chair, maybe I could get my head back to normal.

The patrol returned with a chair and placed it next to Jamal, tapping him on the shoulder and gesturing for him to sit down. He quickly sat, putting his head between his knees.

"Anything else I can do for you?" the patrol officer asked. "Can I get you some more water?"

Jamal was sweating profusely. "Please!"

Thud. Cheer. Chant . . . Thud. Cheer. Chant . . .

Instead of making him feel better, his position seemed only to magnify the ill feeling, so he laid on the platform and raised his feet to rest in the seat of the chair.

"Here is another water," the patrol said, twisting off the top and handing it to Jamal. "I got to tell you that you look a lot better. Some of your color is coming back. Do you think you have the flu?"

"I believe so," lied Jamal, content for now just to feel better.

Thud. Cheer. Chant.

"How many is that?" asked Jamal.

"Let me see if I can count the bodies." The patrol went to the edge of the platform for a moment and came back. "I count seven and here comes number eight on his way down." His tone sounded nonchalant, as though he were describing the clouds.

Two more after this, and then I can go—if I'm able to walk. Jamal pushed himself up onto his left elbow, drank the water, and noticed that his racing heart rate seemed to slow down. "I'm doing much better, thanks to you." If he could keep talking to the patrol, then he wouldn't have to watch what was happening above. But the patrol seemed just as interested as the crowd, fist pumping as the eighth body smashed onto the pavement.

Jamal focused on his breathing and tried not to jerk with each thud he heard. After two more men hit the concrete, Jamal watched the flagmen begin waving two flags, jubilantly signifying the end of the event.

Jamal picked himself off the ground and resumed his place at the podium. The mob didn't want it to end. "More! More! More!" they roared in unison.

"This is all," he said into the mic. "There is no more. You need to leave this area." Jamal scanned the crowd and could see the same pulsating movements, the arms in the air joining in the beat of the chant, the throbbing and hopping in unity. Clearly, he understood that his admonition was going unheeded. He turned to the patrol and raised his shoulders as if to ask, *What now?*

The patrol stepped next to the podium. "This crowd is completely whipped into a frenzy. In my experience as a police officer, I would say we need to get you out of here before something bad happens. Do you feel well enough to come with me?"

"I think so. Lead the way."

The officer grabbed Jamal's arm and pulled him in the direction of his car. "It's a powder keg and the fuse has been lit! Follow me. Now!" Into his shoulder mic, he spoke some short instructions as they worked their way through the crowd.

Halfway to the car, Jamal heard multiple gun shots followed by screams and chaos. Loudspeakers from police cruisers began instructing the people to disperse. "Clear the area immediately!"

"What just happened?" Jamal asked.

"Our guys fired blanks into the air. I'll get you to your car, and we'll have a lane cleared out for you. You will soon be on your way."

"I don't know what I would have done without you," Jamal said, patting the officer on the back as he climbed into his car and followed two police cars leading the way out of the downtown area, their emergency lights flashing.

Four blocks from the crowd, the police cars stopped and waved Jamal's car on. Jamal gave them an appreciative wave in return. *I have never experienced anything like that in my entire life.* Even though he was still reeling from what he just witnessed, Jamal knew it was time to turn his mind toward his own dangerous situation. He turned at the next intersection and made his way toward Tom's office building.

CHAPTER 13

12:34 p.m.
Monday, March 1

ROSIE SAT IN the unit at Cooper's bedside, chatting to him as if Cooper were hanging on every word. Cooper still remained comatose, but this was a normal lunch break routine for Rosie when she could fit it in. She was telling Cooper all about last night's excitement and how God had allowed her to escape through the provision of her friends, the Larsons.

"God is faithful; even when you do something foolish, like leave the house unprepared, He still protects you. Not all the time, but He did last night, and I am so thankful." Rosie took another bite of salad. "Someday you will be able to say God brought you through this entire ordeal, and this will be part of your story." She speared another piece of lettuce when the alarm blared, warning of a problem in the next unit down the way. "Looks like Mama has to get going." She raced out of Cooper's unit, putting her unfinished meal on the top of the central desk counter, and hustled to Jimmy's unit, soon to be face to face with one of her patients.

"Can you hear me, Jimmy?" Rosie leaned into the fury of an epileptic seizure as the young boy with the heart issue twitched. "Look at me! Breathe in and breathe out." She exaggerated her breathing motions, puckering her lips and her cheeks and then blowing the air out of her expanded cheeks. "Now it's your turn to breathe,

Jimmy, just like I showed you. Come on now, I know you can do it." Jimmy focused on Rosie, and his contorted facial tension began to relax. He slowly mimicked her breathing.

She looked around the hospital bed at the three other nurses and two aides who were helping to restrain Jimmy to keep him from hurting himself. She signaled to release their hold on him. He was coming down from another epileptic episode in which all his muscles were taut as a bow string. Wringing wet with perspiration, he looked exhausted.

"Whoa Jimmy, did your mama ever tell you how strong you are? I don't want to get in your way, little man." Rosie lovingly patted Jimmy on the head.

I'm sorry, Miss Rosie," Jimmy whispered sheepishly. "I'm not sure what happens to me, but all of a sudden, my body begins to sweat all over, my mind goes blank, and the next thing I see is all of you in here holding me down."

"No need to apologize, honey. That's why we're here and why we're trying to help you fix that magnificent brain of yours, so these attacks won't keep happening to you. We want you outside playing and in school learning with the rest of your friends." Rosie studied his eyes to see if he was truly finished with his episode. She rested her hand on his chest and gave a sign to the others in the room that it was over, and they could go about their other duties. "Can I get you some orange juice or something else to drink?"

Jimmy smiled. "Orange juice, please."

"Coming right up, my friend." Rosie walked toward the door and hesitated. "Did you know you're one of my favorite kids on this floor?" She looked at him with a smile, and he beamed back at her.

As Rosie walked toward the breakroom for the orange juice, she saw Dr. Wilson come through the PICU doors wearing green surgical scrubs, a colorful Mickey Mouse surgical cap, and a concerned look. "I thought you were in surgery all afternoon. What brings you back here so soon?" She put her hand up to her mouth to shield her next statement, whispering, "Aren't you supposed to be on 'probation?'"

Dr. Wilson chuckled and said under his breath, "Don't think you are off the same 'probation' hook as Betsy and me."

Rosie grinned and feigned shock as she walked to an aide to ask her to take orange juice to Jimmy and sit with him for a couple of minutes until he quieted down completely. She then went back to Dr. Wilson to see what was going on with him.

Dr. Wilson took a deep breath and sighed. "I need a break, and one of my patients was delayed. I just got off a troubling call with my wife, Helen."

"How is she doing since the announcement?"

"She heard all the relocation details on the news and from several friends who called to make sure she was in the loop. She was pretty emotional when we talked, but we should have known something like this was going to happen after the takeover."

Rosie patted his hand. "How could we know how bad things were going to become?"

Dr. Wilson agreed. "She's upset that we're being forced to give up our house. That house we have called home for more than thirty-two years has been a bright spot in our lives. It is where we saw our children off to school and where all the family gatherings have taken place. It is the home where our children brought their future spouses to meet us. We hosted multiple birthday parties, engagements, and anniversaries. There is so much life in that house." He exhaled. "It will be hard to think of that place as anything other than our refuge, our 'party central,' as the kids and grandkids have called it."

Rosie smiled. "I can still see Helen in that red, white, and blue hat when we had the medical center floor party there last Fourth of July."

Dr. Wilson chuckled quietly. "She did look goofy in that huge patriotic hat, but it was fun, and she enjoyed it thoroughly. I guess we didn't realize it at the time, but that was the end of an era for us. Now we forfeit our homes to enter a new chapter in our lives."

"Tell Helen I'm sorry that you have to give up that wonderful home." Rosie stuck out her lower lip in sympathy. "We're all in the same boat now."

"A college classmate of mine, who works at the hospital in Waxahachie, was on a phone consult with me on this last surgery. After we conferred, he told me that he's watching a lot of construction on the west side of I-35, like fencing, leveling the huge field, and erecting several enormous tents. All this is too big to be just a new lumber yard or a big box store or whatever. He thinks it might be the site of a camp. Perhaps that's our future home."

"Waxahachie. Why there? It's out in the middle of nowhere."

"That just may be the point—to put us out in the boonies, away from everyone who could help us," said Dr. Wilson. "It's not like we will want to keep up with our social lives while we're there, and I doubt they'll provide internet service." His hospital cell phone went off. "I have to go. Don't lose heart. This is not the end for us but the beginning of a new adventure. I have to believe that God has some plan for us in this entire process. Besides, I've always wanted to investigate the tunnel system of the abandoned Superconducting Super Collider that's down in Waxahachie. If we'll soon live there, I'll have a chance to learn more about it."

She furrowed her eyebrows, thinking that was an odd way to respond to their new challenges. "What's the Super Collider? Where did that come from?" When he only smiled his response, she chuckled. "Dr. Wilson, you are always the optimist. You could find an opportunity in the most difficult of conditions."

"Well, I look at a broken leg, and in my mind's eye, I see a person walking. That is what we orthopedists do, we take the calamitous and bring out the fabulous. With God's help and the patient's determination, we see some very remarkable results. So, leaving our home and having to move off to some obscure flat prairie south of here won't be ideal, but it is the hand we are being dealt. Somehow, we'll make it work." He waved his arms across the PICU floor. "Don't forget, we all have accomplished some pretty remarkable things, not the least of which is Cooper's progress. And for those conditions that are impossible, it just takes a little longer to make those work out as well." With an exaggerated facial grimace, he whispered, "I'm on probation indeed!"

His hospital cell phone went off again. "Now they're getting anxious upstairs. I guess they're ready for me." He wheeled around and walked briskly out the doors.

Such a dear man. I hate to think of him put out of this hospital where he's made such a difference. I hate that he and his family will lose the home they love simply because of what he believes—or doesn't believe. Her thoughts turned to her own situation and all she would lose as well. Then as she started to walk back toward PICU, she thought about her work. *What will this place be like in a month without us infidels?*

CHAPTER 14

12:55 p.m.
Monday, March 1

"WE STILL NEED to talk." Before Tom could respond, Jamal continued speaking into his phone with strained cheeriness. "I'm driving back from downtown, so I'll be at your office in five minutes. We can go over some of the estimates for the camp size when I get there." He trusted that Tom remembered that the statement about camp size was their prearranged code for *we can't talk over the phone in case someone has wiretapped it.*

"I have those camp size estimates you requested," Tom responded quickly and easily. "I'll be in the lobby waiting."

"You will see the company car out front in a couple minutes." Jamal hung up and exhaled his relief. He was grateful he could trust Tom with the coded language. If anyone else knew, he'd be in trouble for sure.

As he drove, the images and nausea from the executions overtook him again. He grabbed his bottle of water and drank greedily, hoping it would help him recover his head and emotions. He continued to alternate between feeling clammy, hot, and then cold. Any relief he felt from the drink was drowned in the guilt of consuming anything during the daylight hours of Ramadan. Even though he sat at a stoplight and could have closed his eyes for a moment to try to erase the images, he didn't dare. He knew that man after man would speed through his mind—falling, screaming, and smashing onto the concrete street. He forced himself to focus on the traffic and his driving.

He pulled into a parking space marked VISITORS in front of Tom's building and waited only a few minutes before he spotted Tom walking toward him. As Tom opened the passenger-side door, Jamal asked, "Do you have your car keys?"

Tom patted his pants pocket and nodded.

"Follow me in your car," Jamal said. As Tom gave Jamal an inquisitive look and raised his palms in question, Jamal put his finger to his lips, wordlessly suggesting Tom say no more.

"We are probably going in different directions after our discussion," Jamal said.

Tom smiled and slammed the passenger door shut. The sound made Jamal flinch. It was too similar to the horrifying sound of the bodies colliding with the ground.

As Jamal led Tom away from his workplace, he wondered where he could go for privacy—a place that wouldn't arouse suspicions. He drove to the parking lot of the Kimbell Art Museum in Fort Worth's cultural district, just west of downtown. Quickly pulling into a parking space, Jamal hopped out of the official car and sprinted to Tom's vehicle, getting in. "Please take me to the botanical gardens."

"Will you tell me what's going on?" Tom asked. "You look terrible."

Jamal responded only by collapsing farther into the seat.

"You feel okay?"

Jamal shook his head. "This is the worst day of my life. Can we talk about it when we get to the gardens?" He put his hands in his lap to try to disguise their shaking.

"I caught the television coverage," Tom said. "Of course, everyone caught it since it was required viewing. It was really gruesome. Channel 1 covered the event in Boston. Channel 2 showed the local coverage for Fort Worth and Dallas on a split screen. I saw you a couple of times. It was definitely 'parental and viewer discretion advised' or however the saying goes."

"Can we stop talking for a few moments? I'm trying to get my head back on, and your chatter is not helping me." Jamal's tone was harsher than he'd meant, but everything within him was shaking and terrified, and he didn't know how to control it. From the corner of his eye, he saw Tom's countenance fall. "That was too severe, I'm sorry," Jamal apologized.

Tom waved him off with his right hand as he drove through the gates of the picturesque gardens. He parked in the spacious but fairly empty lot and turned off the vehicle.

They both sat in silence as Jamal stared out the passenger-side window. His shaking became more pronounced, so he shifted his hands to the armrest and clung tightly. A sob forced its way out of Jamal's mouth. "I can't take it anymore. This is wrong. I am in way over my head." He dropped his head in his shaking hands. "There is no way out. Every imaginable exit means death to me and, worse, death to my family."

Turning to Tom, he felt embarrassed to plead but didn't know what else to do. "You have to help me think of something. I've got to get . . . some relief . . . or I will explode . . ." He sniffled and wiped his nose on his sleeve. "I can't keep living like this. I hate my life. I have no peace with this job." He buried his head again and wept uncontrollably.

The car was quiet, save for Jamal's attempts to compose himself with stifled sobs and heaving breaths, struggling to regain his voice.

"When you left my house last night, everything seemed fine," Tom said once Jamal calmed himself. "What happened?"

"I wish I could go back and relive the last sixteen hours," Jamal uttered with a defeated sigh.

"We both know that is not going to happen. Let's focus on now. After you left last night, what went wrong?"

"Everything! Safi . . . an imam . . . that boy." His eyes widened as he remembered the little boy and his bloody forehead. Perhaps Tom had an update. "Any news on the boy I hit? Did the news say how badly he was hurt or where he was taken?"

"I believe he suffered a broken leg and some cuts and bruises but nothing life-threatening. I heard the mother and father on Channel 1 talking briefly about the injury. Since they were infidels, the reporter didn't spend much time on the story before he moved on to something else. Police are still on the case, though." Tom looked at Jamal. "The cops have described a car that generally looks like yours, but the child described a man who worked in a circus with a monkey. Were you wearing your tunic and cap at the time?"

Jamal's stomach lurched. "Yes." He lowered his head in shame.

"He must have read a children's book where a character with a monkey dressed like you appeared in the story. Then there was a mysterious person who reported the accident at a convenience store before leaving, but he was in street clothes. The store clerk and the inside camera got a good look at you. Your sunglasses will keep them off the track for a while, but the investigators might figure out that a circus guy with a monkey in an infidel child's eye could be a man in a cleric's robe. You must come clean on this and turn yourself in."

Jamal sighed heavily and opened the car door to get out. "I changed out of my robe when I left the accident. Do you know anyone at the police department? Have any Muslims reached the top of the command center there yet?"

Tom thought for a moment. "I know Captain Aziz at the main station on Calhoun Street. But how will that help? Muslim or not, the civil law is clear. You left the scene of an accident after injuring a child. Evidence will show that you had a cell phone in your possession when you called me minutes after the offense. They will say you should have remained at the scene and used that phone to call 911."

He knew his friend's words were true, but he needed to get out of the car. The air inside was suffocating him. "I need to walk."

Jamal put both hands on the top of Tom's car to steady himself a moment and get his balance before he shut the door. He began to walk slowly toward the trails where he knew they could talk privately.

Tom rushed to his side and put his arm around his shoulder, which helped stabilize him.

They wound their way around the gardens in silence until Jamal found a bench in a wooded, secluded area. He walked straight for it and sat.

They remained quiet for a moment as Jamal tried to gather his thoughts. Then, as though a dam burst, he looked up at Tom, who was standing in front of him, and began to speak quickly and pleadingly. He had to make Tom understand. "I couldn't stay at that accident! I would have been discovered. The caliph would know. I would have disgraced the name of Allah."

"Well, now all of Fort Worth PD is looking for some chump who didn't seem to care about leaving a kid by the side of the road. This needs immediate attention. If they find out who is on the convenience store camera, and they start putting two and two together, you may find a police car at your office waiting for you when you return, along with officers asking you to put your wrists together like this." Tom put the palms of his hands together in front of him. "We need to figure something out fast."

Jamal stared blankly off in the distance. *How can I make this right?* An idea quickly formed in his mind. He stood and shook Tom's shoulders with excitement. "Since the boy and his family are infidels, I could let them stay in their home and keep their job for several months instead of going to the camp. Just until the boy gets better. That should soften the blow of the hit and run. We could negotiate with this Aziz fellow for an expunged sentence against me. You could arrange to get the medical bills paid out of some discretionary Islamic funds, then we could move on to the next problem."

Tom's jaw dropped. "Those are some huge assumptions, my friend. I can check on that and see what I can do, but I'm not sure you can pretend to be off the hook that fast." Tom stared at him confused. "What's the next problem?"

Jamal nervously straightened his tunic as he sat again, gesturing to the other half of the bench next to him. "This could take a while. You better sit down."

Tom joined him and looked expectantly at Jamal.

Where do I even begin? Jamal decided to start with the caliph's call the night before. He left out nothing, including the unnerving murder of the Seattle imam, the stepped-up timetable of the relocation, his encounter with Safi and the subsequent beating, along with the children's reactions. "After all of that, I had to get out of the house and clear my head. That's why I was driving east of town when I hit the boy."

Jamal knew he was jumping from topic to topic, but he didn't know how else to handle it. "Beating my wife is permitted by the Koran. Of course, you know that. I could justifiably beat Safi for her defiance, but this isn't the example I want my girls to see." He stood and paced as Tom continued to sit quietly and watch him. Finally, he faced Tom squarely and tightened his hands into fists. "I'm about to tell you something that scares me to death—and not just for me but for my family. I am in the wrong place! I shouldn't be the city imam. Do you know what that means if they ever find out I feel that way? They will kill me and my family without hesitation!" Jamal sat again in exhaustion.

"How can you be sure of that?"

"Omar told me something this morning." Jamal stopped short in his explanation when, out of the corner of his eye, he noticed a couple walking toward them. They seemed to be looking at the different flower exhibits along the trail. The man and woman were both in spring attire, casual shirts, jeans, and tennis shoes. She was hearing her hajib. The sight of her made his stomach clinch. *Are they spies?* They were rambling slowly, stopping occasionally, and making comments to each other regarding the flowers that were identified by small placards.

They seemed in no particular hurry to get past Jamal and Tom.

"Aren't these pretty yellow daffodils?" he said to them, when they got near, pointing to the flowers at the side of their bench.

"Yes, they are," the couple said, almost in unison, smiling, as they moved on to the next flower exhibit past the bench.

Once sure that the couple was out of earshot, Jamal spoke again, this time almost in a whisper. "Omar told me about the imam's family in Seattle being burned in a house fire. It may have been a terrible twist of fate, but I doubt that. Perhaps I deserve to be put to death, but not my family." He held up his shaking hands to show Tom. "This is getting to me. I'm terrified. I can't think rationally. My mind is stuck on animalistic survival. Who beats his wife because she is showing concern for him and their family?

Who leaves a child in the middle of the road writhing in the pain that he caused? You know me, two months ago, I never would have done that. Can you imagine that when my greatest nightmare is realized, and they discover and confirm my doubts about this job, they will have me killed?"

Tom grimaced.

"Then imagine the next day you drive by my house, and it is burned to the ground with the four charred female bodies of my family among the smoldering ruins. That is the torture of having to keep this job. I can't let that happen to my family!"

The wind suddenly picked up, whistling through the trees, and blew dust up on the trail. Jamal and Tom quickly turned their heads to avoid getting the grit in their eyes.

Brushing himself off, Jamal looked back at Tom. "I'm exhausted and have nothing left to feel except this terror we've discussed."

Tom looked astonished. "This is a horrible way to live."

"You got that right," Jamal's voice cracked with emotion. "If anyone within the caliph's organization heard about my misgivings, I would be shot within minutes. There is an informant in every city where an imam is a leader. I think the mole here may be Uma, my administrative assistant. That is why we are in the gardens, and that is why I cannot relax or let my guard down for a moment."

"So that's why you wanted to come in my car?"

"Absolutely! I am suspicious of people. I am constantly looking over my shoulder. There could be someone watching me even now." Jamal stood and slowly looked in every possible direction. He only saw the couple who had walked by them minutes ago, but they were farther down the path and seemed uninterested in him. "I am sure I'm becoming paranoid, which might be what the caliph had in mind for all of his imams."

Tom stood and also looked around. "I see nothing that would indicate we are being watched right now. Would you just sit down and relax for a couple minutes, and we'll try to discuss this reasonably?"

Jamal shook his head. "Yes, but let's walk over there, deeper into the gardens. That space might be more remote." Jamal pointed west, where the area was darker from the thicker foliage. The trees' canopy was dense, which prevented the sunlight from getting through to the path. Jamal began to trundle away from the bench as Tom came alongside him, trying to keep him steady. They walked slowly to the spot Jamal pointed to. He wanted to keep walking, but overcome with exhaustion, he sat down again.

"This seems better for now," he said. "All of the plans coming down from the caliph were outlined for us in a 'whitepaper' shortly after the takeover. As you've heard, the next event is the relocation. What you haven't been informed about is the coming purge and the camps. All of these steps are part of a larger plan to systematically reduce the unwanted infidel population within the United States of Islam through disease and starvation."

Tom sucked in air. Clearly, Jamal had caught his friend by surprise again.

Jamal gritted his teeth as he spat out the words. "The deaths of over two million infidels who refuse to convert to Islam is now my responsibility! I cannot just quit. But what am I supposed to do?"

"I don't know what I would do if I were you," Tom admitted.

"The caliph definitely will not care to hear about my turmoil," Jamal said, his tone mocking. "All the caliph is concerned about is obedience and the strictest adherence to the plan. I now realize that he cannot tolerate weakness in any form. His one and only concern is about the progression of the United States of Islam and the transformation of this land into an Islamic state. The next step will be world dominance as we prepare for the Day of Judgment."

Tom cleared his throat and looked oddly uncomfortable. He glanced around and then swallowed hard. "If you feel safe here, then I want to tell you something that is very personal," Tom said, his voice quiet. His face looked strained, as though he wasn't sure he wanted to speak. "This is something that can get me into trouble. But I share it in the hope that it will make your troubles feel a little lighter."

"We have known each other for years. You should feel free to tell me whatever is on your mind. I told you about my issues!"

Tom stared absently at the flowers. "Shortly after Alex died, my relationship with Lori was tested in every conceivable way. The six months after his death was a hard time to find any peace."

"I know all of that. I walked through it with you. Fast forward to what you want to tell me."

"Be patient with me." Tom rubbed his hands together, then looked seriously at Jamal. "This is hard to admit because the Koran is very clear about the punishment." He swallowed hard. "It could even get me killed."

Jamal's eyes opened wide in surprise. *What could possibly be that bad for Tom?*

"After dropping Rosie off at the medical center last night, I had a dream, a vision. You know how important dreams and visions are?"

"Yes, of course."

"Well, in this one I saw, very unmistakably, the Man in the White Robe."

Jamal was surprised but didn't understand how that vision could get Tom killed. "Go on."

I discovered this man to be Jesus of the Christian faith."

Jamal's eyes grew wide.

"I was terrified as I looked at Jesus, so I got down on the floor. But he had kind eyes and told me in a soft voice not to be afraid. He told me that he was going to help Lori and me with the pain of losing our son. I asked him why Alex had to die. I couldn't contain myself. I wept out the six months of the grief I had repressed." Tom wiped a few stray tears from his eyes. "Something unexplainable occurred while he was there. I knew I was in the presence of Allah. I am not sure what that means, but I do know there was purity and a sense of holiness there. I knew that I needed to humble myself before him. Although he didn't demand contrition, I knew it was right to ask Jesus for forgiveness. I asked him what I was supposed to do."

Jamal sat dumbfounded. *My best friend of almost twenty years is telling me some blasphemy about seeing Jesus. I should be livid, but he has peace on his face. This doesn't make any sense.*

Tom slid from the bench and knelt in front of Jamal. "He told me to love, and he told me to help you and Safi and your three girls. He said your five names out loud. Obviously, that means Jesus knows who you are. I asked how I was to do that, and he said to listen to you and to pay attention to what is around me. I was halfway expecting you to call me today, but when you actually did, I didn't know what to say or do. You said you needed peace. Well. . . I found true peace last night for the first time. I am here to love you and listen to you and tell you about that peace."

Jamal rubbed the top of his head and felt disgusted. "Get up! I don't like you kneeling in front of me. It isn't right. We only kneel before Allah and the prophet, not before man."

Wearing an anguished look, Tom seated himself back on the bench.

Jamal blew out a long breath. "I-I don't know what to say. You have backed me into a corner. You know, of course, that I am supposed to report you as a blasphemer. You should be killed immediately. I am surprised that this Jesus, about whom you spoke, knows who I am and that he knew I would need help today. I . . . I don't know . . . I am confused. I don't know what to say."

Tom spoke haltingly. "I am not convinced I understand all that occurred last night, but I do know one thing for certain. I saw the Man in the White Robe. I know it was Jesus, and I know my mind and feelings are calmer and clearer today. I believe there can be peace in this process for you, Safi, and the girls if you were to embrace Jesus too. I believe you could be a family again."

Jamal looked off in the distance at the thickness of the tree coverage. *It sounds too good to be true. See Jesus, embrace him, whatever that means, and suddenly I'm off the hook? I don't know. But . . . what if it is true?* Jamal sat in conflict between the beliefs from his past, his present circumstances, and the preposterous story Tom had just told him. Slowly, a smile washed over his face. He took in a deep breath. "I thought I was coming here to fill you in on my problems. I am still not sure what I should do, but I do feel strangely encouraged. I'm not sure what to believe, but I have known you a long time, and I trust you. I don't know that I *can* believe while still being the leader of the Islamic movement in this area. My inner conflict would magnify tremendously."

A moment of silence passed between the two. Tom reached down and pulled a weed by the bench and began to tear it apart. "I am going to pray that Jesus will intervene and give you the same peace and comfort I received from him last night. You and I both know about the past. I will be with you and try to get you some peace. I will admit that your circumstances are overwhelming and dangerous. I don't think Jesus would have come to me last night and mentioned your names if he didn't have some sort of plan for you. Can we agree on that?"

Jamal gave a weak smile. "I will take you up on the offer to help. Your Jesus needs to do something relatively fast, or I will be a topic of conversation much like the Seattle imam. I would like to live and have a chance to see my relationship with Safi and the girls restored. You must understand that my eternal destiny is at stake. There are particular sins in my past . . ." His voice trailed off. Then he shook his head, trying to clear the fear he suddenly felt again. "If I died tonight, I am convinced I would be doomed to Jahannam. You have heard me preach on hell and its seven levels, each more severe than the previous level. *Allah save me from this fate.* The only guarantee from this fate is that I become a martyr. My martyrdom would mean that my family and I get to paradise without question or risk of default."

"Whoa! We don't need to jump into martyrdom yet. Let's see what the next couple of days bring," said Tom. "You are, after all, still the imam for the Dallas Fort Worth area."

"My immediate job is the relocation, to see that it goes as planned, and to stop any impending rebellions that might be brewing among the infidels."

"Okay, Jamal, why don't you make a list of all the other issues you can honestly say that you and the caliph agree on. That way you will be ready to agree with him as each of those things come up."

Jamal began to mentally enumerate the points he and the caliph had in common. "We both want the infidels moved into the camps by April 1. We both want the assets and businesses of the infidels appropriated into the Islamic bank as soon as possible. We both want the DFW financially independent by the end of the year. And we are concerned about the Day of Judgement." *I am assured of my own future, but in my present state, it is overwhelming to think about the end of the world, the day when Allah, the All-Just,*

will judge all mankind for their deeds, good and bad, and send us to
paradise or eternal hellfire.

"Don't just tell me these things," Tom said. "Write them down so you will have them in front of you on your desk. When your goals are out in front of you, you will start talking like an imam."

Tom glanced at his watch. "We need to get you back to the office before Uma becomes concerned about your absence. You need to exhibit the confidence that you are the man for the job. Uma, and anyone else who might be watching, will pick up on this confidence and compliance, which will buy you some time. In the meantime, I will check with Captain Aziz to see what we can do about possible charges in the hit and run. We'll talk about the Man in the White Robe again later. Just know that I'm here for you."

"I appreciate you listening to me," Jamal said. "You went out on a limb to tell me about your dream with Jesus. I want help, but I have a lot of caliph work to do before I can even stop to think about that. You're right that I need to get back to the office and show Uma I'm still in charge." They stood together. Jamal offered a weak smile and a slight shrug, then they headed toward the car.

CHAPTER 15

3:00 p.m.
Monday, March 1

JAMAL WALKED PURPOSEFULLY into the office with an even stride to demonstrate his confidence and stopped in front of Uma's desk. "What did I miss while I was out of the office?"

"Where have you been since the executions?" asked Uma.

He frowned and put his hands on his hips. "I was with Tom Larson. We were looking at the projections of expenses for the camp and the estimated number of infidels we think will decide not to convert. Why do you ask? Was someone looking for me?"

Uma fidgeted with her hands and looked down, clearly nervous about something, then glanced back up at Jamal. "Omar called. He wants you to call him."

"When did he call? I talked to him on my way to pick up Tom. Was the call after that?"

Uma handed him the pink call-slip reminder, which had the time written down as 1:20 p.m. That seemed odd since Jamal had talked to him about five minutes before that.

Jamal bristled. "Omar probably thought I was back in the office and called my cell. When I asked about what I missed, that is when you are supposed to give me the call slips, not ask me questions."

Uma looked up defiantly. "Well, I have some more questions for you to answer."

"*You* have more questions for *me!*" He crossed his arms, feeling his temper rise. "Okay, go ahead and ask."

Uma's jaw set and her eyes gave him a determined stare. "When you left the office this morning, after you picked up the instructions and your script, why did you stop at the corner of Seventh and Penn on your way downtown? You were there for at least five minutes. Did you pick up anyone at that location? Then you drove downtown, where you parked the car. Did the passenger join you at the podium where you gave your remarks?"

Jamal looked at her in disbelief. "How dare you question me!" He wanted to strike out at her for being so invasive. "Are you a spy?" His lips curled into a harsh snarl. "And if you are, you are a lousy one! You don't even have your facts right. What business is it of yours to know if I did or didn't stop? And if I picked up a *carload* of people, that is not your concern" He scratched his head in mock thought. "Perhaps this is a case of you reading too many spy novels?" He paused, then slowly drew out a question. "Who put you up to this?"

He paused again to let his words sink in, watching her eyes grow wide. "Now I have some questions for you. Has someone directed you to ask me all these questions? How did you even know where my car was? Is it the regional imam who has forced you to be so nosey? Was it someone higher up?"

Uma jumped up as she burst into tears. She lowered her head and covered her face as she ran out of the door, presumably to go to the restroom.

With his mouth agape, Jamal looked down at her desk and searched for answers. He shook his head in disbelief and walked toward his office. *Good grief, what was that all about? How could she have known I stopped at that parking lot on Seventh? If she followed me, she would know I did not pick up anybody. This is just crazy. She has always been a bit of a nag, but this means I have a reason to be concerned. I need to guard my steps more closely from now on because it appears that someone is watching me.* Jamal felt his anger continue to build as he strode into his office and slammed the door. *What are you doing? If you are being observed, you need to calm down and quit acting guilty.*

As he slowly counted to twenty-five to calm his pulse, Jamal slumped down in his chair. He was just beginning to collect his thoughts when he heard a faint noise in the direction of Uma's desk. He stepped toward his door and opened it a crack. He knew he had to calm things, especially if someone was watching. He took several deep breaths and coolly walked out. "Okay. I drove downtown, and the guard who helped me park the company car can tell you how many people I had with me, which was none. I delivered the caliph's message to what, was by then, thousands of witnesses. After the executions, I drove to Tom Larson's office, and I came back to our office to check in with you. You can call Tom and ask him how many people I had in the car when I picked him up." Then he stamped his foot and pointed to the name plate on his office door, "That says Imam for the Dallas Fort Worth Area. Today is the last time you question me. Show some respect!" Jamal finished his statements dripping with sarcasm and anger.

Out of his eye, he caught the glint of a small object in the upper corner of the room. It was one of the many cameras he was certain the caliph had directed on him. With all the composure he could muster, he returned to his office, determined to go over the details of the camp. They would see his loyalty there.

★ ★ ★

3:20 p.m.

Slamming his fists on his desk, the Observer yelled "What an idiot! I never should have trusted her!" the Observer said to himself as he watched Uma on one of his many cameras. She had returned to her desk following the exchange with Jamal. As soon as he watched the imam exit her desk area for the second time, he dialed her and watched her pick up the ringing phone.

"Hello, this is U—"

"What were you thinking?" the Observer said gruffly into his wireless headset. He stood and began pacing around the room. "I watched that entire ridiculous conversation you just had. What a disaster! Now Jamal knows he is being watched because I asked an amateur like you to help me."

The Observer stopped his wandering, looking squarely at the image of Uma on screen three. He pointed at her as though she could see him. "When I asked *you* to get more information, I never intended you to ask those questions directly of Jamal. There are ways to gather information other than through questioning him. We may have made a serious mistake in giving you this much responsibility. I am disappointed with the way this has developed, and I am going to demand that you not ask Jamal any more questions. Do you understand?"

Uma's face turned disappointed. "You asked me to get more information," she whispered. "That is what I thought I was doing. I was trying to please you and find out the facts you requested."

"Uma, you are *not* to ask any more questions." He felt his tone grow even more stern. "That was a complete failure for the caliph. We will find another way to get the facts we need." He cleared his throat and purposefully changed his voice's cadence. With a softer tone, he tried now to be the gracious Observer, to manipulate her to do something different. "Right now, you need to go into Jamal's office and tell him some story—that you overstepped your bounds by following him with your car. He *cannot* know we are tracking his every move with GPS in either of those cars. Tell him you were trying to satisfy your own curiosity and couldn't tell if someone got in the car. Make up something convincing that makes the situation better than it is. Tell him you will stop being so nosey and will leave him alone from now on." Forsaking the "good" Observer persona, he thundered, "Go do it, Uma. Make it right."

Uma began to cry. "I'm so sorry to bring shame upon you and the caliph."

"Control yourself, woman," he warned through gritted teeth. "After you settle the issue of your impertinence, you must act normal and help him get the census estimate for the size of the camp."

He watched on the screen as Uma put her hand over her mouth and took several deep breaths to quiet herself down.

"Now dry your eyes." He returned to his soothing, soft voice and waited for her to follow his command. She smoothed out her hair with her right hand and straightened her back in her chair in response.

"The survey questionnaires you worked on and mailed out are due back to you and your workers this Friday. Jamal needs that number next week to know how large to build the camp. Perhaps you can become useful. Ask him if you can help him come up with a rough estimate on the number of infidels who will not take the offer. That could be your second-highest priority. Now, what is your first priority?"

"Go tell the imam my story about following him and my curiosity and how I'll never do that again," Uma answered dutifully.

"Good, Uma, you are a good girl. Thank you," the Observer said in a condescending manner.

Once he hung up, he immediately called the caliph and lamented, "Uma in the DFW office is a huge liability and must be eliminated tonight."

"Then do it quickly and make it clean."

"There will be a new administrative assistant in the morning. I will snatch someone reliable from the regional office."

"Excellent," the caliph said. The call disconnected.

*　*　*

3:30 p.m.

Jamal heard a quiet knock on his office door. When he told her to enter, a contrite-looking Uma came in with her head bowed slightly.

She stood in front of his desk, nervously fidgeting with her hands. "I-I did follow you in my car out of my own curiosity," she said and then hesitated as though unsure of herself.

Or perhaps because she is lying?

"When you pulled into that parking lot, it all happened so quickly that I had to drive past." She avoided his eyes. "I circled the block three times. The first two times, you were still there, but the third time you must have driven off because your car was gone. The only explanation I could figure out was that you were waiting to pick someone up. I'm sorry. Will you forgive me for being so meddlesome? I promise not to interfere anymore. It is such a privilege to work for the city imam that I sometimes take my job too seriously and want to know what is going on before it happens."

Eyeing Uma warily, Jamal was genuinely surprised at her confession and change of heart. "Apology accepted," he said, remembering the various cameras lurking in the office. "But I must say, I am very surprised by you that you would go to such lengths to follow me. However, there is much we need to do together, and we can't afford to be adversarial."

She remained standing in silence.

"Please, sit down," he said and gestured to a chair to her left. *I do need some help, and I am past exhausted. I can hardly think straight. It can't hurt to have her brainstorm with me about our population projections of the DFW metroplex—or can it? What if she influences me with bad information? It's just a guess. We are just trying to come up with an estimate.*

Jamal stood and faced the round worktable in the corner of his office. "I'm expected to calculate an approximation of infidels for this whole area, which is a blind number without any data, but we need some parameters for the size of the camp to complete our construction by the deadline. As we are in the 'Bible Belt,' I don't expect a huge influx of people taking the generous offer to convert to Islam."

"I'm willing to help if you will let me," Uma said.

"I do need help with the tally, so why don't you sit here at the table, and I'll bring the current report to you. Let's see if we can come up with the information the regional director and the caliph need."

For the next few hours, the two of them worked on the estimate. As the day wore on, Jamal began to yawn every other minute, and his eyes became heavy. He stood in an attempt to get some blood moving and help stir himself awake, then looked at his watch. "Uma, it is almost 7:00 p.m., and I am completely worn out. I'm afraid I'm going to have to go home and see my family and get some rest."

"That sounds good," she said. "Why don't we call it a day and pick this up in the morning? You go home and see your wife and kids."

They left the pages of their work spread out. "Thanks for your help on all this," he told her. "We might be halfway through the process. Now we can use district numbers as the formula for so many infidels per square foot of space, and we should come up with the maximum needed area for the camp. We will do the math tomorrow."

"I'll see you in the morning," she said cheerily.

Leaving his office, Jamal looked over his shoulder for any clue of what the truth might be in the office and in her statements. *Who can I trust? Who was watching me today? Within the last few hours, Uma seemed kinder than normal and a little too eager to accommodate me and my family.* As the mistrust settled into Jamal's mind, he was sure Uma was trying to manipulate him somehow.

CHAPTER 16

8:00 p.m.
Monday, March 1

WHEN AN EXHAUSTED Jamal arrived at his house, to his relief, he saw the other car in the garage. A flood of memories came rushing back. What would he say to Safi? Could he tell her about hitting the child with his car, the executions, his discussion with Tom, or his encounter with Uma? No, he decided.

He walked slowly into the living room and shuddered when he realized this was where he had beaten his wife the previous night. What would he say to her? How could he possibly apologize for how he acted? How could he relieve the fears of the children?

"Safi, are you here?"

Safi sneaked out of one of the children's bedrooms and soundlessly closed the door behind her. She tiptoed toward him in the darkened hallway, one hand against the wall to steady herself and the other raised to her swollen mouth, laying a finger to her lips to indicate that he needed to be quiet. As she drew closer, he began to see what he had done to her face. Her left eye was blackened and nearly swollen shut. Her cheek under that eye had a bulge that protruded out almost to the end of her nose. Her lips were misshaped.

His eyes traveled down to her left arm, which was similarly discolored from trying to defend herself from his attack. *What kind of monster am I?*

He averted his eyes as they filled with tears, his heart flooding with regret. A soft moan escaped his lips. "Oh, Safi. I am very sorry for what I did to you. It was a terrible mistake. I wish I could have last night back. Will you forgive me for hurting you and being so out of control?"

Though Safi smiled weakly, her eyes registered fear and apprehension. "I forgive you," she said, emotionless, clearly saying the words expected of a dutiful wife. "We have a lot to talk about, but not now I . . ."

She had always been honest with him, but now he could see her guarding her words.

"What, Safi? Please say what you are thinking."

She breathed in slowly as though still uncomfortable. Without looking at him, she whispered, "I don't know what I am supposed to think or how to feel as the wife of the imam. You have terrified me. I need to protect the children." She paused again and slowly, almost imperceptibly, shook her head. "We can discuss this later."

"Will the children even see me, or do they think I am a monster for hitting you so severely?"

"They will need some time to see you as their father again and not as someone to fear."

"Would you go with me to talk with them?"

"I put them to bed at 7:30. They are down for the night. As you can imagine, they had a rough time last night. I'll be sleeping with them for now. We moved all four of our beds together into Sarah's room."

His arms, shoulders, and head went limp. "How long will that last?"

"I guess that is somewhat up to you and how they respond to you. You didn't make it easy on any of us. So, this is where we are and where I will be sleeping for the foreseeable future. By the way, for their peace of mind, I had a lock installed on the door to Sarah's room and the adjoining bathroom."

Jamal grimaced, and he lowered his head in shame. "Oh, Safi, I'm sorry you felt you had to go to such measures."

"I was responding to the circumstances. If you want to play tough, then I need to protect myself and our three wonderful girls. Evidently, our safety is up to me."

Jamal rubbed his head vigorously as the consequences of his actions became more of a reality. "You are right to do what you have done. I am not proud of how my life has played out. This morning when I left the house, I drove out by the Trinity River, east of here. I was tired, driving into the sunrise—" *Wait*, he thought, interrupting himself, remembering that the caliph may have his house bugged. *I can't say this out loud. Not here in our home.*

"Well, can't you see it is your job that is causing all of this? Ever since you took the promotion to the DFW imam—"

Holding his finger to his lips, Jamal interrupted Safi with a silent *shhh*. "Can we talk about this tomorrow? I need to get to bed," Jamal said as though he were addressing a room full of people, but feeling his eyes grow wild.

"Okay," she said haltingly, looking puzzled. "If that is what you want to do." Silently, she mouthed, "What?"

He beckoned her to follow him down the hall into their master bathroom. She followed reluctantly, keeping her distance. Entering the bathroom, he turned on the sink's faucet, quietly shut the door, and whispered, "I have very strong reasons to believe that this house, as well as my office, have been under surveillance for some time. I know my job is a problem, but right now I have no choice. In fact, you and the girls have no choice either."

Safi's swollen brown eyes revealed panic. "You are scaring me even more now, Jamal! What are you saying?" She backed away from him, but the bathroom was too small for any significant separation.

Jamal continued to whisper, now more pleadingly. "This morning, I accidentally hit a young boy by the side of the road." He lowered his head to break eye contact. "But I intentionally left the scene of the accident and never returned."

Safi squinted her one good eye as though in question of his admission.

"I'm telling you this because this job has eaten me up and is trying to sear my conscience away. I just witnessed the execution of ten young gay men and was expected to enjoy it, to relish in the punishment." His face paled. He turned toward the sink and splashed the running water on his face. Then he lowered the seat on the commode and sat, putting his head between his knees to recover from his lightheadedness.

"The reason we are in this bathroom with this water running," he whispered, looking up at Safi as she pitifully handed him a towel to wipe his face, "is because I don't believe we can have any conversation inside this home without it going straight to the caliph's ears. I suspect that every city imam's house and office are bugged. How else would they know what the Seattle imam was thinking?"

Jamal stood unsteadily and took several steps closer to Safi, hands behind his back, to let her know she was safe. Even though he was right next to her, he talked in a low voice. "The caliph and his goons knew the Seattle imam objected to the caliph's timeline before the imam stated it. His murder was well orchestrated with cameras and theatrics to scare the rest of us into submission. He was shot, and his family was mysteriously killed in a house fire right after."

He gave her a few moments to let that news sink in. "It's clear that the caliph is a radical Islamic terrorist. I now see he illustrates this fact every day, apparently without hesitation, by having people killed. I can't do that. I want out, but he will have me killed if I back out now. And that means you and the girls are in danger. This is all part of the circumstances that have made me so agitated and out of control. I'm not excusing my behavior, just explaining it. I feel like a cornered rat."

Safi gently patted his hand, which was more than he had hoped for or felt he deserved.

He squeezed her hand in return. "Go on to Sarah's room and lock the door. You will all be safe tonight."

He hoped she believed him. Later that evening, just as he was drifting off to sleep, his phone rang. A voice on the other end of the line stated in a matter-of-fact tone, "Uma will no longer be working in your office. Her replacement, Faiza Abbas, will arrive tomorrow by 8:00 a.m."

Before Jamal could utter a syllable, the unknown man hung up.

He quietly hung up the receiver, curious about the man behind the monotone voice and what it all meant. One thing he knew for certain—whatever had happened, it hadn't been good. Wasn't this confirmation that Uma had been a compromised and clumsy spy? Would this mean that Faiza or whomever will be just as nosey, only better at it? He would have to be better at his deception too, and so the game of cat and mouse begins. *I just don't know if I am the cat or the mouse.*

CHAPTER 17

7:00 a.m.
Wednesday, March 10

"TODAY SHOULD BE quite a day," Rosie said as she winked at Betsy. "We are telling the world by mailing in our census questionnaires that we are not taking the—" Rosie made air quotes "'generous offer' of converting to Islam, which, in fact, would be denying Jesus. And so . . .." She paused briefly and swallowed, "We get to go to the camp." Doing her best to shake off the fearful images of what that could possibly mean, she smiled. "Moving on to today, I get to train my own replacement."

Betsy returned a tight smile.

"Frankly, this is a day I hoped would never come. This job and these kids have sustained me for more than three years. I hate for it to have to end this way," Rosie said as she shoved her rolling desk chair back from the central nurses' station and stood.

"And now you get to show —" Betsy looked down at the name at the top of the email lying on the top of the desk, "Dura Hasson, what we do, and then she takes over, whether she's good for the job or not," Betsy said with disgust on her face.

No longer able to control her anger, Rosie smacked her fist on the desk. "That is not right, and you know it! We've got to train her to do the job well because we care about these kids!" She immediately regretted her tone and inhaled deeply to calm herself. "You have been here twenty-seven years, and I've been here over three," she said, now whispering. "They expect us to somehow teach this new person all about our kids within two weeks? The only thing I know about her qualifications is that she is Muslim." Rosie made a sweeping gesture with her arms. "What about these kids and their needs and the fact that they trust us and light up like a Christmas tree when they see us coming? How are we going to teach the love and appreciation we have for them? That can't be taught." Rosie paused, and her tone changed to sarcasm, "Need I remind you that the stellar performance we have done trying to save lives led us to probation? What do we know anyway?"

"You are going to have to let that go, Rosie. It's not like we are taking our HR files with us to the camp. Put that behind you and move on. Simply train your replacement."

"You didn't like it either when we were dressed down," Rosie fired back, feeling embarrassed by Betsy's admonition.

Betsy's eyes spotted something past Rosie, and she pasted on a quick tight-lipped smile. "Here she comes."

Rosie turned to see Roger Barnett from human resources escorting the new replacement toward them. A dark-skinned woman, whom Rosie assumed was Dura, wore a bright pink hijab and pink nursing scrubs printed with green hippos in white ballet tutus.

"Rosie Chavez," Roger stated pleasantly but professionally, "I'd like to introduce you to Dura Hasson, who will take over for you." He turned his attention to Betsy. "This is Betsy Thompson, the charge nurse for the floor."

Rosie extended her hand to Dura, attempting to warmly shake her hand and greet her. "I love your outfit," she said with a smile. "The kids will love it too."

"Ms. Hasson is well qualified," Roger continued before Dura could respond. "She worked as a certified nurse assistant at Tarrant County Hospital. She specialized in early childhood intervention. Please help her get established in her new job here." Roger turned abruptly and walked away as quickly as he had arrived.

"Are you from the Fort Worth area?" asked Betsy.

"Born and raised here," Dura said. "And I got my CNA certification from Tarrant County Junior College."

"Then you will fit in very nicely here," Rosie told her, genuinely wanting to help Dura feel at home. "I graduated from high school here on the south side and went to UT Arlington. Shall we?" She gestured toward the first room, ready to give Dura the tour.

As Rosie discussed the routine on the PICU floor, she pointed to the glass-walled units where the patients lay in their beds, then to the middle of the floor where the central desk was positioned to view all the patients. Dura asked basic questions regarding the purpose of the middle desk, if the glass walls were intended to remove privacy in the rooms, and where the nurses usually sat during their shifts. Rosie thought this cursory understanding of the workings of an ICU, much less on the pediatric side of nursing, was alarming. Her questions had nothing to do with the actual care of the patients. *How could I help re-direct her thinking to patient care?* "Can you tell me about your normal day at County?" asked Rosie.

"Sure," Dura said. "Our main job was to work with patient services, specializing in social and mental health for the low-income population on the east side. We were always involved with home studies to give the children and parents the best environment possible for nutrition, learning, and positive social interaction within the family and community units."

"That sounds like your experience could have a strong, meaningful influence on a lot of children," Rosie said, smiling, though inwardly noting that Dura said nothing about meeting the medical needs of the children or checking vital signs or providing medicine management or observing the patients' daily needs. Although Rosie had expected a significant gap in knowledge and experience for this type of intensive pediatric care, still, she had hoped for more.

She cringed as she thought about her own son lying just down the hall. *They are shoving me out the door, but Cooper isn't ready to leave the hospital. What am I gonna do? I can't push a comatose kid on a gurney all the way to a camp. But if he stays here, the level of care is going to be compromised. I can't win! I thought asking if I could stay until Cooper was better would be approved, but it wasn't.* She took in a deep breath to calm herself. *Okay, come back to this moment, girl. You have a replacement to train on a floor where things can and do go wrong.*

She took another deep breath and tried to shake off her worries. "I think the best possible training would be to take you through several charts, Dura. My son, Cooper, is in this unit. Almost two months. A car accident. Let's—"

"I had no idea your son was here," Dura said, her eyes wide with concern. "That must be really difficult! I'm so sorry."

Rosie swallowed hard. She felt touched that Dura cared enough to offer her condolences. "It is crummy. I just want to be with him. But I have to keep working to pay for his medical needs." She looked away and cleared her throat, trying to hold her surprise tears in check. She blinked a few times and then smiled weakly. "Well, let's start with his chart. It's fairly uncomplicated because he is in an induced coma while his brain and leg are healing." She led Dura to the central desk, where they sat together.

But the pain of Cooper's condition and Dura's kindness weren't easily tucked away. She needed to hide her emotions. "I think I'm going to get a bottle of water first. Want one?"

At Dura's nod, Rosie headed for the breakroom. *You've gotta focus on the task at hand and remember you're doing this for Cooper.* She grabbed two bottles and returned to the desk. Sipping from one and handing Dura the other, Rosie carefully introduced Dura to the "brains" of the PICU floor, where the monitors for the various units clicked, beeped, and displayed vital information about each patient. "You will eventually tune your ears to listen for the beeps and alarms." She pointed in front of her. "These folders are the charts related to each child, and the whiteboard behind us displays the flowchart listing which nurse is assigned to each patient."

They walked together to Cooper's unit.

"Hey, Cooper, how are you? Have you been able to move around very much today?" Rosie greeted her son as if he were sitting up watching Texas Ranger's baseball at spring training instead of lying peacefully in a coma. "This is Dura, our new nurse, and she is here to take my place when you and I leave in a couple of weeks."

Rosie turned to Dura and explained the coma and how that condition was reflected on the chart. She walked her through each aspect of charting the vitals and any change in condition. Rosie was pleased that Dura seemed to understand the way to chart; however, working on paper and actually dealing with a conscious patient's needs were two different things. "Of course, I'm partial to my own son, but now I want you to meet Jimmy, one of my other favorites here on the floor. Let's start by going back to square one, the central desk."

After a thirty-minute overview and pointing out how the main monitor could be switched to zero in on a particular patient's vitals or zoom back out to see the entire floor, Rosie asked Dura to practice by locating Jimmy's vitals on the monitor. "Take a couple of minutes to find his particular chart in this row and read over his history. Then you can take me to Jimmy's unit. All the data is in the chart, including the unit number. Remember, I'm right here to help you."

Dura found Jimmy's chart and pointed to the unit number that was on the outside of the aluminum binder holding the chart. She opened the chart and began to read.

After several minutes, Dura looked up.

"Ready to go?" Rosie said. "I know this is very elementary, but we need to start at the beginning." They stood, with Dura leading Rosie to Jimmy's unit. As they walked in, Rosie said, "Now we are going to get personal."

When Jimmy saw Rosie, his bright smile lit up his face, but that smile faded when he noticed the stranger.

"How is my little soldier this morning?" Rosie asked as she walked slowly to the head of his bed and stroked his hair lightly. "I want you to meet a new friend of mine." Rosie reached out and grabbed Dura's hand, pulling her in and wrapping Dura in a sideways hug. "This is Nurse Dura. Doesn't she have on a great smock? Really soon, Nurse Dura will be doing a lot of what I have been doing for you."

Jimmy shyly looked at Dura and then back at Rosie. "Will she be as nice to me as you are?" His eyes begged for an affirmative answer.

"Did you know that Miss Dura has been working with children just like you for six years?"

"And I have loved every minute of it and loved every child I have worked with," Dura smiled broadly. "The children I helped thought I was very nice. But only you can tell me if I am as nice as Miss Rosie."

"It won't be long before you will be asking for her instead of me," Rosie told Jimmy.

"Have you had your breakfast yet this morning?" Dura asked Jimmy, as she stepped closer to his bed.

In an instant, Jimmy's demeanor changed drastically as he stared blankly off into the distance. His monitor quickly spiked on heart rate and respirations. Profuse sweat bled out of his forehead, and his muscles cramped up all over his body as he began to squirm uncontrollably.

Rosie reached over and quickly hit the nurse "call" button on his wall above his bed.

Dura backed away. Her brown eyes wide. "What did I do?"

"It wasn't you. Just follow the lead of what you see the other nurses do. Try to hold him and keep him from thrashing around and hurting himself. He is having a seizure, so we will have to secure him."

Two women and two men hurried into the room and took their places around Jimmy's bed, just as they had done with this procedure twenty times before. Each nurse and aide automatically took one of Jimmy's limbs, restraining him and holding him still, even as they spoke gentle, soothing words to him.

But Jimmy continued to loudly moan something imperceptible in his obvious confusion.

Dura reached out and held the arm closest to her.

"Can you hear me, Jimmy?" Rosie leaned close to his face as she attempted to cradle his flailing head. "Look at me! Watch me now. Breathe in and breathe out. Your eyes are open, but you need to focus and look at my face over here." She did another cycle of breathing exercises and encouraged him to do the same.

Jimmy's eyes slowly began to focus on Rosie, and his contorted facial tension lessened.

Rosie looked around his hospital bed and saw a still-wide-eyed Dura helping the other nurses and aides who were protecting

Jimmy and keeping him on the bed. She looked back at Jimmy. "You went away again. This time right in the middle of our introduction with Miss Dura. Do you remember this nice lady?"

Dura stepped forward, and Rosie took Jimmy's and Dura's hands and placed them together. "Can you say, 'how do you do?' to Miss Dura? I bet you are thirsty after that episode. Would you like some orange juice?"

"How do you do?" Jimmy said as he took the back of his hand and wiped his forehead with his bed sheet. "I need a drink. Thank you."

"Well, let's give a job to Miss Dura. She will get you your drink." Rosie walked to Dura and whispered, "It's in the breakroom behind the central desk. Would you mind?"

Dura nodded and headed out of the unit. As soon as she returned, she handed the chilled can of OJ to Jimmy with a straw, which he sipped gingerly.

"Okay, little man, why don't you tell Miss Dura where you were born and where you and your parents live?" said Rosie.

Dura listened kindly as Jimmy launched into a lengthy explanation of his birthplace and his current home in Hillsboro, Texas. "You know, that's where I-35 splits into East and West I-35. One goes to Fort Worth, and the other highway goes to Dallas." Then he and Dura were off to a conversational duet, which could have easily lasted thirty minutes.

"Hold on just a moment," Rosie chuckled. "Miss Dura has to meet some of your other buddies up here on the floor, so why don't we save some of this for later?"

Reaching out and squeezing Jimmy's arm, Dura said, "I'll be back to hear about your soccer skills, okay?"

"Sure," Jimmy grinned.

Dura and Rosie left the unit and walked back to the central desk area.

"How do you feel about the exchange with Jimmy?" asked Rosie.

"He was a little stiff at first, but asking questions is key to getting him to talk. He obviously loves to talk about himself," Dura smiled. Her eyes fell, and she looked more serious. "But I wouldn't have known what to do for him during the seizure if you weren't there. That scared me. Maybe I am not prepared for this, and I am in over my head."

"Well, I *was* there, and I'm here to help you through the training." She smiled. "Now, please have a seat. We have four more children to work through, and then you will be the resident expert. See? This isn't so bad for a first day on the job."

Dura's face held concern. "But all we've done is check on Cooper and hold Jimmy down."

"We do critical medical care here, but along with that, we work at loving these kids with positive interaction to hopefully bring them back to good health." Rosie brushed her hand along the lineup of multiple charts in the holding rack. "Many of these kids, like Jimmy, are not from the Fort Worth area. Consequently, the parents are traveling back and forth between here and their hometowns, trying to keep the household together with brothers and sisters and their jobs. As you can imagine, the parents are racking up enormous bills while the child lies here trying to get well. You were most definitely doing something when you were talking with Jimmy. You were showing him love and concern, which, as a PICU nurse, we must include in the work we do here. I know about that need personally, as you saw with my son. We all seem to have our separate battles. Some get very close to home and affect us in ways that are difficult to measure." Speaking of Cooper made her want to sit quietly with her son, but she knew she couldn't do that, so she turned their attention to the four other charts in the rack.

About an hour later, Betsy came out of a unit carrying the chart of a child just admitted to PICU who was under observation post-op. She lay the chart on the top of the high counter in front of Rosie and Dura. "She's yours," Betsy said. "I'll wait here while you and Dura go through the child's file in case you have any questions."

Rosie picked up the chart and handed it to Dura. "Now we need to focus on this patient." Rosie opened the chart and pulled a blank piece of paper from the desk beside one of the monitors. She placed the paper over one side to hide the answers from Dura as they went down the chart step by step. The first issue they encountered was the spike in the blood pressure. When Dura had no idea what to do, Rosie slid the paper down line by line to give Dura the sense that she was dealing with each issue firsthand. Rosie also explained that as nurses, they must report what they see to the doctor, then wait for the issuance of doctor's orders before they can change medications and other courses of treatment. Rosie hoped this exercise gave Dura a point of reference to use if she encountered children with similar problems. Perhaps these clues could one day spur her memory until it became second nature.

Dura looked overwhelmed.

"This is a lot, I know," said Rosie. "Do you have questions?"

"Yes!" Dura blurted out. "If the doctor orders medicine, where would I find it? How do I measure the dosage? What if I don't understand what the doctor is asking of me?"

As Dura continued with her list of questions, Rosie was comforted with the fact that, even though she had not trained as a nurse, Dura seemed to want to do the best she could. Unfortunately, Rosie realized Dura was only one of the multiple replacements that were forced, totally unprepared, into these essential jobs. *Wow, the once-renowned Children's Medical Center of Fort Worth will be experiencing a severe loss of highly qualified medical staff with some well-meaning but unprepared staff. Dura is an indication of all of our board certifications that will be leaving to populate a camp south of here.*

By the time Rosie was finally able to go home, she felt physically exhausted and desperately in need of an uninterrupted night of sleep. As she lay on her bed, however, she couldn't turn off her mind. Instead of resting, she got up and slowly paced in a circle, going from the kitchen to the living room, to the hall to the breakfast room and back again. With her fists clenched, she wept.

"Where were you when—" Her mind quickly ran through her accumulated losses. "My parents and husband died!" she blurted out. "Now my son is hanging on through the unknown of this coma. . . I'm losing my job and my house simply because I believe in *you*, and I refuse to renounce *you*. What about your promise to take constant care of me?" She paced on, raging her way around the house. Her rant stopped abruptly, interrupted by the piercing ring of her home telephone. She quickened her steps to the cordless phone, took a deep breath to compose herself, and answered with a throaty voice.

"This is Dura. I know you are home getting some rest, but the inevitable occurred. Sweet little Jimmy's alarm went off with an elevated heart rate. I thought, oh no, please not another seizure! So, I ran to check his vitals and turned off the alarm. He was sleeping away like nothing was wrong."

"What did you do?"

"I checked everything with my own stethoscope. Heart rate, BP, and oxygen were all normal, so I looked at the young man and thought that something was not adding up. Checking him over, I noticed that he had wiggled out of his monitor connection. Scared me to death! I thought something was really wrong, and no one was here to bail me out. I hate to bother you, but I had to tell someone."

Rosie chuckled and momentarily felt like a mother hen. "Way to go, Dura! That will probably only happen once. You will be able to tell when the alarm is different for a disconnect. Good job!" Inwardly, Rosie was afraid the conversation was ending because she would have to be alone again with her depressing thoughts of her crushing losses.

"Thanks. See you when you return. Good night, Rosie."

"Good night," said Rosie wearily as she hung up the phone. She had to admit that she liked Dura. *If circumstances were different, and I was going to be around longer, I think we could be good friends.*

But the thought turned her attention back to the real circumstances. *Please, God, don't let me go back to the place of hopelessness. I need to be strong for Cooper so he can pull through this trauma.*

Still standing by the phone, Rosie rubbed her throbbing forehead and remembered that her pastor always told her she had a choice in how she responded. She straightened her back, shook her head fiercely, and looked up at the ceiling. "I choose not to let this set of circumstances be my demise!" she yelled. "I will depend on you, Jesus, as my light and strength to get me through this trial. I will face my foes and see what comes in these impossible times. I *will* do whatever it takes to survive, along with Cooper, in order to get to the other side of this ordeal. If I die trying, so be it, but I refuse to be reduced to a sniveling idiot overcome with fear." Rosie felt a renewed sense of strength and peace to move forward. She was finally able to go to bed and get the rest she needed.

CHAPTER 18

8:45 p.m.
Saturday, March 13

TODAY MARKED NEARLY two weeks since the patrol chased Rosie to the point that she took refuge in the Larson's home. She learned the hard way not to go anywhere without her escort. But tonight was a night she seriously considered breaking the rules. She was frustrated with the requirement to have a male escort every time she stepped outside of any building by herself. To avoid it, she practically lived at the hospital for the last week, which was nice in terms of seeing Cooper more often, but Rosie needed some changes of clothes and a break from the cafeteria food. She considered a stop by the grocery store on her way home.

She dutifully called the service early Friday afternoon, according to the Sharia-mandated instructions, to request an escort/driver to pick her up at the hospital after her shift change at 7:20 p.m. The Muslim male attendant was to arrive at the front portico and check in with the security guard, who would then call Rosie.

One hour and ten minutes later than the prearranged time, the driver finally showed up, with no excuses and no apologies.

When Rosie got into the car, she collapsed against the backseat in disgust. "We need to stop at the corner supermarket close to my house to buy a few things."

"No, we can't do that!" the escort yelled over his shoulder. "This is halftime, and I need to get back to the basketball game. This is March Madness, you know, the college tournament. Maybe the last one. Who knows."

"No, sir. When I called your service dispatcher, I told him what I needed. My contracted ride included a stop at the grocery store for twenty minutes. That is part of the deal. I already waited for you over an hour past my pick-up time. You must comply with the terms of our agreement."

He didn't respond.

"How can your company expect to get another call from me or any of my other friends?" she said, through gritted teeth. She sat with her hands fisted in her lap. *He is so annoying!*

Fortunately, the driver stopped at the store. Though he said nothing else about the basketball game, she clearly felt his displeasure as he made an amplified point of reading his watch.

She looked at her watch as well. "Let the record show the twenty minutes begins now." She quickly got her cart and headed toward the breakfast aisle. She knew when she got home, she would gather these groceries, at least a week's worth of uniforms, check the mail, pay some bills, and pack snacks she had stored away at the house. This way, she could stay at the hospital another week.

As she made her way through the store, she kept running into a couple who seemed to be shopping off her list, always in the same aisle as she was. The man looked familiar, but the woman wore sunglasses, and her hijab sat higher than was the custom. Rosie knew she had seen the man before, but she couldn't quite remember where.

Aisle after aisle, they passed each other. When both women stood in front of the rice, quinoa, and noodle shelves on aisle 23, the woman came very close to her. "Are you Rosie Chavez?" she whispered.

Hearing her name from this stranger startled and concerned her. "Yes, I am," she answered slowly. "How do you know me?"

The lady smiled. "I read it on your name tag."

Rosie immediately put her hand on the lanyard hanging from her neck, which displayed her name, as well as her PICU credentials, her medical center entrance pass, and her parking garage key card. She had forgot to remove them from around her neck when she left work. "Well, yeah, I'm Rosie. Can I help you?"

"My name is Safi Kadib," the woman said, still whispering. "I remember meeting you when you attended Alex Larson's funeral prayers at the courtyard of our mosque. My husband, Jamal, is the imam. He led the prayers for the Larson family. Alex's death was such a tragedy."

Rosie glanced at Jamal, who stood by the shopping cart, oblivious to their conversation. "Yes, I have met him. Isn't he the new DFW imam?"

"The very one. The Larsons are good friends of ours. Tom told me about that night when you went to their house. I understand you've experienced some tragedies of your own."

"Yes," she said simply, feeling caught off-guard that a stranger knew private details about her life. "I have had some heartbreak in the last months."

"Did you convert to Islam so you can stay?"

"No. My Jesus means too much to me to forsake him when times get hard, as they seem to be now. That is why I will be relocated to the camp."

Safi reached for a bag of quinoa. "I must talk with you soon."

Rosie looked at her surprised, wondering what the imam's wife could possibly have to say to her. "I am at the medical center day after tomorrow. I will be there all day, almost every day."

"Come say hello to my husband, Jamal," Safi said loudly, clearly wanting to change the subject.

Rosie stepped with Safi to the cart where Jamal was standing. "I remember meeting you the night I was at the Larson home about two weeks ago," she said. "You made the call that probably saved my life from the patrol. Thank you again for taking care of me. Just so you know, I paid my February and March jizya, so I am up to date." Rosie gestured toward her escort. "As you can see, I never leave home without an escort, and my hijab is in place." She touched her head scarf. "Although this new way of life is different, and these changes have come at us quite rapidly, we are all trying our best to observe the orders given to us over at the Compliance Network."

Jamal smiled awkwardly. He nodded to Safi and made a sideways nod toward Rosie. "It's nice to meet you again, Rosie. Right now, we need to move along before people begin to figure out who I am."

She thought his statement odd but smiled. "Yes, I need to be going too. I have only twenty minutes in here, and I fear my escort is going to leave me if I don't hurry it along." She glanced once more toward Safi before turning away.

She checked her watch, noting she had five minutes left. She stepped to her escort. "This was different from my normal grocery store visit, I'm sure. That was the city imam, Jamal Kadib. I needed to take a moment to respectfully meet him."

Her escort didn't seem impressed and looked purposefully at his watch again. She decided not to push his limits.

Back in her escort's car, she couldn't get the brief exchange with Safi out of her mind. It was troubling. *I must talk with you soon,* echoed in her mind. *What on earth would Safi want to talk about with me?* Surely Rosie hadn't done anything wrong that Safi could know.

And yet Safi's statement sounded like a desperate plea for help. How would Safi be able to make arrangements to come to the medical center and then find Rosie? *Since Alex was at the medical center, perhaps Safi will remember where the PICU area is.* She shrugged lightly, believing it was strange the secretive way Safi spoke and then how she changed the subject so quickly when Jamal came near.

There is definitely more to this story. But what?

PART 3

THE PURGE

CHAPTER 19

6:50 a.m.
Sunday, March 14

ROSIE HAD JUST entered the PICU loaded down with her backpack, a grocery sack, and several changes of clothes when Dura came rushing up to her.

"I need to talk to you," Dura said in a hushed tone.

First Safi, now Dura! Rosie looked at Dura's terrified eyes and wondered who else "must" talk to her. "Sure, what's going on? When do you want to meet?" Rosie pointed to her bags. "Can I put this in my locker, or do we need to talk right now?"

Dura's eyes gave a daggered look. "Not so loud! I'll come find you."

"Okay!" Rosie whispered in return, looking defensively at her. *What is it with these people? If another person comes up to me and says they must talk to me, I may just scream, "So talk!"*

Ten minutes later, Rosie was in the PICU pharmacy closet doing the mandatory drug inventory count after the weekend. Dura came into and shut the door. "I am so scared, I don't know what to do," she said, shaking and looking pale. "There is something going on here at this medical center that is way above my pay grade, and it is creeping me out. We didn't have any of this going on at the county facility."

Rosie gently put her hands on Dura's shoulders. "You're trembling! What's going on? What have they done to you?"

"They haven't done anything to me. I only *wish* they had tried to do something to me. I would have fought back with all my might." Her face grew bright red. "What they have done is despicable! But I don't know what to do."

"You can start by calming down and telling me what's going on."

Dura began to whisper so fast that Rosie had a hard time keeping up. "Oh, Rosie, there is so much to say. It's Jimmy. He's gone!"

"What do you mean, he's gone? They already moved him?"

Dura shook her head furiously. "No, I mean he is *dead*."

Rosie stumbled against the back wall of the closet in surprise. "Wha—"

"Yesterday all his vitals were good. I checked them just as you taught me. You told me to look at the hard data and look at the child and talk to them."

Rosie held up her hand. "Stop. No, this can't be true." Rosie began to tear up. Wiping her eyes on her smock. "I don't understand. What happened? A seizure? You must slow down and breathe so I can follow what you're telling me."

Dura let out a heavy breath and then started in again. "We don't have time to slow down. I've got to tell you this quickly. I was in his room, and all the data looked right in line: temperature, blood pressure, pulse, oxygen—all good, similar to what we charted earlier. I checked his color and felt his arms, hands, legs, and feet. I was talking to him the entire time. He told me he felt good and called me Miss Dura for the first time and, of course, he asked for Miss Rosie. He was so cute, and we were really connecting. He even began to talk about going back to therapy. He was really talking to me. It was wonderful!"

"So, what happened?" Still crying, Rosie watched Dura's eyes.

"Later, his labs came back, which showed he was about the same." Now Dura started to tear up. "Jimmy felt better, he looked better, and he had hope that he was healing." Her tempo finally slowed down.

Rosie patted Dura's arm, partly to comfort and partly to encourage her to keep talking.

"About 1:00 in the afternoon, an orderly came to take him to a test. I did not see the orders or anything. He just came out of the blue. The man said he had orders to take Jimmy. That was so strange because they always run the tests in the unit." Dura gestured over her shoulder toward Jimmy's unit, and the tears flowed more. She wiped at her tears and her nose before continuing. "Here is our little Jimmy being unplugged from his monitor and rolled down to the elevator. Little did I know that would be the last time I would ever see him. I waited and waited, and he never came back from his test." Dura burst into sobs.

As terrible as it was, Rosie had seen these types of things happen before, so she reached over and hugged Dura. "You must have felt awful not knowing what happened to your patient. These kids on our floor are often very sick, and we just never know—"

"It was the worst day of my life. Later that afternoon, Betsy received an email that said Jimmy died during the test. She told me, and we cried together. We all agreed that his condition was serious, but I certainly didn't expect him to *die*. Not that day. We had talked, and for Jimmy, he was feeling fine."

Dura tried to compose herself, putting her hand on the pharmacy shelving to steady herself. "But Rosie, that isn't the strangest thing. Betsy got word that there were eight other deaths that same day."

Rosie studied Dura's face for a long moment. She tried to rationally wrap her mind around what Dura said, but she couldn't grasp the words. What was this rookie replacement standing in front of her telling her . . . that *nine* kids all experienced unexpected deaths? All within a matter of hours of one another? This didn't make sense.

"Betsy was asking around in the other parts of the hospital," Dura said. "She was told to stop asking questions and do her job."

Rosie wiped tears from her face. She could well imagine how that went down with Betsy. She envisioned Betsy's red curls bouncing and her cheeks flaming to announce her inner rage over her desire to protect her kids at the hospital.

"Betsy seemed more determined to find out what was going on. She told me that each of the nine children was very sick with differing maladies. All of them had various illness and had long-term hospital needs. Every one of them was taken off their particular floors for some type of 'tests.' None of these children returned to their floors. When Betsy began to ask for more information, she was abruptly sent home."

Rosie's mind began to spin. "I noticed Betsy wasn't here today even though her name was on the schedule. Being sent home is a pretty drastic maneuver to get her off the floor and stop her from talking. This is the worst news ever."

"That is the least of your concerns," Dura spoke sternly in between heaving sobs. "I am really afraid that something bad is going on here." She lowered her voice to a whisper and glanced at the door. "You need to seriously consider getting Cooper off this floor and out of this hospital. He could be next. He has serious 'long-term hospital needs.'" She added air quotes. "Those were the exact words they used to describe the other nine kids who died. Why nine deaths on the same day, all taken for tests, all really sick, and all ended up dying in the process?"

Raw fear struck Rosie. She sucked in her breath and felt the blood leave her face. She turned to face the inventory paperwork to hide her panic, crying for Cooper now. *I think I'm going to throw up.*

"If I were you, Rosie, I would not turn my back on this new administrative team. This new set of managers are not people to entrust with any child. Betsy confided in me, 'These nine are only the ones we know about.'"

Waves of nausea washed over Rosie as she backed up to the wall again between the shelving to brace herself. She raised a finger of caution to Dura. "Just a second." She slid down the wall to the floor and raised her knees to rest her head against them until the nausea passed.

Not now, Lord! I can't lose anyone else. Don't let me lose Cooper too! I don't know what to do. I need some divine intervention. Please! I need your help.

Dura stood, wringing her hands. "Are you going to be okay? What can I do for you?"

Rosie focused on breathing in deeply until she felt calmer, then stood upright again, wiping her face. "Don't worry about me. What can we do for Cooper? His medical outlook is better each day, but there is nowhere to place him right now. I certainly don't want him to go to another hospital around here. Since I am with him, I am his advocate." She shook her head. "Is there another way?"

"I understand, but we *must* find a way to get Cooper out of here soon. We need to get the doctor's orders and find a facility that will take him. As you know, all the big city medical facilities are being overtaken by radicals, and there isn't a better place than this, particularly since you are here so much of the time," Dura said, her panicked breathing finally slowing down.

"But I can't watch him all the time. I wish Dr. Wilson wasn't booked up with training his replacements. I need his advice right now."

"I can help. You have helped me. I will take this challenge of keeping Cooper free from harm. I will watch over him as if he were my own. You can count on me."

Rosie looked into Dura's eyes again and saw new compassion. "I know you mean well, but how can you say that? What would prevent an orderly from coming up right at this moment and taking Cooper? For all we know, they might be circling other floors as we speak, picking up children for tests. No. You're right. I have to come up with a plan to get Cooper out of here."

"I know this is hard for you and Betsy," Dura said. "Working with you both, I see how much these kiddos mean to both of you and especially Cooper being on the floor. I was thrown into your lap, and you were forced to train me, but you bent over backward with kindness and extra coaching. It is hard transitioning into your job. But you have made me feel welcomed and appreciated. You are trying to give me a positive experience here. I could understand if you didn't want to—because of what's happening to you. Because of what my people are doing to you."

Rosie was touched by Dura's words and concern, and she squeezed Dura's arm.

"I know you are a Christian," Dura continued. "I realize that makes you an enemy of the new government of Islam, but you are more than just nice. So, thank you. And please, let me help you." She squeezed Rosie's arm in return and smiled.

As Rosie smiled back and began to step toward the door, Dura held onto her arm. Dura's dark eyes had changed. They looked . . . Rosie wasn't quite sure, but she thought she saw fear mixed with excitement there. This time, Dura held up a finger and said, "Just a second."

Dura walked to the door to pull on it. When it remained shut tight, she turned again to Rosie. "I want to tell you something else."

Rosie's stomach churned. *What else can she possibly tell me? Aren't nine kids being murdered bad enough?*

"Something happened to me last night that I can't explain. I want your opinion."

"Please, just hold that thought." Rosie said, "I can't stand it. Come with me, I have got to go and check on Cooper." Rosie grabbed Dura by the arm and walked briskly from the pharmacy closet down to Cooper's unit. Rosie stood over Cooper's bed to watch him, crying silently. Dura walked over to the opposite side of the bed. Rosie reached out to stoke his curly hair one more time, then straighten his sheet and blanket and then check his monitor. Smiling down at him, "Mama's here. I love you, and I am going to protect you and make sure you get the best care ever." She sniffed, wiped her face, and turned her face to Dura. "Okay I feel much better. You were saying?"

Rosie sat next to the head of the bed and watched Dura shut the unit door and pull the privacy curtain across the wall of the unit.

Rosie waited while Dura dragged the other side chair next to Rosie and fidgeted with her smock.

"There is no easy way to say this, but . . . Jesus was in my room last night."

Rosie's eyes widened. "How do you know it was Jesus?"

"Because he told me. Just like that!"

"What did he say to you? What did he look like? How long did he stay? Why did he come to you?"

Dura held up her hand. "Whoa! I think he looked Middle Eastern. He was dressed in white, I believe, because his face and clothing were so bright—actually too bright to look at. I had this overall feeling of being loved. I know that you have love me, Rosie, because you are always trying to bring out the best in me. Jesus had a love for me that far outshined your encouragement and care for me. He told me not to be afraid and that he loved me, and I was right where he wanted me to be." She paused and looked pleadingly at Rosie. "What do you think that means? Right where he wants me to be? At the medical center? Or next to you and Betsy? Or with my family? It is all so very confusing. But this one thing I know, without any doubt, Jesus loves me."

Rosie clasped her hands together over her heart and smiled broadly. "I've never experienced Jesus's presence like that, but I believe you, Dura. That is so awesome!"

"He loves me, and I am not supposed to be afraid," Dura said, beaming with delight. Then she lowered her eyebrows in concern. "What's next? Am I supposed to prevent more tests from going wrong? Am I supposed to steer clear of the leadership that is taking over this hospital? Or am I supposed to sit back for more instructions? I am perplexed. I need some help."

Rosie thought for a moment. "I think Jesus came to you for a very specific reason. I believe he wants to share his love with you and forgive you. He wants you to believe in him. This is what he wants for everyone. He is very predictable on those three truths: love, forgiveness, and belief in him. I am so pleased that you got to see him. Now I am curious. Tell me how this happened? What time of night? Or were you even aware of the time? Were you asleep, and he woke you? Or was it like a dream?"

Dura considered the questions. "I don't know about the time, but I was asleep. At least, I thought I was asleep. His face or voice or something very distinctive woke me. So, I would guess it was not a dream, but after Jesus left me, I was still in bed, and I hadn't moved. It was sort of like I awoke again to think about what had happened. I don't know, Rosie. It was really scary, and yet it was peaceful and comforting. The one thing that haunts me, in a good way, I guess, was the simple way he looked at me with penetrating, clear green eyes. The way he said my name. 'Dura.' He said it as if he was my father, only much more lovingly. I couldn't take it all in. I can't stop thinking about him and his visit. It occurred so fast, and yet he seemed to dwell with me for quite a while."

Rosie sighed. "You must be careful because accepting the love and forgiveness that Jesus has for you makes you the enemy of Islam. You know this."

Dura nodded.

"You know the Islamic teachings are very clear about a Muslim who accepts Jesus. As I understand it, there are some very real threats that come to a person, especially a woman, who becomes a follower of Christ. As wonderful as this is, and as much as I hope you accept this truth, I cannot stress this enough: you must be very careful who you speak to regarding this experience. Telling the wrong person can get you killed."

"That is why we are having this conversation in private!" Dura said in an excited whisper. "I intend to be very careful about whom I will tell. On the one hand, I am so excited about my experience with Jesus and thrilled with the possibilities of what is in store for me. On the other hand, I am scared of what may happen as a result. I have a strange peace about my future here at the medical center and wherever Allah or your God seems to be leading me. I am just glad to tell someone. I knew I could trust you, Rosie. I knew you would understand what all this means."

Rosie smiled, genuinely happy for Dura and where she may be heading spiritually. But the news about Cooper's predicament crashed into her thoughts again. "Please pray with me over the next few days about what to do with Cooper. I am very concerned about him being here."

"Of course, I will."

Rosie prayed silently. *Is it really possible that someone might try to kill my son? Lord, can it be that your appearance to Dura might be a key piece to this puzzle of getting Cooper removed from PICU?*

CHAPTER 20

5:05 a.m.
Monday, March 15

ROSIE AWAKENED WITH a start, her heart racing. She stood abruptly from the chair next to Cooper's bed. Grabbing the bed railing to steady herself, she instinctively looked at Cooper, who hadn't moved from the last time she observed him. He seemed to be sleeping soundly. She then looked at his monitor to view his vitals, which were normal for him.

She'd had a rough night as her emotions felt crushed from the previous day's events. *How dare the hospital kill my kids? This is infuriating.* She spent the night next near Cooper's bed to protect him since she no longer trusted anyone in the hospital administration. She stayed awake most of the night praying about Dura's outrageous suggestion of getting Cooper out of the hospital before he became its next victim.

What would Ramon do in a situation like this? He would always have me write down the pros and cons. She went out to the central desk and retrieved a sheet of paper and a pen. Sitting back in her chair, she began to scribble notes. On the con side, she wrote "CD" to remind her of "certain death" if Cooper stayed and was taken for "tests." She scratched "PD" on the pro side for "possible death." *Either way, it doesn't look good for team Cooper,* she thought.

As she continued with the list, Dura came in. "Your shift is going to start soon. Do you want to go down and get something to eat in the cafeteria?"

Rosie's stomach growled at the thought. "To tell you the truth, yes, I would." She paused before getting up. "Would you mind guarding Cooper and stalling them if they come to take him for any tests? I'll be back in five minutes."

"Of course."

On her way back from the cafeteria with her take-out breakfast of muffin and eggs, Rosie saw Betsy. She smiled and fell in stride with her as they walked toward the security check-in desk for their floor. "What happened yesterday?" she asked just above a whisper. "You were sent home? They said you got a call from Mr. Sunshine, Ali-Com."

Betsy's face turned red, and she fumbled in her purse to retrieve her key card. She stopped just shy of the security gate. "Someone in the hospital thought I was asking too many questions. Me—trying to be an advocate for these children whom they apparently have no qualms about eliminating with impunity." Her hands trembled. "Why wouldn't I be asking questions? No other charge nurse was coming to their defense."

Betsy stepped to the card reader and scanned her card. The reader beeped its acceptance. Then it beeped again twice. The gate wouldn't open. "What is wrong with this device?" She tried her card again and again it denied her access. The redness in her face crept down her neck.

Rosie bumped Betsy's hip. "Here." She handed Betsy her breakfast to-go box and pulled down her key card from her lanyard. "Let me use my card to get you in."

As the reader accepted Rosie's card, Hank, the security guard, appeared. "You know better than to let someone in on your card,

Rosie. Betsy's card has been deactivated." He looked at Betsy. "Will you come with me? We need to walk to Mr. Ali-Com's office."

"Hank, what is the problem here?" Rosie had known Hank since her first day of work.

Hank turned around and smiled at Rosie. Taking the breakfast box from Betsy, he placed it back into Rosie's hands. "You should go upstairs, Rosie. This doesn't concern you."

"But it does concern me!" Rosie said, feeling anger wash over her. It was one thing to have the administration do their dirty work, but Hank was one of the good guys—one of them. "Betsy is one of my best friends. I thought she was a friend of yours too."

"You know I like Betsy, but I'm just following orders. You can't shoot the messenger." Hank lowered his voice. "You need to back off, Rosie, and let me do this. I'm not happy about it either, but I need to keep my job."

Rosie felt a twinge of remorse as she watched Hank escort Betsy down the hall and around a corner.

Lord, it feels like everyone is against us, even old friends. Give me grace.

She headed back to Cooper's unit, where she gratefully saw Dura still there. "Thanks, Dura."

Dura nodded and left, and Rosie settled into her seat next to Cooper, where she opened her breakfast box. "Hey, Cooper, Mom's back. I got some breakfast." She took a few half-hearted bites of her egg sandwich and wished she could stay in this chair all day to watch over him, but she comforted herself with the thought that she would be on his floor to monitor any orderlies who came and went.

Once she finished her breakfast, she checked the wall clock. It was time for her shift to begin. She pushed Cooper's hair off his forehead. "Hey Cooper, you need a haircut. We will get you one soon."

Things on the floor went without incident throughout the morning, though later that afternoon, Rosie realized she still hadn't seen Betsy. She tried calling her work phone but got no answer. She sent Betsy an email just to see what would happen. She received an immediate automated response: "Betsy Thompson is no longer working at the medical center."

Rosie's jaw dropped. "Just like that," she said out loud, not bothering to hide the disgust she felt. "No 'Thank you for your years of service here.' No 'You were such an inspiration to children and other nurses alike.' No 'Sorry to see you go.' What a sendoff."

"What's up?" Dura said, stopping at the central desk in front of Rosie.

Rosie motioned for Dura to come around the desk and look at the computer screen. "What do you make of this?" She pointed to the message.

Dura read the email. "That looks ominous. They didn't even give us a chance to say goodbye to her."

"I saw Betsy this morning trying to get her key card to work. When it didn't admit her, Hank appeared and ushered her to Mr. Ali-Com's office." She sighed. "Do you think you can nose around and see what's happened to our Betsy? Or maybe even call her at home unless you think the phones are bugged." Rosie stopped, looked around the floor, and frowned. "Does this mean I'm officially getting paranoid?"

Rosie and Dura looked at each other, and Rosie felt the blood rise to her cheeks. Dura's eyes held the same fear that settled on Rosie. She knew why Betsy wasn't coming back, but she wanted to hear more details.

Rosie considered her dilemma. "I know all this is too little too late, but can't we have minds that remain curious and interested in the facts? I'm glad I won't be here if these 'tests' become the norm and we aren't allowed to investigate what's happening."

Rosie stood and walked around the length of the central desk as if sizing it up. "Refusing to let us ask questions is another erosion of freedom. If I ask the wrong questions and get run off by the new management, I will not help Cooper's recovery at all. But if I bite my lip and say nothing, what will I accomplish to help him and the other kiddos?"

Dura reached out her hand to Rosie. "I'll see what I can find out about Betsy. But it's best for *you* to stay quiet. You don't want to do anything to compromise your time here with Cooper. Besides, we need you. If we lose you too, it will benefit nothing except the ego of the administrator who will see you as another notch on his belt to show the floor and the other nurses who is boss."

Rosie nodded reluctantly. Although she wanted to get to the bottom of what happened to Betsy, she knew Dura was right.

I'm here still here for a reason. She put her head in her hands. *Help me, Jesus. If I'm in the spot where you want me, what am I supposed to do now?*

CHAPTER 21

8:30 a.m.
Monday, March 15

BZZZZZZ. THE PHONE vibrated in Jamal's pocket. The sensation caused him to jump. *Oh yeah, it's my new cell phone.* Normally, that kind of call would automatically go straight to his hands-free system in the car. He smiled to himself at the ingenious ways he had circumvented the Observer's surveillance system.

I'll call Tom back when I'm out of the car. This new burner phone from the discount store was the ticket—a secret only he, Tom, and a college friend, Navid, shared. Navid because he had his ear to the wall on what was happening regionally with the radical leadership.

As the phone in his pocket continued to buzz, a call came through on his hands-free system. The car screen read "OFFICE WORK" with the ten-digit number appearing beside the text. Jamal's countenance immediately fell. It was Faiza Abbas, Uma's replacement. She was pleasant enough and seemed more efficient than Uma, but he didn't trust her.

Pushing the "Accept" button on his screen, he said, "This is Jamal."

"Hi, Imam, this is Faiza. You have several appointments this morning and later today. I was wondering when you would be coming into the office so I can confirm your times with them."

"I'm a few miles away. I should be there in about fifteen minutes."

"Very good," said Faiza. "I'll see you then." She hung up, leaving Jamal time to review his circumstances. *I now have two cell phones. I must turn off the vibration of the burner phone unless I'm by myself in the car. Right pocket burner, back pocket regular phone with the ringer on . . . easy to remember.*

He arrived at the DFW office, parked, and walked toward the entrance of the office complex. He patted the location of both phones as he walked along, trying to remind himself and make sure they were where they should be. When he got under the cover of the building, he pulled out his new phone and listened to the voicemail from Tom, then called Tom back.

"Where did you come up with the idea of an area code for the east coast?" Tom asked.

"I don't know, it just seemed like a good idea when I was buying it. Plus, if they were ever looking at your phone record, you could always say you have an accounting client out east. Be creative. That will be your story if and when that comes up. What about lunch today?"

"Sounds good. Should I pick you up at the Kimball as usual, let's say around 11:40?"

"Sure. And have you made any progress with the police concerning the parents of the kid I hit?"

"I can't believe you are asking me that on the phone. We can talk about that when we meet. I'll see you there."

Jamal hung up, placed the phone back in his trousers, smoothed out his tunic, and entered the building. Faiza greeted him from her place at the front desk. She was a nice-looking woman. Jamal guessed her to be in her early fifties. Actually, she reminded Jamal of his own mother. Faiza had worn a different business suit each day since she started, with a matching jacket and skirt or dress slacks and hijab. She was always very tastefully put together. He was impressed over the way she represented the office as well as the values of Islam. Yet in the back of his mind, he knew there were cameras in the corners and the listening devices likely remaining, so he could trust no one except Tom.

Jamal stopped at her desk to discuss the day and the flow of his appointments.

"The first person you need to call is the regional imam to discuss the progress on the camp construction," she said. "Then there are a couple more men I think you could simply call instead of meeting with. I mean it's your choice. It didn't sound too urgent. Then Mr. Siddiqui called again. He wants to drop by during lunch to talk about his daughter's death at the medical center. This is his third call since I've been here. Sounded pretty insistent. Should I have him come over to meet you?"

"That timeframe will not work," Jamal said. "I have talked with him once. He will not be satisfied. He and his family are humiliated about some infidels viewing his daughter before she died. Besides, I already have lunch plans out of the office." He anxiously checked his watch. "Tell him I will see him two weeks from today. The march and relocation will be complete. And the infidels he is so angry about will all be relocated. I can deal with his issue then." He turned toward his office to call the regional imam when she stopped him.

"And today's lunch? How shall I put that down on the schedule? You are having lunch with . . . ?"

Looking back over his shoulder, he saw the professional assistant looking ever the part. He squared up so he stood looking straight at her. How could he refuse that inquiry? And what would it hurt if she knew it was Tom? "I'll be at a working lunch with Tom Larson, our accountant, my friend. After my call with the regional imam, I'll have to figure out how we are going to pay for all this expansion at the camp. Tom seems to pull strings to make money appear out of thin air."

"Very good. I'll put down Tom Larson for lunch," she said. "Do you know when you will be back?"

"Not for certain. We have a lot of ground to cover."

"In the meantime, I'll call Mr. Siddiqui and head him off until after the dust settles on the big events in our future."

"That's fine." He closed his office door behind him and sighed lightly. *Yes, let's handle those big events in our future.*

* * *

8:50 a.m.

The Observer smiled as he watched Faiza interact with Jamal on the screen. He noted on another screen that Jamal was in his office calling the regional imam, so he reached for his phone and dialed Faiza's desk phone.

"Good morning, this is Faiza. May I help you?"

"Nicely done, Faiza. If what Jamal has told you is true, you have retrieved more information voluntarily out of our imam than your predecessor did in all her time there. He is having lunch with his friend Tom Larson. Now earn your keep and find out how Jamal is making the arrangements to meet with Tom. I have no record of Jamal talking to anyone about a lunch plan today or any other day."

"Jamal seems happy to work with me. Please give me some time to figure it out," Faiza said, her voice betraying a sense of desperation.

"Unfortunately, because of the inadequate job your predecessor did, I don't think we have any time to spare. We will know where Jamal meets Tom for lunch because his car's GPS will pinpoint that location. The missing piece is how they communicated prior to the appointment. He is not calling from home or from the car, otherwise we would have a recording of that call. If Tom is randomly coming by his house, then we would hear the doorbell ring. I need to know, Faiza, and you need to discover this new mystery! I know I'm pushing you, but we cannot let his communication continue to go undetected. We must have more intel. Get on it."

The Observer watched Faiza respond with a start. He smirked in a satisfied way as he stroked the scar on his face. He upset her peaceful setting as intended. *I despise using females, but we need them to get this information. Ah well, they are expendable.*

After he hung up, his phone immediately rang. He looked at the caller ID and quickly answered. "Hello, sir, peace be upon you. How good it is to speak with you this morning."

"You must tell me about the DFW imam and the Austin imam," the caliph said. "Do we have any more evidence on either of them? Can we trust them through the relocation and the march, or do we need to have them eliminated? Gut feeling right now, what do we do?"

"My gut feel is that Jamal Kadib and the Austin imam are both trustworthy enough to at least get through the relocation. Kadib's camp is ahead of schedule and appears to be ready for occupancy come the due date. He is still too independent for my tastes, however. There is a deviousness about him that I can't quite put my finger on. He talks normally in his home with his family but then whispers imperceptibly with his wife when they appear to be alone."

"Is he on to us?" The caliph's voice rose sternly. "You are the one with all the equipment that you insisted on acquiring. Go down there and find out!"

The ending words thundered so loudly that the Observer had to hold the phone away from his ear to keep from hurting his eardrum. "Yes, your excellency." But his words hung in the air, unheard. The caliph had already hung up.

CHAPTER 22

10:45 a.m.
Tuesday, March 16

AS ROSIE AND Dura were interacting with a new patient and her parents, helping her feel at home as much as possible, Betsy's replacement, Margie, the new charge nurse in the PICU, entered the unit.

"Good morning, Nurse Margie," they both said, nearly in unison.

"This is Ruth Wallace, our newest patient, and her parents, Mr. and Mrs. Wallace," Rosie said. "Wallace family, this is our new charge nurse, Margie Atherton."

Rosie wondered about this new nurse hired so quickly. *Margie showed up yesterday, barely one hour after Betsy's departure. She seems nice enough and knowledgeable, but this tall, scrawny Muslim snoop will never take the place of Betsy's love for the children and her red curls bouncing down the hall.* She looked at Margie. The hajib around her gaunt, chiseled face gave her more the appearance of a severe prison guard than a caregiver and child's friend. *Margie. Such a friendly name for such a harsh-looking woman. Why couldn't they find a standby supervisor who at least looked kind? A smile wouldn't crack her face . . . and let's put some meat on those bones.*

"Rosie? Rosie!"

Rosie yanked herself back to reality when she realized Margie was talking to her. "Sorry about that," she said and smiled brightly. "I lost myself for a moment there!"

Margie didn't return the smile. "There is a lady at the nurse's station. She has asked to speak with you." And with that, she turned on her heel and exited the room.

Rosie looked through the glass wall. A woman wearing dark glasses and a bright head scarf looked her way. *Is that Safi Kadib?* "If you'll excuse me," she said. "Dura, I believe you can finish admitting this new patient while I take care of this."

Dura nodded but looked at her questioningly.

"Mrs. Kadib?" Rosie said as she approached the woman. When Safi nodded, Rosie smiled and extended her hand. She wanted to make sure anybody who might be listening didn't think anything out of the ordinary over this woman's greeting. "How nice to see you. Have you come to see our facility here?"

Safi clasped Rosie's hand but said nothing.

"Have you come to talk with me," Rosie asked quietly, "or is there another reason for your visit?"

"Please, call me Safi. You said you spent most of your time here at the hospital, so I have come here to see you." Safi leaned in and whispered, "I must be able to speak openly with you. Is there someplace we can talk? My escort has agreed to wait for me in the area beyond those doors." Safi gestured toward the PICU waiting room to the right.

"I was just going to check on my son, Cooper." Rosie let the white lie escape from her lips. "Would you care to follow me there? Since you have come in from the street, you will be required to wear a gown, gloves, and a mask. These children are in ICU for a reason. We want to protect you and them."

Rosie walked Safi to a cabinet next to the white board and pulled out a full-length, paper-thin yellowish gown and some booties for Safi to put over her street clothes and shoes. After sanitizing their hands, Rosie led her to Cooper's room.

This is my turf, so I guess whatever she's here to discuss, we will do it in a safe area with the curtains wide open. Rosie saw Dura out of the corner of her eye and winked, so only Dura could see it, to signal all was well.

Rosie offered Safi the chair, but Safi remained standing.

"How can I help you?" Rosie asked.

Safi looked at Cooper and a soft smile came to her face. Then she looked around the room and out toward the hallway. "We can speak candidly?"

"Yes," Rosie assured her.

"I'm here about my request a couple of days ago."

"Yes, I remember. Your exact words were, 'We must talk.' This is as safe a spot as you can ask for during these days and times." Rosie gently rubbed Cooper's head. "This unit is for my son, Cooper, as we discussed in the store."

She walked back to the foot of the bed, nearer to Safi, and picked up Cooper's chart as if to read it. "I believe you remember why he is here in the PICU, he was in a car wreck? You asked to come and see me, and I am glad you came. Now how can I help you? I don't have much time. We are busy on the floor."

Safi sighed heavily and removed her dark glasses to reveal faded bruises, a partially swollen right eye marked by red and blue lines. "My husband," she said simply and lifted a hand to gently touch the bruised area. "About two weeks ago."

Rosie gasped. "I'm sorry," she said, swallowing hard and feeling regret for mentioning her busyness. *This may explain why she was so nervous that day in the grocery store—having her husband standing right there beside her.*

Safi didn't seem to hear her. "The children could not help hearing the struggle. They came out of their rooms to see what was happening. Nothing like this had ever happened before. When Jamal saw their terrorized faces looking at him, gratefully, he stopped hitting me and left." She paused and closed her eyes. "The entire incident was terrifying. And confusing. I hope my daughters and I don't have to endure the humiliation and pain of that kind of confrontation ever again."

"I am sorry to hear this," Rosie said again. "May I ask, why are you telling me?"

Safi opened her eyes again and a glint of tears sat in the corners. "This is not easy for me." She blinked and lowered her gaze. Her hands fidgeted with the ties of her yellow gown at the waist. "I told some of this to Tom Larson. Tom told me that he has known you for some time and has had religious conversations with you recently. As you may know, he is a trusted family friend, and he suggested that I talk to you. He said you would understand."

Rosie waited, unsure of what to do with this mystery.

Safi looked Rosie square in the eyes. "I don't know how to start." She paused again and cleared her throat. "The Man in the White Robe came to me that night after Jamal left the house," she blurted out. "He said he came to bring me relief. His loving presence was wonderful." Safi's eyes began to glisten again, but now the tears ran down her bruised cheeks.

They stood silently for a moment—the only sounds in the room coming from Cooper's monitors beeping occasionally. Rosie repositioned the side chair to face the couch on the opposite wall. "Please sit down, Safi," she said and pointed to the chair while she moved to the couch.

Safi settled into the chair. "After Jamal left, it took a while to get the children settled down and to sleep. When they were asleep, I lay on my own bed and was beginning to drift off to sleep when I noticed the bedroom was filled with light. Initially, I assumed that Jamal was back in the house and had turned the light on." Safi crossed her legs. She then glanced over her shoulder to see if anyone was at the door.

"It's just us in here. You can talk," Rosie reassured her.

"This light wasn't just light. It was the brightest white light I have ever seen. The curious thing is that it wasn't particularly blinding, but you couldn't look at the source of it, nor could you discern the details of the man's face and body. Just an outline." Her eyes took on a faraway look. "Even now, describing this all to you, it is as if the entire scene is before me again, as if he is still standing in front of me."

"Did he speak to you?"

"This is why I am here. I need to tell someone what happened to know what to do next. It was too wonderful to keep to myself. As I sat in bed and looked at him, I tried to memorize as many details as I could. He began to speak. Do you know the first thing he said to me?"

Rosie shook her head no, but inwardly, she was frantically thinking, *what did he say? What did he say!*

"Safi." She smiled. "He said my name, 'Safi.' Oh Rosie, it was so sweet and loving. I could listen to him say my name over and over. I was stunned that the Man in the White Robe was even there in my house. But that he knew my name! He had come to comfort me. The way he said my name felt as though he was holding me. I was so completely loved and cared for." She glanced around again, then she leaned forward. "This Man was Jesus. It had to be him. He told me not to be afraid of his presence. Then he explained that he was going to use what Jamal had done to me . . . that I had endured Jamal's wrath in order to bring me and my children and Jamal to the truth about Jesus." Safi lowered her face into her hands.

Rosie jumped up and pulled the privacy curtain across the windowed wall. Then she grabbed a box of tissues and handed them to Safi.

Safi looked up at her and smiled faintly. "Jesus assured me that he has a purpose for all of it—the beating, the fact that the children witnessed it, even that Jamal has become the DFW imam. Jesus said I will see his hand of guidance and leading through the whole progression, but Jamal must realize that he can't do this in his own strength. He, too, needs to trust Jesus. Jesus told me that my responsibility is to completely trust him, and he will make a way for us through this giant nightmare."

Rosie's eyebrows rose, and Safi chuckled quietly. "Those are my words. Jesus didn't call my circumstances a giant nightmare. He said my life, with all that has happened, will be a story of redemption for making things right."

The monitor to the right of Cooper's bed beeped, showing that his heart rate and respirations had accelerated. Rosie walked to his bed and stroked his face. "You are okay, son," she said with a gentle smile. "I know you love to hear stories about Jesus because you know he loves you." Rosie turned to face Safi. She wanted to hear more. "Anything else you can remember?"

"Oh yes," said Safi. "I begged to know if this would include a way out of the job that Jamal has. I believe he hates it, the takeover, the relocation, all of it. Jesus smiled and said my name again and told me to trust him. He said his purpose was to bring me and the kids and Jamal to himself. Then he was gone. As quickly as he came, he disappeared. But he left me with the overwhelming love that he had for me. It felt like a bath of warm love. My wounds, although still here, seemed to feel better."

"That's wonderful, Safi. Truly."

"Now understand, Tom and Jamal are good friends, and Tom's wife, Lori, is my best friend. She noticed my bruises when she picked up my oldest girl for school the morning after the beating. She came back and brought Tom with her. I told him all about the beating and eventually told him about the vision. It was a risk, I know. But I had to tell someone, and I didn't know what else to do!"

Rosie smiled and nodded her encouragement.

"Knowing you are a strong follower of Jesus, Tom suggested that I tell you what has happened to me so you could help me understand. When I saw you in the grocery store, and you were so open about your own experience about Jesus, I thought I should take Tom's advice and try to get some time to talk with you. Here is one of my questions: Jesus said to trust him. I have a feeling that this term is common among you Christians. But what exactly does that mean?"

"Well, aren't you supposed to trust Allah?"

"Not really. With Allah, it is all about respect, fear, and retaliation. So how am I to trust Jesus? What am I to trust him to do?"

"We have a lot to talk about, don't we?" Rosie smiled. She wanted to continue this conversation, but she also didn't want to raise suspicions by being in Cooper's room too long. She looked at her watch, then back at Safi. "Since I'm on duty right now, I need to go make some rounds with my patients. Would you have time to take a lunch break with me in about twenty minutes?"

"Yes!" Safi said eagerly.

"It would be downstairs in the cafeteria. The food is really pretty good for institutional chow. Can your escort wait it out?"

"Oh, my escort will be fine." Safi followed Rosie into the hall and removed her yellow attire. "He is used to special circumstances when it comes to the wife of the imam. Why don't you let me buy the lunch because of my intrusion?" She put her sunglasses back on.

Rosie was walking Safi toward the waiting room when Dura rushed toward them. "We need you right now with the new patient. It can't wait."

"I'll be right there." Rosie turned back to Safi. "It looks like I'm probably not going to be able to get away. How about bringing me a grilled chicken sandwich, and we'll find a place up here? Or we can make it another day if you'd rather not wait. Please understand it's like this all the time, but I do want to hear the rest."

"I've got time, and I'm willing to wait," Safi said. "I'll see you back up here when you are free. Look for me in the waiting room." Safi waved her escort to follow her to the elevators.

Rosie turned to head toward the new patient's unit and noticed Dura still standing nearby.

"The new girl's parents have heard about the recent tests that occurred and the subsequent deaths," Dura said. "What do we tell them?"

They walked together into the new patient's unit. The Wallaces immediately looked at Rosie with grave expressions.

"Mr. and Mrs. Wallace, I understand you have some concerns," Rosie said and reached out to touch Mrs. Wallace on the shoulder.

Mrs. Wallace subtly shifted a tissue from one hand to the other, obviously trying not to show that she had been crying.

Mr. Wallace began to speak in a low volume but with a sharp edge. "Nurse Chavez, we couldn't help but hear about what happened to some of the patients, not only from this floor but throughout the hospital. Ruth's health is our foremost concern, and I understand that when we have to leave for the camp, Ruth will likely be going with us. But to have her taken for these so-called tests and not come back—" His voice cracked with emotion. "How do things like that happen?"

"Mr. Wallace—"

He held up his hand. "It isn't just here. It's all over the city. My former job, before the takeover, was as an administrator of a large skilled nursing facility on South Bryant Irvin. They lost ten elderly patients to *tests* yesterday."

Rosie's heart sank. But as a nurse, she knew she needed to keep as professional as possible. "This is alarming—"

"Alarming? This is murder!" Mr. Wallace raged, stifling a yell.

Dura shifted uncomfortably in the doorway.

Regaining his composure, Mr. Wallace lowered his voice. "What else could it be? There were too many deaths with the same bizarre description." He reached for his wife's hand, who was now in a full-on sob. "We are trying to keep Ruth safe, aren't we, dear?" As he looked longingly at her, she returned his gaze with a nod and dabbed her eyes.

Rosie saw some movement from the charge nurse who stood at the central desk and tried to give Mr. Wallace a long squinting blink of a warning to have him slow down or lower his voice even more, but to no avail.

"Should we take Ruth home now, where we know it is safe? But then we have to deal with her miserable adverse reaction to the oral cancer drug that is giving her the hives and whatever else is going on. She is not sleeping. She is miserable. She needs help, not tests."

Margie came into the unit and surveyed the gathering. "Is everything all right in here?"

"Everything is fine," Dura said.

"Well, I heard a loud disturbance. What is going on?"

"Mr. Wallace is understandably concerned about Ruth's reaction to the latest cancer protocol," Dura said.

Rosie was impressed by how quickly Dura thought on her feet.

"Sir, I can see your concern," Margie said directly to Mr. Wallace. "But your voice could be a problem to the other patients. You will need to control the volume, or I will have to ask you to leave."

"Yes, ma'am," he said.

When Margie left, they all glanced at one another.

Turning to Rosie, he implored in a whisper, "What should we do?"

"My heart goes out to you. More than you know." She sighed. "I have a child on this floor myself, and I am also deeply concerned about the strange disappearances." She looked at Dura. "We're trying to come up with a plan now to protect these children, but this all must be kept very quiet, and for now, you must trust us."

"How am I supposed to trust you with our daughter when I only met you forty-five minutes ago? As you well know, this place used to be the best children's hospital in the state. Everything has changed with the takeover." He looked at his wife and then at his young child lying helpless in her bed. "I'm not sure if we shouldn't just take our chances, pack up Ruth, and go home."

"We *are* asking a lot of you," Rosie said. She knew their hearts; she felt the same vulnerability with Cooper.

Mrs. Wallace continued to cry as she gazed up at her husband and shook her head.

Rosie gathered all the conviction she could muster. "Your child's health and medical best interests are our main concern. Dura and I will do all we can to protect Ruth. That is what I mean when I say trust us. That is all I can say at this time."

"Please, Harold," Mrs. Wallace said. "We came here because Ruth is sick. Nurse Chavez has the same problem with her son.

Can we let Ruth get her first couple of treatments before we have to go to the camp?"

Mr. Wallace exhaled heavily and then slowly nodded.

"When can we start the treatment?" Mrs. Wallace asked. "One of us will be here with her constantly."

"I'll tell the doctor you are checked in and ready to begin the infusion, which is on the first floor. I strongly recommend one or both of you go with her. It is a quiet place with a library, so you can read her books or do other things to pass the time."

Rosie exited Ruth's unit and headed toward Cooper's bedside. Her hands shook lightly. *Why on earth did I say we would protect their child? I don't have a clue what we can do for Cooper, much less little Ruth. Lord, please help me come up with something quick!*

Rosie shut the door and began to pace. *What am I going to do, Lord? I have to hear from you. I am way out of my league. Please tell me what to do because I now have more people thinking I have some great idea, and you know I have nothing without you.* She stopped pacing. "Breathe, Rosie," she told herself out loud. "Now go make your rounds."

As Rosie cared for her other patients, she noticed Dura help Safi get the yellow disposable covers on, and Safi sat just outside Cooper's unit, reading a book. Sitting in Safi's lap was an untouched boxed lunch. She was surprised that Safi had followed through on her promise, but she was grateful.

When she finally got a few minutes, Rosie apologized for taking so long, and they went back into Cooper's unit. "I have a thirty-minute lunch break, and Dura promised she'd cover for me, so please finish your story while I eat, if you don't mind."

"I know you're very busy. I should really apologize for hanging around and interrupting your work. But I'm glad you are willing to listen to my story. I think you are right about the presence of Jesus and his love appearing to go together. The feeling of being loved by Jesus is so remarkable. There is no greater feeling."

"Safi, I am thrilled to hear about your involvement with the Lord Jesus. I have to say that this dream or vision is not completely off the charts. In fact, I know about a very similar incident that happened around the same time as you, and that person described it in much the same way. Love and the feeling of being loved is the most consistent portion of the stories that I hear." She paused for a moment, realizing Jesus appeared to Muslims, but as she paced in this very room, begging for help from God, she'd gotten nothing. Strangely, though, she didn't feel envious. Safi needed to know about Jesus and his love—Rosie had experienced that over and over.

"I have to admit," she continued, "I've never experienced what you have, with Jesus in the room, bathed in light, but I can believe it without the experience. That is what we Christians call faith. I experience that same love by trusting in what Jesus has said about me in the Bible. That feeling of love is experienced by faith for most of us. Faith is a key element in learning to trust him. The Bible talks about faith, saying, 'Without faith, it is impossible to please him, for whoever would draw near to God must believe that he exists and that he rewards those who seek him.' I will gladly exercise my faith to try to find God and then be rewarded by him, but I would love to have an experience like you have described. That overwhelming love is one of the ways heaven is described to us."

"How do these other people have a similar tale of the presence of Jesus?" Safi asked. "I mean, do these other events come at night, or has the time been different? Have you heard them talk about what else Jesus said to them?"

Rosie took a quick bite and held her hand up to slow Safi down. "The time of day doesn't seem to matter, though I can tell you the issue that does matter is being in a relationship with Jesus. Since he started the relationship with the special visitation, he will want you to continue building a relationship with him."

"What does that mean? How do I accomplish that?" asked Safi. "Nothing would please me more than to be able to get more of whatever I received from him that night he came into my room."

"God left us with his version of a love letter, which we refer to as the Bible."

"Yes, I know. It is your Koran."

"Not quite. This book shows us how very much God loves us. How he sacrificed his Son so that we could live a full and eternal life with him and—"

Safi interrupted. "This is so amazing, but why would he want me or love me? I've never even sought him."

"Because he wants a relationship. He loves everybody. Read his Book, and you'll see it is more than a love letter to his people. It is a murder mystery, an adventure story, the chronicling of a man named Abraham and his family and how that family became a nation, which would bring a Man in a White Robe to give the world the opportunity for a relationship. This Bible is a presentation of this story of God and his desire to bring us back to himself through a relationship with Jesus."

Dura stuck her head in the door. "I'm sorry to interrupt again. Mrs. Wallace and Ruth are about to go down for Ruth's first infusion. Is there anything else you need to say to them?"

"I think I've already said more than I intended," Rosie said sheepishly.

Dura eyed her and giggled nervously as she closed the door.

"You were saying about your Bible . . . ?" Safi said.

"Yes. The book is strange and funny and beautiful and poetic all in different places. Can you wait here for just a minute? I need to run to my locker." Rosie ran to her locker and retrieved her paperback copy of the Living New Testament and put it in Safi's hands. "Here's a modern-day translation of the second part of our Bible, after Jesus was born on earth." Rosie thumbed through it and stopped at the book of John. "John is a book in this part of the Bible, think of it like a chapter in this part of the Bible. That's a good place to start reading. Now a warning, which I am certain you already understand. You must be very careful to whom you tell this because as you know, talking about Jesus can get you killed."

Safi nodded. "I don't know how I will tell Jamal. And knowing him as I do, this incident with Jesus will be the last thing he will want to hear. He will flip out."

"This will be a matter of serious prayer. God wants us to constantly depend on him. So, this will be an opportunity for you to trust God in this circumstance. Tell you what, Safi, I have memorized some verses many years ago from the book of Psalms, which have meant a great deal to me over the last several weeks."

Rosie stood and went to the window. She stared out over the south side of Fort Worth, which used to be a safe place for her and her family, surprised by the emotions surfacing. She slowly turned back around to face Safi. "Let me quote Psalm 112:6–9: 'Such a man will not be overthrown by evil circumstances. God's constant care of him will make a deep impression on all who see it. He does not fear bad news, nor live in dread of what may happen. For he has settled in his mind that Jehovah will take care of him. That is why he is not afraid but can calmly face his foes. He gives generously to those in need. His deeds will never be forgotten. He shall have influence and honor.'" She paused as she let the words sink in. "Those words have helped me through some very difficult trials." Rosie wiped her eyes with the sleeve of her smock and pointed to Cooper.

Safi's eyes glistened, and she whispered, "I think I will need to know that by heart myself, and I want to say that verse is true of me in all circumstances."

"I'll get a card with Psalm 112 written on it. If you are interested, I can put a couple more verses on several cards, which I think you will find helpful. Please remember the timing and the way God takes care of us will probably not fall right into what you expect." She glanced at her watch. "I hate to end this, but I need to get back to work."

Safi stood and crossed the unit to hug Rosie warmly, her eyes still brimming with tears. "I feel so relieved. I'm glad I came!"

"Me too, Safi."

Safi put her sunglasses back on and left. As Rosie headed out of the unit, she noticed Margie hanging around the entrance to Cooper's doorway, acting strangely, as though she'd heard their conversation. Rosie frowned at Margie but made her way back to the central desk. Later, Dura told Rosie that Margie had been lurking around Cooper's doorway during the last few minutes of Safi's visit.

This doesn't impact me because I will soon be at the camp, Rosie thought. *But poor Safi better watch her back. Margie probably recognizes her as the imam's wife.*

CHAPTER 23

3:20 p.m.
Tuesday, March 16

"CAN YOU MEET me in Cooper's unit?" Rosie whispered to Dura at the central desk.

"Give me a few minutes to finish this chart, if it's not an emergency, and I'll be right there," Dura said without looking up, entering her notes into the computer.

"No emergency." Rosie walked briskly back to Cooper's unit, where she pulled the curtains over the full-length window and paced apprehensively. When Dura arrived, Rosie felt compelled to check down the halls before she shut the door. "Was Margie really hanging outside Cooper's unit? What was she doing?"

"Just call it creepy," Dura said. "She seemed to walk slowly back and forth in front of the door. She couldn't have been listening because when I walked by and stopped at the door, I couldn't hear you or Mrs. Kadib."

"Okay, that's good. On another note, I can't believe I told the Wallace family I have a plan for their daughter to keep her safe. You could have sneezed or done something stupid to keep me from talking. What am I going to say to them after the orderlies come and wheel Ruth away?"

Dura smiled and gave Rosie a conspiratorial look. "That is just it. I think I do have a plan. It may even be a great idea for Cooper and, hopefully, for two more children. One of those could be Ruth, but to get them off this floor, we need to act quickly."

"Oh sure, *you* have a plan," Rosie said sarcastically, even though her eyes betrayed her astonishment. "I'm the one biting my nails, and for the last couple of hours, I've worried myself sick over the reckless statement I made—but here you are, calm as can be with 'the plan.' So, spill it!"

"We both realize there is a lot of risk if Cooper stays on the floor with the status quo, correct?" Dura said. "Those tests came completely out of the blue. And the next round, which I'm sure there will be, will be as completely unexpected. We need to get prepared."

"I know, but how?" asked Rosie.

"When I was at County Hospital, there were several small rural hospitals associated with our network. They were constantly bringing over patients from the rural counties to our bigger facilities to get assistance for the more difficult cases. One particular hospital in Cleburne had an ambulance driver who was Muslim but who was very helpful. Whenever he brought patients, we would talk. He appeared very relaxed about the religious views."

"Relaxed in what way?"

"Yosef would give me hints that he was not following the Muslim creed as closely as some may have been led to believe."

"He just outright shared that with you?"

Dura raised her eyebrows and smiled shyly. "We went on a few dates together."

"That is all well and good, but what does this Yosef have to do with our dilemma?"

One of the new nurses opened the door. She squinted in question at what Rosie and Dura were doing talking in a patient's unit. "Margie is looking for you," she told Dura. "She wants to go over your work schedule for next week."

As soon as the nurse shut the door, Rosie threw her arms up in exasperation. "That scared me to death," she exclaimed, her voice an octave higher than normal. She gasped and threw a hand over her mouth to cover the squeaky tone. "I am so nervous talking about this here. You better go before someone becomes suspicious."

"Yes, this is too important for us to be caught trying to put together an escape plan. It has to be right."

"Could we have dinner together in the cafeteria this evening?" asked Rosie. "I don't know if I can wait that long, but I guess I'm going to have to be patient. Look at me. Is it obvious I'm worked up?" Rosie held up her arms to reveal significant sweat rings under the sleeves of her smock. Her black hair was sticking to her neck. She shrugged her shoulders in resignation and gave a half smile to Dura.

"Take some deep breaths like you told Jimmy to do." Dura's face turned despondent. "I miss that little bundle of conversation. He didn't deserve whatever they did to him. Rosie, you're going to have to concentrate on relaxing and helping me focus on a plan that will get Cooper and others out of here alive."

"Yes, you're right," she said, now feeling embarrassed. "See you at dinner."

Once Dura left, Rosie took in a deep breath and held it to a count of ten before exhaling. *I have faced down the patrol at Tom's house and lived to tell about it. I have a God who is big enough to get me through the death of Ramon and my parents. I can deal with this next step.* But she still felt frightened. *Lord, please, help me.*

* * *

5:40 p.m.

Over dinner, Rosie and Dura sat in a secluded corner of the virtually empty hospital cafeteria with their heads nearly touching as Dura laid out the wild plan to get the children out of the hospital. "Yosef called me yesterday evening to congratulate me on being moved over to the medical center. I told him about my experience with Jesus, and Yosef told me he kind of expected me to look into the Christian faith because of the conversations we used to have."

"Really? Why?" asked Rosie nervously. "Can he be trusted?"

"He and I used to talk into the late hours about the supernatural and how Allah would seemingly only speak to the prophet Muhammad on the topic of killing Jews or getting even with someone. We would always end up discussing how the takeover was so abrupt and unfair to the citizens. So, yes, I felt comfortable talking to Yosef about my experience with Jesus. And, yes, I trust him."

"But how does he figure into this plan?"

"He told me how upset he is about the tests. He doesn't want to sit idly while children die when he has room in his Cleburne hospital system for three more children. He wants to take three of our most likely candidates off the PICU floor and hide them in his hospital. He realizes this is just buying some time, but our alternatives here are final and without hope."

Rosie jerked back in her chair in amazement and looked around to see if anyone had noticed. She knew she'd never get used to feeling spied on. "Am I hearing you correctly?" She subtly looked around again. "This is so far-fetched . . . there are hundreds of issues here! My stomach is tied up in knots just thinking about this. No." She shook her head. "We have the finest facility here in the southwest, and we are talking about turning the care of Cooper and possibly two other sick kids over to some small-town hospital? I cannot believe we are seriously talking about this right now."

"Pretend like I just said something funny," Dura said sternly. "We are drawing way too much attention to ourselves. Laugh right now and don't look around anymore. Simply laugh."

Both summoned a series of fake laughs and chuckles.

Dura took a bite of her tuna sandwich. "Let me ask you this, do you intend to take your chances with the next series of tests and hope it will not involve Cooper? Just hear me out. The Islamic faith teaches that the body must be buried within twenty-four hours of death. We are in charge of the charts here in PICU. We chart the deterioration of Cooper and Ruth, if the Wallaces agree, and one other child. They all die on paper and are buried quickly. According to Yosef, all the morgues are maxed out and congested because of what is being called the purge. He says even some of the small-town funeral homes are taking the overflow from all across Fort Worth and as far east as Arlington. Cooper and the two others are transported to Cleburne in body bags, where Yosef can care for them 'for burial' until you can get them. He will admit them to Cleburne Hospital with false identities. Later, we will transport Cooper to the camp where you will be after your march down to the camp . . ."

"Wait just a second. You are way too far ahead of me here." Rosie ran her fingers through her hair, trying to gain some composure. She slowly looked up at the ceiling and then leveled her gaze on Dura. "You are telling me that I am going to voluntarily give up the care of Cooper and ask two other parents to do the same? Then we are going to send these three kids to some small-town hospital that would have, without question, sent these three kids to us here in Fort Worth? And then, if that is not enough, we are going to get those kids to a makeshift tent hospital at a camp thirty-some-odd miles south of here when someone gives us the all clear? Did I miss anything?"

"Well, it is a lot more complicated than that, but you said the basics."

Rosie pushed her chair back from the table. "I need some more water," she said, her voice strained. She reached down for her glass and walked slowly to the water dispenser by the food line. *I can't believe Dura is asking this of me.*

She got some more ice and filled her glass to the top, then gulped half of the glass down before filling it again. When she felt more in control, she returned to the table.

Rosie sat down with her glass looking off into the distance, "Okay, I understand Cooper, but why Ruth? She is a new arrival; she doesn't fit the long-term stay narrative."

"She is the perfect candidate because she is a recent newcomer," Dura began. "She can make the trip. she has just started her protocols, and her parents seem to be in the boat."

"Where does that put me?" asked Rosie.

Dura smiled and reached over to pat Rosie's hand understandingly.

"You will have Cooper and these two others under your wing again down at the camp," Dura said with conviction. "We must do *something.* I know the risk is extremely high, but the options are limited. I realize this sounds outrageous but leaving these children here to be wheeled off to their deaths seems even more extreme."

Rosie exhaled hard. "I heard that the other medical facilities had to participate in the so-called purge. Wouldn't that put Cooper back into the mix—and at a lesser facility?"

Dura agreed. "That is correct, but Yosef has noticed that the longer any child is in a hospital system, the greater the chances are they will be eliminated in the purge. He can admit these three kids into their system as new patients and effectively reset the clock on their arrival time in the hospital. I know this doesn't quite apply to Ruth, but you promised her parents we would do something."

Both sat in silence for a few minutes. Rosie looked down at her plate and used her fork to push around her uneaten green beans and meat patty. Her mind was thrashing through the innumerable odds of a child surviving the escape, making the trip to Cleburne, then enduring less-than-premiere care in a smaller hospital. Her hands began to shake as the fork clattered to the plate. She looked down as the tears began to flow over her cheeks. "I don't know what to do. I don't like any of these options," she said softly. Rosie looked up to the ceiling, trying to hold back the tears. *Ramon, if only you were here to hold me. It is so hard to be by myself. I don't know what to do. Ramon what would you do? Holy Spirit, please give me peace.*

"I know it's dangerous. We need to think this through. But, Rosie, you know the reality of the alternative if you don't act." Dura took another bite of her sandwich and swallowed, giving Rosie time to cough and pretend she had sucked down some food, allowing her to wipe at her eyes without anyone noticing.

"Yosef is coming in a couple of days. The question is, will Cooper be part of the three he will take? If not, we could leave Cooper here and take another child in his place."

Rosie sighed heavily. "I am not even certain that Cooper can travel. He would have no monitoring during the evacuation. Obviously, you can't have a monitor beeping from a corpse traveling to a morgue. I don't know . . ."

"Okay, then you tell me a Plan B. What else is there to consider? Rosie, I don't mean to be crass," Dura said as she reached over and lightly touched Rosie's hand. "But I'm afraid that if he stays here, he *will* become a corpse. We need to start charting immediately. We must show the weakening condition, such that these three deaths are medically logical and without question. Then you and I can get time of death and the death certificates, along with the orders to transfer the bodies to the morgue. We are lucky that the Tarrant County medical examiner is so overworked that they have allowed us to confirm deaths like this without verification." She paused again. "Do I have your permission to begin this process?"

Rosie felt her tears come again and tried to discreetly dry her eyes with her napkin. "What do we do with Margie? She watches me like a hawk. How do we keep this charting process from her?"

"As the mother losing her son, you would have to stay up here 24/7. That way, we protect the charts."

"Dura, what if it doesn't work?" She knew she was facing the real possibility that this could be the last few days she would see Cooper alive.

*   *   *

7:05 p.m.

Mechanically going through her rounds, Rosie could not take her mind off the danger she and several others were about to voluntarily face. She entered Ruth's unit, where Mrs. Wallace was seated next to her bed, reading to her.

"How did you do with your stay downstairs?" Rosie asked the little girl. "Pretty boring, right? Did your mom find you some good books to read?" Rosie checked Ruth's arm where the infusion was started. "Now let me pull down your gown a little bit because doctor's orders are to install a port. Let's look at the upper chest, right about here." Rosie began tapping around on Ruth's chest below the collar bone where the ribs began on the left side. "Mrs. Wallace, could you come look at this potential port site here, please?"

Mrs. Wallace stood close to see where Rosie was pointing on Ruth's small chest. "Someone will come to take Ruth for some very minor routine surgery. They will install a few tubes right here to create a port for future infusions. I strongly suggest you insist on going with her to the surgery suite." Rosie checked the door with a quick glance. "Then you need to get your husband up here tonight to talk privately about our next steps concerning Ruth's care."

Mrs. Wallace gave a brief nod of understanding.

Rosie stood up straight. "I need to get to the next patient," she said loudly. "But I'll be back to check on you later." She looked at Ruth. "See ya later, gator."

Rosie found Dura sitting alone at the central desk and nodded. "I'm feeling much better when I'm doing something. I like the Cleburne idea."

Dura looked up and gave her the slightest nod.

Later that evening, Rosie talked to the Wallaces in Ruth's unit while Ruth slept. "I realize this sounds too shocking for anyone's sensibilities, but what has already occurred is equally offensive. I think this is a huge risk, but it is a choice I am willing to take for my son. We don't really have a lot of choices for our kids. With God's help, we may be able to pull this off."

Mrs. Wallace wept quietly through Rosie's explanation while Mr. Wallace asked questions. "Where will our daughter be? What kind of care will she receive? When will we be able to see her again?"

"These are all good questions, and I wish I had answers. Right now, all I know is that staying here at Children's has its risks, and for some children, it has already meant certain death. Cooper is a prime candidate for the purge, so I don't have a choice. Dura, the other nurse you met, is talking to another family right now to fill the third slot that is available. Regardless of what you choose, please keep this secret."

"When do you need to know our decision?" asked Mr. Wallace.

"It is already after 7:00 p.m., so we will need to begin charting Ruth's decline immediately. Dura and I must begin tonight." Rosie knew intimately the aching decision they had to make. And she could offer them no guarantees.

The Wallaces studied each other with clear fear in their eyes. "Can we have some time to discuss it privately?" asked Mr. Wallace.

"Certainly," said Rosie. "But if Ruth doesn't take the slot, then we need to find another child with parents willing to join us."

An hour later, Rosie had their decision. She walked to Dura, and seeing that they were alone for the moment in the central area, she said, "Now that the Wallaces are in on the plan, did Mike Hall's parents agree?"

"Yes, reluctantly. They see no other choice. The Halls also agreed to spend the night in vigil over Mike's decline and death." Dura inhaled deeply. "That completes the three kids."

"Everyone knows what to expect and will spend the night in their child's rooms," Rosie said. "Now come with me. I want to show you my plan on falsifying the monitoring. Since shift change has occurred, we are good until tomorrow night, with us pulling double shifts. Let's go to Cooper's unit first. The number-one concern for me is Margie. She can apparently appear out of thin air, and I think she's still on duty. We need to be extremely careful around here the next thirty-six hours."

Rosie and Dura walked together into Cooper's unit. Rosie pulled from her front smock pocket a thick roll of bandaging gauze. She removed Cooper's blood-pressure cuff and wound some of the gauze around his arm where the cuff was. She then replaced the cuff on top of the wrapped dressing and turned back to the monitor to restart the machine. The BP readings were muffled but recorded a decrease in Cooper's blood pressure. Rosie then taped the pulse oximeter to Cooper's index finger with a similar piece of gauze between the fingernail and the bright florescent red light. With this encumbrance on his finger, Cooper's oxygen level dropped to a dangerously low 78 percent.

"Sorry, Cooper," Rosie said, patting her son's arm. "We'll watch you manually." She looked at Dura. "Can you do this for Mike, and I'll go take care of Ruth? But in the process, let the parents see and understand this is part of the deception of showing the decline on their charts. We will have back-up records to match the paper charts we are falsifying. Explain that this is the drastic downgrade in their child's health, at least as indicated on their charts, but realize this is all part of what we are doing to try to save them." All Rosie knew for sure was that Dura was looking a lot more comfortable than Rosie was feeling.

Rosie and Dura agreed to take turns sitting at the central desk as they began to systematically forge the charts on the three patients. The report for each child revealed constant system shut down, organs failing, and all three children looking fatal. If caught, Rosie and Dura both faced immediate dismissal and forfeiture of their nursing licenses and certifications, not to mention Rosie's probation. Rosie wasn't sure it mattered much for her. She didn't know if she would be continuing her profession in the camp or would be assigned to do something else. Plus, they had the other children's parents putting all their faith and hope in them. Rosie knew the risks were real, but the question from Dura echoed in her mind: *What is plan B?* She quietly prayed with each false entry she made. "Dear God, I am beyond what I am trained for and out of my comfort zone, plus I'm lying outright, like Rahab in the Old Testament. I need your help to know what to do."

At about 9:30, Dura came by the central desk, where Rosie sat nervously watching the monitors and charting. Dura wore such a calm expression that Rosie became irritated. *How can she look so normal?* "You certainly don't seem the least bit bothered by what we're doing," Rosie whispered.

"Jesus gave me the idea. He told me what to do, so I really think it will save these kids' lives." Dura pointed to her heart, then to the ceiling.

Rosie looked at her inquisitively and had to smile. "Dura, I certainly hope you are 100 percent correct on this. I'm really scared, Dura. Tell me it will be all okay."

"I wish I could. I have to trust Jesus just like you, so here we go together."

"May God have mercy on us all," Rosie sighed quietly.

Margie appeared beside Dura. "Could I see you in the break-room? Something isn't right," she announced, her eyes piercing Rosie. *Oh, dear Lord, protect us. Blind the eyes of those who would do us and our kids harm. Dura says she got this idea from you. Please confirm your plans to us.*

CHAPTER 24

7:30 p.m.
Tuesday, March 16

JAMAL SAT IN his favorite leather chair and read his Koran, trying to find peace and quiet. He looked up as Safi entered and slid down on the hassock to face him. He held up his hand. "Let me finish this one surah."

Safi waited patiently until he put down his Koran. "Tell me about the new girl at your office. Faiza? Is she working out all right?"

"She seems efficient." Jamal winced, realizing he needed to be on guard for any unwanted listeners. "She's okay, I mean, pleasant. I can't figure out why she is here, and Uma was sacked so abruptly. She is easier to get along with, but she is almost too sweet."

Safi got up and moved to an adjoining chair. "I need to talk with you about another subject."

"Oh my, this sounds serious," Jamal said half-joking, studying Safi's face for a reaction.

"For me, it is very serious. You will recall on the night when you hit me repeatedly."

Jamal stiffened and watched as Safi fidgeted with her hands in her lap.

"Well, something happened that night that has changed my life."

"Could we move to the kitchen table, so we are both more comfortable?" As they both walked to the brightly lit, lemon-scented kitchen, he changed his mind. "It's such a beautiful evening. Want to sit on the back patio?"

As soon as they stepped outside, Jamal leaned in. "Before you talk," he whispered, "I must ask your forgiveness for beating you. I love you. This is not the same job or the same religion that I signed up to be part of." He gently squeezed her shoulders, hoping to win back some of the affection they had prior to the job promotion. He kissed her on the forehead near the fading discoloration of the bruises and sat at the patio table, motioning for her to join him. "Now tell me what happened, my love."

Safi touched where he kissed her. "You are forgiven. I would like to think we have a love that can endure these hardships. I am grateful for your gesture of concern, and I hope this is the beginning of new steps toward change."

Still standing, she looked down at the concrete patio. "I am very nervous, but I feel I must tell you something very private."

Immediately Jamal felt deep concern. *What is she dealing with?*

Safi looked around in the dark backyard and crossed her arms as if protecting herself. "Do you think it is safe out here to talk?"

"Discussions related to the job or any objection to Islam cannot occur inside. I am convinced I'm being watched closely—maybe not with a camera, but with listening devices. We must be very careful." Jamal walked to Safi and cupped her face in his hands. "I know this is hard on you. The pressure of my job and now forcing millions of people out of their homes to the camp, then to sign what amounts to a death warrant for thousands of people by way of the current purge. It all must be very unsettling for you. It's unsetting for me too. I'm the guy who was looking for a way to lead the DFW area into peace and a reflection of how to know Allah and worship him."

She looked into his eyes. "In the early morning, after I went to sleep," Safi started in halting speech, "the Man in the White Robe appeared to me."

He stepped away and cleared his throat. "This is not what I expected you to say."

She smiled faintly. "This entire contrast of you and the struggle with the caliph as opposed to my encounter with the Man in the White Robe is so stark. It is a constant source of comparison in my mind."

"Go on." *I want to see how similar this encounter is with what Tom described to me. This is so strange for my two closest relationships to have seen this man in a white robe.*

"I'm not sure if I was asleep or if I had never gone to sleep."

"Was the room lit up suddenly, and did this man know your name? I mean, did he call you by your first name?"

"Yes," Safi exclaimed loudly, surprised that Jamal could describe details of the experience. She then covered her mouth, realizing the volume was too loud. She lowered her voice to a whisper. "How did you know? The room was filled with a very bright light, and the light seemed to come from the man. Then he called me by name. He said, 'Safi.' But first, he told me not to be afraid. Can you imagine Allah telling someone not to be afraid?"

"That is quite a contrast," Jamal conceded. "I sometimes think Allah and the caliph would just as soon squash me like a bug as to put up with my presence. Did the man have a message or a purpose for the visit?"

"I felt loved as I never have before. He said he had a purpose in all that has occurred so far. Do you want to know what he said the purpose was?" Safi waited a couple of seconds until Jamal nodded.

"It was to bring me, the girls, and *you*, to himself. He wants us to know him in a personal way."

Safi reached out to take Jamal's hands in hers. "I love you, and I am well aware that according to Sharia, you are supposed to kill me if I start to follow this Man in the White Robe." She swallowed hard as if unsure about what she'd just admitted. But then her back straightened. "He, Jesus, had such a loving presence. His kind eyes were captivating. I could not stop looking into them. Those eyes conveyed as much love as his voice did. I got the impression he watches over our family. He said that you and I are part of a bigger story. He wants you to know him as well."

Jamal felt sweat pop out on his face as he glanced around the empty backyard, instinctively looking for anyone who might over-hear the conversation. "Safi, if the caliph even knew I was talking to someone about this and didn't take action, I would be instantly shot. Someone else had a similar experience and risked telling me too. Interestingly, in both situations, this man brought up my name with comparable purposes. One was to 'help' me, and the other is to 'bring' me to this man."

"This should be good news for you." Safi's face held hope.

Jamal sighed. "Exactly what am I supposed to do with this information? I might as well begin to plan my own funeral prayers." He turned from her, feeling weak and helpless. "I feel so hollow inside as if my life is leaking away. Why me? I don't deserve this attention."

"Jamal, listen to me. Why would this man appear to me and say he wants you to come to him if he knows that means certain death for you? That doesn't make sense. The other person you spoke about said he wanted to help you, but to help you die?"

Jamal removed his skull cap and began to wring it in his hands. "But how can I trust someone I don't even know if I believe is real?"

"Come on, Jamal! Please listen to me. There is something positive in here for you. Besides, you couldn't possibly earn whatever it is that Jesus is offering. He is all about grace, which means a free gift to you. What if he has a plan to get you out of your job and a place for us to go and live in peace? I believe it is the same peace that you were seeking from the very start when you got this position."

Jamal spun around, feeling pressured and frustrated by Safi's words. "The only place to get away from here, at this point, is to the camp with the infidels—and that is not a place of peace. It will be more like hell for those poor people." Jamal recited the caliph's goal: "The camp will not be a pretty place for the millions who are going there." He shook his head. "I think my funeral prayers might sound better."

"Don't say that!" Tears sprang to Safi's eyes. "We need you as a father, and I need you as my husband. Don't you understand that I love you and want to help you?"

"I am thankful for your love and forgiveness, but we are talking about eternity here. If I'm martyred, I and the entire family—you, the girls—we will all get into paradise. There would be no more worrying about my past sins or having concern over the family's struggles."

Safi shook her head vigorously. "No, this man, Jesus, he told me he offers forgiveness as a free gift to those who believe in him and confess him before others. Our Muslim paradise may not be the real thing, and whatever good you do here on earth to earn your way may never get us there, even if it does exist. He came to me when I needed him most. Face it, Jamal, what do you have to lose?"

"Everything! My life! And the lives of those I love!" Jamal fought to keep his voice down. "Don't you see there is no way out for me? If I stay with the caliph—" He thrust his arm toward the house. "You've seen me in there. I'm crushed by his constant surveillance."

He swept his hands broadly around the patio. "I can't go anywhere without looking over my shoulder or second-guessing myself. His minions could be over that fence. That is no way to live. But if I follow you as you go after this Jesus, I'll be gunned down." He crossed his arms. "Which way would you suggest?"

"Come with me," Safi said with pleading eyes, grabbing his hand. "I don't know what will happen, but I have to believe there is an escape for you and our family. He said for us to come to know him. Surely there is more than just knowing him and then being put to death."

Jamal held her hand and looked deeply into her eyes. He wanted what she said to be true. But Jesus? *She is talking nonsense. She is trying to convert me to Christianity! And for what? All those Christians are going to end up dead. They are all going to be relocated and persecuted. Is she honestly suggesting that kind of a life for our family? Has she lost her mind?*

He jerked his hand away from her grasp, then walked into the house and away from her and this Jesus.

CHAPTER 25

10:15 p.m.
Tuesday, March 16

"WHAT WAS THAT all about?" Rosie watched Dura return from meeting with Margie. "What did Margie say to you? Did we get in trouble?" Rosie looked carefully at Dura's face, trying to read any difference in her demeanor. Were they under any suspicion for spending so much time in Cooper's room together? "Are we still under the radar?"

Dura picked up a chart and lifted the aluminum cover, apparently to read over some of the contents, but then Dura began to speak quietly, her eyes still on the chart. "Evidently, I hadn't signed my time sheet on the correct line, and she was trying to get me straightened out early before it became a habit." Dura sighed in relief. "Then she wanted to go over next week's schedule. We are getting close to your end time here in the next couple of weeks, so we need to get all the positions covered before you and the others are gone. This is all happening too fast." She gave a slight smile. "But do you want to hear some wonderful news?"

"Of course!"

"When we were going over the schedule, Margie mentioned that because she came to Children's in such a hurry to cover for Betsy, she needs to go back to her previous workplace to clean up a few things. She will leave at shift change tonight and won't be back here for two days."

"God be praised," Rosie said, trying her best to remain straight-faced. "This is an answer to a prayer that I didn't have the faith to believe God would answer." The charge nurse was going off the floor—and they would be unsupervised. This was exactly the kind of good news they needed. But even still, she knew too many other things could go wrong.

"I have other good news," Dura said. "I'm going to see Yosef at lunch today."

She watched Dura pick up two charts and walk off to her patients. *I sure hope Dura and Yosef's plan works so we can get our kids out of here quickly.*

*   *   *

1:00 p.m.
Wednesday, March 17

Rosie was at the nursing desk, trying to maintain the look of the grieving mother of a dying child and nurse to two other failing children, when she spied Dura coming through the door after her lunch break. Rosie kept her poker face. "How are the events in the outside world? I need some hope because Cooper is starting to crater." *At least on the falsified charts,* she thought.

She nodded. "Crater? Oh no, Rosie, I'm sorry. Let's have a look."

"I think I saw something disturbing on his monitor." Rosie kept a frown in place and led Dura to Cooper's unit.

She took her place next to the monitor on the side of Cooper's bed and went through a charade of pointing to different indicators of the vital signs, while in hushed tones. "Okay, spill."

"I told him we started charting the decline and death of our three patients." Dura's voice held no emotion, as if she were reading a recipe for baking biscuits. "The parents are in the units and are acting the parts out well. Yosef will see that body bags from the morgue will be delivered to PICU tomorrow with the oxygen bottles hidden within the bags, his compliments. We will place each of the children in the bags and hook them up to the oxygen. Their 'deaths' will be staggered about every twenty to twenty-five minutes, so the placement in the bags will be reasonably timed."

"Stop! Stop!" Rosie whispered. "We are talking about my child and two more living, breathing children here." Rosie felt her voice shake and tears pool in her eyes. The dry description of the proposal got to her. She walked to the window to compose herself.

"We need to go over the details with as little emotion as possible," Dura insisted soberly. "This is our best time. You must know what to expect and how to react, or we can't pull this off." She touched Rosie lightly on the shoulder to turn her and pointed toward Cooper. "This is your patient. People might be watching us. It is essential that we get back on message. Can you do this?"

Rosie knew Dura was right. She took several deep breaths to calm herself and nodded.

"Are you ready for me to continue?" Dura asked.

Rosie looked up, giving another reluctant nod.

"Good, because this is where you come in." Dura pointed at the monitor as if that were the topic of discussion. "As I was saying, after we place all the children in the bags and hook them up to the oxygen, you and I will push the gurneys down to the loading dock. Yosef will be waiting with his ambulance. He'll have oxygen and monitors so he can keep track of their progress on the trip to Cleburne. You will be the grieving mother. You can show your grief with tears and emotions, which I am sure will be genuine at that point. There will likely be others on the way down and others there watching, so make sure they think it is real. If you are able, help us load the gurneys into the ambulance and stay until Yosef leaves. You will have to stay here at the medical center. Yosef will stop the ambulance somewhere along the way, exchange the fresh oxygen bottles and hook up the monitors."

What am I doing? What am I saying yes to? Can I really trust Dura? And her friend Yosef—some Muslim man I've never even met?

Dura reached across the bed and put her hand on Rosie's hand. "You can do this. It's Cooper's only chance to get out of here, as well as the other two kids."

"I know," she sighed. "Well, it won't be hard to play the part of the emotional mother. I'm already terrified. What if I never see my boy again?"

"Just so you know, Yosef will call the Cleburne dispatch and tell them he has two inbounds from Hamilton and one from Hico, the little towns north of Cleburne. He will proceed on into Cleburne as if coming from Hico, where he has two friends who will help him set up the patients under new names. The hardest part on the kids will be the ride. That's the biggest blank spot in the plan. If one of the three goes critical on the trip there, then we're sunk. We will have to pray that all this goes well and that these kids respond positively to the treatment when they arrive in Cleburne."

"We chart them dead on Thursday—" She paused as her voice broke. "And that is when the two stretchers with the bags are delivered, but at what time?"

"They will be up here around the 7:00 a.m. shift change to add to all the confusion, so let's chart their deaths fairly soon after morning rounds. That will all take place tomorrow morning. That means this will be my first double *double* shift." She shook her head in wonder. "We will be ready."

"I am so nervous I can't sleep. I can't think about anything else. I am tied up in knots, Dura! I'm the one who is supposed to remain calm about all this, but this is my *son*. He's all I have left in this world." The thought of these kids going to the morgue without sounds or movement inside the bags was the issue she worried most over. "We need God's grace and mercy to pull this thing off. Forget losing our jobs. If this doesn't work, it will get us all killed."

★ ★ ★

2:00 p.m.

Walking from one unit to another, Rosie heard a new nurse speak loud enough to get her attention. "Excuse me, Nurse Chavez, Safi Kadib is here to volunteer on the floor."

Rosie inwardly groaned, berating herself. "I can't believe I completely forgot Safi said she was coming back this afternoon." Rosie looked at her watch. "Have Mrs. Kadib put on a gown and mask. She will know what to do, and please, put her in Cooper's unit. Tell her I will be there in a minute."

Rosie went to her locker in the breakroom to get the paper sack that held the Living Bible and the verse cards she had prepared for Safi. Then she returned to Cooper's unit and greeted Safi with a hug. "I'm pleased that you came back to see Cooper and me," she said and handed Safi the bag. "There are a few other cards with Bible verses in there. I took the liberty to include these verses because they are particularly helpful to me in my times of struggle." She chuckled uneasily. "These days, it seems as if I am in a battle almost all the time."

Safi smiled and nestled them deep into her oversized purse. "How is Cooper doing since I last saw you?"

Rosie's breath caught. She hated that she had to lie to this woman who had shared a deadly secret with her. But she couldn't risk it. With a downcast face, she shook her head sadly. "Not good. Cooper's condition is deteriorating, and he is not responding to the medicine. His kidney functions are failing, and the brain trauma is bringing no help to the other injuries." Rosie's eyes effortlessly teared up. She pulled a tissue out of her front smock pocket, dabbed at her eyes, and wrapped her arms around herself. "The neural storms that we thought diminished are now returning with a vengeance. He has fought long and hard, but I don't know that he can recover. At this rate—" She paused and continued in a whisper. "Cooper . . . may not make it through the night." She slumped into the side chair next to Cooper's bed with her head down.

Safi gave a sharp intake of breath. "Oh, Rosie, I am so sorry! Is there anything I can do? What about God taking care of you and Cooper?"

Rosie looked up. She couldn't lie about God. "God has taken care of me and Cooper. There is so much I want to say right now, but please pray for us. We need to hear from God on what to do. The next few days are very important. I will require some much-needed guidance." Tears came again to Rosie's eyes. She knew the time was short and that she needed to change the subject. "Remember we talked about the verse in Psalm 112? The verse that starts out, 'Such a man will not be overthrown by evil circumstances. God's constant care of him will make a deep impression on all who see it'?"

"Yes, I remember. It seems that we are both in the middle of evil circumstances." Safi's own eyes welled with tears.

Now it was Rosie's turn to comfort Safi. She patted Safi's hand. "God will take care of us both. Tell me what is going on with you."

"Jamal came home from work the other day. He was very contrite and humble. He did something very strange. He asked me to forgive him for beating me, then he kissed me on the forehead."

"And he's never done that before?"

"No. And then I told him about the Man in the White Robe."

"What did he say? What did he do?"

Safi began to shed more tears. "Jamal is under a lot of stress from work, and I am concerned that I am a contributor to that stress. Ultimately, he said he thought he should begin planning his own funeral prayers. He believes my meeting can't be anything but bad news for him, even though he mentioned that someone close to him had a similar experience. I think that might be Tom Larson, but Jamal wouldn't say."

Rosie nodded in understanding.

Safi looked Rosie in the eyes and sighed. "We just became acquainted, but I feel like I can trust you. I wish we could have more time together. There is so much more to learn from you. I realize your beliefs are costing you everything, and yet you still want the best for me and my family. I will not forget you."

Rosie was touched. "Thank you. I am concerned for you and your girls and Jamal. God always writes the last chapter in our lives. He is the one who can change a man's heart toward himself. I will pray that you will see—"

Dura came charging into the unit. "I'm sorry to interrupt, but Mrs. Wallace is having a meltdown."

"I'll be right there." Rosie turned back to Safi. "I'm sorry to rush you, but I must get back to work. Can you see yourself out?"

"Of course. And Rosie?" Safi smiled kindly. "I will be remembering you and Cooper too."

CHAPTER 26

2:30 p.m.
Wednesday, March 17

ROSIE AND DURA raced into Ruth Wallace's unit. A sedated Ruth lay on her hospital bed with Mrs. Wallace sitting next to her, sobbing loudly with her arm draped over the unresponsive child.

Mr. Wallace stood next to his wife. "Please quiet down!" he told his wife, pleading softly. "This will not bring Ruth back."

Rosie touched Mrs. Wallace's shoulder. "Mrs. Wallace, we can hear you all the way into the central area, and it's unsettling to the other patients. I know this is very difficult to watch your daughter slip away, but there is nothing else we can do at this point. Please try to calm yourself."

Mrs. Wallace jerked her body from Rosie's touch.

Rosie offered a questioning glance to Mr. Wallace, looking for assistance. "If we can't get her to calm down, I'm going to have to ask you and Mrs. Wallace to excuse yourselves and go to the waiting room. This is not helping Ruth. Let me remind you, we are acting out a role here, and your wife needs to play along."

"I know. I'm sorry. She understands, but she just suddenly started this meltdown."

"I understand it's scary and that we have no guarantee," Dura said, stepping closer. "But we must stick to the plan. She *must* calm down."

Mr. Wallace nodded and turned toward his wife. "Martha, listen to me. You must come with me." When she didn't respond, he grabbed her arm and lifted her to a sitting position. Still, she refused to quiet down. He maneuvered his arm around her waist. "Come on now, stand up. We need to take a little walk."

Her sobs began slowly to subside. She nodded. "I know. I know."

Rosie mouthed *thank you* to him as they left. That kind of sobbing would make sense if they'd pronounced Ruth dead, but not at this point. She stepped closer to Dura and whispered, "Would you mind taking a note to him, asking if he would like us to give her a Valium to help settle her down? I feel sorry for her. I understand this is emotionally hard on her. I'm feeling the strain myself."

"You are asking me to give her a narcotic without doctor's orders?" asked Dura.

"Yeah right, what are they going to do to me? Fire me? Or send me to some internment camp south of here?" Rosie reached into her smock's pocket and jingled the keys to the drug closet. "I am so deep into the tank of doing corrupt things around here, what is one more pill going to do?"

Dura smiled.

"Speaking of shady dealings, do you have the extra death certificates pre-signed by the medical examiner? I will need to get Dr. Wilson to sign off on these three kiddos to have them ready to go in the morning. He is aware of our timing and plot and has agreed to sign."

"Margie showed me where they were in her office. She kept them in case there was another purge, and we needed to verify multiple deaths throughout the hospital. It would be impossible for the ME to keep up with the overcrowded conditions," Dura said. "I will have them ready for you in a few minutes."

* * *

6:45 a.m.
Thursday, March 18

Sitting next to Cooper, Rosie dropped her head onto her son's bed and began to beg God. Her fist clenched Cooper's falsified death certificate. Looking to the ceiling through puffy eyes, she whispered, "Lord, you know my heart. I'm scared. I need your comfort and peace to wash over me during the next several hours. Protect my little Cooper. He has fought so hard to stay alive, and I am releasing him from my care and the watchful eyes of this place. You know this is a huge step for us. Please be with him and continue to fight for him and Mike and Ruth. Please close the eyes of those who would seek to stop us today." She put her head back down and sobbed.

"I'm so sorry to interrupt you." Dura stood in the doorway. She moved closer to Rosie so she could speak in a whisper. "We've had a slight change in plans. Yosef has arrived with the gurneys, body bags, and concealed oxygen tanks. Because Margie is gone and I'm the interim charge nurse, I should stay on the floor to quell any concerns if anybody saw both of us gone with the three deceased children. Now just you and Yosef will take them down to the loading dock."

Come on, girl, she scolded herself as she sat upright. *How you react right now will determine if we succeed with our plan or not.* She felt a warm embrace from Dura who had come to her side.

"Come with me to meet Yosef. You will like him," Dura said. "He has kind eyes. I know this is excruciating, but the clock is ticking. According to Sharia Law, the dead are buried within twenty-four hours." Dura slid Cooper's death certificate from Rosie's

217

hand. "I'll take that and add it to the other two to keep things in order.

Dura helped her up, which she appreciated, since her legs now seemed unsteady. They walked out of the unit and saw a dark-haired young man dressed in a blue uniform positioned next to the gurneys. His long-sleeved shirt had some sort of EMS insignia on one side of his chest and his name tag sewn on the other side. On the shoulder of his uniform was the new green and white stars and stripes flag of the United States of Islam. The cargo pants he wore had the usual medical equipment of scissors, tape, and utility belt, which held a two-way radio and a cell phone. And yes, he did have kind eyes.

"Nurse Rosie, I would like you to meet Yosef. Yosef, this is my friend Rosie who tragically lost her son last night after a long battle with a severe brain injury." Dura glanced at Rosie, who, as if on cue, gave a slight sob and wiped at her eyes. "Rosie wants to spend as much time with her son as she can. She would like to prepare the children for transport and help you take them down to your ambulance."

Yosef solemnly extended his hand to Rosie. "I am sorry for your loss. I got a call from Dura early this morning. I hear you need help with the overloaded conditions in the hospital morgue. I can take three of your deceased children to the mass burial plot west of Cleburne for the appropriate handling. They will be prepared for burial there, in the makeshift morgue. Under the circumstances, this is the best I can do."

"You never think that you will outlive your children, but the end came so quickly." Rosie leaned against one of the gurneys, her eyes brimming with real tears she could no longer hold back.

"There is no nice way to say this," Yosef said, almost apologetically, "but I can help you ladies get the bodies on the stretchers."

This was it. The moment they'd all planned for. But now that it was upon her, she wasn't sure she could go through with it. She bent over in pain and put her head down on the padding where her son would eventually lay. "Wasn't it enough to have to give up my parents and then my husband and home? Now I've lost the last person so close to my heart. I hate this!" Rosie had no trouble playing the part of a grieving mother in front of the other staff.

Dura and another nurse rushed to comfort her. Rosie heard the condolences coming from her coworkers. "You were a good mother to Cooper. You are a good nurse to him and to others."

"I knew Cooper was having trouble, but I thought he could hang on and get better." She took a few shaky steps toward Cooper's unit, then stopped and shook her head. "I can't do this by myself." Rosie turned back to Dura. "Would you help me prepare his body? Then we'll work our way to the other two. The other parents are grieving too."

Rosie and Dura entered the unit, where Cooper lay still in his bed. All Rosie could think about was the danger to Cooper and the others and the possibility of getting caught. *This is not helping me.* She began to silently pray through the 23rd Psalm. *The Lord is my shepherd, I shall not want—but I do want your protection, and I am about to enter the valley of the shadow of death! Protect me there. I do fear evil . . . please let goodness and mercy be with me. Oh, how I need that.*

Yosef came in with a gurney and rolled it next to Cooper's bed. He then unzipped the body bag and laid it open.

Rosie stood for a moment and stared at her young son. "Look at him. That beautiful black curly hair . . ." Rosie let her tears flow freely down her cheeks as she gently touched his face. "You have always been my angel boy. Such a sweet child, so loving and sensitive and kind. Your dad and I would lie in bed every night and laugh at all you said that day. You are such a joy!" Rosie bent over and kissed him on the forehead.

Dura put a comforting hand on Rosie's shoulder. "I have loved that curly mop from the first day . . ." Dura continued gently, "Okay, Rosie, it's time. You need to think of the end results here. We have the potential of saving his life. Keep thinking about that and perhaps how you will get to see him again."

She inhaled deeply and sighed. "Okay, let's do this."

The three of them immediately went to work. Dura moved Cooper to his side while Rosie tucked a portion of the bag underneath his body with a tri-folded sheet on top of the bag but underneath where Cooper was to now lay, then Dura returned him to his lying position. Rosie unfolded a part of the sheet, and with a *one, two, three* count in unison, Rosie and Dura lifted Cooper to the center of the body bag. They neatly folded the sheet over his head, chest, and legs after they connected the nasal cannula to the oxygen bottle that they placed between his legs. Rosie couldn't bear to have the sheet covering his face, so she pulled it back to expose it.

Dura began to zip up the bag from the feet up to Cooper's chest, then she backed away and motioned to Rosie. "The rest is yours to finish."

Rosie shook her head. "I can't do that to my little boy. What if he can't breathe inside the bag? That is so final. It makes it look too real; so dead."

"That is the point!" Dura said. "We made provisions for his breathing with the oxygen tank."

"Then can we zip him last?" Rosie asked fearfully. Her clasped hands began to shake as she held them to her chin, looking down at Cooper's face.

"And have someone wander in here to see that canula in his nose?" Dura whispered. "This is painfully harsh, but this must be done."

She straightened her shoulders. "Yes, you're right. I'll finish it up." She kissed his face again. "I love you, angel boy. Godspeed. I will see you again." She put the sheet back over his face and zipped up the bag to the top, then patted his chest.

The three of them looked at one another. Rosie breathed deeply again. "That's one; two more 'bodies' to go."

The Wallace family waited in the dimly lit unit where Ruth lay in repose, sedated to appear dead. Rosie saw an inconsolable Mrs. Wallace, sobbing as she lay next to Ruth's body. Mr. Wallace stood next to the bed, patting his wife in an endeavor to comfort her but struggling to hold back his own tears.

"I'm sorry, Mrs. Wallace, but we need to get Ruth ready for burial transport. I'm afraid I will have to ask you to step away so we can work on her," Rosie whispered reverently, trying to keep the ruse moving.

"Please don't take my baby!" Mrs. Wallace wailed out. "This can't be happening."

"Come over here, honey," said Mr. Wallace. "We have to let Nurse Rosie do her job."

Rosie held up her hand to stop them preparing the gurney that would carry Ruth and Mike on the same stretcher. She turned to Ruth's bed. "Mrs. Wallace . . . Please, we talked about . . ."

"No, this is not real," Mrs. Wallace cried out, "I'm so afraid!"

"I understand," Rosie whispered, "But we only have so much time to . . ."

"You can't take her. I won't let you have her," she wailed out.

Rosie looked at Mr. Wallace with an imploring look. He reached over to his wife. "Martha, you *must* help us. You have to work with us and get out of their way. Nurse Rosie understands our pain. Remember, one of these little bodies is her own son. I know this is hard, but these two ladies and this man have a job to do, and our delay will just make it worse." Mr. Wallace walked over to the edge of the unit and tapped a side chair. "Martha, come sit here," he said gently.

Rosie gave a sideways look at Dura. "I thought we gave her something for this?"

"We did, but that was almost *twelve* hours ago. It is too late for another round right now," Dura said.

"Okay," Mrs. Wallace said slowly. She bent over the bed and kissed Ruth on the forehead and then whispered something indistinguishable into her ear. She backed from the bed as Mr. Wallace came back to guide her to a side chair against the outside wall of the unit. They sat holding each other as their eyes were fixed on their daughter.

Going through the identical routine with the concealed oxygen hooked to Ruth, all was going smoothly until the nurses started to cover her head with the sheet prior to zipping up the bag, when Mrs. Wallace cried out. "Stop! You can't do that to Ruth. She's not—"

"Martha," Mr. Wallace snapped. "Not another word." Mr. Wallace reached over and held her face against his chest.

Rosie bent down close to Mrs. Wallace's ear. "This was the hard part for me with my son too," she whispered. "But Nurse Dura reminded me that the children will be on oxygen under that sheet."

Mrs. Wallace looked at her and, finally, slowly nodded her understanding.

Rosie covered Ruth's face. As Dura held the two parts of the bag together, Rosie pulled the zipper to the top of the bag. She held up two fingers. "That is two."

The third and final child, Mike Hall, didn't take much time. His compliant parents had also requested permission to stay in the unit to say their last goodbyes. Mike's small body was loaded up on the same gurney with Ruth's body bag. Their feet were touching with their heads at opposite ends. With each child she bagged and placed gently on a gurney, Rosie's heart hammered away as though she was doing wind sprints for soccer training.

"I'm thinking a Valium for me might be a good idea right now, but I need all my wits about me," she told Dura.

Rosie and Yosef maneuvered the two gurneys toward the elevators as several other nurses offered Rosie their condolences. Rosie graciously accepted their kind words but kept pushing the gurneys toward the elevator doors. "I've said my goodbyes to Cooper. I'm just getting my boy off to the transport. I'll be back in a few minutes," Rosie said through genuine tears of sorrow.

Hurrying to push the "down" button, Rosie was shocked to see the elevator door open with its distinctive ding and Mr. Ali-Com the hospital administrator, facing them. He was the last person they wanted to see. He stumbled into the two gurneys. In his cheerless fashion, he regained his composure and stood upright. "What is going on here?"

"We had three deaths last night on the floor, and we are taking them to the morgue," Rosie blurted out. She gripped the side of the gurney where Cooper lay and wept as she tried to gain some control. Through her tears, she looked around the central area and took in the five nurses who wished her well, along with the Wallace and Hall parents who were following from a slight distance. Dura stood close by her. Yosef attempted to push the other gurney onto the elevator, but now the bungling administrator was building up a head of steam.

"Don't we have orderlies for that? Don't you have better things to do than this, Ms. Chavez?" Mr. Ali-Com gestured to the gurney Rosie was pushing. Then he turned his attention to Yosef and pointed his finger straight into Yosef's face. "Who is this man here? Is this what goes on when Ms. Atherton is not here? Why is everyone standing here and looking around? Get back to work. *Now!*"

"As the temporary charge nurse," the quick-thinking Dura spoke up clearly, "I had orchestrated a send-off of three of our best loved patients."

"For heaven's sake, Rosie lost her son this morning!" one of the other nurses yelled out. "Can't she tell him goodbye?"

The elevator door began to shut, and Rosie pushed the "down" button again. With a ding, the door reopened, and Rosie pushed Cooper's gurney halfway into the space to hold the car.

Dear God, blind the eyes of my adversary who would seek to stop this escape and snuff out the lives of these small children. Please intervene on our behalf and rescue us. Her heartbeat quickened even more.

"I have all the paperwork right here," Dura said, holding up a clutch of papers in midair. "The death certificates, the transport notices, and the sign off from the ME and the doctor. It is true one of the deaths is Rosie's child. This other gentleman here is the transport driver who will be taking the bodies to the morgue and burial site west of Cleburne since our own morgue is past its maximum capacity. Now can these two take the children downstairs?"

Rosie couldn't help herself as she let out a sob, fear building as she dabbed her eyes with her sleeves.

Mr. Ali-Com slowly surveyed the room again. Then he snapped his fingers at Dura and held out his hand, palm up. "Papers. Let me see the papers."

Dura complied.

224

"Get back to work, the rest of you," Mr. Ali-Com said tersely. "This doesn't concern you."

The nurses dispersed as the elevator door began to buzz and close automatically on the half-in-half-out gurney. Rosie quickly put her hand into the path of the closing doors to stop them from jostling the gurney to keep from bothering Cooper. All they needed was for him to sigh or moan with the disturbance.

"Keep all the bodies on the floor," Mr. Ali-Com said. "No one is going anywhere until *I* say they may go."

The Wallace and Hall families erupted into tears, the wives falling on their husbands' shoulders, weeping forcefully.

"Would you look over there?" Rosie said boldly, in a loud whisper. "Those are the parents of these deceased children. Look what you're putting them—and me—through. I am the parent of the third dead child. This hospital was known for its excellent care." She inched closer to his ear so only he would be able to hear. "Don't exacerbate their grief by doing this. Grieving parents have just said their final goodbyes. You may want to punish me for whatever reason, but please don't disrespect the dead by some show of force." She paused and inhaled deeply. "What can I do to make this work?"

Mr. Ali-Com stared hard into her face. "Ms. Chavez, come with me." He gripped her by the elbow and pulled her toward a darkened unit. Over his shoulder he yelled, "Charge nurse, call Dr. Wilson and have him report to this floor immediately. I see that he signed these death certificates and I want him to verify his signature."

Rosie jerked her arm to try to get him to release it. "Please let go of me. That hurts!" With her other hand, she tried to pry the administrator's grip from her elbow.

He roughly escorted her into the unit, where he released her with a shove. She stumbled back against the outside wall and rubbed her arm.

He slammed shut the unit door and covered up the window to the central area by drawing the curtains. Then he pulled the side chair to the end of the vacant bed to sit facing the entrance. "Now, Ms. Chavez, stand right there." He pointed in front of him.

Walking to the designated place, Rosie stood trembling and crying, unsure of what was going to happen next.

"I am well aware of what grieving parents look like, so I don't need your instruction. Further, Ms. Chavez, if I wanted to punish you, I would not include the delay of someone else's deceased child. I do not appreciate being dressed down in front of my workers. I simply wanted to see what was happening on the PICU floor in the absence of Ms. Atherton. How interesting that I would show up at the time you, not an orderly, were taking down *three* fatalities to the morgue."

Rosie unsteadily wiped her tears. She hoped she could pull this off. Her son's life depended on her acting ability. "Why won't you let me take my son down to the transport? It is my last time to see him before he is buried! Is that too much to ask? Are you that cruel to a mother?"

"How did they die? Tell me how each child died. Then if Dr. Wilson confirms the same cause and his signature, they can be taken downstairs."

"Is this really necessary?" Rosie shook her head in disgust. "You are making me relive the loss of each child!"

"Get on with it, before Wilson gets here."

Sighing heavily, she looked out the window. "Cooper, my son, was in a car accident in January. He suffered brain trauma and a broken leg. He was comatose. His little body finally gave up." She wiped her face with her smock. "Ruth Wallace had cancer and she was taking chemo. She reacted poorly and her blood count dropped like a rock. She never recovered. Mike Hall had leukemia.

He came to us in bad shape and never got better. Tragic, but that is what it is like on PICU. Some get well and get to go home and some leave on a stretcher like these three. I don't know what else to say." She now stared him down.

The door opened without a knock. Dr. Wilson entered, dressed in surgical scrubs. "Surgery has been delayed for this interruption. I hope this is important." As soon as he spotted Rosie, his face turned concerned. "So sorry again for your loss, Nurse Rosie." He gave her a brief hug. "I noticed the gurneys are still out in the central area. Why?"

Rosie's eyes pointed toward Mr. Ali-Com, who was now riffling through the pages of the three death certificates. Without getting up, he handed them to the doctor. "Tell me how these three patients died, and is this your signature on each of those pages?"

"Okay." Dr. Wilson looked down at the certificates. "Cooper Chavez, acute brain trauma, comatose, never recovered. Ruth Wallace, bladder cancer. She reaction to chemo, red blood cell failure, sepsis ensued. She died. Mike Hall came to us with acute myeloid leukemia. If his parents had known earlier, Sloan Kettering is the best place for that form of leukemia, but it was too late. We never had a chance to really help him." Dr. Wilson looked again at the pages, examining each one before handing them back. "Of course, those are the pages I signed after I examined each child. Why on earth would you doubt their deaths and my signatures? Is that all? There is a hurting little patient and a surgical team waiting on me. And frankly, this is nonsense."

The administrator rubbed his forehead, perhaps contemplating his next move. He dropped his hand to his lap. "Dr. Wilson, as you say, you better get to work since they are waiting on you," he said gruffly. "As for you, Ms. Chavez, I will allow you the privilege of seeing your son down to the transport but make it quick. We will see that he is buried properly according to Shirai Law and the ways of Islam. Need I remind you that you and the others on probation defy the dictates of this fine medical center and chose to do procedures the infidel way. You have other patients and duties waiting on you."

"Thank you, sir," Rosie quietly sighed.

"I guess that settles that," Dr. Wilson said and turned toward the door. He paused long enough to sympathetically say to Rosie, "I certainly hope you will take some time off to get some rest and process and grieve the loss of Cooper. That is good for your own mental health."

"Thank you for your concern, but it would be no use for me to sit around the house. I do better when I keep myself busy. I'll be here tomorrow." She turned her attention to Mr. Ali-Com. "May I be excused?"

"Certainly, but hurry. I'll be waiting for your return."

As she exited the unit, she caught sight of Dura and gave her an enormous eye roll followed by a grim look. Dura quickly put her hands together in prayer mode and then dropped them to her waist. Rosie walked briskly to the two gurneys where Yosef was waiting. "Let's get these kids down to the transport."

"Yes, ma'am. I will get the elevator." Yosef pressed the "down" button.

When the elevator doors opened, neither Rosie nor Yosef wasted time getting the gurneys loaded into the compartment. As the elevator door began to close, Rosie saw the Wallace and Hall parents and gave them a somber look. They nodded. With the doors now shut and the elevator moving downward, Rosie breathed a sigh of relief, although her heart rate was still racing, and she felt she might be getting dehydrated. "How much time do we have left on these oxygen bottles? I didn't count on that delay."

"They are hour containers for an active person up walking around. Our little people are essentially asleep, so we should be fine, but there is no time to burn. I will have to stop sooner than I had planned to switch the bottles out."

Rosie made a mental note to assure the other two sets of parents that the oxygen supply was sufficient for the drive. "You know to start the IVs on all of them after you refresh their oxygen?" Rosie said. "I just wish I could go with you. But I know that isn't possible. Did you see any movement or hear anything from these three while I was in the unit with Mr. Ali-Com?"

"Thankfully, they were quiet in your absence."

The elevator doors opened at the basement loading dock level. To Rosie's surprise, the area was packed with fifteen EMS vehicles, ambulances, and other types of medical transports. "What in the world is going on?" Rosie asked. "This looks like they are planning for a disaster or setting up for triage."

As they weaved their way between several trucks, a couple drivers who were leaning up against their parked vans, recognized Yosef. "Hey man, what's with the two stretchers? Hospital is really keeping you in business, right?" They laughed.

Yosef laughed back. "What can I say?" he told them and quickened his step.

"Do you know those guys?" whispered Rosie.

"Yeah, we see each other at pick-up and deliveries like this. That one is mine," he said, pointing to the white ambulance with a distinctive red stripe.

Rosie could now see the bold letters emblazoned on the side: Cleburne EMS, and under that, Emergency Ambulance.

Yosef wheeled his gurney behind the van and opened the back doors. "This is a little tricky, so I'll take it from here," he said, moving to her gurney.

Rosie backed away and watched Yosef slowly guide Cooper's gurney up to the back of the ambulance. When the undercarriage of the gurney came into contact with the bumper, the wheels collapsed underneath the bed. Yosef leaned his left hip into the weight of the gurney and rolled it into the ambulance, where he locked it into place on the left side of the truck's floor.

"I didn't see the bag jiggle once in that loading process. Thank you for being so gentle with my boy." Still with a foreboding fear, Rosie furtively looked around, expecting something else to go wrong. *Lord, keep us all safe. Blind the eyes of those who would want to stop us. Stand guard over these little ones.*

"Sure. It is all in the hips." Yosef's voice sounded nervous as he strode to the other gurney and repeated the process. Again, the long spindly wheeled legs neatly folded up under the conveyance as Yosef boosted the gurney into place on the right side, leaving a narrow aisle between the two gurneys, down which he could eventually walk.

"Yeah, those must be some early arrivals for the second round of deaths supposed to happen later this morning," one of the men said.

Rosie gasped and quickly caught herself. *Remain calm,* she thought. *Act like you know what is coming down.*

"What are you talking about?" Yosef said. "Is there another group of deaths coming?"

"You might say that," one man said and chuckled, casually striking a match on his shoe to light a cigarette. "We were told to be here by 11:00 a.m. for another round of the purge. We were told to expect another 60 or so from here and another 350 from the city of Fort Worth alone. They indicated we would carry out more than one thousand bodies in the DFW Metroplex today. You didn't hear about that? We will have our hands full. We need to get these bodies prepared for the funeral prep and burials before sundown tomorrow. That is a lot of body disposals for us. But good money."

Thank you, Lord, that your plan had a destination far enough out of the DFW Metroplex to protect these children.

"My supervisor must be waiting to tell me about it once I get back from delivering these bodies," Yosef said coolly.

"Well, it is good that you got here early because, in another three hours, this loading dock and every other morgue loading dock will be packed out and swirling with activity."

Rosie's lower lip began to quiver as she realized how close they came to not getting these three children out of the hospital in time. Before she stepped back from the ambulance, she placed her hand on Cooper's body bag and whispered her constant prayer. "Oh, Jesus, please watch over my baby boy who needs so much care and attention. Be close to him during our time of separation and heal him. He desperately needs your touch." She looked at the other body bags. "And, Lord, do the same for these others, your children, as well."

Her hands lingered as she could feel the form of his chest through the bag. Rosie turned to Yosef. "Please, you must tell Dura every detail of these three," she whispered. "When Cooper wakes up, have the doctors tell you, then relay that information to Dura immediately. I need to know how he is doing. Promise me."

He patted her hand and smiled kindly. "I will."

She stepped back and watched Yosef get into the driver's seat. Nausea overcame her as the realization sunk in that Cooper and these two others could have been slated to be callously eliminated because they had no use to the radical Islamists in the "grand plan," whatever that was. *If we had waited . . .* She closed her mind to that possibility, certain now that God had his hand in the timing.

Now Cooper was completely out of her hands. She would have to trust people she didn't know to care for him. She was totally agitated and in new emotional territory. She was assaulted with a fear that she had to counter with faith and trust. Silently trembling, she reached down to touch her wedding ring and began reciting the 23rd Psalm to calm her spirit. Sighing, it was too late to doubt her decision because that ambulance had already left the hospital. All she had to cling to was her faith, hope, prayer, and trust that she would see him alive once they all moved to the Waxahachie Camp in about sixty days if he survived that long.

She stood long enough to see Yosef pull away from the loading dock toward Rosedale Street and onto the Chisholm Trail Parkway. This route would take him on the forty-mile trek to the hospital in Cleburne. Rosie thought of the sixty children the man mentioned just minutes ago. Those children would not have a chance at any alternatives like Cooper, Ruth, and Mike had.

Thank you, Lord, for helping us.

When she returned to PICU, she spotted Dura huddled with Ruth's parents in Ruth's unit, talking softly with them. Rosie cleared her throat and approached them. "What happened when I left? Is Ali-Com still here?"

Dura and the Wallaces looked up expectantly. "Did you get them loaded and on their way?" Dura asked.

Rosie nodded.

"Our administrator left as soon as you did. He said nothing, just left."

"Where are the Halls?" Rosie asked. "They should be in on this conversation."

"I think they are in the next unit gathering up Mike's personal things. I'll go get them." Dura quickly rose and left the room.

"Tell me, what—" Mrs. Wallace started, but Mr. Wallace placed a hand on her arm and shook his head, as if telling her to wait until the other parents entered the room.

As soon as Mike's parents joined them, Rosie looked at the door to ensure no one was lurking about. "We got downstairs with the gurneys only to find out that another mass killing is going to take place today at 11:00 a.m."

An audible gasp went up in the room, and the parents all wept.

Rosie tried to shush them. "We have dodged a bullet due to the quick planning of Dura and the grace of God. There are fifteen vans downstairs waiting to haul the deceased bodies off to the same site we were claiming to send our own children to. It is terrifying how close we came to actually losing our kids this morning. Now we need to pray that Yosef gets them placed safely where they need to go."

"This is so terrible, but I am very grateful they are off the floor. Did they leave safely?" asked Mr. Wallace.

"I watched Yosef drive off until I couldn't see his ambulance anymore," Rosie said. "The next two hours will be very long until we hear from Yosef that they arrived."

"After you collect your child's belongings, why don't you sit in the waiting room?" Dura suggested. "The cleaning crew will want to restore the rooms for the next patients. And you staying in the waiting room will appear normal, as though your loss is too much to bear leaving right away."

The group agreed and walked slowly out of the room, leaving Dura and Rosie alone.

For the first time, fear appeared in Dura's eyes. "We had no idea how close we really were to losing them."

* * *

10:45 a.m.

Rosie had been checking her watch every few minutes since saying goodbye to Yosef. Time was standing still as she anxiously awaited some word from Cleburne. Now she stood next to Dura at the central desk, thinking she was about to go out of her mind. Both women jumped when Dura's cell phone buzzed.

"Is that a text?" Rosie asked, apprehensively watching Dura's face for any type of reaction.

Dura nodded and read the screen. A broad grin lit up her face. She handed the phone to Rosie.

The text from Yosef stated simply, "See you later"—their agreed-upon coded message that all was fine. Apparently, the kids were settled into their new surroundings, and they were supposedly hooked up and receiving care under their new assumed names.

Rosie erupted into tears of joy and grabbed Dura into a hug. "It worked!" she whispered. "You heard from God, and he was faithful to allow it to happen, almost just as you suggested it would. What a relief!"

Dura's eyes also beamed with joy. "I am so pleased all seems well. We couldn't have accomplished this without your willingness and the calm way you handled the obstacles that came our way."

"As the charge nurse, would you go tell the wonderful news to the other parents?" Rosie asked. "It would be good to have it come from you."

Dura lowered her hand so they could exchange a fist bump under the desk before she left. Minutes later, Rosie watched as Dura and the Wallaces and Halls got onto the elevator, presumably to share the news in private.

Must be others in the waiting room, she thought.

Still watching, she didn't pay attention to the two orderlies, one tall and heavyset man and another short rough-looking man, approach.

"We're looking for the charge nurse," the short one said.

"She isn't on the floor right now, but perhaps I could help you."

"We're here to pick up some patients for offsite tests," the big man said, offering a list with the patients' names.

She hopped up from her chair and grabbed the list. "No! You cannot do this right now. We need the charge nurse to release them."

"But we're under orders from the administrator to take these patients down for tests."

Rosie read the list carefully, trying to hold the paper steady enough to read. She noticed three familiar names on the list—Michael Hall, Ruth Wallace, and her own son, Cooper Chavez. Though they were crossed out and names were handwritten next to them.

Rosie was overcome with grief but also grateful that they'd just escaped certain death. *No wonder Ali-Com was so upset,* she realized. Now she could scarcely bear to read the other names of sweet children on the list—all slated to die.

"Were you two here the last time this was done? I mean taking these children down for tests?" Rosie asked, her voice accusing.

"We are doing what we were told to do," the big guy said. "I need to make a call."

"This is wrong," Rosie said. "Go ahead and make your call."

The orderly pulled out his cell phone and spoke quietly. After he hung up, he looked pointedly at Rosie. "We will need the charts on Oscar Sanchez and the other three remaining patients, and we *will* carry them to their tests. We are to take two now and be back for the other two."

Rosie shook her finger in the big orderly's face, anger flashing from her eyes. "I said you need to talk to Nurse Dura, who will be here any moment. There are two chairs you can sit in to wait."

She watched the orderlies defiantly slump into chairs down the hall. She knew she had only delayed the inevitable. *This is just one wing of the floor in just one hospital in a city that has multiple hospitals. What about the DFW metroplex? What about the other medical facilities in the other major cities? And what about the small Cleburne hospital where Cooper is fighting for his life? What evil is happening?*

CHAPTER 27

8:30 p.m.
Thursday, March 18

AFTER WORKING THREE shifts in a row, Dura left at the 7:00 p.m. shift change because of her exhaustion. Rosie had planned to spend the night again in the PICU's sleep room. She wanted to go to bed around 9:30 when events on the floor would somewhat settle down. A new interim charge nurse stepped in during Dura's absence, which meant little would change. And now they had less work to do since the patient census was lowered by seven children.

Though she and Dura had both argued against the orderlies taking the children, they were overridden and watched helplessly as four little lives were wheeled off, never to return.

How can this be? she wondered, feeling desperate and powerless. *This hospital used to pride itself on saving lives. Now we are a platform for finding kiddos as candidates for murder.*

She dropped her head on her folded arms as she sat at the central desk.

"Nurse Rosie, are you all right?" a man's voice drifted into her ears.

Startled, Rosie looked up to see Harold Wallace.

"How long have you been standing there?"

"I just got here. Martha is over by the elevators."

Rosie glanced toward the elevators and saw Martha give a slight nod of acknowledgment. "I was resting my eyes. I'm okay, just really tired and emotionally depleted."

"Is there somewhere we can go to talk?"

She looked at her watch. "The cafeteria is closed. Our own waiting room should be fairly empty right now, though. Why don't we try that?"

"We will meet you there." Harold went ahead to collect his wife.

"I'm going to the vending machines in the waiting room," she said to a nurse standing nearby. "Can I get you something?"

"No, I'm good," the nurse said.

As soon as Rosie walked into a waiting room, Ruth's parents approached her. "Have you heard anything else?" they asked in unison.

Rosie shook her head. "I haven't heard a word other than that text."

Ruth's parents invaded Rosie's personal space to form an impromptu huddle.

"We all want more details," Harold said. "Dewayne Hall, Mike's dad, thinks the four of us can drive together on the back roads to Cleburne. We could get to the hospital, check on the kids, and get back to Fort Worth before curfew."

Rosie's eyes brightened with the possibility of hearing first-hand news about Cooper, but then she frowned. "You do understand that the patrol has all the major roads blocked, and they are very rigid about keeping all the infidels in the cities? How are you going to get past their checkpoints?" Rosie needed them to be realistic. They could end up blowing this whole plan sky high with their impatience. "We have to—" She stopped abruptly as she saw someone enter the waiting room. She had to switch tracks and

238

appear cool. "I know I should have asked earlier, but was Ruth your only child?"

The intruder walked to the vending machine. Rosie noticed their new middle-aged "guest" appeared to be visiting her mother or a friend. She was dressed in typical street clothes—jeans, a sweatshirt, tennis shoes, and the mandatory hijab.

She seems harmless, Rosie thought but caught herself. *Trust no one.*

The woman dropped what seemed like ten dollars' worth of coins into the deposit area as the money slowly clinked into the cash box. She made her selection with a loud buzz and a convincing crash, picked up her beverage, and retreated from the room.

"She is our only child," Harold said softly as soon as the woman left.

"I understand. Cooper is my only child too." She paused, unsure of why she was about to agree. "When do you leave, and what do you need from me?"

He looked at the door and instinctively lowered his voice. "Dewayne has the route figured out. We are leaving tomorrow at first light so they can't see our headlights."

Rosie inhaled and exhaled slowly. "So how can I help?"

"When we get to the hospital, what do we say? Who are we asking for? What are the names of our kids?"

Rosie rubbed her chin in thought. "Yosef should know, but I don't know how to get ahold of him. I could use our hospital phone to call Dura to get his number. The children were supposed to be brought in from Hamilton and then to Hico and then on to Cleburne."

The same intruder re-entered and half-sighed, half-laughed. "Sorry, I need chips now," she announced loudly.

The three collectively and, Rosie hoped, casually, moved to the corner of the waiting room where they settled into chairs.

Still aware of the intruder's presence, Rosie decided to start a new decoy conversation. "Have you spoken to your pastor about this death?"

Martha began to cry. "No, he has been busy with so many other deaths that he has been hard to get ahold of," she said, falling right in line with Rosie's direction. "I just don't know what else to do."

The intruder held her chips and stopped near the door. "Forgive me for the interruption. I think I got it all this time. I didn't mean to disturb a serious conversation."

"Thank you," Rosie called over her shoulder and then waited until she heard the door close. "Are we alone again?" she whispered.

"That appears to be true until the next hunger attack," said Martha. "I'm sorry, I can't keep it together. All this is so fresh." She continued wiping her tears.

"You are doing amazingly well for a mother who just went through the process of losing your daughter. I will call Dura and get Yosef's cell number, which I will give to you before you leave the floor. Call Yosef. He will give you the children's names. Write them down so I can get them from you later. But make sure to hide the paper in case you're caught, okay?" Rosie looked sternly at the two of them. "You *must* come up with a story for the four of you to rehearse and review so that it is on the tip of your tongues. If you get stopped by the patrol along the way, any one of the four of you can spit out some story like, 'We all need to go see Aunt Sue, who is dying in Cleburne.'"

The Wallaces both gave Rosie a blank stare.

"To Martha's concern, if you get stopped, you need to appeal to the mercy of that officer by saying, 'We have this one last time to see whomever before we have to go to Waxahachie.'" She felt her exhaustion getting the best of her. "Come on, am I the only one with an imagination?" She inhaled and smiled reassuringly. "Put your combined heads together and come up with your own story that is easy to remember and makes sense. Okay?"

The Wallaces looked at each other and back at her and nodded.

"You got this." She then solemnly looked directly into Martha's eyes. "When you get there to see Ruth and Mike, will you go by to see Cooper? Will you lay your hand on his head and tell him that his mama loves him and—" Rosie began to choke up and had a hard time finishing her request. "And that she will see him as soon as she can?" Now Rosie wiped her own tears.

"I will." Martha took Rosie's hand and patted it. "We owe a lot to you. You gave us hope. And from the report of the orderlies, Ruth would no longer be alive if we hadn't followed your lead. Thank you again."

"Let me go call Dura, and I'll be right back." Rosie stood. But before she could take a step, Martha jumped up and hugged her. They needed each other, Rosie realized. Two mothers, unsure if they'd ever see their sweet children again. Rosie held tightly to her and allowed herself to cry with Martha.

Oh, dear God, if you don't come through again, we are sunk. We need to hear from Yosef and Cleburne Hospital. Please help us.

They released their hug, and both wiped at their eyes. Rosie left.

Rounding the corner into the central area, Rosie nearly bumped into Margie Atherton.

"Well, Rosie, I've heard you had an interesting couple of days. Why don't you come into my office, and we can talk about it?"

* * *

10:00 p.m.

After the meeting, Rosie pulled the door shut to Margie's office and walked toward the PICU waiting room. She was beyond exhausted but knew she had to keep moving. She checked her watch. She'd been in with Margie for an hour. She hurried into the waiting room, which she expected to be empty, but still wanted to check. She stood motionless with her hands on her hips, trying to think where the Wallaces could have gone during her interruption with Margie. She slowly looked around the room for any clue they may have left.

She eased herself into the corner seat that Martha had occupied and glanced at the end table. The previously shuffled and disheveled magazines were now neatly stacked. A scrap of paper, like a bookmark, peeked out of the top magazine.

She pulled out the paper. The front side was blank, but when she turned it over, she saw small lettering.

HEARD YOU GOT STOPPED. WE LEFT.
MW

She decided to look at Ruth's chart to find their telephone number. *Nuts!* She remembered that Margie had all three deceased children's charts in her office. She willed herself to think. Immediately it came to her: *the computer files.* But getting into those files was risky—especially because they left digital trails. With her new idea formulated, she headed upstairs to the surgery floor, where she tiptoed down the hall until she found an open computer on which someone had not logged out. She smiled at her good fortune.

Quickly taking a seat, she typed in Ruth Wallace's name and found the phone number she was looking for. Grabbing a ballpoint pen from the desk, she quickly scribbled the number on the palm of her hand, logged out, and headed to the surgery's lobby where she spied a wall phone. Rosie picked up the phone and dialed Dura's number, which she'd committed to memory when their plan was beginning.

It took six rings before Dura answered. Her greeting sounded sleepy.

"Don't ask why I'm calling," she whispered, "but I need Yosef's mobile number. Can you give it to me?"

"Of course," Dura said without a hint of curiosity.

Rosie wrote the number on the same hand, thanked Dura, and hung up. She got another outside line and dialed the Wallaces.

CHAPTER 28

9:00 a.m.
Friday, March 19

JAMAL BREEZED OUT of his office and headed toward the lobby door as he threw a quick "I'm going down the hall" alert to Faiza. Before she could respond, he walked to the building's back entrance. He exited and stepped into the bright Fort Worth sun. Squinting as he looked around to make sure he was alone, he pulled out his burner phone and called Tom.

"Can I come pick you up at 10:15 before our Friday prayers?" he asked as soon as Tom answered. "I need to ask you a few questions."

"I'll be ready. Text me when you get to the parking lot, and I'll come down."

Jamal quickly reentered the building, went into the men's room, and washed his hands, then returned to his office. The clock seemed to tick by more slowly than usual, and Jamal felt himself grow more on edge. By 10 o'clock, Jamal decided it was time to leave. "I'm heading out to get ready for Friday prayers," Jamal announced to Faiza. "Do I have anything pressing before the weekend?"

She looked at her appointment book. "It looks like you're fairly open until Monday. If someone calls, may I tell them where you'll be?"

"I'll be with Tom Larson for financial planning, then I'll be going over my sermon notes." Jamal stopped momentarily in front

244

of her desk. "If anyone asks, you can tell them I'm at the mosque. Then our family will be together for the al Sabt, the sabbath weekend."

"Okay, sounds good to me," she said, appearing uninterested.

When Jamal got in his car, he started to whisper the Shahada, the Islamic declaration of faith, a daily requirement for all Muslims to repeat. He whispered it twice, then he snapped on the radio to Channel 1 talk radio with the volume much louder than necessary. He grinned as he pulled out of the parking lot. *What do you think of that, Mr. Observer?*

$$\star \quad \star \quad \star$$

10:03 a.m.

The Observer tore the studio earphones off his head, jerking his body back against his leather chair, then threw his fist down on his desk. "Oh, Jamal, you think you are so smart, trying to get me to listen in on a whisper then blasting me out with the radio." He sneered. "I will get you for that."

He leaned back in his chair and thought deeply. *He told Faiza he was going to meet with Tom Larson to work on financial planning. . . . but how did he make the arrangements? He has made me look the fool.*

He picked up the phone and dialed the Fort Worth office.

"This is Faiza," Jamal's assistant said after the second ring. "How can I help you?"

"This is the Observer. I just watched and listened as Jamal told you he is meeting with Tom Larson. How do we *know* that he is meeting with Tom?"

She didn't skip a beat. "Because I asked him what he was going to do for the meeting."

"Exactly, but there is *still* a missing piece to this conversation, which you haven't figured out. We have a bug on his phone, in the office, in both his personal and company cars, and in his home. How do he and Tom arrange these meetings? We know he doesn't text Tom because we would see that. Last time the GPS showed that Jamal went to Tom's office and then to some museum where the car and his phone sat for several hours. Then Jamal drove back to the office."

The phone rang in the office. "Please hold sir," Faiza said, "I have to answer this." Before he could respond, she put him on hold.

He became furious that she did such a thing. He watched and heard her address the other caller and then punch the button to make his line active again. "I get so tired of those sales calls."

"Stop right there!" the Observer said, his voice reaching a thunder. "Do not *ever* put me on hold *again!*"

"I am so sorry! Oh, please forgive me for my carelessness." Faiza's voice quickly turned to fear.

"Never again. Do you understand? Now discreetly find out why they go to the museum. Are they having lunch outside the car or maybe in the museum? Do you know what kind of car Tom drives?"

"I apologize again, sir. And yes, I know what kind of car Tom drives. It is a Ford Escape. Light blue. They could talk about their meetings at morning prayers. They both attend morning prayers."

"My informants tell me that they hardly look at each other, much less speak to each other during those prayers. If you can't come up with some other answers, you are going to make me come down there and do your job myself. It won't be pleasant for you. Am I clear?"

"Yes sir," she said. "I—"

He hung up on her before she finished.

* * *

10:10 a.m.

Jamal got into Tom's car as soon as he saw him in the Kimball Museum parking lot. "What do you hear from the police on the hit and run?" he asked as Tom headed toward their usual spot at the gardens. "Have they agreed to our plea deal about staying in their home and so on?"

Tom grimaced. "Chief Hasson at Fort Worth PD is more than a little upset that the situation is playing out this way, but the parents are amenable to your suggestions. I think we're getting close to a settlement."

"That is a relief. Keep working the chief." He stared out the window at the passing scenery. "Now my real problem is the march next week. I have lined up thirty-thousand-armed militia mercenaries who will be ready to shoot anyone on sight who show the slightest hesitation to follow the rules. The population of the DFW metroplex is an estimated 8.5 million. Subtract the 2 million who are converting to Islam, along with the half million previously committed to Islam like you and me, and that leaves 6 million infidels on the forty-five-mile march. This all has to be completed in two days. That is the nightmare that keeps me from sleeping. How will I corral that crowd without killing the old and weak, the stragglers, the stubborn, and the ones who see this as their opportunity to get away?"

They'd stopped at a red light, but when the light turned green, Tom didn't drive. The car behind them blasted his horn. Jamal looked in his sideview mirror to see the driver making a nasty gesture as Tom drove through the intersection.

"Are people just getting more impatient these days?" asked Jamal.

"Sorry, I was thinking about the logistics of moving six million people," Tom said. "Where will they spend the night?"

"On Highway 287 and I-35, but even that is a problem. We've ordered thousands of temporary light plants to illuminate the highway to keep an eye on the crowd, but it will be intense with potential escapees."

"Do you really think the infidels will not want to go to the camp?" Tom asked.

"Would *you* like to be forced from your house, then marched off to some unknown spot as your new permanent residence?"

Tom shook his head.

"I wouldn't either. The caliph says to expect 3 to 4 percent rebellion. That is somewhere close to two-hundred-and-forty-thousand people who will be shot, and that estimate is on the low side. The wounded will be executed. We will not be bandaging anyone, then the mess of clean-up with funeral pyres to dispose of the bodies. Events will get ugly very fast. And who is at the top to blame when that happens? Old Jamal sitting right here." He pointed to himself.

"I can see your heart on this. Blaming yourself won't help. You know you are just doing the job you were told to do."

"Yeah, well, that didn't work so well for the Nazis like Goebbels, Mengele, Ribbentrop, Speer, and Himmler, did it?" Jamal felt his anger rising. He hated that the regional imam and the caliph were putting him in this position. He hated what his religion was doing to these people. *This* was Islam? *What about peace?* he thought again.

They rode in silence for a few minutes. "Do you know what Safi is trying to convince me to do now?" he finally asked.

"No telling."

"She is encouraging me to pray to Jesus." Jamal looked to Tom for a reaction.

Tom's face broke into a grin. "Well?"

"She had a dream the other night, and Jesus came to her in a white robe, similar to your experience. He told her he wanted to help me. Well, he could sure help me by getting me out of this mess."

Tom pulled the car into the parking lot at the gardens, found a spot to park, and turned the car off. Then he looked at Jamal. "Here's the deal. According to Safi, Jesus says he wants to help you, correct?"

Jamal nodded.

"Then why not give it a try? Pray to Jesus. It is my experience, when Jesus was with me, that he already knows your name."

Jamal ripped his skull cap off and flopped it at Tom. "No! You can't possibly understand what—"

"Calm down and let me finish! You pray to Jesus, and no one has to know. We watch what comes of the help with a wait-and-see approach. I am well aware of the Islamic constraints concerning even having this conversation. Look at yourself. You're emotionally tied in knots with a very short fuse. You are concerned about throwing homosexuals off buildings and displacing millions of people from their homes." He gestured toward Jamal's pants pocket. "You are even carrying a burner phone to deceive your bosses. You have to admit you are *not* the picture of a sold-out imam for the cause of radical Islam."

Jamal lowered his head and sighed as he put his cap back on. He gazed unseeing out his window at the parking lot. He couldn't believe he was actually having this conversation or even considering praying in this way. "Okay, let's say that I pray, and nothing happens. Why would this Christian God care about me and my problems anyway? See these cars here? The people who own these cars might be the folks I am going to displace. I'd think Jesus would consider me to be his enemy, not someone he would offer to help." Jamal lowered his head again. "I am forever caught between doing what I think is right and obeying the bosses who rule my life."

"That is just it," Tom said. "Jesus loves you like he loves me and Safi and your children. He wants to see you made whole and have a life worth living, not this life you dread and want to escape." He paused. "Come on, what do you have to lose?"

Jamal snapped his head up and pointed at Tom. "That is precisely what Safi said to me a few nights ago. I told her I . . . I may lose *my life* over this." Jamal's hands were now shaking with anger. He thrust his back against the seat and yanked on the door handle. "I need some air."

He got out, slammed the door behind him, and walked toward the gardens.

CHAPTER 29

7:45 p.m.
Friday, March 19

"COME AND SIT with me," Rosie said excitedly to Dura, pointing with her eyes to the empty chair beside her at the central desk.

Dura took the seat. "What's up?"

"I just got off the phone with Yosef," Rosie whispered. "I'm taking the weekend off. He will pick me up at my home later tonight, and I'll ride in the ambulance to Cleburne as a patient. I can't believe I'm finally going to see my boy! Yosef told me that Cooper opened his eyes. And get this. He asked about me! Can you believe it? That is such an answer to prayer! I just hope I can remember the crazy alias we gave him—Craig Wilson, which makes me Rosie Wilson. I hope this isn't too confusing." She squeezed Dura's arm and giggled with delight.

"Hush, girl!" Dura's face contorted into a mock scowl. "Or Margie will be asking why Nurse Chavez is on an adrenalin high after her child just died, and she got chewed out at yesterday's meeting."

Nothing was going to dampen her spirits, especially not Margie. "Yosef also said the other two are doing well, but Mike has some issues they are watching. And the Wallace clan will be up here in a few minutes to debrief me on their trip."

Rosie started to giggle again, then passed her hand over her face in a vain attempt to change her mood and facial expression. "Okay, while I'm gone, you've got this, correct? I'll be off the air; no telephones, no nothing. YOYO—you're on your own."

"I won't be completely on my own," Dura said and smiled. "Remember, I'll have Jesus with me."

The elevator door gave its familiar ding, so Rosie looked in its direction. Harold and Martha Wallace were strolling toward them, looking grim-faced and grieved—as they'd been directed.

"Hello, Mr. and Mrs. Wallace," Dura said. "How are you?"

"We aren't doing well. That is one of the reasons we're here," Harold answered. "We would like to speak with Rosie. We need some encouragement."

"Yes," Martha chimed in. "We need to comfort each other." She sniffed.

Rosie walked around the desk and gently hugged them both. "I know you must miss your daughter terribly. I think about Cooper every minute of every day. Would you like to go into the waiting room to talk?" She wrapped her arm around Martha. "Nurse Dura, would you mind covering for me?"

Dura nodded. "Of course."

As soon as they entered the waiting room, Rosie reached in her smock pocket and pulled out the note Martha had left. "Pure genius," she said and waved it in front of them before returning it to her pocket. "I thought you'd left, but it was good reassurance when I read it. Thank you for thinking that through."

"The credit goes to Harold," Martha said, taking the same seat as before.

Rosie didn't want to waste time with pleasantries. "You made it okay? No troubles?"

For the first time, Harold's face relaxed, and he smiled. "Everything went like clockwork."

"All three of them look really good," Martha said, smiling as well.

Rosie was glad to see Martha smile and realized it was the first time she'd seen her that way. Martha looked lovely when she smiled, her face taking on a much younger appearance.

"They seem to be getting excellent care for such a small hospital," Martha continued.

"What can you tell me about Cooper?" Rosie said and felt ashamed. She should have asked first about Ruth, but her mama's heart couldn't bear to wait. "Did he wake up while you were there? Is he moving his arms and legs? Is he opening his eyes? I heard he asked for me. Is that true?"

Harold and Martha both smiled. "We did see his big brown eyes," Martha said.

"And he did move his arms," Harold said. "We heard him ask—"

"Oh, it's true! Thank you, Jesus. What wonderful news." Rosie put her hands to her face and cried out loud. Feeling overcome with her emotion, she allowed herself to feel it fully and buried her head in her lap as her shoulders shook over the joy, pain, and relief she felt.

Martha placed her hand lightly on Rosie's back and rubbed gently. It felt as if Rosie's mother were there caressing, comforting her. *Thank you, God, for Martha's mother heart of compassion.*

Once she was able to compose herself, Rosie sat up straight, embarrassed not just that she'd lost control. "I apologize."

"No need," Martha said. She looked like a new person, as though her ability to comfort Rosie had given her a purpose. "We are so happy we were there to see your cute little Cooper and his miracle so we could share it with you. There is no other way to explain it."

Rosie smiled appreciatively. "How did he look? How long did you get to stay? What were the roads like? I mean, did you get stopped?"

"Well . . ." began Harold as he looked at Martha for confirmation. "We and the Halls arrived about 8:45 yesterday morning. All the way over in the car, we worked on memorizing the assumed names of the children."

"And our own new last names," said Martha.

"That's right," Harold said. "It was a little tricky at first, but we got into the swing of things with our new identities, and we got checked in. We walked straight into Ruth's room, and the Halls went to see Michael. It was quite a reunion. It was hard to get Martha out of Ruth's bed. Mike, by the way, is not doing well. The Halls told us on the way home this evening that his blood count is low, and it doesn't look good long-term. They are going back tomorrow if they can get through."

"I am so sorry to hear about that. Mike was in rough shape when he left here. When did you get to see Cooper—or Craig Wilson, as he is now called?"

"When Martha and Ruth were in an inseparable clutch on the bed, I slipped out and went to Cooper's room. A nurse was there exercising his arms and his good leg. I asked if I could watch, and the nurse wanted to know who I was. I mentioned I was a good friend of his mother's and that you had asked me to look in on him since I had a child there as well. Cooper turned his face toward me and said, 'What?'"

Rosie slapped her hands together. "Wow!"

"I looked at his confused face and said, 'Your mother is working very hard to come see you. She wanted me to tell you she loves you.'

Cooper said, 'Where is she?' I told him that you'd get there as fast as you can."

Rosie's tears erupted again. *Cooper has survived. And he's coherent. He's responding to direct stimuli, and he can form a question—and he remembers me!* She inhaled deeply and wiped at her eyes.

Martha reached into her purse and pulled out a stack of folded tissues, then handed Rosie two.

"Thank you," Rosie said, wiping her eyes and nose with the soft tissue. "I have some of my own news for you. Yosef promised to take me to the hospital tonight. Lord willing, I will spend the weekend with Cooper. We will have a lot of loving to catch up on. My dear little soldier. It will be so good to see him."

*   *   *

10:00 p.m.

Rosie stood at the front window of her unlit house with the curtains parted ever so slightly, anxiously watching for her ride. At her feet sat her backpack with the bare essentials for an overnight trip to Cleburne.

Dear Lord, help Yosef find the address in this darkness, and please keep us safe on our trip to see Cooper. Thank you for the cloud cover to dim out the nearly full moon.

No sooner had Rosie completed her prayer, she saw the large form of a vehicle without any exterior lights quietly roll up the street to her front walk. The driver opened his door, but the interior lights didn't come on. She shut the gap in the curtains, grabbed her backpack, and hurried to the front door.

"Thanks for picking me up," she whispered. She stepped out into the night, shut and locked the door, then walked with Yosef toward the ambulance. She stopped briefly to look at her home and make sure all the lights were indeed out.

Funny, this is where we brought you home, Cooper. Now I'm thirty-five miles away from seeing you, hopefully, tomorrow morning, with your wide-open eyes.

Yosef opened the passenger-side door. "Let me get in here first. This is a tight fit, and I will be able to guide you through the maze."

She followed him in, trying to let her eyes adjust to the unfamiliar surroundings. "Wow, it's dark in here. Where do I go?"

"Hold on." His feet shuffled along the floor, inching away from her, and then his hands moved above her head, probing for something. She heard a click, and a faint red night light illuminated the block forms near where she stood hunched over. She saw the metal edge of an overhead compartment that was only inches from her face. "That could leave a scar," Rosie said patting the hanging obstruction. "They remind me of an airplane's overhead compartments, only these hang down very low."

"That is exactly correct, except our passengers are lying down and don't need the head room. This way, we can stow all our emergency equipment and medical supplies up top." Yosef held out his hand, encouraging her to sidle his way. "This is your bed." Patting the stretcher, he exaggerated the spot on the right side of the truck until her eyes adjusted to the reddened dimness. "The dark interior helps disguise what we are doing. You will have to ride on the stretcher in case we get stopped."

Yosef helped her maneuver onto the narrow stretcher. "Roll up your sleeve on your right arm and lift it up," he said, as he ripped what sounded like adhesive tape.

She did as he instructed, and she felt the tape fastening a plastic tubing to her arm, probably to look like an authentic infusion.

He carefully adjusted an oxygen mask to her face and mouth, then covered her with a blanket and strapped her in. "You're all set. Now get some rest."

He maneuvered back to his seat, then began driving. "First things first," he said after a few minutes. "When you get there, remember that Cooper has a new name—Craig Wilson."

Rosie knew this already since she and Dura had created the names. She'd named him Craig, because of the Craig Brain Trauma Rehab Center in Denver, which had given Cooper so much help after the accident. And Wilson to honor Dr. Wilson.

"Also remember that I am your escort, so don't try to get ahead of me when we get there. You are from a small farm north of Hico. I just picked you up from work." He paused, and his voice took on a more compassionate tone. "We have a while to go, so set your mind at rest and enjoy the ride. God is in control. He has guarded us so far. I'm almost on the toll road, and that will make it hard for us to hear each other. This is your time to spend with Jesus."

Rosie closed her eyes and listened to the tires race over the highway. She tried to think through every possible trouble spot she might encounter.

God, I am trusting you with all my heart. This weekend has many things that are completely out of my control. But I will acknowledge you in all my ways, so please make my path straight. I ask that Cooper will be improved beyond what I can even imagine and that we will have a sweet time together. And keep us safe.

She continued to pray and soon felt peace come to her spirit. She focused on relaxing, and soon she noticed the truck slowed down and made a series of turns.

We must be getting close. God, protect us.

The vehicle slowed and turned into a bright area.

After parking and releasing Rosie from the gurney and its bindings, Yosef escorted her into Cleburne hospital and straight into the ICU ward.

A large woman in her late fifties with graying hair, glasses, and a loose-fitting red uniform with the hospital logo stitched above the left pocket looked up and smiled. "Yosef!"

"Rosie Wilson, I'd like you to meet Frances, the charge nurse," Yosef said.

"Nice to meet you," Frances said. "I've known Yosef for years. So, any friend of his is a friend of mine."

"Thank you," Rosie said.

"You just get off work, honey?"

"Okay, ladies," Yosef interrupted. "I'll take my leave. See you later." He gave a slight wave and headed back the way they'd come.

"Yes, ma'am," Rosie said, ready to spout off her well-rehearsed background. "I work at the Rangler's Store right there at 281 and 2nd. Do you know Hico?"

"Sure do, honey. I used to take my kids to the Billy the Kid Museum. But that was a long time ago. Is that thing still there?"

"The museum is just down the street from the Rangler," Rosie said, feeling anxious about being asked too many questions about a town she'd never visited. "I guess you know I'm here to see my son, Craig."

"Of course. But since you've been working with the public all day, assuming that's what you do, I'm going to ask you to wash up and put on a gown, hat, and gloves before you go in. Those are right over there." Frances pointed her jiggling arm to the left of her desk. "Craig has had a big day. He had X-rays yesterday, but today the doctor on call worked with him and his PT nurse to start his exercises."

Rosie saw a sink tucked close to the desk and began to scrub her hands. Putting on the protective gown, hat, mask, and gloves, she looked at Frances. "How do I look?"

"Kinda normal for around here. Where'd you learn to wash up like that? Hico Clinic teach you that?" Frances said with a smile. "You got to deal quietly and softly with your son. He needs his sleep." She walked Rosie two doors down from the nurse's station and stopped at a doorway. The sign on the wall next to the door said, "CRAIG WILSON."

Rosie walked to Cooper's bed and stared at him. *There you are, my angel.* She studied his dark curls and eyebrows highlighted by his father's darker skin. *And those eyelashes any girl would kill for. You are such a handsome child.*

Her tears of joy flowed as she reached down and took his hand. "How's my fighter? Your mama has certainly missed you." Without thinking and going into nurse mode, she looked at the monitors and pulled out her own stethoscope to double check the monitor's readout.

Frances stepped into the room, her arms filled with a blanket and pillow.

Startled too late, and sure she was caught, Rosie quickly stashed the stethoscope into her backpack.

"Here are your things, honey, in case you plan to stay. I know you've had a hard day." Frances handed her the items and left without another word.

How could I have been so careless? She hoped Frances hadn't seen—after all, she argued, it was dark in the room. She pulled the room's one chair next to the bed and settled down, wrapping herself in the blanket. She grabbed Cooper's hand again. "Good night, my sweet prince."

CHAPTER 30

2:00 a.m.
Saturday, March 20

THE VIBRATION FROM Jamal's burner phone lying next to his stomach awakened him from a hard sleep. He instantly went on high alert. *Who has died? Or who is warning me of someone trying to kill me?*

He looked at the caller ID. *Navid. This can't be good.*

He swiped his finger across the screen to secure the call and got out of bed quietly, holding the phone to his chest to keep the lighted screen from disturbing Safi.

Too late. She stirred and lifted herself on her elbow. "Are you okay?"

"Yes, just getting up to relieve myself. I'm fine." He willed himself to speak calmly. "You can go back to sleep." He made his way to the bathroom, then circled quietly toward the outside patio, gingerly opening and shutting the door behind him. In bare feet and wearing only a T-shirt and boxer shorts, he was unprepared for the chill of the night air.

"Navid, what is going on?" he whispered into the phone to his friend from their college days at the University of Texas. Navid Uzell was now the imam and informant from the Austin area.

"Here is the latest from my secured source." Navid's baritone voice sounded strangely somber. "And, Jamal, it is not good news."

He paused and then inhaled deeply. "You, me, and the imam from San Antonio are on the short list of the next round of imams. We are all three being scrutinized closely, possibly even targeted by the Observer. One or all of us could go the way of the Seattle imam after the march next week."

Jamal's knees went weak. "What are you talking about? We are completely ready here in the DFW area and have been for a week. In fact, when the caliph, peace be upon him, moved up the march by two days on his last conference call, I jumped on the change." He paced forcefully around the perimeter of the patio. "How will this happen?" he asked. "Oh, Allah, I hate this job!"

"When we signed up for this, we had no idea what we had in store for ourselves, did we?" Navid asked.

"Have you told Ibrahim Kravit in San Antonio about all this?"

"No, you are the first call. My source just called me. I believe it is credible, obviously, or I wouldn't be calling you. My guy has access to some snooping devices and is able to hack into and track down all manner of intercepted encrypted messages—probably even this very phone call. Say hello to Hal."

"I—" Jamal stopped. A noise came from the patio door. The full moon had broken through the clouds, so he stood still under the shadow of a tree in his backyard.

"Jamal." Safi's whisper floated to him in the darkness. "Are you alright?"

Holding the phone to his chest again, Jamal stepped into the moonlight. "I am doing fine. I need some time to think. I'll be inside in a few minutes."

"Would you like me to bring you a jacket? It's cold, and you don't have much on. Or I can come out, and we can talk? I'm worried about you."

"No," Jamal said dismissively, then realized how his tone sounded. He softened his voice. "But thank you. I'll be okay."

Safi reentered the house, and Jamal returned the phone to his ear. "The more I think about this call, the angrier I get. I have busted my tail for the caliph. We here in the DFW had a higher percentage than *they* predicted of infidels refusing the conversion deal. We had to make the camp boundaries bigger to accommodate the larger crowd. Then we did it in record time, and we were ready early. *They* were always moving the goal line—and my team always met or exceeded the challenge every time! And all I might get for doing his bidding? A bullet to the head."

Jamal began pacing again to shake off the crisp chill in the air as well as his anger and now fear.

"You and I don't deserve this," Navid said, his own voice cracking with emotion. "But the truth is, it's what is coming down. I'm here as your friend to warn you. Be extra kind to Safi and the family so they can remember you kindly. Pray more, lead an exemplary life, and Allah will be pleased."

"Stop it!" Jamal shouted into the phone, then realized his error. "Excuse me, Navid. I know you are trying to help, but right now, I am so frantic that I want to punch something or do some serious damage to someone's face." His hands now shook so fiercely he could hardly keep the phone close to his ear.

"If they kill you and me, that will make us martyrs for Allah, which will guarantee our positions in paradise for our families and ourselves. This is wonderful news. It is what I have been clinging to, something you and I will never again have to worry about. But I must warn you to expect that your family and your home will be destroyed very soon after your death if it is at all similar to the Seattle imam's removal. I have a plan in place for my family. I encourage you to prepare your family and do the same."

"Thank you, my friend. I should be grateful for the call. But it is impossible for me to think straight anymore. How am I to sleep after this call tonight?" Jamal paused. "Are you sleeping at all?"

"I am not as prepared as you for the march. Our camp in Lexington, which is due east of Austin—a little more than fifty miles away and in the middle of nowhere . . ." Navid's voice trailed off.

Just as well since Jamal had lost his ability to concentrate. He could hear Navid start talking again, but he couldn't understand what he was saying. "Have you told your wife?"

"No, not yet," Navid said. "She has enough to worry about."

"Thanks for the call, Navid. You have been a good man to know through all of this. Call again if you have any more information." Jamal hung up and lowered his head.

They're going to kill me. They're going to kill me. They're going to kill me.

He thought about going inside to change into workout clothes to go for a long run. Maybe he could run so hard that he would cause his own heart attack and be done with it all. *But changing clothes would wake Safi. I don't want to confront her right now. Not at this hour.*

He quietly opened the patio door and entered the house. His body was shaking so violently that he had a hard time closing the door with the ease he had hoped for, clumsily locking the deadbolt with a noisy clunk. He grabbed a nearby chair and waited so his eyes could adjust to the darkness. His panicked breathing still came heavy in uneven gasps.

"Can I help you?" Safi said, sounding alarmed. She was to his left.

"Don't do that!" he said, slurring his voice. "You scared me. Where are you?"

"I'm seated by our fireplace in the green chair. Since I can see you, I'll come to you. You sound as if you are cold and exhausted."

"I am freezing. Do you have one of your blankets in here to put on me?"

He heard her get out of the chair, reach for something, and then walk toward him.

She touched his cheek. "You are frozen!" She draped the cover over him and led him to his chair a few steps away. "What was going on out there? Really."

With Safi near to comfort him, he pulled her face down to his mouth and whispered into her ear, "We can't talk in this room. Go start the shower in our bathroom. Turn it on hot, I'll be in a second. The steam will warm me up and the noise of the shower will cover our talking."

"What is that cold metal in your hand? Is that a gun?" she whispered in a panicked voice.

"No." He placed the burner phone in her hand and closed her fingers around its form. "See? It's nothing. Now go start the water. I'll be there soon."

He remained in the chair for a few moments to get control of his emotions. He could not let her see him this way. His eyes adjusted to the dark interior, and he looked around. *Where are you hidden? What are you thinking right now?* He knew the Observer was intruding on their privacy.

He stood and walked to the master bath. Steam billowed out, as he stepped inside the room and shut the door, still wrapped in his cover. Safi was seated on the marble countertop next to the sink, studying the phone that Jamal had given to her. He saw in her concentration a look as if somehow there was a hidden secret locked within it. She stared up at him, her eyes boring into him.

I don't know if I'm ready for this, but I need to face her questions. She deserves to know.

"Your breathing sounds better." She held up the phone between her thumb and forefinger, wiggling it a bit. "What is this for, and why do you have it? What was going on out there?"

"It is certainly warmer in here than outside," Jamal said, stalling the conversation.

"Jamal?"

"It's a burner phone." He smiled sadly. "I purchased it with cash. It has a weird area code and number, and I pay cash only for the minutes I use. It is untraceable, and only three people have that number. It is extremely secretive and safe." He drew in a deep breath and exhaled. "I have been sleeping with it at night to receive emergency calls, just like the one I received a short while ago." He was warming up and beginning to feel better temperature-wise, though he felt an ominous weight on his chest. "It was from Navid." He knew she was fond of Navid and his family.

"Navid? Why?"

"He called to say that he, Ibrahim in San Antonio, and I . . . might be killed next week."

"What?" Safi cried out. "I-I don't understand."

Jamal put his finger to his lips. "Shh! You must keep your voice down. This is the report that Navid has heard, so he called to tell me."

"What are you going to do about it?" Tears began to pour down her cheeks.

"What do you mean, what am I going to do? There is nothing I *can* do. I'm trapped in this job. I've done all they asked me to do. Somehow, they still don't like me and what I'm doing. The three of us are on a watch list, whatever that means. We might be targeted similar to the Seattle imam."

"I'm scared, Jamal." She harshly wiped at her eyes. "You say there is nothing to be done. That is the wrong answer! Don't you see there is something that *must* be done?" She inched closer to him and gestured to the door. "Not long ago, Tom picked me up while Lori watched the two little ones, and we went for a short drive. He told me about his concern for you. He told me about his vision with the Man in the White Robe. It was very similar to my vision. Jesus came to both of us and was talking about *you* to both of us. Has he come to you in a vision?"

"What right does Tom have to involve my wife and interfere in my relationship with Allah? That is treason! I should report you both."

Safi touched his face gently. "These visions are examples of Jesus loving you. He knows your name. He is wanting to bring you to this love. Please, Jamal, this is really important. This is *eternity* we are discussing."

Jamal felt his anger build again. "Navid assures me that my death will be as a martyr, so we have a guaranteed entrance into paradise. That is straight from the Koran. I need no further assurance. End of discussion!"

CHAPTER 31

7:00 a.m.
Saturday, March 20

ROSIE AWOKE TO see a short, slender, bald man with a closely cut beard standing in front of her. He wore a white lab coat, green scrub pants, and white tennis shoes. *This must be the attending physician.* "Good morning," she said, her voice still sleepy.

He smiled. "Good morning. I didn't mean to wake you. I'm Dr. Roger Ingram." He extended his hand over Cooper's bed.

"I'm Rosie Wilson, Craig's mom." She stood, still wrapped in the warmth of the nighttime blanket, and shook his hand.

"I heard that you met our lovable Frances last night. She tells me you work at a convenience store in Hico. Are you going to tell me that's where you purchased your stethoscope?"

Rosie tried not to squirm while she pulled the blanket tighter around herself, feeling exposed. "I'm not sure what you mean about a stethoscope, but I did meet Frances. She seems to be a good person to be over the unit."

"She is all that and more." He stood straight. "Let's get right to the point. Your son is very lucky, or he has had some extremely good physicians. His leg surgery, for example, was not done by locals in Hamilton, Hico, or even here in Cleburne. The X-rays before surgery do not exist in this hospital, but the X-rays we took here yesterday illustrate the bone-setting skill that I have only seen from one doc around here. Would you happen to know Dr. Boyd Wilson in Fort Worth?" He paused, giving her a stern look.

Rosie fidgeted with her wedding ring under the blanket. *I don't like the way this conversation is going. Lord, please help me know what to say!* She shrugged her shoulders, hoping that would satisfy him and end the conversation.

Dr. Ingram sighed. "So, it's more evidence that you want. Okay, here we go. As for Craig's brain injury, he is very fortunate to be under my care. I happened to have completed a fellowship at Craig Hospital in Englewood, Colorado, before coming here. Craig is a renowned rehabilitation hospital that specializes in, among other things, traumatic brain injury or TBI, which is what I believe happened to your son. I was skyping with my colleagues up there to discuss Craig's case until the Islamic regime disallowed the exchange of information. Mrs. Wilson, I have to say, those docs up there in Colorado tell me your son's case sounds very familiar to a child they were working on under the care of a Dr. Wilson in Fort Worth."

Rosie felt her face flush, and she stepped back, feeling with her hands for the chair behind her, still clutching the blanket. Her head began to spin as she sat and anticipated more explosive revelations.

"Mrs. Wilson, are you feeling ill? Can I get you some water?"

"No." She held up her hand. "I must be having a hot flash or something. I'll be fine. I have been keeping long hours, and this wasn't the best place to catch up on my sleep."

He looked at her skeptically. "If you're certain you are fine, let me finish. The child's name in the case study was Cooper Chavez. That child had a mother named Rosie Chavez, a very skilled nurse at the same hospital with Dr. Wilson. Does any of this ring a bell?"

Her chin began to quiver, and she spoke in very deliberately, punctuating her words so she conveyed her plea carefully. "Dr. Ingram, I'm sure you are a good doctor, and it sounds like you have been trained well to meet the conditions of my son. He will need your skill to fully recover. My job as his mother is to love and care for him to the best of my abilities." Rosie's quivering became more pronounced.

"But you haven't answered my question, Mrs. Wilson."

"Again, you are a doctor. I am his mother. My loyalties are to this boy to see that he gets well and out of this hospital, hopefully walking on his own. I respectfully ask you to do your job as a healing physician, so please continue to help him." She looked at her son who was still asleep. "Do you have children, Dr. Ingram?"

Dr. Ingram sighed. "We're discussing you at the moment." He walked to Rosie's side and stared into her eyes. "I want you to know I take no pleasure in this, but you must understand that Frances and I know something is up with you and this sweet boy." He looked down at Cooper.

As if on cue, Cooper stirred. He blinked a few times and looked at the doctor and then turned his eyes to Rosie. The sleepiness disappeared as his eyes grew wide. "Mama, is that you?"

"Yes, it is, sweetheart. I'm so glad to see you," she said, grateful for the break in the tension. She allowed the tears to fall freely as she reached down to hug him, covering him with her body. "It's so good to hear your voice. You were gone for such a long time."

Cooper pushed his mother back. "No, Mama, I was here the whole time. You were gone. This man here," he said as he pointed to Dr. Ingram, "and another lady are helping me." He looked around the room again. "Where is Daddy?"

She knew this question would come at some point, she just didn't expect it so soon. And she couldn't handle it right now. "Oh,

I have missed you so much." She hugged him tightly again. "Daddy can't be here right now," she whispered in his ear as her heart broke again, reviewing in an instant all that they missed together over the past two months. She could feel Cooper's hot breath on her cheek as he squirmed underneath her.

She tousled his hair and kissed him multiple times on the cheek, which he promptly wiped off. "Hey, don't do that," she said in a mock scolding voice to complete the game they had played for years.

Cooper giggled and wiped his cheek again, seemingly begging for more kisses. Rosie lunged toward him, and Cooper put up his arms in defense.

"Let me see if I can get next to you in your bed, okay?" She finally looked back at Dr. Ingram. "Can we crank up his head to a sitting position so I can sit next to my son?"

To her surprise, he was smiling tenderly at them. "That would be fine, Mrs. Wilson."

"Can I sit you up a little so Mama can sit next to you?" Rosie said. "Would that be all right?"

Cooper nodded as he rubbed the sleep from his eyes.

Without thinking, Rosie reached over to the controls and expertly pushed the button to raise Cooper's head, then she lowered the guardrail and slid in to hug him.

Cooper grinned at his mother. "Why did he call you Mrs. Wilson? That's not your name."

Without moving closer, Dr. Ingram cleared his throat. "You know I might ask to see your driver's license or some form of ID—"

"I am trying to give my son the best—"

"*But*," Dr. Ingram continued, "I think we both have probably lived with too much forced interrogations and IDs lately, don't you, Mrs. . . . *Wilson?*"

Rosie swallowed hard and nodded.

"If Craig were mine, I would do whatever I could to keep him alive," he said as he patted Cooper's shoulder. "And yes, I do have children. Two."

"I can see that he is getting excellent care under your direction," she said, now looking directly at him. She wanted him to know that she appreciated what he was doing for Cooper.

He took a few steps back. "You can rest assured that this is a safe place for Craig . . . and for the other two who arrived with him—but only for a while. Frances and I will watch out for you."

"Thank you."

"But," he said, lifting his hand in warning, "not everyone here is sympathetic to what has occurred here in the last few days. You will soon discover there are well-meaning people here who are very particular about details." His eyes softened a bit. "You and I will finish our conversation later." Dr. Ingram turned to leave the room. "See you later, Craig."

"Cooper. I told you, my name is Cooper," Rosie's son said with a gleam in his eye. "That is a game we play every time he leaves the room. Now he calls you Mrs. Wilson. He is being silly. But where were you? And where is Daddy?"

Rosie hugged Cooper again and stroked his face, still amazed that he was awake. She inhaled deeply and decided to answer as gently as she could. "Do you remember that day when it was your turn to take snacks to your school? That was the day when Daddy came to pick you up. You remember?"

"I kinda remember going to school. I had my new backpack I got for Christmas." He scrunched his face, as though trying to bring up the memory. "I think I wanted to carry the snacks, but they were heavy, so you did."

"That's right, do you remember anything else?"

As Cooper shook his head, the morning nurse entered with a breakfast tray. "Are you hungry, Master Wilson?" She caught sight of Rosie, and her face turned to surprise. "Who might this be?"

"This is my mama. She was gone, but now she's here!" Cooper said with enthusiasm. "She is really smart, and she is—"

"His mother," Rosie said quickly before Cooper announced that she was a nurse. "I'm Rosie."

"Hello, Rosie," the nurse said. "We were beginning to wonder if you would ever make it to visit him."

Rosie tried to act casual. "My job kept me busy." She turned back to Cooper. "How about I feed you?"

"Mama, I can feed myself. Don't you know anything?"

"We mothers do get forgetful." Rosie watched in amazement as her four-year-old son dug into his scrambled eggs and toast, washing it down with orange juice.

With Cooper occupied, she decided now would be a good time to continue her conversation with Dr. Ingram, if she could find him. "Hey, buddy, I need to go ask a question really fast. Keep eating, and I'll be back before you're finished. Okay?"

Cooper looked up between bites. "Okay," he said through a mouth full of eggs.

Rosie left the room and didn't have far to look. Dr. Ingram was leaning over the central desk with his elbows on the ledge talking to Frances. She walked up to the two, who quickly stopped talking. "May I interrupt?"

They both turned their attention to her. Dr. Ingram straightened to a standing position.

Rosie looked around and then quietly began. "My name is Rosie Chavez. I can explain all this later, but I must know how to handle a situation with my son immediately."

"Oh-kay," Dr. Ingram said. "What is the problem?"

"That little guy in there, Cooper, my son, he was injured in a tragic car accident that killed his father. He wants to know where his dad is. Would the shock of such bad news do damage to what you think is best for him, you know, with the brain injury?"

"That is an excellent question," Dr. Ingram said. "Does he even know he is in Cleburne? We certainly haven't told him. Have you asked him what he remembers from the day of the accident?"

"I don't think he has a clue where he is. He only realizes that I wasn't here when he woke up, and he can't remember anything past me taking him to school that morning. His dad picked him up after work. As they were driving home, their car was broadsided by a drunk driver going sixty after running a red light. We believe Cooper was knocked out from the collision. Ramon, my husband, was killed instantly." She breathed in slowly. Saying it aloud brought back an ache that was still raw.

"I am so sorry to hear about your loss, Rosie," Dr. Ingram said compassionately. "To your question, I would suggest his brain shut down the memory for a reason. Tell him his history backward. Time will help heal his brain. Your job is to walk him backward from the present to the accident. The last thing you tell him is that his father died in that car crash. Keep the story essential to the facts and know that you will be requested to tell the story again and again. Therefore, remember what you say the first time."

She had always been the professional nurse giving parents this kind of news. Now she was on the other side. She felt the tears threaten to appear again and blinked hard.

Frances walked around the desk and hugged Rosie, giving her a tissue. "Listen, honey, Yosef told us about the terrible goings on over there in the DFW area. Little kids and old people just snuffed out like they were nothing." Frances snapped her fingers in the air to punctuate the quickness of the victims' deaths. "I knew it must be bad for you to send these three kids over here, but I didn't know the half of it. I will support you in any way I can."

"Why does it have to be so hard?" Rosie sniffed and used the tissue Frances had given her to wipe her nose. "Poor Cooper just woke up, and now I have to tell him what he missed." Fresh tears began to fall. "I'm sorry for all these tears, but I just haven't had time to really grieve Ramon because I've been so focused on getting Cooper well."

Frances gave Rosie another hug and patted her on the back. Rosie melted into the hug and wrapped her arms around Frances, slowly giving way to sobs.

"You let it all out, sweetie. When I lost my Edgar, my world came to an end for a while. You can tell me everything, and I will try to help you get through this."

"If you'll excuse me, I need to get on to a few more patients," Dr. Ingram said. Rosie figured it was a good time for him to excuse himself. *Probably all the emotion is too much for him.*

"Do you want to practice on me what you want to say to your son? I know it's important, and you need to get it correct so you can say it again the same way," Frances said after Rosie's sobs slowed.

"No, I'm better now," Rosie said. "I think I've got it in my head." She wiped at her eyes. "You have no idea how long it's been since I've been hugged like that. Maybe weeks, and I was used to being hugged by Ramon every day. I have a physical ache, missing that touch. Thank you, Frances."

Frances smiled. "I have plenty of hugs. Any time you need another, you just let me know."

Rosie walked to Cooper's room with a new plan and purpose. As she entered, she saw that he'd cleaned his plate. *At least his appetite hasn't changed.* She pulled the tray away from his bed and sat next to him, stroking his black curls.

"Cooper, there is something I must tell you, and it is very sad. You aren't at Mommy's hospital. You're in a hospital farther away from home. You have been asleep for almost two months."

Cooper's eyes widened in surprise.

She nodded. "You had to sleep that long to let your brain and leg heal. Most of that time, you slept at Mommy's hospital, but we moved you where you're very safe and you'll be taken good care of."

His little face scrunched as he tried to understand what she was telling him. "But . . . why?"

She rubbed his face gently. "Because you and Daddy were in a bad car accident, and you got hurt. Daddy came to pick you up from school the day that you remember. But while you were on your way home, someone hit the car. You both got hurt really badly."

"Is Daddy sleeping too? Is that why he isn't here?"

How do I tell him? she wondered and commanded herself not to cry. "No, baby. He died. Just like Grandma and Grandpa died. Now Daddy is in heaven."

Cooper shook his head. She could tell he was trying very hard to process what she was saying. Finally, he began to cry. "That's not true, Mama."

Rosie put her arm around him and hugged him tight to herself. "You worked so hard to come back from all your sleeping. I know Daddy is proud of you, and I am too. I miss Daddy so much, and I know you will too. We will never forget him, and we can talk about him as often as you want to. But right now, I need you to be brave for me and keep getting better. Can you do that for Mommy?"

He nodded slowly.

"Okay, here is a new game we need to play just between you and me and the people here at the hospital. It is a name change game.

We need to play like your name is Craig Wilson and that would change my name to Mrs. Wilson."

"That's the game Dr. Ingram plays with me every time he leaves the room."

"Well, we are here at the hospital as guests of someone very special, and that person wanted us to use these new names so we won't get mixed up with other people. So, *Craig Wilson*, can you play along?" Rosie tweaked his nose with her fingers, which brought another smile.

"I guess so. I hope I can remember. It sounds easy. But I want Daddy."

"I do too, sweetheart. You are such a good boy. You are amazing, and I love you, my dear little man." Rosie hugged him as they both began to cry again.

"Good morning, Craig!" came a loud voice. A petite African-American lady in her mid-thirties with a bouncy blond afro tied up in a yellow scarf wearing a bright red uniform came into Cooper's room. Her voice seemed impossible to come from such a small frame. "Well, who do we have here?" She strode quickly to Rosie and stuck out her hand. Her arm was adorned with multiple, multicolored bangled bracelets. They shook hands with a noisy flourish. "Hello, my name is Chrissy. I'm Craig's physical therapist."

"I'm Rosie, his mother."

Chrissy looked between Rosie and Cooper, her eyebrows furrowing. "Why does everybody look so sad today? Something is definitely *not* right here with my happy Craig." Her eyes landed questioningly on Rosie.

Rosie stood and motioned for Chrissy to follow her outside the room. Out of the earshot of her son, Rosie said softly, "I'm so glad you are here to help him, but you must understand this little man just found out his father died in the same car accident that injured him. This is the first time he is learning about it." Rosie pressed her hands together to mime praying hands and tilted her head back to Cooper's bed.

Chrissy gave a large nod and frowned.

They returned to Cooper's room, and Rosie patted her son on the chest. "He is kind of sad right now."

"Oh no, child, I am so sorry to hear about this."

"I don't want to work on my arms and leg today," Cooper announced.

Chrissy feigned an exaggerated expression of shock. "What did I hear from you? Of all the times to exercise your body, today is the most important day! You and I need to work that sadness out of your body. If I'm not mistaken, I think you are a man full of action, and you want to get moving, right?" She looked conspiratorially at Rosie. "They call me Dr. Feelgood. First, I make them hurt, and then they feel good." She burst out laughing. "Isn't that right, Craig? So, we need you to climb out of that funk and get started. Which arm do you want to start with?"

Cooper raised his right arm with a forced smile. "Ready."

"Then here I come. Watch this, Mother." Chrissy gently began to manipulate his arm, shoulder, and wrist. Rosie watched closely from the other side of the bed as Chrissy explained every squeeze, push, and maneuver. "This is what Mom gets to do when you are home." Addressing Rosie, she asked, "Where is home?"

"North of here," Rosie said, trying to relay as little as possible.

Chrissy looked back at Cooper. "We should have you ready to leave in no time." Then she nodded toward Rosie. "Be sure to get a good stretch here by putting your hand under the elbow and gently pressing down."

"Ow! That hurts!" Cooper said with a frown.

"I know, sweetie, but you will thank me tomorrow when you can move your arm with ease."

After an hour of Rosie watching Chrissy maneuver Cooper's arms and his good leg, taking notes on the back of a menu, and doing some hands-on work herself, Chrissy clapped her hands together. "Okay, we are finished for this morning. I will see you this afternoon at about 3:00, so get your nap in because I'll be back." She stuck out her fist, which Cooper met with his own. They touched tenderly, then jerked away from each other in simulated explosions, leaving both laughing hysterically.

"See you later," they both said, almost in unison.

"I'm sorry about your daddy," Chrissy said, then looked at Rosie. "You too." Then she left.

She would be a great employee for our hospital . . . in another world. "Well, bub, your mama needs to get something to eat. Can I bring you anything?"

"Ice cream," Cooper suggested excitedly.

She laughed. "That sounds like a celebration request. If they have it, you got it." She bent over and kissed him on the forehead. "I love you."

She found the cafeteria and grabbed a sandwich, along with two ice cream sandwiches that she tucked inside a white paper sack and placed on top of her lunch tray. As she headed back to Cooper's room, walking past the administrative staff offices, some artwork caught her attention, so she stopped briefly to gaze at it. A woman a little older than Rosie came around the corner without paying attention and collided with her, causing her to drop her lunch tray.

"I'm so sorry," Rosie and the lady apologized simultaneously. Rosie bent over to pick up her food while the other lady knelt to assist her.

"Mrs. Wilson?" the woman said.

Rosie's eyes grew big. "Do I know you?"

The woman pointed at Rosie's visitor's tag.

"Oh!"

"My name is Alice Denny. I work in the admin records." She held up her mobile phone as she stood. "I was just texting. They say don't text and drive, but I can now confirm not to text and walk either. Sorry again."

"It's okay."

"Are you the Mrs. Wilson, the mother of the new arrival, Craig?"

Rosie tensed and tried to keep her demeanor calm. "Yes. As a matter of fact, I was taking him a treat for doing so well with his physical therapy. What was your name again?" Rosie looked at the woman's name tag, which read, "Alice Denny, Supervisor of Admissions and Records."

Pointing to her name tag, she smiled. "Alice. I was actually wanting to talk with you. I have a few questions for you. Would you mind stepping into my office for a moment? I heard that you were in the hospital visiting your son. I need you to help me fill out some information on Craig."

Rosie lowered her eyes to her food. "Now isn't really a good time. I have a hungry youngster back in the room. I need to get back to him. Chrissy, his PT, gave me some rehab exercises to do with him as soon as he finishes his ice cream sandwich, which is melting in this paper bag. That's his reward."

Alice smiled. "Of course. Well, would you come back to my office after you eat? My questions won't take long. More curiosity than anything else, I suppose."

"Um, yes, okay." Rosie hurried away and wondered what the questions could possibly be. She was still considering the conversation when she entered Cooper's room.

He waved at her the moment she rounded the corner. "Did you get the ice cream?"

"Right here." She handed him the white sack then pushed the rolling stand up under his bed so he could eat without it dripping all over his sheets.

He pulled out the first wrapped sandwich, then grabbed the second one. His face fell with disappointment. "They're melty."

"I'm sorry they are. We are just going to have to be extra careful when we eat them. Here, let me get you a paper towel to catch the drips." Rosie walked to the sink in the room and pulled off three paper towels and handed them to Cooper who was busily unwrapping the package and licking the edges.

"Actually, I think I better eat my ice cream first, so it won't be completely melted before I start on my chicken sandwich. What do you think?"

Cooper nodded vigorously, ice cream running down his chin.

"How is that tasting?"

He moaned in delight.

She laughed. "I sure have missed talking to you."

Frances came into the unit and stood next to Rosie's chair. "I understand you have met Alice," she said unceremoniously. "Could we step into the hall for a minute to discuss that?"

Once they were out of Cooper's hearing and all was clear in the hallway, Rosie looked incredulously at Frances. "How could you have possibly found out about my run-in with Alice so quickly?"

Frances spoke very quietly. "Listen, honey. Alice is like a hound on a rabbit around here. She's that way with everyone, so it isn't just with you. She is like the neighborhood lady with the curtains parted. She is in the know. Since you have been back to the room with your lunch, she has cruised by ICU twice, presumably to check on you. One of those times, she and I made eye contact, so she stopped to talk with me." Frances again looked up and down the ICU hall, then narrowed her eyes at Rosie. "Knowing of your relationship with Yosef, when I saw you come in last night, and you told me you were going to be here all weekend, I changed my schedule to be here. I don't have anything going on at home, and I had a hunch that you would need some help with Alice. Be careful with her. Ever since your son and the other two arrived, she has been sniffing around, trying to figure out where these three kids came from. She told me she was unable to locate any records from Hamilton or Hico, and she plans to widen the search to nail it down."

Rosie nearly choked. "What do you mean? I thought it was safe here. Dr. Ingram so much as told me that. Doesn't she have enough to do trying to run this hospital?"

Frances chuckled for a moment and turned serious again. "Rosie, I know you are not a poker player because that face would give away your hand, so relax. We here in the ICU know all about the purge. We know the three kids were probably smuggled here from Fort Worth."

Rosie winced. "What *don't* you know about me?" Her mind was spinning with anxiety. *What else am I obviously exposing for everybody to see?*

"Just don't play cards with a professional gambler. I see all kinds of people in here, and I can read faces fairly well." Frances chuckled again. "Dr. Ingram and I know all this information on you. However, Alice does *not*. The minor grilling Alice wants to put you through will attempt to fill in some blanks. I think, in the long run, the origin of your three children and the circumstances that led to them being brought here will create trouble for everyone."

"What do you think I should do?" Rosie looked into Frances's eyes and then covered hers with her hands. "Jesus, help me, I'm in over my head." She dropped her hands to her sides. "I'm sorry. I just need some ideas."

"Our Jesus is big enough to take care of you," Frances smiled kindly. "Honey, Alice could be an obstacle to what we want to see happen here with these three kids, *or* she could be an ally. She is just doing her job. Perhaps if you told her some of what is going on here, she might help. She is a little strange and hard to get close to, but in general, she is a nice, if not thorough, person, and she keeps the hospital running smoothly."

"But can she be trusted? What would keep her from calling the authorities to say she has three escapees from Fort Worth once she figures it out?" Rosie began to toy with her wedding ring, twisting it around her finger and moving it off and on. "I thought I was coming over here to spend a nice, relaxed weekend cuddling with Cooper and catching up on some loving, but *bamo!*" She struck the air with her fist. "I'm here revealing all my life stories, and I'm possibly on the edge of turning myself in. Not what I had in mind." She gave a pleading look to Frances. "He *has* to remain safe here."

"Alice wants to know that she is a player in the game and not some outsider looking in, but it's not my story to tell. She's gruff, but she really can be a good lady. She's a single mom with a special needs daughter, so I think she could be understanding." Frances placed her hands on Rosie's shoulders. "I don't pretend to know what to do, but I do know we are to trust God for the results of our lives, whatever the outcome. She is expecting you to tell her something."

"I just . . ." She took in a deep breath. "I know I go back to Fort Worth, and at the end of next week, I leave my home and march with a couple million of my closest non-Islamic friends to a detention camp somewhere close to Waxahachie. There we are expected to live until we either starve to death or die of some disease. You, however, have the good fortune of not living in one of the top one hundred metropolitan areas in the former USA and are therefore exempt from such punishment." Rosie stuck out her tongue as if she'd just tasted a bitter poison. Frances shook her head in disgust.

Rosie sighed. "Now isn't that a happy thought? Actually, I will find some purpose with several others working in the medical tent, serving those four million plus 'campers' as we make it our new home."

Frances shook her head in disgust. "The future prospects just get worse with each day. I guess I could go to my church and see if we could take in these kids until something breaks open. But right now, you have to tell Alice something. If she is with us, so much the better. If this plan backfires, then we deal with it. I'll be here with my ear to the wall. Alice isn't the only one around here who can figure things out, as you well know." Frances looked around to make certain they were alone. "We need to get out of this open area."

Frances led Rosie back into Cooper's room. "Okay, honey, you and Craig get some time together." Frances called to Cooper, "When you get ready for a nap, I'll come in and read you a book. I'm never too busy for that." She looked at Rosie. "Mama, it's time to go get registered with Alice and tell her everything you need to say."

CHAPTER 32

2:15 p.m.
Saturday, March 20

ALICE WAS HUNCHED over her desk but looked up as soon as Rosie knocked lightly on the doorframe. "Oh, Mrs. Wilson, come in." Alice, an attractive, thirtysomething brunette in a tailored blouse and slacks, stood, offered her hand to shake, then indicated the chair across from her desk.

Rosie closed the door behind her and scanned the room. Except for the files on her desk, Alice's office was tidy. Some institutional artwork hung on the walls, and an outside window overlooked a courtyard with a tree. A bookshelf with an eclectic collection of books, awards, and pictures of her with other presumed notables stood carefully arranged on the shelves. Rosie's eyes fell on what she hoped would be helpful. She studied two family pictures with Alice, two older adults, and a child. *Bingo!* Next, she spied on Alice's desk another photo of Alice with the same young girl.

Rosie took a seat. "I see you have a little girl." She pointed to the photo on the desk. "In that picture, she looks about Craig's age."

Alice smiled and looked at the photograph. "Yes. My daughter, Angela, is now nine. She was five when this picture was taken."

"I can imagine, as a mother, if anything happened to your little girl, you'd do anything you could to save her."

"Of course," Alice said. "She's my life."

Rosie smiled and nodded. "As you know, I am the mother of one of your patients. What you may not know is that he is my only child. He and his father, my late husband, were in an accident. A drunk driver smashed into my husband's car, killing him instantly and seriously injuring our boy with a brain injury and a broken leg." Feeling emotion seeping up to the surface, she paused to compose her voice.

Alice opened a drawer, pulled out a box of tissues, and passed it to Rosie, who took two and dabbed her eyes.

"I suppose someday I can get through this without crying, but obviously I am not there yet. This morning was the first day in two months I have seen my son awake. He was in a coma because of his brain injury. He is talking and glad to see me, which is wonderful! But do you know what one of his first questions was to me? He wanted to know where his daddy was."

Alice's eyes filled with tears, and she grabbed a tissue as well. "What did you tell him?"

"It was heartbreaking, as you can imagine, to have to tell him that the day he was injured, which he can't remember, his father was killed."

"I don't know how you have survived. I saw you a couple of times in the room with Craig, and you seem like such a sweet mother with him. Even now, you seem calm. I couldn't do that."

"It is hard," Rosie admitted, then paused to let everything sink into the discussion. She took a deep breath and dabbed at her eyes and nose. "Dr. Ingram told me that I will need to keep telling my son how all this happened for several weeks until he understands. Right now, he thinks he just woke up from a long nap, and everything should be like it was. I have to be there to fill in the gap over and over with the timeline."

"I can't even imagine. My Angie is mildly autistic, but she is able to learn. She works hard at socialization, but we discovered she has apraxia, where the brain and the tongue don't communicate, causing her difficulty with all communication skills. Her PhD father couldn't handle the disparity between his intellect and her difficulties in expressing herself, so about a year and half before this picture was taken—" she pointed at the photo, "he left. I moved to Cleburne to be close to my parents and their support." Alice looked adoringly at the picture. "She is such a pretty child. Those deep brown eyes and that beautiful brown hair. Those closest to her can understand what she's saying. She knows she is not speaking normally yet, but she is happy and learning each day. She is a joy to us all." She sighed softly.

"I'm sorry you've had to deal with all of that," Rosie said, hoping Alice would respond favorably to her confession.

Alice rubbed her chin thoughtfully, then focused back on Rosie. "Mrs. Wilson, you seem like a nice enough lady, but your son being here is creating problems for me. You two are in my hospital without a trace of any background on you or the other two children who came at the exact same time. Let me show you something." She grabbed one of the files from her desk and held it up so Rosie could see. It was about an inch or so thick. "I had my assistant print this from the computer records. This is one patient, and I have all kinds of information on this particular individual. Full name, date of birth, home address, telephone number, social security number, HIPAA releases, attending doctor, diagnosis, treatment, and emergency contacts. On and on the information goes."

Then Alice reached into a right-hand file drawer and pulled up a flat file and turned it so Rosie could see the title: "THREE MYSTERY PATIENTS." She raised her eyebrows. "Not a single name could be confirmed with the name given at check-in. No names corresponding to the population records in Hamilton or Hico or in the entire Hamilton County. I have no other information, yet they are taking up ICU beds down the hall. What do you suggest I do?" Alice leaned back in her chair, fingers clasped on the desk, and gave a direct stare at Rosie.

Rosie realized this conversation was certainly not going to allow any secrets. *Well, here it goes. Help me, Lord.* She breathed in deeply and let it out. "I'm sure you've heard of what has occurred in the DFW metroplex over the last week."

Alice's nodded sadly, then narrowed her eyes.

Rosie shifted uncomfortably in her chair and cleared her throat. "I cannot tell you how difficult this is to say, but I had no alternative. I . . . I was responsible for removing those three children who were slated to be killed in the hospital where I work. Your fine facility was close and out of the sphere of the radical Islamic influence, at least for now, so this is where we brought them. I am begging for your mercy to let them stay in disguise, just for a short period." Rosie held her breath. Everything they'd worked toward was now in Alice's hands. Could she be trusted?

"I suspected as much." Alice rocked forward in her chair. "I just couldn't prove it. I was aware of the atrocities against the hospitalized children and elderly over there. News like that travels fast, and when I heard it, it really did turn my stomach. I had to know how those people believed they could get away with that kind of horrible treatment." She pursed her lips in thought. Finally, after what seemed like eternal moments, she nodded. "There is good and bad with your story. Obviously, I am pleased you got the children here safely, *but* . . . they are here without any records or shred of evidence of who they are. Cleburne is the county seat of Johnson County. That means this hospital is also the county hospital." She pursed her lips again and wheeled around in her chair, appearing to look out the window behind her desk. "Let's think about this for a moment." She paused for another thirty seconds before turning back around. "We do indigent care, but we also get audited monthly. Your kids can be part of our impoverished percentage for the county, but I need real, verifiable names to satisfy the county goons who breathe down my neck every month. They can't stay here long, though. How much time do you need?"

"I don't know, maybe a week or two," Rosie said, feeling relieved that at least Alice didn't intend to report them. *At least she isn't asking us to leave immediately.* "I'm working with the parents of the other two kids, and they are looking to me to lead on this deal. I wish I could promise that I will find a way to get them out of your hospital, but we are in very difficult circumstances with the radical Islamists. If you will just help us a little longer. We want them in the care of their own parents more than you can possibly want them out of here. We need time for these kiddos to regain some strength and get well. At this point, we have no other options."

Alice creaked back in her chair. "I could maybe give you—"

The telephone rang at Alice's desk, causing both women to jump. "I'll ignore that for now." But when the phone rolled over to voicemail, it immediately began to ring again. "Someone seems mighty insistent, don't they? Our hospital system is far superior to anything in Hamilton County. We can work out something, but I need names before you leave this weekend."

"Thank you."

"These are scary days indeed. If it were my Angie . . ." Alice stared at the photo again, then sighed. "We will do what we can."

A loud knock came at the door.

"For heaven's sake, what is it? Come in," Alice said loudly with undisguised exasperation.

A nurse poked her head in the door. "Excuse me." She looked at Rosie. "Frances wanted you to know that Chrissy is back with Craig doing physical therapy."

"Oh, okay," Rosie said. "Thanks for letting me know."

The nurse shut the door.

"Go see what Chrissy is doing with your son," Alice said. "Why don't we talk again in an hour or so?"

"Thank you, Alice. You have no idea how much I appreciate what you're doing for us."

As Rosie entered the ICU and walked past Ruth's room, she spotted two other nurses huddled with Frances and Dr. Ingram around Ruth's bed. Alarm bells of concern went off in Rosie's mind, so she slipped into the room. Frances began unhooking the monitor leads that ran to Ruth's arm and chest. Ruth's face and skin had an ashen pallor, and her lips were not the natural color.

"What's going on?" Rosie asked Frances when she got close enough to whisper a question.

"Rachel's BP has dropped too low. We suspect internal bleeding," Frances whispered back, with her hands still working feverishly to get Ruth ready to be rolled out the door. "We are getting no returns on her pulmonary artery past the spot where the lung tumor displayed on the MRI. Dr. Ingram is taking her to the OR to assist the surgeon who will staunch the bleeding and possibly remove the tumor."

As they started to wheel her out of the room, Rosie stepped up next to Ruth's head and whispered into her ear, "I'm right here with you, Ruth. You are in good hands now."

"I'm going down to get scrubbed up," Dr. Ingram announced. "Bring Rachel down to OR #2 as fast as you can. The anesthesiologist will meet you there to get her prepped."

"Are we cleared to roll? Come with me, Rosie," Frances said. "You keep talking to Rachel to encourage her as we push her down the hall."

Walking beside the hospital bed with her hands on the rails. "Come on, Ruth," she whispered. "We are nearly there. You got this. You can make it, sweetie. Hang in there. I'll be there when you wake up to see that pretty smile of yours."

As she walked toward the elevator after delivering Ruth to the OR, Rosie noticed Alice standing in the main area looking squarely at Rosie.

"She is one of my kids," Rosie told her, when Alice approached. "I never made it to my son's room and his PT, which is the direction I'm heading now."

"How about I see you around 4:00? I think I have an idea."

Rosie contemplated calling the Wallaces but decided to wait for the outcome of Ruth's surgery. She didn't want to worry the parents when there was nothing they could do.

CHAPTER 33

3:10 p.m.
Saturday, March 20

"ISN'T THIS OVERKILL?" Tom asked, sitting on the trail bench at the botanical gardens and watching Jamal pace back and forth. "Haven't we done this about ten times already?"

"There will be an announcement this coming Sunday on Channels 1 and 2 that the march has been moved up to this Tuesday. With everybody looking over my shoulder and second-guessing me, I can't afford any margin of error. This has to flow like clockwork." Jamal looked around for anything out of the ordinary. His senses had gone into overdrive, and he felt his paranoia driving him to be overly cautious. His anger rose over his friend's apparent lack of concern. "This is *serious*, Tom."

"I know," Tom said and tapped on the space next to him on the bench. "Would you sit down? Why would they suddenly change the date of the evacuation?"

"The caliph wants to throw the infidels off their ability to plan any escapes." Jamal gritted his teeth.

"You look like you're about to explode. What's up? Your appearance says *I'm guilty* as if you just robbed a bank. Come on, Jamal, relax and compose yourself. You got me out here to talk about the details of the march. This is new information, but I am the wrong

291

audience. I can't do anything about the plan changing. What is really eating you?"

Jamal resurveyed in every direction, then with a deep breath, he plopped down on the bench and exhaled loudly. "I got a call on my burner phone at 2:00 a.m."

"Your burner phone? I thought that was just between you and me, so we could get together without—" His face changed to concern. "Who called? Is that what has you all stirred up?"

"I gave that cell number to two other imams whom I've known from college days. One is Navid Uzell, whom you remember from UT. He is now the imam over Austin. The other imam is Ibrahim Kravit in San Antonio. I don't think you know him. But the call came from Navid. Long story short, we are all three being scrutinized closely, possibly even targeted by the Observer. This feels just like what happened with the Seattle imam." Jamal removed his skull cap, then ran his trembling hands nervously through his hair. When he replaced his cap, he gave Tom an edgy sideways glance.

"Hold on. When you say the Seattle imam, we both know how that ended. Are you saying . . ." Tom stroked his chin, clearly connecting the dots. "This is very serious . . . and certainly won't end well for you, if you're saying what I think you are." Tom shook his head. "But didn't the Seattle imam resist the dates of the march or behave like he wasn't completely in compliance with the caliph and his wishes?" This time Tom stood and paced, then faced Jamal. "Have you done anything to provoke the caliph's wrath?"

Jamal pulled out the burner phone and held it up, shaking it in his hand. "Your presence here and this place were all orchestrated in secret and rebellion with the caliph's directives. This phone was used to coordinate these meetings. In a word, *yes!* I have thwarted their ability to watch my every move, and they would qualify that as a provocation."

"Do you think it is true? You get a call in the middle of the night from Navid," Tom shrugs "Where did he get his information?"

Jamal could feel the paranoia creep over him, and he looked around again. "Don't ask me how Navid knows," he spat out. "He was told that the three of us are on a watch list. Do you know what it is like to live as if there is a nefarious person always watching you? Someone constantly recording your every move, ready to do you harm?"

Jamal deliberately released the tension in his hands and jaw. His attention was immediately drawn to the left as a lone male walker headed in their direction. "We better get moving." He examined the trails, then pointed to the right of where they were standing. "This way." He walked ahead without waiting for Tom.

Tom jogged to keep up.

"When the phone vibrated and woke me, I carried the phone *outside* to the patio to say my first words. Navid confirmed to me about the surveillance. His sources tell him that the three of us are to be eliminated, most likely after the march. The march takes two-plus days, then clean up, maybe four days. That means I probably have ten days to live." He stopped short, feeling his heartbeat quicken with terror. "What would you do?"

Tom paused, as though concentrating. "Have you thought anymore about Jes—"

Jamal poked his finger into Tom's chest. "Don't. Do not tell me Jesus is my friend or has all the answers. You called Safi and told her about your vision. You can't do that. You are my closest friend, and now you are ganging up on me—with my own wife?"

"He is the one who appeared to me and told me that I was to help you. Very same thing with Safi. Jesus is trying to get your attention. He can bring peace to you." Tom shrugged. "I have no idea what that will look like, but right now, he is your only hope."

Jamal shook his head. "That is no choice."

"What is wrong with this choice?"

"It would make me an apostate, which is an act of treason—a sin and a crime against Islam, punishable by death. Are you *trying* to get me killed?"

Tom's eyes widened. "Do you hear what you are saying? Think about it. Either way your Muslim brothers are going to kill you. Come to Jesus. His promise is eternal life, love, and acceptance. And don't forget forgiveness. You can walk with him in true peace. You are striving all your life for forgiveness and the acceptance of Allah."

"How dare you mention my Allah and your Jesus in the same breath!" Jamal stared with disgust at his friend. He looked back down the trail to see where the stray walker was. "You should be ashamed of yourself for bringing this up again. Jesus was a prophet but is not a savior. Bringing him into this conversation only clouds the real issue, which is about keeping me alive. I cannot abide by any conversation that includes your experiences. That doesn't help me." Jamal's body began to tremble with fear and anger.

Tom waited for the tension to ease as they stared at each other. "Jesus is offering this to you freely when you pray in belief and receive him. All you are trying to get rid of from the past, Jesus can wipe away. He makes you clean. It's the best offer you will ever get."

Jamal's torment felt as though it would overtake him. He took a threatening step toward Tom. "Did you not hear me?"

But Tom did not back away. "Loud and clear," he said, as he kept his eyes locked with Jamal's.

"You really do believe this stuff?" Jamal's heart continued to pound.

"I do. And I feel more convinced than ever that he is the only way—the only hope we have."

Jamal blinked and broke the stare, but he was still trembling. Looking down the path, he saw the person he had seen earlier now approaching them. "I can't talk about this anymore. I appreciate you coming out with me, but I am past done. We better go."

"I will continue to pray for you and your family," Tom said, now whispering. "I really do love you." Tom gestured to the right as they approached a "Y" in the trail. "My car is over here."

Jamal looked over his shoulder and breathed a sigh of relief as he saw the other garden visitor veer to the left.

CHAPTER 34

4:15 p.m.
Saturday, March 20

"SORRY I'M LATE," Rosie said as soon as she entered Alice's office. "It is so good to see my son that I'm having a difficult time pulling myself away."

"Have a seat." Alice pointed to the chair Rosie had sat in before. "How is our patient, Rachel, doing in surgery?"

"The surgery nurse made a routine call to ICU to tell Frances they'd been able to stop the bleeding and reestablish the blood flow. Rachel took two units of blood, and they've just begun to remove the tumor. Looks like it is all good so far."

"That it is good news for now." Alice picked up the skinny folder marked "THREE MYSTERY PATIENTS" and placed it in the middle of her desk. "Being in the position I am, I have access to a lot of data, including the property tax rolls of Hamilton County. With a population of about 8,400, you would think there would be a fair representation of the surnames Wilson, Reynolds, and Martin."

Alice picked up a computer-generated list from the side of her desk. "Only one Martin in the county records. Of all the names you guys picked to give to your smuggled patient Mike Hall being Matthew Martin is unfortunate and highly suspicious. Seems that our only Martin in the county was a Spencer Martin, who is in his nineties. He's a well-known fixture in the city of Hamilton and is now in a retirement home there. Spencer had all girls." Alice nodded toward the read-out. "You could see my investigation was not that difficult. On the other hand, my contact and access to this database is very useful."

Rosie wasn't following. "How could this help?"

"We find three names from the tax rolls that we can temporarily assign to the children and use those names to register them in this medical center. But . . . just like me finding this from the public record, it can also work against us. If I can find names to use in our scheme, someone else can use the exact same database to prove we used the names as a fraud. I can't afford that, and neither can you. For me, it's my job. But for you and these kids, it would likely be much direr."

Rosie's mind raced through the unknowns. "I see the dilemma. What kind of warning do you think we might have?"

"That would be hard to say. I've been here almost five years. I get along well with the director and the hospital board. I don't think I have any enemies, so an ambush on me is fairly unlikely. But we are in a hostile situation since the takeover."

Rosie bit the inside of her cheek. "Could you know in advance if someone else is probing the data?"

"No. It is public information. We are playing a deadly game."

Rosie shivered at the thought of someone finding Cooper and the others. "Who else would be looking into this? Why bother three kids in a small hospital in Cleburne?" She began fidgeting with her wedding ring, nervously taking it off and on, off and on. "Okay, which name do we start with first?"

* * *

2:30 a.m.
Sunday, March 21

Rosie was sound asleep, lying next to Cooper in his bed with her arm wrapped protectively around him, when she felt the bump of someone trying to stir her awake.

"Wake up, Rosie. We have to go now." Yosef was standing over her, shaking her body.

"What time is it?" Rosie asked, rubbing her eyes and standing quietly, trying not to wake Cooper. She reached down and covered him with a blanket where she had just laid, then kissed him on the forehead. "I'm going to miss you, my strong soldier," he told him. "May God be with you." She put her hand on his shoulder and silently prayed for God's protection and for Cooper's endurance while they were separated. She blinked back tears of pain that she had to leave him again.

"We must go," Yosef said, walking to the door.

She nodded, keeping her attention on Cooper. She needed to take one long, last look at him. "I love you," she whispered. Her eyes filled as she thought about their conversation before he fell asleep. She'd informed him she was going to have to leave, but she'd come back. He hadn't handled it well. It felt to him that he was losing both parents.

Yosef cleared his throat.

She nodded and then followed him into the hallway and past Frances.

"I'll keep him safe," Frances told her. "Don't you worry about it. Just trust that God's hands are big enough to take care of both of you."

"Thank you." *May it be so.*

CHAPTER 35

4:00 a.m.
Sunday, March 21

YOSEF'S AMBULANCE ROLLED to a stop in front of Rosie's house with all the truck running lights off.

"You are home," Yosef told Rosie as he quietly rattled around his driver's seat and shuffled back to the spot where she lay confined to the narrow gurney.

"I cannot thank you enough for giving me over a full day with my son, Yosef," she said, sitting up, watching him loosen her restraints. "The timing was perfect because he was rested and ready to talk and full of life. He was about 75 percent of his pre-accident self. You made the trip possible. You risked your life for me."

Yosef smiled at her. "We took the long way home. I watched at every stoplight and corner to be certain we were not followed. I saw no tail."

Except for the faint red interior light, Rosie could see only the streetlights and house lights of her neighborhood, along with the illumination from the waning moon. Before reaching for the side-door handle to exit, she touched his arm. "Once again, I will never forget how you've helped us. You and Dura will always be on my heart and in my prayers. Thank you."

* * *

9:50 a.m.

Rosie yawned and stretched after her brief night's sleep, which left her feeling emotionally drained and physically ragged. She glanced up at the rearview mirror and caught the bored and seemingly uncaring eyes of the escort who was driving her to Betsy's house to talk about the upcoming forty-something-mile march to their new living quarters in Waxahachie.

Rosie paid the escort and strode up the sidewalk toward Betsy's front door. Before she got to the porch, Betsy flung open the door, red curls bobbing. "Come in this house and tell me something I don't know."

"Betsy, it's so good to see you." Rosie ran the last ten feet into her dear friend's arms.

"It is by the grace of God that I am hearing about your boy from the 'underground' nurses and Dura, but I want to hear the details from you. Come into the breakfast room. I've fixed some home-made chicken salad." Betsy took Rosie's arm and intertwined hers into a guiding motion toward the back of the house. The kitchen table was already set.

Rosie walked to the big picture window looking out onto Betsy's picturesque backyard, filled with neatly trimmed trees and bushes with colorful flowers peeking from the mulch beds.

"Wow! This is beautiful! Is this what you've were working on since your 'leave'?"

"All the bulbs were there from previous years—the tulips, daf-fodils, and crocus. But I've had some time to rake the leaves, pull the weeds, and reapply the mulch. I've enjoyed myself." She sighed.

"We won't get to enjoy it very long, you know, with our forced evacuation. I hope the new occupants enjoy the view."

"Can I help with anything?"

"No ma'am," Betsy said. "Take a seat and relax." She brought the bowls of lettuce and chicken salad and a plate of croissants to the table. "Let me pray over this food, and then we can start eating."

She gave a short but heartfelt prayer, blessing the food and their conversation, then encouraged Rosie to dig in and not be shy.

"It all looks delicious," Rosie said, helping herself to a heaping spoonful of chicken salad. "We'll need to get our strength up for the march at the end of this week."

"That was something you missed while you were in Cleburne. Yesterday, Channel 1 announced that our march has been moved up—to this Tuesday."

Rosie's hand stopped midair. "Why? Did they say?"

"Oh, it doesn't seem to matter, does it? They'll get us moved out of town one way or another. Ugh, let's change the subject. Tell me about your weekend in Cleburne. Did you get to see Cooper? How did he look?" She took a bite of chicken salad with her fork and looked expectantly at Rosie.

"Can I say that yesterday was one of the best days and one of the worst days of my life? Best—" She held up an index finger on one hand. "Cooper looks great. He was awake and lucid. We talked, and he remembered Ramon and me. Worst—" She held up the index finger on her other hand. "He wanted to see his dad. We dealt with our emotions regarding Ramon's death, just as if Ramon had died that day. And for Cooper, Ramon's passing *had* occurred that day. It was terribly sad. But another best: the medical staff are excellent, and the charge nurse, Frances, is an older version of you. She is wonderful. Cooper's attending physician did his fellowship at Craig Hospital in Denver, which makes him fully prepared to handle Cooper's case. But another worst: when that doc called Craig Hospital to explain Cooper's situation, there was already a file on Cooper, not a boy named Craig, from the time Dr. Wilson called from Fort Worth months earlier, wanting to know how best to treat him. There we were with his and my name all over the file. There was no use denying it. I went into Cleburne in disguise as a gas station worker from Hico." She shrugged and tilted her head with a silly grin. "My cover was blown in the first five minutes."

"Oh no!" Betsy clapped her hand over her mouth.

"Oh, yes. But wait, another best: thankfully, he was a compassionate doctor who understood why I am doing things this way. And I found a sympathetic administrator, who has agreed to hide our three stowaways until they get better, or we get a place for them."

"That's great!" Betsy said in between bites.

Rosie shook her head. "But worst: now she is in a big mess because we came to them with bogus names that were not verifiable. She now has to hide these three in the shadows until some smarty pants asks the right questions, figures out who they are and where they came from, and blows the whistle."

"Ooh, not good."

"But best: I got to spend the most wonderful time with Cooper. We talked about everything. We talked and cried and hugged and cried some more. I met his PT helper, and she is a dandy. What a dynamo she turned out to be, full of life and enthusiasm. She got Cooper lined out, and he is about ready to walk. She would fit in well at Children's Hospital—in another world." Rosie paused a moment, put her hands on the table, and looked out into the backyard. *Another world.* Her eyes reddened and began to tear up. She reached down, took the napkin from her lap, and put it to her quivering lips.

Betsy reached over and patted her arm. "It's okay if you want to stop talking about it."

"No, I need to get through the worst part of the whole day. That is when I told him I had to leave and come back here to Fort Worth. He didn't understand. He thought I was there to get him out of the hospital and take him home so he could see his room and play with his friends and go to school." A sob broke through her throat.

Betsy patted her arm once again, which only made Rosie cry harder. "I knew this would hurt you. You were only there one day. Both you and Cooper were on an enormous emotional roller-coaster ride the whole time. I am so sorry for both of you."

Rosie lifted her chin and looked at Betsy. "I can't forget the look of betrayal on Cooper's face. We had this great day together. He was smiling, talking, and enjoying the evening, and then I told him I would be gone when he woke up in the morning. He cried and said he wanted to come with me. I *wanted* him to come with me. He couldn't survive the march. It was like a knife in my heart all over again. I lost Ramon, and now I feel like as soon as I've gotten Cooper back, I may lose him again." Rosie wiped her face with the napkin, waited a few moments, and took a couple of deep breaths to compose herself. "The reality is there is a chance I'll never see him again. I am simply having a hard time with that thought. Let's talk about something else for a while, okay?"

For the next several hours, they reminisced about their days at Children's Hospital and all the good times they'd shared. They rehearsed their lives together, experiencing the hand of God through the good doctors and staff and the positive atmosphere the hospital administrators and leaders promoted and encouraged.

"The best place on earth to work," said Rosie.

A heavy silence fell between them. Everything had changed and was changing.

Finally, Rosie broke the silence. "What can we expect about the march?"

"I still plan on spending the night with you Monday, so I guess I will have to use the escort one more miserable time," Betsy said. "That way we can be together. Most roadways will be blocked come about midnight Tuesday. According to Channel 1, the alarms will wake us at 6:00 a.m., and they are expecting us to 'muster,' as they called it, at 7:00 for a roll call. I have registered at your house, which is three miles closer to Waxahachie than my house. They expect us to cover twenty-five miles the first day. We will spend the night on the road, literally on the pavement, and then march the remaining twenty-plus miles the next day on into the camp."

Rosie shook her head in disbelief. "We are really going to do this?"

"I wish we had a choice."

"We can renounce Jesus and join Islam, which is really no choice. I can hear my youth pastor's admonition to memorize Isaiah 59:19." She looked up as though reading the verse in her mind. "'When the enemy comes in like a flood, the Spirit of the LORD shall lift up a standard against him.' Never have I seen such lawlessness. The enemy has come in like a flood. Let's see what God's standard looks like when it is raised up."

Betsy squeezed Rosie's arm. "Don't miss the obvious. God's hand raised up and spared Cooper and two others from the death angel when you smuggled them out of the hospital. The underground tells me that our place in the camp has already been secured. The medical workers are living in actual houses near the opening in the fence. There is a huge medical tent with a red and white striped top very close to our home."

"Amen. Don't forget comfortable shoes and plenty of water and something to eat. I looked at the weather, and it looks pretty good all week. The night will be cool in the forties but no rain. Lucky us!" Betsy said with a deadpan expression, then smiled.

A horn honked in front of the house.

"Your ride has arrived," Betsy said.

"I'm terrified about what is going to happen. But I'm also excited to see what God has up his divine sleeve. All we can do is trust him."

CHAPTER 36

9:45 a.m.
Monday, March 22

FAIZA SAT AT her desk organizing the files needed for the day when the office phone rang. She picked it up on the second ring. ""This is Faiza. May I help you?"

"This is the Observer. Where is Jamal? I see he is not in his office, and according to the bug at his house, he left there one hour and forty minutes ago. I know he hasn't called you."

Faiza sat up straighter and combed her fingers through her hair, obviously remembering she was on camera. She nervously cleared her throat. "You are correct, sir. He has not called in yet, but I do expect . . ."

"Of course, I'm correct! Find him and have him call me immediately." Frustrated, the Observer hung up. He watched Faiza gently cradle the phone, probably appreciating the fact that she was still on his screen. *She has good self-control. Let me see how she finds him.* He seethed with hatred for Jamal. *He is sticky sweet, yet I am convinced he is dishonest toward me—even though I haven't caught him in his deception. Keep going, little Jamal; your day will come.*

The Observer stroked the scar on his face.

* * *

10:00 a.m.

Jamal's phone rang. He'd just stepped out of Tom's car and was headed toward his own. The caller ID announced, "WORK OFFICE." He looked back at Tom and shrugged. "Hello, Faiza, what is going on?"

"The Observer. He seems very upset. Imam, I have been calling for the last fifteen minutes trying to find you. He wants you to call him. I think it has to do with the evacuation."

"I've been working on this march all weekend, including this morning," Jamal said, his voice amplified. "I know he must be on edge, but every detail has been reviewed at least three times with my team." He paused a moment and then sighed in disgust. "I will call him so he can relax. He should be as confident as I am that this will come off without a hitch."

He hung up and dialed the Observer's number.

"Where have you been?" The Observer's voice trembled with rage.

"My evacuation team had an offsite meeting to go over the march details one last time. Since the timeline has been moved up, we were making certain all essentials are covered, and as predicted, they are."

"Why didn't you answer the phone when I called earlier this morning? That is an act of complete insubordination. What if I, or the caliph, had wanted to get your attention on some pressing matter?"

"We are talking now, sir. How can I help you?" Jamal wanted to reach his hands through the line and strangle the man, but he knew he must stay in control. His life literally depended on it.

"I needed to talk to you earlier this morning, not now!"

"Sir, I was in a meeting with my subordinates, but I am available to talk right now. I noticed that your first call was at 9:35 a.m., just thirty-five minutes ago. How can I help you now?"

"I do not have time for playing games, Jamal. You are testing me, and I do not like to be *tested!*"

"Sir, I was with my team. Please call Omar to verify the time and place. All the team agreed before the event to leave our phones in our cars to minimize distractions during the meeting. I don't see how this is testing you. The results of the evacuation will show that we are all taking this very seri—."

"Shut up, Jamal. I am sick of your excuses. We will talk again tonight during the caliph's call."

As soon as he heard the call disconnect, he threw the phone into his car and went on a walk around the cultural district of Fort Worth to calm down. *Even when I try to do the right thing, I get chewed out. Is Allah as angry and difficult to please as they are?* His mind shifted to what Tom and Safi kept talking about: for-giveness through Jesus. *But if I accept Jesus, that is an instant death sentence for me and my family. . . . But so is getting on the wrong side of the Observer. There is still no escape.*

After his walk, though still angry, Jamal got back to his car and picked up his phone. He noticed a voice mail. He sighed and thumbed the password to hear the message. *What else can possibly go wrong?*

"Jamal, Omar here. The Observer called and wants us to have the same meeting in your office at 11:00. I called all the parties, and they are on point. See you then."

He glanced at his watch and realized he could just barely make the meeting on time. He really wanted to throw a fit, bang his head, and yell, but he knew that was exactly what the Observer wanted—proof that Jamal wasn't playing by the rules.

Come on, Jamal, keep it together. Don't let them get to you. Turn the car on. Drive back to the office. Play their game.

* * *

7:30 *p.m.*

The Observer sat in the control room and stared at the video image of Jamal. The forced repeat meeting went as well as could be expected. The preparations seemed airtight. But something still bugged him.

What am I missing? Jamal is doing everything we are asking him to do, yet, according to Uma and now Faiza, he disappears for several hours at a time. That makes me feel anxious. I must know what is happening.

Pushing himself from the desk, the Observer stood to clear his head. *There must be more clues on the video. I can't give up this easily.* He sat back down, queued up the beginning of the meeting, and this time he focused on the friend, Tom Larson. *Both Uma and Faiza think these departures are always with this Tom Larson. Where are they going, and what are they talking about?*

After scrutinizing the meeting and Tom, the Observer threw his arms up. "I don't get it! Tom looks like an ordinary person off the street."

Should I go to Fort Worth and follow them? He sat back in his chair and massaged the scar on his cheek. *I will be watching you tonight, Jamal, during our next call with the caliph. During this evacuation march, we will be moving upwards of 180 million infidels with no margin of error. You and the other imams will not mess this up.*

The caliph has made it plain to me this must run smoothly . . . or I will be killed.

PART 4

THE MARCH

CHAPTER 37

6:25 a.m.
Tuesday, March 23

"THAT WAS THE last hot shower for who knows how long," Rosie said as she walked into the kitchen. She wore her nurse's attire and her favorite walking shoes and carried a backpack. "How'd you sleep?" She dropped it on the counter and grabbed a muffin.

Betsy, similarly dressed, sat at the breakfast table, her open Bible lying in front of her and a half-drunk cup of coffee to her right. "Well, I woke up at 3:02 a.m. and couldn't go back to sleep, so I tossed back and forth. Then I got up and started reading Jeremiah."

"Now *there* is the feel-good book of the day," Rosie said.

Betsy gave a hollow laugh. "Israel kept ignoring God and walking—no, running—away from him. Clearly, I don't have God's mind, but I have to wonder if he didn't just say to Israel, 'Okay, have it your way.'"

"Is that when the bad guys came in and destroyed Jerusalem and hauled the rebellious Jews off to Babylon?"

"To slavery, yes." Betsy poked at the pages of her Bible. "Not without warning, though, which was Jeremiah's job." She sighed and shook her head. "I hope we aren't in that camp for seventy years because we didn't listen."

"The Jews were in Babylon for seventy years?" Rosie was surprised. She knew the story but hadn't realized how long they'd remained away from their homes.

"Yup." She stared off blankly for a few seconds, then clapped her hands together. "We need to get going." Her voice was filled with false bravado.

Rosie unplugged the coffee maker, rinsed out the pot, and wiped the counter down. "I simply can't leave behind a dirty house. Somehow my sweet mother would rise up and scold me." She turned toward Betsy. "Have you weighed your backpack this morning? Mine tilted the scales at twenty-two pounds. Do you think that's too heavy?"

"How much of that weight is water?" Betsy asked as she wandered to the front window and parted the curtains to look out.

"I guess about one-third of the total. I think I'll take some more water." Rosie grabbed four more bottles from the fridge and stuffed them into her bag. "What are you seeing out there?"

"The crowd has started to line up. Do you think we ought to be out there now?" Betsy walked over and picked up her pack. "One last potty stop."

"I'll be outside." Rosie slowly exited the front door, then turned and looked at her home for what she assumed was the last time. A deep sadness rolled over her.

This is where Ramon and I brought Cooper home as a baby. We planted a tree in the backyard, dreaming that one day Cooper would play under it, and we would plant a garden next to it, grow our own vegetables, and enjoy life together. She sighed. *Goodbye, my little house and all the dreams you held.*

Betsy stepped outside and shut the door behind her. "Stupid to ask, but . . . ready?"

"No, but then it doesn't really matter, does it?" Rosie asked as they began to walk down the street toward the crowd.

The tension was palpable as neighbors filed from their houses and looked on with anxious anticipation.

Two men from the patrol came trolling along on two separate four-wheelers, shouting instructions. "Each man, woman, and child must register. Have papers and armbands ready."

"Good morning, Velma," Rosie said, greeting her elderly neighbor, who looked frail and was shuffling along slowly, clinging to her daughter's arm. "Where is Eldon?"

"Daddy got sick, so we took him to the hospital," Linda, Velma's daughter, said, her eyes red from crying. "While at the hospital, they took him for tests, and he died."

"The doctors killed him!" Velma cried out.

"I am so sorry," Rosie said, redirecting her steps to hug and comfort Velma. But a patrol came between them.

"Keep moving. There are others behind you trying to get registered."

Rosie and Betsy exchanged looks, knowing full well what took place with Eldon. "I'm willing to bet my house that he was part of the purge," Rosie whispered. "You would have liked him—loved his wife, kids, and grandkids; yard-of-the-month guy and always had a story to tell. He just retired last year."

At the registration area at the end of Rosie's street, fifteen workers, each with a computer and a scanner, sat behind long tables. One of the workers barked out, "Next!"

Rosie stepped forward and held out her wristband so the worker could scan it. They never made eye contact until the computer screen brought up her face.

"*Confirm* if the information is correct," the cheerless worked stated, pointing to the confirm button on the screen.

She did as he directed, and he gave her a bib tag, which was immediately printed with the same bar code. "Pin this to your front. Must be seen at all times. *Next.*"

Rosie helped pin the bib tag to the front of Betsy's shirt, and then Betsy returned the favor. "Very stylish! Do you feel planned for?" asked Rosie with a cynical eyeroll.

"More like spied upon by the one and only—our big brother, the caliph," Betsy quipped under her breath.

Before they joined the gathering throng, each had to pass through a line-up of about twenty metal detectors and then be individually subjected to a wand for those who made the detectors squeal. This entire process of frisking the marcher did little to calm down the crowd before the start.

At precisely 7:00, a patrolman on a four-wheeler came along, shouting into a bullhorn, "Begin marching down Piedmont to Southwest Boulevard, which turns into 183, which becomes I-20, then on to Highway 287, where we will spend the night. You will notice the group will become increasingly larger. You must keep moving swiftly. Do not slow down! We will keep you motivated. Move out." He shot a large caliber handgun into the air several times, startling Rosie.

"Was that the equivalent of a 'pretty please'?" Betsy said.

In the distance, she heard more gunshots, signaling the beginning of their long march.

When they arrived at the corner of Southwest Boulevard, their group made the left-hand turn as directed. She slowed down to watch her group blend into the longest span of people she had ever seen. Thousands of walkers were already there, with an equal number to the west coming toward the intersection where her neighborhood merged with the boulevard. All four lanes of traffic filled with reluctant people, weighed down with backpacks, and some carrying walking sticks. Many of the participants wore sunglasses and hats, in case of unexpected sunshine on this cloudy day. The noise of people walking and talking, combined with the ever-present blasting from the megaphones to "hurry up, keep it moving, and pick up the pace," became a deafening cacophony.

Merging into the eastbound marchers, Rosie saw a family who looked familiar from her days at the medical center. The little girl was crying loudly.

"Estell Smith, is that you?" Rosie yelled cheerfully toward them. "It's Nurse Rosie! Will your mommy let you come over here and give me and Nurse Betsy a hug?" She looked at the little girl's mother. "Mrs. Smith, remember me? Nurse Rosie from Children's Medical Center?"

Estell stopped crying and looked at her parents for permission. They smiled reassuringly at her. "Yes, it's okay," her mom said.

Estell ran to Rosie and threw her arms around her.

"How long has it been since you were in PICU?" Rosie asked. "You sure do look good. Is that a new pair of walking shoes?"

"Yes!"

"She got out four months ago," Mrs. Smith said, joining them as they walked. "Her chronic asthma has not flared up until this last week when we started to talk about the march and leaving the house."

Rosie nodded, unsurprised. The stress had affected them all.

"We heard there had been trouble at the medical center, so we knew that was not the answer for her asthma attack," Mrs. Smith continued. "It is so good to see you and know you are close by for Estell. This must be the Lord's provision. You two worked such a miracle on her when she was with you at the center."

Rosie took Estell's hand. "Tell me about school. What grade are you in now? Because you look so big, I bet you're in the third grade. Am I right?"

"Nope," Betsy chimed in, reaching to take Estell's other hand. "She has to be at least in the fourth grade. I guessed right, didn't I, Estell?"

Rosie delighted in seeing this cute little cherub smiling up at each of them with her two front teeth missing and giggling away like any self-satisfied six-year-old.

"I'm only in first grade!" Estell announced, beaming with pride. She now had a skip in her stride that reflected a change of attitude. "I know I look old, and I'm really smart for my age cause that's what my teacher told me."

Rosie looked over her shoulder and winked at Estell's mama. "She has the confidence to get us all through the day, Mrs. Smith."

"Oh, please call me Virginia, and this is Max." She patted her husband's hand. "Now that we are out of the medical center, we should be able to drop the formalities, right?"

"Sounds good to me." Turning her attention to Estell again, Rosie asked, "When you were in school, did you have lots of friends? I bet you were one of the leaders in your class. Where was your school?" If Rosie could keep Estell occupied and distracted, they could make the best of a terrible situation. And possibly, this little girl could keep her mind off her own son. Though she missed Cooper, she was grateful he wasn't taking this long march with them. He'd never make it, she knew.

They passed the morning by making up games, including whispering 'secret' phrases like "God has a plan for us," then Estell would whisper back, "What is the plan?" "That we march all the way to the camp. Can you pray that with us as we march along?" Rosie and Betsy did their best to keep everyone's spirits up. That seemed especially important given the hundreds of menacing-looking patrolmen in their camo uniforms on their four-wheelers. All the riders wore ammo bandoleers diagonally strapped across their chests and pistols on either side in holsters, which made them appear even more aggressive and stern. They rode on both sides of the column of people, who stretched across the interstate. These men seemed to thrive on terrorizing the marchers with threats and insults.

By midday, Rosie, Betsy, and the Smith family were growing tired of trying to keep in step with the thundering multitude. Modesty was quickly becoming a thing of the past. The group handled calls of nature as discreetly as possible in the center median. Most learned to watch their step. Rosie saw and participated in a "huddle," where several women went to the median and took turns being in the middle while the other women faced outward, providing some bit of privacy. As embarrassing as it was, how else could they get their needed relief? The guards were certainly not allowing rest stops.

"Not to sound too much like Estell, but how far do you think we've gone?" asked Virginia.

"I have a folded map I put together for this very purpose." Rosie pointed toward her backpack. "Would you mind getting it out for me? It's in the section with the top yellow zipper."

Virginia pulled out the makeshift road map and handed it to Rosie, who studied it as they walked. "I think by the road signs, we've passed Forest Hill. That means we are here." She pointed to the spot with a prewritten sticky note that read, "Thirteen miles completed. Thirty-two miles to go." A crooked smiley face stared at them next to the announcement.

Betsy wandered over. "Where are we?"

"See here?" Rosie's finger skidded off the mark slightly. "You get the idea. We are almost to the right turn to 287, where we will start going southeast, which is nearly a straight shot to the camp."

Betsy nodded and pulled out a sandwich from her bag and began to eat it.

Rosie checked on Estell, who was in Max's arms. "Estell looks exhausted. Can you imagine how the other two or three hundred thousand children are managing this walk? Poor kids. And think about the pregnant mothers. And look at all these elderly people. We've got to pray for them."

"Those poor parents and old people," said Betsy between bites.

"I'm simply trying to visualize myself at the camp tomorrow night," Rosie said, wiping the sweat off her brow with her sleeve. She looked up at the cloudy sky. "We have the Lord to thank for the clouds, but somehow I'm still drenched."

Shots fired out, making the group around them jump in surprise. To the right side of the highway, Rosie saw marchers craning and pointing to a young man running down an exit ramp from the highway. Her gaze followed their pointing.

The fourth shot, from a rider on a four-wheeler, dropped the runner into a crumpled heap in the ditch.

"Such a needless waste of life," Rosie said out loud, cringing inside with grief. *Did his family have to witness his murder?*

The driver turned to the marchers and waved his gun. "I need three of you guys to come over here to drag this idiot back to the main road," he shouted from his bullhorn. "Right now. Three men, or I will shoot into the crowd." Nothing happened immediately. He shot but no one dropped. The marchers ducked and covered their heads in fear. Rosie looked around but saw no one wounded. "I think he fired over our heads."

Right after that single shot, five guys came out of the ranks to pick up the runner and pull him back to the side of the road. The patrol took the opportunity to shoot the dead man in the head, right in front of all the marchers. One of the patrols got out his scanner and held it up high for all to see, then he read the dead man's armband and bib tag. "Don't you ever try to run on me; this is where you will end up," he shouted into the crowd. "Your friends will be stepping over you to get down the road. Now get moving. Pick up the pace."

The scene awoke Estell, who clung to Max in terror, crying at top volume and joining the wails of about fifty other children in the surrounding area.

Once again, the patrol rider got back on his megaphone. "Get those kids to shut up. I can't have a bunch of screaming babies in my group!"

"That settled the kids right down," Betsy said under her breath. The mothers and dads seemed to collectively get the kids to calm down, but they all walked faster.

"What was the point of making such a show of reading the runner's bar code?" asked Rosie.

"Maybe the Muslims are as meticulous at record keeping as the Germans were of the Jews during WWII," Betsy said. "I would guess that we'll be scanned in when we get to camp tomorrow night. That way, they know who started, who got killed, or otherwise didn't complete the march, and who checked into camp."

"Sure, if I were the caliph, I would want to know that. But who is going to keep track of us inside the camp?" Rosie tripped over a pothole, making her feet explode in pain. "Ugh. Are your feet sore yet?"

"They're killing me." Betsy took a friendly swipe at Rosie. "I don't need you to remind me of my total discomfort."

An hour later, Rosie's attention was distracted from the normal march when she saw two young men break from the column and begin running into the oak brush in two different directions.

They must have discovered the patrol's routine, she thought, realizing that they made their break right after he drove past them on his four-wheeler. *I'm not sure those guys are going to make it.*

Another patrolman, guarding a group farther back, saw the escape and came roaring up, shooting his pistol in the air to grab the attention of the unaware patrol rider.

The men began yelling on their radios to bring in a jeep with a machine gun. As the column marched on, within moments, the sound of heavy automatic gunfire filled the air. And not long after, the four-wheeler patrol brought the bullet-riddled bodies back to the group, so all could see the foolishness of trying to escape.

The two bodies were stacked on top of each other on the back of his four-wheeler with their limp heads and arms bumping into each other, allowing the marchers to get a repulsive view of the runners' bloody fate.

"These two idiots didn't listen to me. When I told everyone not to run, I wasn't kidding," the patrolman said into his bullhorn.

"I think he is making his point," Rosie said. "We don't need to see all this gore. These innocent children certainly shouldn't have to endure this torture. This is pure evil."

"I need two volunteers to take these two thugs off my machine," he bellowed.

Three men came forward, then one returned to his spot with a relieved look on his face. They chased the four-wheeler rider who sped up about fifty yards. When the two helpers caught up, the rider was off his vehicle, pointing to the ground where he wanted the bodies laid—right in the marchers' path. Then for sick pleasure, Rosie assumed, the patrolman shot both the blameless assistants.

From the crowd came a stifled scream, presumably from a loved one of the helpers. The rider immediately held up his weapon and cocked it, and slowly scanned the group with an evil side-eyed glare as if looking for the mourner. Rosie noticed everyone quickly put their eyes to the front. If this heartless rider was trying to instill more fear and remove any hint of compassion, it was working. Nonchalantly, he scanned the wristbands of all four dead men, then carelessly dropped their limp arms. The remains of the unfortunate were left in the road, forcing the marchers to step over them. The guard yelled into his horn again. "Don't let your friends run off, or I will shoot you too. You must complete your march to the camp. Now pick up the pace."

*   *   *

3:50 p.m.

"It's a pretty blue sky today, isn't it?" Rosie said to Estell, who was back walking with her.

Before Estell could answer, a patrol rider sped past and stopped six to eight rows ahead of them and began hollering at a particular marcher. "You in the blue shirt. Yeah, you, pick up the pace, old man. Can't you see you are slowing down the line behind you? Don't make me come in there after you!"

Estell tightened her grip on Rosie's hand. "I don't like that mean man," she said in a loud whisper.

"He hasn't been my preference either," Rosie said, bending down to speak into Estell's ear. "He may be a mean man, but he is not our concern. We must keep marching as he suggests, no matter how mean he is. This time tomorrow, we might be where we need to be—at our new home. Our job is to keep marching."

The belligerent patrolman kept driving up and down the column and shouting obscenities at the slow movers, continuing to pay specific attention to the struggling man in the blue shirt.

The older man was losing ground in his pace and was now just one row ahead of Rosie. She could see he was not being defiant; he seemed to be giving his all for his age. His walk was becoming a limp, perhaps from the pain of the long journey.

"Hey, old man in the blue shirt. You're walking like an old lady now. What's the matter with you? Don't you have any pride? Straighten up and walk like a man, clumsy old fool. I told you, don't make me come in there. Even little snot-nosed kids are passing you. Pick up the pace, you miserable clown."

Rosie was close enough that she could hear the old man praying. Her heart went out to him, praying for him herself that he would be given renewed strength to finish the march.

"Are you alone? Do you need any help?" Rosie leaned forward and asked him.

"My daughter and her family live in Houston with three of my grandkids. I couldn't get moved down there in time before the march." He could barely respond between wheezes.

The bullying patrol shouted in Rosie's direction. "Hey, are you talking to him? Shut up and leave him alone. Step away from him, *right now!*"

She began to despise the heartless enforcer for his lack of compassion. She knew she had to guard her heart to keep from wanting to claw the mean man's eyes out.

Nothing seemed to change with the blue-shirted old man, who fell back another row from Rosie. She kept looking over her shoulder to see what was happening to him.

But when a shot rang out, she instinctively knew. She looked back, and when she couldn't see the man, she moved to the side of the road. There he was. Dead. The patrolman was scanning his wristband.

The gunshot, now so close, caused Estell to panic. She began thrashing her head back and forth, struggling to breathe. Max pulled out Estell's inhaler and tried to get her to take it. But with her thrashing, he couldn't make a successful connection. They would have to stop walking, which, as they all knew only too well, could get one or all of them shot.

"In PICU, we would give her a slight sedative to calm her and then administer the puffs of albuterol," Rosie said. "Can we talk to her, while you hold her, Mom, and Dad pushes the plunger for the medicine? We have to be quick so Grouchy doesn't get trigger-happy."

The words of the bullhorn came. "Hey, you in the group. Move it. If I have to come in there, my pistol will be out and ready for use."

"Okay, let's give it a try," Max said, ignoring the threats.

Hurry, please calm down. Come, Jesus, and give her peace.

"Come on, baby girl," Virginia said in a soothing tone. "We need you to breathe this medicine. Mama needs your help. Please open your mouth and take a deep breath when your daddy pushes the button."

"That's right, Estell," said Rosie, stroking her hair. "Remember how we did this in the hospital? You took two short breaths, and then we pushed the button on the big deep breath. It's easy. So here we go. One, two . . . three."

Max pushed the button, and within moments, Estell started to settle down.

From the right side, Rosie could feel the evil of the patrolman approaching her, when out of nowhere, someone hollered at the top of his lungs, "They are running on you, moron."

Rosie turned to see the patrolman, who was only feet from her, race back to his four-wheeler. *Those runners may have saved Estell's life with their distraction. How quickly fear tactics change everything?*

She was grateful that Estell was unaware of what just happened. The little girl relaxed in her mother's arms and took a huge draw of breath into her lungs.

"Thank you, Jesus! We better get moving now; nothing good is going to come from those escapees," said Rosie. Just then, blasts of a machine gun went off, and everyone seemed to quicken their pace.

Rosie heard murmurings coming from behind them that the runners were indeed dead. Eyewitnesses reported that the wounded escapees were brought to the road and shot execution style. Rosie felt the fear level elevate in the marchers when they began to trek at a faster pace without anyone needing to shout at them. A lady, five people over, screamed out, "I don't know how much more I can take!"

"You can make it," a few women around her said. "They are trying to scare us into giving up. We are all in this together."

It's like we are cattle being driven to the market. The threats were punctuated by the random acts of violence and harassment. Clearly, all the marchers were tired and their nerves on edge. Conversely, the patrol seemed to increasingly enjoy their power.

The exhaustion and emotion were getting to be too much for Rosie, so she finally asked Betsy, "Can you remind me of some of the good we used to do at the medical center?"

"That's easy," Betsy said. "Remember Paula who came in with a clubbed foot? Dr. Wilson got her foot turned around, but you and I helped her through the dangerous allergic reaction she was having. Her parents brought her back to show us she could walk out of there."

Rosie smiled. "Yeah, I remember." She inhaled deeply and wondered about their future. "We did some good, didn't we?" Betsy nudged her. "And we will again."

CHAPTER 38

Tuesday, March 23
8:30 p.m.

THE SUN WAS setting through the trees behind them. Rosie's throbbing feet, sore legs, and aching back was telling her they had seen enough action for the day.

"See that overhead sign for Mansfield?" Rosie said. "That means we're almost to Texas 360 Toll Road. I remember the toll road on my map because I placed a huge star there. We have eighteen miles to go to the camp. We're more than halfway there. Thank you, Lord."

"I am more than ready to rest for the night. I bet they have foot massages and nice warm baths for the ladies." Betsy's sarcasm caused Rosie to smile.

Rosie nudged Betsy and pointed. "Have you noticed those poles?" Tall poles with clusters of perhaps twenty lights on the top of each stood erect along the side of the road.

"Yeah, we started passing them about an hour ago. I bet those are our night lights."

The patrol came racing by, yelling, "Everyone, stop walking. This is where you will spend the night. Spread out but stay on the road."

"Great," Betsy said. "Our lodgings are literally on the pavement of this highway."

With no location more appealing than any other, they all collapsed where they were.

"I'm whipped," Betsy said, removing her shoes to rub her feet.

Rosie lay on her back, using her backpack as her pillow and closed her eyes. But the lights were bright, and the gasoline engines to run the lights were noisy. People around her in every direction were moaning or crying. She also heard children crying, wanting a blanket or a drink of water. Exhausted parents were doing their best to comfort them.

If I'm grateful for anything, Lord, it's that you've got Cooper in a safe place where he doesn't have to endure this nightmare.

When she finally drifted off to sleep, gunfire jerked her awake. She could only hope that the runners' deaths had been quick and painless.

* * *

10:00 p.m.

Jamal looked up from the frenetic pace of the incoming march information to see his cherished family photo taken a year ago. *Such happy faces. How far we have come. How I miss those simpler times when we were a loving family.*

"Hey, Jamal, just got another call." Omar's voice snapped Jamal back to business. "They are reporting the crowd is mostly lying down for the night with minimal movement."

He'd been receiving reports throughout the march, collecting data from the three hundred open-air jeeps with drivers and spotters. The first reports had come in from all over the DFW area at 9:00 a.m. that the infidels were beginning to move south as planned and that there hadn't been much trouble.

Jamal had anticipated runners, slow walkers, and stubborn people, so he gave the patrol a wide latitude for using fear tactics and outright murder to keep the crowd moving. The spotters informed him that the random shootings had accomplished that goal, and the terror tactics had kept the infidels moving according to the timetable the caliph had established.

His big concern, and the wildcard of the entire march, was the overnight stay on the highway. The cover of darkness was overcome by the five thousand gasoline-generated light plants, which turned the night into day along the highway, so no one got the idea of escaping. He hoped the marchers would be so exhausted that no one would have the strength or inclination to attempt running or rioting. But he also recognized that prisoners would take any opportunity, so he called on the local law enforcement to walk the perimeter to beef up the security.

"Are you going to take a nap?" Omar asked Jamal, nodding toward the couch in his office, their makeshift command center.

"Not a chance," said Jamal. "This is too important." *No way will I take a chance resting and have something come up that could give the caliph any excuse to take me out. Was the caliph using the same tactics on him that he was using on the marchers? Fear, intimidation, and bullying with a huge advantage like a rat trapped in a corner with no escape. Is this how his marchers felt?*

During the night, Jamal had multiple reports of isolated runners trying to escape into the shadows of the night, all of whom were shot before they got to the service road off the highway. The most egregious attempt was a mass effort by twenty-plus infidels. As the report went, evidently, their plan was to lie next to the edge of the road to get the shortest distance to their escape route. They all stood simultaneously and ran for the buildings of the town near the highway. The guards immediately began shooting, and the patrol believed they got all the participants in the attempt.

"How can you know that *all* were shot?" Jamal asked.

"It was dark," said the spotter who was giving the report, "so we counted the best we could, and we collected that many bodies. Unless someone knew one of the homeowners, and he went into that house, we got them all. What do you want us to do?"

Jamal glanced up at the cameras pointing at him. "What is the margin of error that we are talking about? Did you see any house lights come on?"

"With all that gunfire going on around you, would *you* turn on your lights?"

"I guess not. Let's leave it and say we got them all." Jamal knew full well this conversation and the entire evening was on the Observer's radar. Jamal was doing as much as he could by the book. He would know in a week, when the final tally came in on the computer read-out, of the balance of infidels who were scanned in and were not accounted for when they checked into the camp.

I am getting weary of such close scrutiny. Safi was correct in wondering how long I can live like this. Truth is, I don't know.

* * *

6:30 a.m.
Wednesday, March 24

The sounds of the lights and engines shutting off broke through Rosie's fitful sleep, and she opened her eyes and groaned. "What a horrible night," she muttered, remembering the nightmares that had terrified her when she'd finally fallen asleep. She had relived all the terrifying events they'd experienced the day before—the executions and the people becoming so jaded that they'd stepped over bodies and even pushed bodies to the side in their continued march forward.

Betsy stirred. "I need a good massage and some chiropractic care."

"How many gunshots did you hear last night?" Rosie asked, hoping they were all just in her dreams.

"Too many to count. I hope today will be better and that people will focus on the task and realize the escape to glory will not work. What do we have in that backpack for breakfast?"

"Looks like trail mix." Rosie pulled out a bag and handed it to Betsy.

"You have thirty minutes to eat your breakfast and take care of business, then we are all walking south," the patrolmen yelled through their bullhorns. The guards seemed too fresh to be part of the night patrol. "We've got another day of marching ahead of us to get to the camp. Then you can find your living quarters and start your new life. It is a shorter walk today."

Rosie looked at Betsy. "Ooh, doesn't that sound promising?"

As they began to walk, Rosie thought her feet were going to explode. She'd felt blisters starting and prayed they wouldn't get worse.

The morning went much the same as the previous day's walk, except everyone struggled to keep up a fast pace. Even with the threat of violence, the group couldn't manage a quick tempo. The elderly and children were having a particularly difficult time. Rosie ached for them.

"Look at that cute old couple holding hands over there," Rosie said, pointing to her left. "You can see him kind of stooped over with a tan straw hat, and she is in a red garden hat." They shuffled along, not even attempting to keep up with the group.

"The red hat caught my attention way up ahead. Now we're about to pass them," Betsy said. "Hope the red hat doesn't get the attention of the patrol."

"My heart goes out to them for trying to keep up. What were they supposed to do? Stay home and become Muslims? We all know what the first step would be." Rosie and Betsy looked at each other knowingly. "Renounce any previous other gods or religious affiliations," Rosie said, shaking her head. "Never."

Rosie cringed a few minutes later when a patrolman predictably called out the couple. And a few more minutes passed when she heard two gunshots. Tears came to Rosie's eyes. As they continued to march, murmurs reached her that the elderly couple were still holding hands when they died.

Rosie could see the strain on the parents of the small children, newborn babies, and even pregnant mothers. She could tell that for many, the first day was all they had in their reservoir of stamina. Even Estell no longer complained but marched dutifully next to her parents when Max refused to carry her any longer on his shoulders. In just one day's time, they had compliant, obedient followers. The caliph was a master at mind control and manipulation, but Rosie still had a fire in her. She knew God was not finished yet. He had to have a purpose in this process.

Occasionally a family flagged down a guard and begged for leniency on behalf of an expectant mother, an utterly exhausted child, or an injured walker. In each case, the guard belittled the request through the megaphone. "Get back in the line or get shot" was always the answer. Sadly, too many of them ultimately gave up and took the death option.

Help us, Lord, to reach our goal.

Approaching the noon hour and watching the mile markers, Rosie mentally calculated their location. "I think we're about three to four miles from the goal," she announced. "We can do this. We can make it."

By 2:30, up in the distance, Rosie noticed the reflection of the white tops of tents. "Look ahead of us. You can see it!" she yelled as the camp became visible with its sea of tents. Soon a twelve-foot fence with concertina wire on the top came into view on the right.

"Hallelujah, we are nearing the end," Betsy exclaimed with a big grin. They gave each other a high five. It was amazing how a place they had dreaded for weeks became a reason to celebrate.

"We're going to make it, Estell!" Rosie turned and yelled to the little girl. "After all this walking, you can see where you will live. Look right over there." She pointed ahead.

Max lifted Estell onto his shoulders so she could see.

Cries of "Almost there!" echoed down the line of marchers behind them. The walking pace picked up. Rosie noticed that a huge section of fence, maybe a half mile in length, was missing as part of the extraordinarily wide entrance to the camp. Getting closer to the border, Rosie could hear multiple bullhorn announcements.

"Each person must be scanned in before entering the camp. Dip your right index finger into the purple dye after you have been scanned." These messages repeated over and over. Rosie saw hundreds of roped-off cattle chutes for the walkers to get in lines to get scanned and fingers dipped. This process took only a few seconds for each person, so the momentum of the crowd barely slowed down.

Once through this small registration process, the huge multitude poured into the camp, like water spilling over the top of a dam during a flood. The people began running in stampede fashion to find their own living quarters. The patrol was now forced to keep the peace within the camp, directing the five-million-plus marchers to the unoccupied tents farther back from the entrance. Again, any sort of dispute was handled by gunshots to the head—only now, no one seemed shocked.

Approaching the confusion of the chutes, Rosie and Betsy hurriedly said their goodbyes to the Smiths. "We are so proud of you, Estell, for making it the entire way," said Rosie. "You won't have to sleep on the ground tonight."

"But where is my house?" asked Estell, looking at her mother.

"Don't worry, we'll find it," Virginia said. She turned her attention to Rosie and Betsy. "We couldn't have made it without you two. Max and I will always be grateful for all your help."

"Our pleasure," Rosie said. "Make sure you come to the main medical tent with the red-and-white-striped roof near the main gate to tell them where your home is. We will get together later when we all get settled."

Once Rosie and Betsy were scanned, Rosie wondered where Dr. Wilson was. "Dr. Wilson told me that the medical staff would be staying in houses close to the fence entrance and near the main medical tent."

She and Betsy found a utility pole to stand next to, getting out of the rush of people. "Can you see the red-and-white stripes of a medical tent? And any houses near them?"

Betsy squinted. "Way over there," she said, pointing to the east across the stream of people.

Grabbing the utility pole for stability, Rosie got up on her tiptoes and looked in the direction Betsy was pointing. "That has to be our spot." Rosie felt exhausted. "This will be like swimming upstream."

Together they crept across the half mile of the strong flow of cranky but motivated people looking for their own place of rest.

"Will you look at that," Rosie said, approaching the row of six houses, glad to be away from the collisions and bruises she'd just received. The patrol stood guard with their legs shoulder-width apart and rifles held in both hands. They were located at the four corners of each home to ensure that the homes were not entered or otherwise vandalized.

"We get to stay in one of these houses?" asked Betsy under her breath as they walked past the second house. "How are we supposed to get past these goons to get inside?"

"I'm not sure," Rosie said. "Let's go over to the medical tent to see if we can find Dr. Wilson."

Rounding the corner to the front of the medical tent, they discovered more guards, along with a line of people apparently waiting to be seen by the medical staff. "Here goes," said Rosie, stepping to the front of the line.

"Hey, no cutting!" someone shouted angrily.

"Do you want our help or not?" Betsy yelled back in her best New York accent, with a grand gesture of running her hands down her obvious nurse outfit. "We work here."

When Rosie and Betsy got inside the tent, the "receptionist" who sat at a folding table asked how she could help. Rosie scanned the interior space. A hand-printed name tag on a folded piece of cardboard placed on the table read "Cheryl." Stacks of papers were neatly placed around her table, and boxes stood stacked up behind her along canvas walls, making for spartan accommodations.

"Cheryl?" Rosie said, pointing to the name plate.

The receptionist nodded.

"Hello, my name is Rosie Chavez, and this is Betsy Thompson. We are here from Fort Worth Children's Medical Center. We have come to help Dr. Wilson. Can we see him?"

The receptionist gave them both a quick once-over. "What are your names again?"

This time Cheryl wrote down their names and excused herself. She returned in only a few minutes. "He would like to see you right now. Follow me."

The three of them walked through what seemed like a maze. "This looks pretty sterile for a mobile-style hospital," said Betsy. "Look, this is washable canvas floor, there are air filters, and I see poles to hold the walls separate for the exam rooms, I would guess."

"Dr. Wilson designed this tent," Cheryl said and pointed over her shoulder. "Had we made a left back at that corner, you would have seen the triage room, which is a huge place, about half the tent. That is where the people in line will first go to get evaluated." She stopped in front of a flap. "Here you are. Behind this flap is Dr. Wilson."

When Rosie and Betsy pulled back the flap, there sat Dr. Wilson in a white lab coat, along with his wife, Helen, who was dressed in nurse's scrubs. He jumped from the table he was sitting on and hugged them both.

"It is so good to see you and to finally be here after the long march," Rosie said, with an exhausted sigh. She pointed to Betsy. "I couldn't have made the trip without her. What a nightmare."

"Here, sit down and drink some water." Helen handed them each bottled water.

Dr. Wilson reached into his satchel and pulled out two picture IDs on lanyards and handed them to their respective owners. "This will get you past the guards and into building B. There are eight of us medical workers in that house. Always drink boiled or bottled water. I believe we have a water problem—or we're undoubtedly going to. Maybe a possible outbreak of cholera. With the infusion of millions of people, it will spread through this camp like wildfire. Intended by our captors or not, it will surely get grim around here in very short order."

"What is the evidence of cholera? Isn't it a little too soon to be detecting this?" asked Rosie before she guzzled down the fresh water.

"Interestingly, two of the patrol guards came in yesterday with severe diarrhea and vomiting and an inability to retain fluids. Incubation period is anywhere between two hours to five days. They have been tested, and it is cholera. These guards have easily been at the camp five days. I asked them about their water source. They were using well water close to the main gate. Both were shipped off to who knows where. I wish I could send off some samples to the lab back in Fort Worth to confirm. Incidentally, the entire patrol has switched over to bottled water, which will become a premium. Now we are under a boiled water restriction. Always use the boiled water, even to brush your teeth, by the way."

Rosie cringed.

Dr. Wilson sat on the table again. "I had a wild hunch before coming down here that the conditions would be primitive, so I fished around and was able to get my hands on fifty thousand doses of the cholera vaccine, which is stored in building B. Helen will take you two over there so you can get cleaned up and grab a bite to eat. She will also get you inoculated after the meal. Get a good night's rest. Tomorrow, we hit the ground running."

"Where will we be?" asked Betsy.

"In the big room for triage. We will see a lot of foot, leg, and back trauma before the big stuff begins in the next two to ten days, if my predictions are correct."

"What about the remaining doses of the vaccine?" asked Rosie.

"There are about five thousand healthcare workers spread out in the three hundred medical centers and clinics that are distributed across the camp. Those workers got the vaccine as they arrived over the last week to help set up the medical facilities. Then I guess we are picking winners and losers after that on the remaining dosages, and that bothers me a lot. Even if we had 2 million doses, we would be several million doses short."

"This is like a death camp, isn't it?" asked Rosie.

"There is reason to believe that," said Dr. Wilson grimly.

"Though all this sounds scary, we do still know how to pray. We are bold enough to believe that God isn't finished with us yet." Rosie smiled. "See you tomorrow."

That night as she lay in bed, her thoughts went to Cooper. She sighed from missing him but was grateful he was still someplace safe. All the children here, she knew, were having their childhoods stolen from them. No playgrounds, no place to call home, and care that was not up to decent standards. When he got better, this was the environment to which she was going to bring her son. How was she going to explain to him how this had happened to him and his friends, even when she couldn't understand it herself?

Welcome to your new life, Rosie Chavez.

CHAPTER 39

3:35 *a.m.*
Thursday, March 25

JAMAL READ ALOUD the items on the report from the spotters: "One, the slowest marchers have long since made it across the fence line. Two, the contractor who built the fence has moved twenty of the light plants from the area where the marchers spent the night down to the camp. Three, the illumination from the lights allowed the crew to put up the fence and razor-wire topper. And finally, four, the camp perimeter is secured, and the march itself has been completed."

The small group gathered in his office spontaneously applauded. Jamal leaned back in his chair, folded his arms across his chest, and beamed with satisfaction. *We did it.*

The camp was now officially sealed, the presumed threat of the infidel uprising was over, and the leadership should be able to breathe a sigh of relief. Jamal's remaining task was now to prepare a wrap-up for the conference call with the caliph, including the tallies for the number of rounds of ammunition spent and the estimated number of dead infidels who were shot trying to escape. Then he needed a number for the separate category of infidels who died from exhaustion, exposure, or natural causes. The spotters and the patrol scanners had collected all these figures. Jamal knew the caliph would use these records to contradict a potential groundswell of world opinion against the seeming radical Islamic cruelty.

Jamal looked at Omar and the others, then he looked over the report one more time. "I have been worrying about this march since I heard about it back in January. Now it is over. What a load off our backs this represents, gentlemen. Why don't you guys take tomorrow off and get some rest? Send word to the other workers that they, too, deserve a day off. I'll see you the day after tomorrow."

That raised everyone's spirits even more, and they all laughed and chatted easily as they headed out of Jamal's office. By 4:30, Jamal was happy to drive home to get some long-awaited sleep.

When he turned off the freeway and drove down the avenue of his housing subdivision, he noticed the homes of his former neighbors who chose to remain infidels. *What is going on?* He slowed to take in the numerous pickups and U-Haul trucks backed into the driveways of these homes.

Anger boiled up within him. *I've been working my tail off, while these guys are stealing?* He drove by three houses where men were hauling furniture and electronics out.

Jamal pulled up to one of the driveways and parked, leaving the car running. He took his mobile phone out and snapped pictures of the license plates of the pickup and U-Haul. Then he got out and took pictures of the other vehicles along the street.

"Hey! What are you doing?" one of the "movers" shouted.

Jamal clicked "send" on his text to the regional imam, which included the license pictures. "This is the Alvarez home. They were friends of mine. This family left yesterday morning to go to Waxahachie. What are *you* doing?"

Three men stopped their activity. Two were carrying a large flat-screen television, and the other put an armload of electronics with their loot onto the tailgate.

"We are cleaning out their houses," one of them stated. "This stuff is ours for the taking. The word is out on the street that the houses are unprotected, and everything is free for whoever wants it. We want it. They were unbelievers."

Marshalling up all the courage he could, Jamal shouted with bravado, "This property is owned by the caliph of the United States of Islam. This house was locked when you arrived, was it not?"

The three guys looked at one another with a brief recognition of reality. "What about those guys over there? And there?" Another of the men pointed to several different houses where similar looting was in full swing.

"They are, indeed, breaking the law as well," Jamal said. "Now since you are stealing from the caliph, and I am the officer of the mosque and the imam for the Dallas Fort Worth area, I have photographed your license plate numbers and theirs. They are already texted to the regional imam and are now in the possession of the caliph." He crossed his arms. "I strongly suggest you start putting that property back into the house. The caliph does not like to be trifled with or made to be a fool. Fact of the matter, our dear caliph, peace be upon him, loves to use the authority that he possesses to set the record straight. Stealing from a fellow Muslim has a punishment. Do you know what that is?"

Jamal looked each of them in the eye as he pulled up the sleeve of his right hand and extended the hand out stiffly. With his left hand high above his shoulder, he brought his hand down like a karate chop. His right hand went limp. "Under Sharia Law, you will lose your hand. Since I have the license plates of those guys as well, you should go tell them immediately. Oh, and just so you know, the caliph has a long memory and a very quick temper. One of my men will be by tomorrow to check these houses, and then he will come by and check all your houses."

Jamal turned and walked back to his car. *I may have exaggerated the caliph having the photos already, but I did enjoy seeing their eyes pop out.*

* * *

7:00 a.m.
Thursday, March 25

Rosie, Betsy, and a lot of the medical staff now lived in Building B and in the other five brick homes that were confiscated when the camp was designed and constructed. The rest of the camp consisted of thousands of tents laid out in a square grid with twenty feet of walkway between each row going north and south and twenty feet between the aisle going east and west. Four tents were in each square, twenty people per tent, with a cluster of outdoor porta potties in the middle.

Rosie's feet crunched over the gravel as she and Betsy walked toward the hospital tent. She'd had a fitful sleep, but at least she hadn't had to rest on the concrete of the highway. Both women carried a lighter version of their backpacks slung over their shoulders and were wearing clean nurse's uniforms, which they had packed. Rosie's was a bright red top and pants, while Betsy's was cobalt blue. Each wore the same white athletic shoes they had worn to the camp, each with forty-five miles of extra road grime on them.

"When the alarm went off this morning to wake me, I was disoriented," said Rosie. "I didn't know where I was or why I was here until I tried to get up to turn off the alarm. Then my body reminded me all about the march."

"My left hip is trying to loosen up, and I wish it would hurry," Betsy said, rubbing her side and walking with a slight limp. "I realize that Dr. Wilson wants us to keep a lid on the cholera concern, but if that becomes a true outbreak, it will get messy very fast. The water and sanitation alone will become a breeding ground for the disease. As I understand it, the camp is on well water with dugout latrines and porta potties."

Rounding the corner to the front of the medical tent, Rosie noticed the long line of people already waiting. She estimated at least forty to fifty people stood waiting for their turn to be seen. "These are probably our patients for today." She looked over the group who had just endured a hellish two days of walking. Their heads were down, and they seemed dejected. "Look at them. Their eyes look sullen, emotionless, and without purpose."

"Of course, they do. They just saw their homes being ripped from them. They have experienced their friends and neighbors being shot in cold blood, and then they had to step over them as if their dead bodies were simply trash."

"These poor people have injuries deeper than their physical lacerations, blisters, and bruises," Rosie said. *They are not hot yet, but they will soon be thirsty, grumpy, and growing more irritated and impatient as the day goes on.*

She mentally thanked Helen again for giving them both a tour of the place and the location of everything they would need.

Walking into the main entrance, Rosie spotted Cheryl, already seated at her desk and getting organized. "Good morning. When are we supposed to open up to see patients?"

"Officially at 8:00 a.m. There should be seven more nurses coming. They're staying in building C."

Rosie looked around. "Is Dr. Wilson here?"

Cheryl nodded. "Helen will help me hand out the surveys and direct the patient load. We only have five chairs in this area. It will quickly get crowded in here."

"Where are we supposed to be stationed?" Betsy said.

"Dr. Wilson suggested you initially start in the great room, then you will accompany each of your patients to an exam room. When the other nurses get here, I'll have them set up in triage as well. We will get into a routine as the day goes along, and we'll see what works best."

Dr. Wilson poked his head into the reception area. "Good morning, ladies. Good to see you standing upright. Looks like it will be a busy day. Helen is on her way." He checked his watch, then looked around the area. "Ready to see your first patients?"

Rosie glanced at Betsy, who gave her a nod. "We're ready."

"It's only 7:20, but why should we keep them waiting any longer? Betsy, would you mind tying back that flap?" Dr. Wilson pointed to the six-foot section of the canvas tent that was draped over a pole, which, when pulled back, was going to be the doorway.

As soon as Betsy tied it back, the crowd began moving in. "Here we go!"

Rosie was impressed with Cheryl's administrative and organizational skills. Upon entering the reception area, she made sure that each person was given a bottle of water and a questionnaire. All sat down and began drinking the water and filling out the forms.

The first patient to finish was an older gentleman. He looked at Rosie, who took his forms and introduced herself. "Let's head back to the triage area. You can follow me."

They came out of the hall and into the cavernous triage room. Several makeshift desks and chairs stood between seven-foot-tall folding screens, each about ten feet long, set up to give a small sense of privacy. The screens lined each of the two long walls. On the short walls of the rectangle were ten chairs against each, and in the middle section were file cabinets and shelves for the nurses and aides who would be interviewing the patients.

"Welcome. You're my first patient in the camp," Rosie said and smiled, trying to put him at ease. She looked down at his form. "Your name is Neal Jay Parker, and your birthdate is February 26, correct?"

"Yes," he said flatly. "I can give you my social security number too, but I guess that doesn't matter anymore."

She placed the form on a chair and grabbed a blood pressure cuff. Then she took Neal's left arm and wrapped the cuff around it. "Stick out your index finger on your right hand." She clipped the oximeter to his finger. After taking his vital signs, she removed her stethoscope and looked her patient in the eyes. "Mr. Parker, you are in remarkable shape for your seventy-seven years. How can I help you?"

"That march nearly did me in. I ended up with blisters on my feet. The ones on my right foot look pretty ugly to me. I'm concerned about an infection since the camp seems plain of the bare necessities, and hygiene could be a low priority."

"Okay, would you follow me to an exam room?" They walked through the triage room into a hall, then into a ten-by-ten exam room made from the canvas, which consisted of a rolling stool and a metal table with a pillow on which Rosie indicated he could sit. There was a five-foot-tall chest of drawers on wheels like the one Ramon had in their garage back home in Fort Worth. Instead of RIDGID or Knaack Tool brand, it was the biggest portable Red Cross medicine cabinet Rosie had ever seen.

Once Mr. Parker got settled, Rosie requested, "Can I get you to take off your shoes and socks? Then lie down so I can have a look."

Neal easily removed his shoes, but the blood-caked socks were a different story. "Let me get some warm water," she said, patting him on the shoulder.

She soon returned carrying a towel and a plastic foot tub half full of warm water and placed it on the floor. "Here, put your feet in this."

He sat as instructed with his feet, still in their socks, in the water. "That stings!"

"I'm sorry, but I need to clean this up." Rosie stepped over to the Red Cross cabinet and opened several labeled drawers, until she found the one holding sterile scissors.

When she turned around with the scissors, Neal held up his hand. "Whoa, you can't cut these socks off. I only have two pair, and this is one of them. I'll help you peel them off. I'll need these socks later."

"Okay, but it will hurt more."

The water turned pink as Rosie began to work her gloved hands against his blood-crusted socks. Though he grimaced, he didn't offer one complaint. After removing them, Rosie hid her own grimace as she looked at his heels. "You were smart to come in. I'm amazed that you're able to walk at all." She placed the towel on the floor for him to stand next to the table.

"I figured walking on sore feet would hurt a lot less than getting shot." Slowly, he boosted himself onto the table and laid down.

"You are a brave man, Mr. Parker. I'll get you cleaned up and out of here in a few minutes. Stay off your feet as much as possible." She dried his feet, then applied a topical antibiotic to the wounds before she dressed them. She placed his wet socks in a baggie and handed them to him. "I put an extra layer of gauze to act like socks for you. Put your shoes on, and I'll walk you out. I want to see you in two days to see how those feet are doing. Come back to this flap around 10:00 a.m. on Saturday, and I will come find you." She walked him to the exit flap and watched him hobble away. *Poor guy. There has to be thousands just like him.*

As Rosie returned to the triage area, she heard a rising swarm of voices clamoring for help and explaining their issues. She felt overwhelmed by the sheer number of needy people and silently prayed for words of hope to give each who was lined up to see her.

*   *   *

8:55 a.m.

After getting in a nap and cleaning himself up, Jamal drove back to the office for the scheduled call from the caliph. The teleconference call began with the perfunctory congratulations to all the city imams for accomplishing the record-breaking, monumental task of getting the infidels caged up in camps.

"These camps will bring the Islamic state one step closer to the Day of Judgment," the caliph said, revealing his true intentions. "The infidels will pay for their stupidity in not following Islam, and by their own ignorance, they will slowly die without food or water or proper shelter."

Jamal was startled that this world leader would allow himself to be heard using this condemning language regarding such a large section of humanity. Though he pasted on a smile, his thoughts were anything but happy. *He has no shame or conscience. I was part of a scheme to move more than 180 million infidels to their deaths, and I am supposed to feel good about it?* He refused to believe that the Muslims he always knew and respected could be so calloused and evil. He shook his head slightly to clear his thoughts. *I just need to get through this call, then I can go home and see my family and—*

Something broke through his thoughts. His name was being spoken. Tuning back in mentally, he heard it again.

"Jamal, I'm speaking to you," the caliph said. "Are you awake?"

Jamal focused on the screen and saw his face on a split screen with the caliph, and the caliph was not smiling. "I am so sorry, your eminence," he said. "Please forgive me. I am without excuse. Certainly, other imams are as tired as I am."

"Are you unwell?" asked the caliph. "Should we call a doctor?"

"No, sir, as I said, I believe I am merely exhausted. The DFW area did accomplish your goal getting the infidels evacuated into the camp."

"Shut up, Jamal!" the caliph snapped at him. "Do you think I cannot read? You must keep your mind on this call."

Jamal swallowed hard and nodded as he sat up straighter in his chair. With his heart racing and his adrenaline level replacing his spent emotions, he felt the terrible pangs of fear back on high alert. He listened intently, but the voice of Safi echoed in his mind, *You can't continue to live like this with them constantly watching you.*

His wife was right. *I must figure out a way to get out of this trap.*

* * *

9:25 a.m.

The Observer called Faiza after the conference call with the caliph had ended. "I have to get to the bottom of Jamal's extended absences and schedules. You were supposed to call me when you found out where he was going. Do you remember that conversation? You were to help me find the answer to this. Now what do you know?"

"As you know, Jamal calls his friend, Tom Larson," Faiza said. I know that Jamal and Tom drive off for lunch. But I don't know where they go. I believe you had me put a bug in Jamal's car, which now may not be functioning?"

"I know what I did," the Observer said, banging his fists on his desk. "But they drive to a location where they evidently get into Tom's car, which is *not* bugged, and I lose their voice signal."

"Yes, sir," Faiza tentatively responded. "But—"

"We know by the phone's indicator, which ends at the Kimbell Museum, that they must be switching cars there. Where do they go from there?" He spoke in slow, monosyllabic phrases. "*You* are the one on location. Do I need to spell it out for you? Do some detective work for me and for the caliph, peace be upon him."

"I noticed that they have gotten together a lot in planning the march," Faiza said, her voice rising eagerly. "With the conclusion of the march, it is my guess that in the next couple of days, they will probably talk. Perhaps later today or tomorrow."

"I am going to fly there myself. Be prepared for my arrival."

"Yes, sir."

"I assume you gathered all the items on the list I sent you recently. Put them in a duffel bag and deliver them to the rental car agency. I will email you the rental car address with instructions."

He slammed down the phone. *Jamal, I am going to find out what you're up to once and for all.*

CHAPTER 40

7:25 a.m.
Friday, March 26

JAMAL RETURNED TO the house from morning prayers and found Safi sitting at the breakfast table. "It was good to be back with the congregation for our prayer time together," he told her. "We had the usual crowd." He made a rolling motion with his hands, one hand over the other, then pointed to Safi as if to indicate it was her turn to talk.

She looked questioningly at him. "That sounds good."

He waved her off. "Can you guess what the big topic of discussion was after the final amen?"

"I have no idea." She still looked confused.

"The march and how well it went here in the DFW area and nationwide. Your husband and his team did exceptionally well." Jamal again moved his hands in an upward movement. "We should be congratulated."

"Good job." Her face changed to a blank, then she looked into Jamal's eyes and shook her head again.

He smiled. "Thank you. That means a lot." He walked to the kitchen counter, opened a drawer, and pulled out a pad of paper and pen. He turned on the faucet, and as the water rushed out, he scribbled a quick note, and held it up for Safi to read: "We need to make regular kitchen noise."

She read it, then looked again at him.

"Would you make some breakfast for me?" he said as he wrote his next message: "*I don't need food. Please make noise with me.*" He walked to a cabinet and pulled out a frying pan, then lightly banged it on the stovetop while he grinned at her, beckoning for her to come over.

Safi took the pan from Jamal and began to undertake the actions of someone cooking. She opened and closed the refrigerator door and the silverware drawer, and she placed items heavily upon the granite countertop.

As she went through the motions, Jamal scribbled on the pad. "*The caliph remains suspicious of me,*" he scribbled on the pad. "*He called me out in front of everyone on the call by stating that you and I argued before the conference call. I want to present a united front this morning to the listening ears. Thank you for helping me.*"

He handed her the note, and after she read it, he pointed to the ceiling and smiled weakly.

Safi took the pad and wrote her own message then pushed it to him to read. "*I want to be supportive,*" her note read. "*The other night, I spoke too bluntly to you. I was particularly tense because the kids kept asking me where you were and would we ever be a family again. I still don't know how to answer them.*"

Jamal read it and sat at the table. His mind was spinning. *I want to be a family too. But the caliph wants a full-time imam, not a family man, to implement his plan. Therein lies the conflict.*

He saw that Safi was diligently contributing to the charade of making a meal. The toaster popped up with a real piece of bread. She buttered the toast and put it on a plate. She filled two glasses with water and placed them on the table with silverware. Then she set two plates, one empty and one with the toast, on the table—the empty one in front of him. "Here you go."

She sat and picked up her toast. "Tell me about your day today. What is planned?"

"I'm going to have lunch with Tom to go over the march costs. This afternoon I'll be playing catch up on all the items that got shoved to the side. Then the sermon and al Sabt, the sabbath weekend."

As she listened, she wrote on the pad and shoved it toward him. *"When do you catch up with us? Why can't you talk with me?"*

He read the note, studied her tired, lifeless eyes, and wrote, "I *wish I knew. Plus, I know what you will say to me about the Man in the White Robe."* He lowered his head, feeling sad, then pushed the note back for her to read. He stood abruptly, wishing desperately that life could be different. Gazing at her, he again recognized the discouragement covering her countenance. Leaning over, he whispered in her ear, "Maybe we can talk tonight . . . as a family." He tried to kiss her on the cheek, but she turned away.

Jamal cleared his throat. "I am sorry, I have to go," he said aloud. "Thanks for breakfast." Without a look back, he walked out of the house.

Before getting into the car, Jamal used his burner phone to call Tom. "See you at the parking lot of the Kimbell at 11:45 today."

* * *

9:00 a.m.

The Observer drummed his fingers on the steering wheel of the rental car, waiting in a traffic jam. He picked up his cell phone and dialed, but the number rang and rang without anyone picking up. He cursed loudly.

"Hello, this is Faiza," Faiza answered, just as he was about to disconnect the call.

"Where have you been? You sound like you have been running. You know I expect you to answer the phone on the first ring."

"Forgive me, I—"

"Is the traffic in this miserable city always this bad? I expected that once we got rid of all the stinking infidels, our society would run a lot smoother. Find out why the traffic is at a standstill on 121 going southwest to Fort Worth. Going northeast, there is hardly a car on the road. Call me back quickly so I know what to do. I can't be late. Jamal is meeting Tom for lunch, and I—"

The sound of sirens broke up his words. Looking in the rearview mirror, he saw a black-and-white police car coming up behind him, then rushing past him on the left shoulder of the highway with emergency lights blazing. Not long after, a firetruck and ambulance followed another police car, all making the same uproar. "Hold on, it must be an accident up ahead." Two more police cruisers passed him.

"So, you don't need me to find out what is going on?" asked Faiza politely, her breathing back to normal.

"Of course not, you fool! I'm right here seeing it as it happens. Find out where they meet for lunch."

"You mean Jamal and Tom?"

"Yes, Faiza, the meeting place. And directions—by text. Now!"

Five minutes later, his cell phone buzzed with an incoming text. "Their normal lunch meeting location has always been the Kimbell Museum parking lot. Can only assume it is the same." Detailed directions to that spot followed.

"You'd better be correct on this one."

He noticed that the far-right lane was beginning to move. He cursed the fact that he was in the far-left lane, put on his blinker, and began to honk the horn impatiently, trying to move over.

"I despise Texas." He jerked his car forward, edging out the driver who was trying to occupy the same space. Then he laid on the horn and shook his fist, bringing out a similar gesture from the other driver. Not one to leave an argument unanswered, the Observer quickly rolled down his window and irately exchanged points of view with all who surrounded him. Others joined in the squabble as more horns, fists, and yells ensued, adding to the drama. He inched and lurched his rental car through the morass, finally getting into the proper lane. Eventually, the traffic in his lane began to pick up speed to three miles per hour. He offered one more rude gesture out his open window and boomed out, "Go to hell!"

* * *

11:30 a.m.

Jamal got to the Kimbell Museum first and parked in a remote section under a tree. He stowed his personal cell phone in the center console, then ran his eyes over the parking lot and the sur-rounding area. He noted that all the cars were empty except for one car. *Hmm.* The driver wasn't parked in the shade.

He must not be from Texas.

The driver appeared to be reading as he was intently looking down. Jamal looked again, out-of-state license. Why wasn't he inside looking at art? Jamal took a studied glare at the occupant. It seemed odd, but Jamal removed it from his mind as he saw Tom's car pull into the parking lot and stop perpendicular to his.

As Jamal switched cars, he looked once more at the driver of the car, then thought nothing more of it. "Tom, tell me something. With the march complete, what is the biggest threat we face today in the United States of Islam?"

"What kind of a question is that?"

"The caliph has a call scheduled for tomorrow night, and he will have something on his mind. That guy is never satisfied, so I am trying to get ahead of him, seeing if I can anticipate the next big deal, the next issue. We got our congratulations, but that was yesterday."

"Now, don't get all Superman on us. The caliph has the entire world to worry about, and your kingdom is limited to the DFW area," Tom responded.

"True, but I'm concerned about the infidels now in the camps. The caliph did state that the conditions in the camps are acceptable for the participants. Maybe the next potentially concerning issue could be a disease. With that many people in such a concentrated area, there will be no relief, no quarantine. It will become an experiment of the survival of the fittest. How will our camp compare against the ninety-nine other camps across the nation? I think this will be a very interesting time to watch, don't you?"

Tom rolled into the lot at the gardens and parked. He turned and scanned Jamal's face. "You actually look more relaxed than I have seen you since the first of the year."

"I feel like the weight of the march is behind me. I have lost twenty pounds in the process of getting that monkey off my back." He slapped the dashboard of Tom's car. "Let's go find our spot."

* * *

11:50 a.m.

The Observer had followed Tom's car from a distance, going south on University Blvd. He'd received Faiza's text that told him when Jamal had left the office and that he should be arriving at the Kimbell in five minutes. He'd backed into a slot at the Kimbell in an area that allowed him a view of the entire lot, so he was able to see when Jamal parked four slots down from him. He'd kept his head down—not that he or any one of the other imams would recognize him since they'd never seen him. But he still wanted to play it safe. He observed Jamal get into Tom's car, and once they pulled out, he began following at a distance.

He looked ahead as he followed Tom's car and made a right-hand turn into a huge, gated area displaying a sign that read "BOTANICAL GARDENS."

Where is this guy taking me? He watched Jamal and Tom get out of Tom's car and walk off to the west. He quickly parked, popped the trunk, grabbed the duffle bag that Faiza left for him at the rental agency, and began to assemble his listening device. He installed the headphones, pointed his parabolic microphone dish at a tree with a bird roosting in it, and listened for a sound check. He clearly heard the bird chirping and smiled to himself as he returned the dish to the bag. Next, he patted down the bag, searching for a long narrow box. His hands found the desired container, which he opened pulling out the razor-sharp Ka-Bar knife.

He immediately attached the scabbard to his belt and pulled his shirt tail out to hide the twelve-inch weapon. Donning a big floppy hiking hat over his headphones, he adjusted his sunglasses with non-see-through lenses.

Time to find these traitors and learn what they talk about.

He shut the trunk with a thud, picked up the duffle bag, and walked to the pedestrian entrance to the gardens. It took him several minutes to find Jamal and Tom sitting on a secluded bench, then it took him another few minutes to find a spot to set up where he could hear but most likely not be seen. He carefully placed his bag on top of some flowers with a sign of identification, "CLAYTONIA AKA MINER'S LETTUCE" with further descriptors on the placard. The small delicate flower was now mostly covered up with the black duffle. Paying no attention to the English ivy that surrounded the exhibit or the clearly marked notices, stating, "Give Our Gardens a Chance. Please Stay on the Designated Trails," he tromped the area with his size-eleven hiking books. Considering the sign, *Hmmf,* a smile curled up on his lips. *Even these flowers will bow down to me.* Leaning against the backside of a tree, he settled himself and clicked on the listening device, pointing it at the two men deep in conversation.

"What else did Safi say?" asked Tom.

"She wanted to talk, but I told her I had to go to work," Jamal said.

A gray-haired man and a woman in a hijab came slowly walking along the path between the Observer and Jamal and Tom. They methodically stopped to read each flower exhibit's placard along the pathway and comment on their beauty. Their constant chatter interfered with the Observer's ability to hear the exchange between the men.

"Move along, you idiots," he muttered under his breath. "I can't hear these traitors."

"Sir? Sir, excuse me." A voice behind the Observer caught his attention. When he didn't acknowledge the voice, it became more demanding. "*Sir. Excuse me, please. Is this your bag?*"

A renewed annoyance filled him as he turned to find a young man wearing a dirty tan set of coveralls that had the Fort Worth Botanical Gardens emblazoned above the left pocket. His work gloves, huge cowboy hat, and sunglasses communicated that he was a staff gardener, and he was pointing to the Observer's duffle.

"Please leave," the Observer whispered, his words soaked with condescension. "Can't you see I am working here? I need some privacy."

"Excuse me, sir. Can't you read, sir?" the gardener said, raising his voice. "The sign *clearly* says to stay on the trail. Now kindly get out of the exhibit. You need to remove your bag and get back on the trail." He inhaled and exhaled loudly to show his displeasure. "*Now*, please."

The Observer lowered his dish and turned his body to face the gardener. With a tilted head to one side and a frown, he decided to give the gardener one more chance to back off. "I need some time here. It may not seem important to you and your precious little flowers, but you need to get lost for a while. I'll pretend this discussion never happened."

He turned back around and was relieved that the older couple had moved down the trail. Again, he pointed his dish at Jamal and Tom and clicked it on to tune and activate the recorder.

"You can't ignore me," the gardener said, his voice now near a yell.

Jamal looked in his direction and elbowed Tom. "That guy is spying on us," Jamal said, coming clearly through the listening device. "Could that be the guy from the Kimbell parking lot?" He jumped up and began walking briskly toward him.

The Observer quickly pushed the gardener out of the way and began packing up his belongings.

"Hey, you, who are you?" Jamal shouted, coming closer. "What do you want? Why are you following us?"

The Observer began to run toward the parking lot, but he could see that Jamal had the angle on him and was catching up. Soon Jamal grabbed his arm and pulled him back.

"Who are you?" Jamal demanded, facing him.

"You are not good enough for the job of city imam. You should not have grabbed my arm. Remember Seattle?" With a swift turn, he took Jamal's right arm with his left and lifted it. Drawing his

Ka-Bar knife, he thrust it into Jamal's stomach, up toward his diaphragm, and ran it from side to side, cutting the suprarenal abdominal aorta with the skill of a professional assassin, causing a massive bleed out to begin.

Jamal's face registered surprise and agony as he collapsed to the ground.

Knowing he had little time to get away, the Observer ran to his rental car and threw his duffle into the trunk. Wasting no time, he got behind the wheel and sped off.

*   *   *

12:30 p.m.

Jamal pressed the gaping gash in his stomach and stared up at a blurry image of Tom bent over him. He reached out his bloody and shaking hand and grabbed Tom's arm. "My hands feel wet," he said through slurred speech. "I am getting really cold. Can you get me something to cover me?" Jamal knew he was dying.

"Who did this?" Tom said, his voice full of emotion. "Hey! Call 9-1-1!" Jamal assumed he was speaking to the gardener. "Listen to me, Jamal. You have to cry out to the Man in the White Robe. It is not too late. He knows your name. Jesus wants to help you."

"Take care of Safi and the girls like we talked about," Jamal said, his breathing becoming more labored. "They will burn the house tonight. Don't delay. He had a knife. He told me, 'Remember Seattle.' Please help my girls."

"I promise you I will protect Safi and the girls. You just need to cry out to the Man in the White Robe. Please, Jamal, please! Dear God, please help my friend find his way to you."

"It is getting darker and colder," Jamal whispered. "Awfully dark. Dark." His throat rattled as he struggled with another breath. His last.

* * *

12:35 p.m.

Tom felt Jamal's hand go limp and lifeless. His tears came fiercely as he put Jamal's arm down to his side. The eyes of his friend were fixed in a blank stare at the overhang of tree branches. He gently closed them. He looked back down at Jamal. "Goodbye, dear friend." Another wave of emotion washed over him as he heard distant sirens, and he embraced Jamal's body.

* * *

2:10 p.m.

After being interviewed by the Fort Worth police for an hour, a grief-stricken Tom called his wife, and together they headed out to break the news to Safi. He knew the police would also tell her, but he wanted to be the first.

Safi took one look at Tom with his blood-stained shirt, and her eyes grew large. "He's gone, isn't he?" As soon as Tom nodded, she collapsed into his arms.

"It all happened so fast," he said quietly. "We were at our usual place in the Botanical, sitting on a bench, talking through the normal business of the work that Jamal and I always talked about." He maneuvered her back into her house and placed her gently on the living room sofa, then remembered Jamal told him the house was bugged. He put his finger to his lips and pointed to the backyard.

They all quietly moved, with Lori helping a still-sobbing Safi to a shaded concrete bench, which backed up to their backyard fence. Lori and Safi sat together, holding hands.

"Safi, I am sorry to shorten your grief and discuss plans, but time is of the essence," Tom said, standing over her. "One of the last things that Jamal said was that his killer told him, 'Remember Seattle.' I'm convinced—as I'm sure Jamal was—that the man who killed him was from the caliph, and he will be coming after you and the girls tonight or the next night. I promised Jamal I would not let that happen."

Safi gasped and looked at Tom with fear in her eyes. "What on earth are you talking about? Are you saying Jamal was deliberately murdered by the caliph? So, it was true."

"I know this is all coming at you fast. But if the Seattle imam's death has any parallels to the death of Jamal, we can expect some sort of 'accident' to befall you and the girls within the next few days. The Seattle imam's family, along with his parents' and in-laws' homes, were destroyed by fire the same night as the imam's death. They all perished. This seemed like too much happenstance when Jamal and I discussed it weeks ago. He and I talked through a very specific plan to be implemented if he were murdered."

"He told me he was supposed to be on a list to be killed after the march, but I never thought something like this could happen." She began weeping again. "My dear Jamal. He thought of me and the girls with all the pressures that were upon him." Her hands shook as she wiped at her eyes. "What was he planning?"

"Lori will help you pack up a trash bag of necessary clothes for you and the girls. We will take all of you away from the house when they get home from school and daycare this afternoon. You all will spend the night at our house and then eventually at a place not far from here where you will never be recognized. We have arranged for four female bodies, who perished in the march and are about your sizes, to be delivered to the house this evening and placed in your beds. If there is a fire, they will assume these bodies are yours."

Safi looked from Tom to Lori and began to tremble violently. "Why would they do that to me and to our girls? I don't even know what happened to Jamal, and now you are telling me this master of the universe wants to kill me and our babies because of . . . what? Because you and Jamal were talking in the park?"

The front doorbell began to ring repeatedly. Safi drove herself deep into Lori's arms. "Why is this happening to us?"

"That's probably the police," Tom said, as he looked at Lori and mouthed, *we need to go—now.* He ran to answer the door and came face to face with the same police investigator he'd left at the botanical gardens.

"Good afternoon, Mr. Larson," the detective said. "I see you have made your way to the Kadib home. I need to speak to Mrs. Kadib, if I may."

Tom stepped aside, making way for the man to step into the living room. "I'll get Mrs. Kadib for you. As you can understand, she is very upset to hear about her husband."

"Of course."

Tom found Safi and Lori in the kitchen and ushered them in to greet the detective. Safi's eyes were swollen and bloodshot.

Without any apology or condolence, the detective pulled out a small pad and pen from his pocket. "Did Jamal have any known enemies in the area?" he asked dispassionately. "Have there been any recent disputes between Jamal and anyone else that you know of?"

Safi shook her head to each question. "No," she said over and over.

Tom was glad she knew enough not to say anything about the caliph or his henchmen.

The detective's phone rang, and he looked at the caller ID. "Excuse me, I have to take this." He stepped outside the front door.

While he was gone, Tom, Lori, and Safi looked at one another quietly. Tom nodded and mouthed, *good job*. He could tell from her eyes that she didn't feel it was such a good job. He knew Safi didn't like the lies or the position Jamal had now put her and her children in.

I should have listened when he was so afraid. I should have done something.

"Mrs. Kadib, thank you for your time," the detective said, returning to the living room. "I have no more questions right now. Goodbye." He turned abruptly and left.

Tom shook his head in disgust and gestured that they should head back outside. "Let's get you some fresh air."

Once back out in the yard, Tom saddled up close to Safi. He wasn't sure how far the bugs' hearing could actually reach. "Jamal did warn you that this house might be bugged, correct?"

"Yes," Safi said weakly.

"What we just witnessed in there is an example of the caliph, or someone in the caliph's office, calling the cops off Jamal's murder investigation. This confirms that we need to get you out of here and keep you safe. You and the girls come over to our house tonight for dinner, and we can talk freely about some ideas of what to do. I know Jamal was an only child, and both of his parents are dead. Tell me about your parents."

Safi's face went white. "You don't think they could be in danger too?"

"There's no telling what the caliph might do."

"I . . . I have siblings . . . But they, like my parents, are scattered all along the East Coast, from New Jersey down to Georgia. They are all Muslims, and it would take a lot of work to track them down. What should I do?"

Tom breathed a bit easier. "In the case of the Seattle imam, their families were all right there in the same town. Let's just hope that they are lazy, and they leave the research to the bigger fish they have to fry. Have your parents moved since you left for college?"

"Yes, they moved to a different city."

"That should help quite a bit. I pity the poor person who lives in their former house if they do decide to retaliate against your parents without doing any research." He rubbed his chin in thought. "I have some planning to do, so I will see you tonight." He turned to Lori. "Would you stay with her and get the girls ready?"

Lori began to nod, then stopped abruptly, looking behind Tom. Her eyes lit up, and her face shone like the sun. Safi's face reflected the same.

Tom whirled around. There, in the brightest of light, stood the Man in the White Robe.

"Jesus!" he whispered, his knees immediately becoming weak.

Jesus's eyes focused on Safi, and he smiled kindly, compassionately. "Don't be afraid."

Tom tried to open his mouth to speak, but no words seemed adequate. He was filled with awe.

"I'm here to comfort Safi and assure her of my love for her. I will prepare you for what is to come."

CHAPTER 41

6:35 p.m.
Friday, March 26

ROSIE WALKED WITH Betsy back to their living quarters. "I could have treated the exact same blisters on at least five poor souls in a row and not looked up. It was as if they were wearing the same shoes and socks."

"I saw the same thing," Betsy said. "It's more than the physical abrasions that worry me. The terror in their eyes is still right at the surface of everyone I saw today. They *know* the truth."

"Yes," Rosie said and paused, trying to think of a way they could truly help people's emotional states. They were now living in death camps. *That's what this was meant to be all along.* "Is there any type of counseling or support here for emotional wounds? Surely there have to be counselors in the camp somewhere. Those were real friends and loved ones they were stepping over." Her mind raced back to the images of blood spurting out of people's heads as they were shot. She closed her eyes tightly. "That was a war zone. I think we're seeing PTSD. . . . and we can't give them a bandage for that wound."

"You know me," Betsy said. "I wanted to ask them about their minds, to really talk to them. All I could do was hug them and move on to the next twenty patients assigned to me for that hour." She hung her head in clear remorse. "We are nothing more than a first-aid clinic right now. The serious stuff—" She pointed to her heart. "That's just under the surface."

"And if everyone keeps their raw emotions bottled up, it won't be long before someone is going to blow." Rosie shook her head sadly.

They passed a patrol guard who let out a huge belch and patted his stomach as though he had eaten an immensely satisfying and rich meal.

"Truly repulsive," Betsy said under her breath. "I hope he gets terrible indigestion."

"Nurse!" Rosie covered her mouth in mock shame. "Carrying on like you have no compassion for his natural bodily functions. Tsk. You should be ashamed." She chuckled and tucked her arm into Betsy's. "We have to get this nervous tension from no rest and no breaks out of our system before the really bad stuff hits."

Rosie set her gaze farther up the path toward their residence and slowed her gait. Leaning against their home was a man with his arms crossed who looked like . . . Tom Larson. *That couldn't be. Why would he be here?*

As she got close, she was certain it was him. "Tom, is that you?"

Tom nodded and stepped forward.

"What on earth are you doing here?"

"We need to talk," Tom said, his expression somber. "Is there somewhere to go with some privacy?"

Rosie's stomach clinched in fear. "Sure, why don't we step inside?" She looked at Betsy. "You may remember Nurse Betsy. Do you mind if she joins us?"

"Of course, I remember. No, I don't mind."

After getting settled in the only "private" room they could find in building B—a room toward the back that housed supplies— Rosie and Betsy sat and stared at the now-pacing figure of Tom.

"My presence here, I know, is quite a shock," he said, apprehensively. He began to say something else, but he choked up, sniffled, and looked away.

Rosie looked at Betsy, whose eyebrows raised in surprise, and then back at Tom.

"I don't know where to start, but here it goes in a condensed version. Jamal was just killed in a brutal knife attack. The assailant gave every indication that he was acting under the direction of the caliph."

"I am so sorry for your loss," Rosie said. Rosie's mind was racing. *Poor Safi! Why is he telling me this? What does it have to do with me? Why is he here?*

Tom took a couple of deep breaths, then offered a sideways smile. "This is where it gets weird." He sat cross-legged in front of both women at their feet.

When would a Muslim man ever do such a thing? Rosie thought, feeling surprised.

"Today after the murder, Lori and I went to Jamal's house to tell Safi about what happened. You've met her. I understand you've had some . . . conversations with her, yes?"

Rosie felt her stomach tighten. *What's going on?* She slowly nodded.

"Lori and I told her the horrible news. The police came and went—that's another story—but more to the point, if this is a caliph hit, then I need to get Safi and the girls out of the house tonight. If Jamal's murder follows the pattern of the last imam's killing—an imam in Seattle, which Jamal witnessed on a conference call—the family will be next, incinerated in their own home."

Rosie and Betsy gasped.

Tom jumped to his feet and began pacing again. "It's true and let me tell you another shocker." He stopped directly in front of them. "While Safi, Lori, and I were talking, the Man in the White Robe appeared to all of us. I mean, Jesus, my Savior, was right there with us all!"

Betsy grabbed Rosie's hand and pulled it up close to her chest. Rosie knew exactly what Betsy was feeling. *Jesus is showing up. He's actually showing up and showing himself. The radical Muslims came in like an enemy with murder and hatred. But Scripture says, "When the enemy comes in like a flood, God will raise a standard against him." Jesus, what a mighty standard you are!*

"We all saw him," Tom continued, his eyes bright with intensity and awe. "He told us three specific things." As though unsure of his own story, Tom punched his fist into his other hand and walked away, then turned back toward them. "It was unbelievable!"

"You saw him," Rosie said, making sure she'd heard correctly. "He was actually there with you?"

"Yes!" Tom's voice raised in awe.

"That is amazing!" Betsy said.

"What were the three things he told you?" Rosie asked.

"So, it *is* believable?" asked Tom.

"Yes, of course! Though I have never seen him, I know Safi said she had."

Tom cleared his throat and licked his lips. "Jesus was so tender with Safi about Jamal's death. We were all crying, even Jesus. He told her he would be with her and the girls." He lifted his thumb as if counting and then put out his index finger. "He then said to me that his people who are down here need more food and water." He moved his third finger out to join the other two. "Then he said to move Safi and the girls to this camp."

Rosie blinked hard. *"Here?"*

Tom nodded. "That is when I asked him how I was supposed to do that. And he said—" Tom paused and looked directly into Rosie's eyes. "Ask Rosie Chavez."

She let this message sink in and then smiled broadly.

Tom shook out his body as though he could relax now that he'd delivered the message. "Does his message mean something to you? Please tell me it does and that's why you're smiling."

"Yes," Rosie said, her eyes filling with tears.

Tom exhaled loudly. "I need some good news about now. What are we supposed to do? I got in tonight by conning my way past the front guard to discuss with Dr. Wilson the costs of the medical supplies. That trick won't work again with a grown woman and three little girls tagging along."

"Do you have a cell phone?" Rosie asked.

He looked confused but reached into his pocket and presented it to her.

"May I dial a former nurse colleague of mine named Dura? I think she and her friend, Yosef, may be part of the plan."

Tom nodded and raised his shoulders in question.

As Rosie dialed the number she had committed to memory, she turned and winked at Betsy.

With Dura's hello, Rosie's excitement grew. It was wonderful to hear her friend's voice. "Dura, this is Rosie. I'm calling from the camp. Bet you didn't expect to hear from me."

"Rosie! My goodness, how wonderful to hear from you. I watched the news when the march took place. How awful. But you're okay? Wait, how did you get a phone?"

Rosie had to laugh at Dura's quick and breathless chatter. "Betsy and I are fine. Yes, it is exhausting work, but we are okay. Listen, I can't talk long. Can you dial Yosef for a conference call?"

"Of course, of course! Hold on."

Rosie could hear Dura fumbling with her phone. But a few moments later, the familiar voice of Yosef came through the speaker loud and clear.

"Yosef, this is Dura. I have Rosie on the phone. She wants to talk with us. Take it away, Rosie."

"Hi, Yosef. I'm with Tom Larson, a friend of mine. Tom and I are down at the camp. Uh . . ." She hesitated. Was it too much to ask her friends to do this, knowing they could get into big trouble? But then she remembered who sent Tom with this task. "I have another favor to ask."

"At your service, Rosie. Whatever you ask me to do always requires trusting God and challenging my faith. If it requires trust, I'm in!"

"Well, this is a big ask—but it comes from the Man in the White Robe himself."

Yosef let out a muted cheer. "I'm so deep into possible trouble, what's one more thing? Besides, it has been a little slow since I took you home Sunday night."

Dura laughed over Yosef's response, causing excitement to course through Rosie.

They think they've won—the people who forced us on this march and into this camp. But God is greater. Another thought hit her. Maybe there is a way Yosef can help me get Cooper to the camp as well. Maybe we haven't been forgotten. Maybe we didn't come here to die but to thrive.

"Hang on, you two. I'm going to hand the phone back to Tom, so you can hear what we need and then exchange contact information. You have some plans to work out."

Rosie quickly passed the phone to Tom, who began telling them what he'd shared with Rosie. She thought of all that happened since the militant Islamists had bombed and taken down her country. She'd lost her parents, her husband, her job, her home. She'd nearly lost her son. *But God has a plan. The bad stuff doesn't surprise or worry him.* She inhaled deeply, feeling hope rise within her. *What a great time to see God on the move—and he wants me to be part of it!*

She looked at Betsy as a chuckle escaped Betsy's lips. "Oh, this isn't over."

Thinking of Cooper, Rosie set her jaw and replied, "Not by a long shot."

ACKNOWLEDGMENTS

First and foremost, I want to thank my spouse of fifty years, who read and pre-edited these words multiple times. To the following individuals, I extend eternal gratitude: to LeAnn, who pushed me over the edge, to Jeff for getting me started with Chicago, to Ginger for reminding me that I was redeemable, to the prayer team who carried me throughout this entire process, to Benjie for his insights into the content and theology, and to Lydia for her artwork on the book cover. This project couldn't have been completed without the help of all of you from the Red Cliffs. Thank you.

REFERENCES

I spent years reading many books on Sharia Law and the intent for the Coming Day of Judgment. Several books by Joel Rosenberg speak of the caliph and the timing of the days ahead. Bernard Lewis, in his book *Crisis of Islam*, speaks of the current-day problem of intellectualism with radical Islamic terrorists. But when I read *Dreams and Visions* by Tom Doyle, I knew I could tell the story and bring to light the high value the Islamic faith puts on dreams and visions inasmuch as that is how the prophet Muhammad got his start. All Biblical refences unless otherwise noted come from The Living Bible.

Lewis, Bernard. "*The Crisis of Islam.*" Random House Trade Paperbacks, 2004.

Doyle, Tom, with Greg Webster. "*Dreams and Visions: Is Jesus Awakening the Muslim World?*" Thomas Nelson, 2012.

https://joelrosenberg.com/

CPSIA information can be obtained
at www.ICGtesting.com
Printed in the USA
BVHW030816260423
663030BV00001B/1